P9-BJO-839

A Toast
To
Tomorrow

Manning Coles' story, *Drink to Yesterday*, marked the introduction of a new type of spy story. A TOAST TO TOMORROW, covering the period from the close of the last war to the crisis at Danzig, is as superbly written as the earlier book with a new twist which adds immeasurably to the tension and excitement. It is as different from the old spy stories as a Hitchcock movie is from silent pictures in the days of Lon Chaney.

We would like you to forget any ideas you may have about spy stories and approach this as a novel with humor, three-dimensional characters, realistic narration and breathtaking suspense.

A Crime Club Selection

This Book gives Insights on The Rise of the Reich -- While fiction -- there is an abundance of fact interwoven. Interesting to keep as an insight on that Eria In Germany Between 1919 - 39 - Danzig was the the beginning of The Panzer Krecht ---

A Toast
To
Tomorrow

MANNING COLES

PUBLISHED FOR
THE CRIME CLUB

By Doubleday, Doran and Company, Inc.

New York

1941

PRINTED AT THE *Country Life Press*, GARDEN CITY, N. Y., U. S. A.

To
A. M. Y.

Remembering the Free City
of Danzig

CONTENTS

A Toast
To
Tomorrow

HE WALKED INTO HIS STUDY, switched on the reading-lamp, drew the curtains and threw more logs on the blazing fire, for it was very cold in Berlin that evening in March 1933. He pushed an armchair in front of the fire, a huge padded leather one which looked much too large for his short spare figure, and put beside the chair a table with a box of cigars on it, matches and a thick wad of papers in a cardboard cover with a label inscribed, *"The Radio Operator,* A Play, by Klaus Lehmann." He had the air of a man who is preparing to enjoy a long-expected pleasure and does not intend small discomforts to spoil it. Every few moments he glanced at the clock. Finally he opened a cupboard door and looked inside, scowled, and rang the bell; a manservant answered it, a man as long, thin and melancholy as his master was short and cheerful.

"Yes, sir?"

"Franz, did I not say there should be beer?"

"I could not say for certain, sir."

"When in doubt, Franz, provide it."

"Very good, sir."

"I rather think, Franz, that I have told you that before."

"If you say so, sir."

"Of course I say so, haven't you just heard me? Don't stand there arguing, go and get it."

The servant's long wrinkled face assumed exactly the expression of a pained bloodhound, and he slid out of the room leaving the door ajar and admitting an icy draught. "Now I've annoyed him, Franz always leaves the door open when his feelings are hurt."

Franz came back with a tall jug, put it on the table and prepared to leave, but his master said, "Just a moment," took two glasses from the cupboard, filled them both and handed him one.

"Drink success to *The Radio Operator*, Franz," he said. "This is a great moment, when one hears one's first play being performed for the first time."

Franz's ugly face lit up. "It must be, sir. *Prosit! The Radio Operator*."

They drank with appropriate solemnity, and Franz put his glass down.

"I know how you feel, sir, if I may say so. I felt like that myself once."

"I didn't know I had a fellow-author in the house."

"It was only a little thing, sir. It went:

> *'Though she was old,*
> *Her heart was never cold.*
> *I'll never see another*
> *Like my grandmother.'*

My parents put it in the paper, sir, when she died."

"I see," said the successful playwright. "An epitaph, and very nice, too. I always think epitaphs must be so difficult. Either you delight the family and nobody else, or else you delight everybody except the family."

"Yes, sir," said Franz. "Excuse me, it is time."

"Heavens, yes," said the author, springing at the wireless set and switching it on, to be rewarded with the closing bars of a Beethoven concerto. Franz left the room, shutting the door this time, while his master poured himself out some more beer and settled down in the big arm-chair with the manuscript upon his knee to listen to his very own play.

"You are now to hear," said the announcer, "the first broadcast of a new play, *The Radio Operator,* by Klaus Lehmann. There is only one character, the radio operator himself——"

The play opened with the usual background of morse, starting very softly, growing louder and more insistent, then dying away again to a whisper as the only character began to speak. It would seem that even the morse, un-intelligible jumble of letters though it was, delighted its author, for he snuggled down into his chair and a self-satisfied smile illuminated his scarred face even before the speech began.

"To-night I sit for the last time," said the radio opera-tor, "in the little cabin they call the wireless room, sur-rounded by the familiar instruments——"

"I hope to goodness that's right," muttered the author. "Don't believe I was ever in a wireless room in my life."

"——the table before me, for to-morrow we reach Ham-burg and I go ashore for the last time. Next voyage an-other man will sit here in my place listening to the myriad voices of the air——"

"Nice touch, that."

"——instructing, warning, comforting——"

The morse rose in intensity again, drowning the opera-tor's voice for a moment, and again the author smiled.

"For my life at sea is ended, and to-morrow I retire. How well I remember when I first went to sea!"

The operator had started his career in a Jewish-controlled shipping line, where starvation wages, revolt-ing food, and disgusting accommodation had combined with the slave-driving habits of the owners to make his young life a misery. "Cockroaches," said the operator, in a tone quivering with emotion, "cockroaches in my bunk, cockroaches in the wireless room, even cockroaches in the coffee, and if a free-born German dared to complain he was met with hectoring disdain and bullying laughter."

"Not a good phrase," said the playwright, frowning. "I meant to alter that and I forgot. Hectoring something else and disdainful laughter would be better."

Then the war came, the wireless operator joined the Imperial Navy, and was wounded at the battle of Hiorns Reef. He seemed to have had the singular gift of being in several different parts of the North Sea at once, but what of that?

"On that great day," he said, "I saw with my own eyes numerous gallant destroyer actions between the bull-terriers of our Fleet and the darting, stinging wasps of the enemy; I saw our cruiser squadrons sweep the English ships out of their way as a broom scatters autumn leaves; I saw the proud English battleships blow up with a thunderous roar and become as it were dust in a moment, while their cries for help came to my ears over the air."

Again the morse rose and sank again, and the author took a pull at his beer.

"And I sincerely hope that makes the English sit up and listen," he said.

When the operator came out of hospital he was sent to the shore station at Ostende, where the U-boats, returning from their nocturnal adventures, reported arrival in the chilly dawns—or did not return nor report. The war came to an end and there followed the dreadful years of defeat, when the mark slumped, food was bad or unobtainable, and the people perished.

"I walked the streets of Hamburg," said the wireless operator, "out of work, out of money, out of hope, starving, destitute, wretched. 'Will this go on for ever?' I cried, 'will no one deliver Germany from her chains?' But heaven was merciful and sent us a Deliverer."

"Came the Dawn," commented the author, lighting a cigar.

"Our Leader," continued the voice from the radio set, "had an uphill task indeed, such as only a superman could have performed, but he has done it, and what do we see to-day? A Germany free, powerful, respected and feared. Her sons walking the world with stately tread and unbending necks, her ships, well found, well provisioned and equipped, sailing the seven seas again with ship's companies proud to serve in them, and the tramp of her armies shaking the earth. At home her people are busy, contented and happy, and her children grow up healthy, strong and fair. We know to whom we owe all this, to whom all praise and honour is due, and we shall pay it, we and our children and our children's children; in days to come the whole world shall pay it too, saying as I do, 'Heil Hitler! Heil Hitler! Heil!' "

The morse broke in again, rising to a staccato climax, only to be drowned in its turn by the strains of the Horst Wessel Song. The author closed his manuscript and relaxed in his chair.

"That ought to please Adolf," said Klaus Lehmann, Deputy Chief of the German Police.

.   .   .   .

The s.s. *Whistlefield Star* was a biggish cargo boat six hours out of Hamburg for Cardiff, and she carried two wireless operators. The senior operator was approaching middle age, red-haired, stocky and freckled. He had seen service in destroyers in the Great War and was a little too apt to tell people all about it. The second mate, on the other hand, was the possessor of a wireless set which he claimed would bring in anything except the morning's milk, and he kept it in the saloon. The wireless operator came in off duty, looking for supper, and found the second mate producing hyena-like noises varied by cat-fights in an attempt to tune out an over-powerful German station which was broadcasting a Beethoven concerto.

"For the love of Larry," said the operator, "pipe down. Can't a man get a bit of peace from the blasted wireless in his spare time?"

"I shall in a minute, if I can't get anything but this high-brow stuff. Give me something with a tune to it."

"You might know you can't get anything but Hamburg off here. Ow! Oh, Lord, don't do that, you're turning the sardines liverish."

The concerto drew to its close and there followed an announcement in German. "Sounds like the end of the concert," said the second mate, "perhaps we'll get something decent now." The next item started with morse, at first very soft, working up in a crescendo and then falling quiet again.

"Here, Sparks," said the unfeeling second mate, "something to amuse you." But the wireless operator was too busy telling the steward what he thought of the tea to pay any attention. A voice on the radio started to talk, and after waiting a moment in the hope of something better the second mate was just beginning to tune away from it when the morse broke in again. "Taa," it said, "tit—taa—tit—tit, taa. Taa, tit—taa—tit—tit, taa." This time the wireless operator sat up listening.

"Here," he said, "hold that a moment. T-L-T. T-L-T. Where have I heard that before? It's a call-sign. I used to know it."

The morse died out when the German voice went on talking, talking, while the wireless operator scowled with thought, till the second mate got fidgety.

"I'm fed up with all this yap," he said, "I'll have a look round to see if I can't find something else."

"I have it," said the wireless man suddenly. "One of our people in Germany. We had a list of call-signs to listen for, and I'm sure that was one of 'em. T-L-T."

"What?" said the mate. "Britishers broadcasting from Germany? When?"

"During the war."

"But did they? Who were they? What were they doing?"

"Spying, like. Intelligence work they called it, an' I'll say they had to be pretty intelligent to get away with it. There was a few of them used to transmit with spark sets, used to get messages out that way. In code, of course, couldn't make head nor tail of what the mesage—— Listen!"

The morse began again, and the wireless operator snatched a pencil and an old envelope from his pocket and jotted down letters as they came. "T-L-T. RKEHO——" When it ceased again he looked mournfully at the result.

"Well, there you are," he said, "and what it all means I've no more idea than a blind kitten."

"P'raps it doesn't mean anything," said the second mate. "Just trimmings, like, like what you get on the National sometimes."

"Don't believe it, not starting T-L-T like that. I don't know if I ought to do something about it, but I don't know who to send it to now. Now, when I was in the Service——"

"Oh, Lor'," said the second mate, and unostentatiously quitted the saloon.

●　　　●　　　●　　　●　　　●　　　●　　　●

Young Emsworth settled himself down in his chair before the receiving set in the Foreign Office, pulled the

earphones over his head and listened with pleasure to the
last movement of a Beethoven concerto, magnificently
rendered. "If only we could always hear stuff like that,"
he murmured, "instead of all the awful tosh we have to
listen to." He glanced with distaste at the programme. A
play by Klaus Lehmann called *The Radio Operator*,
doubtless some of that dreadful propaganda stuff, news,
a talk on the Hitler Youth movement, a concert of light
music. He sighed and drew a writing-pad towards him,
for it was his business to listen to what Germany was being
told, and report upon anything rich and strange. Also
within his reach was the switch of the recorder, an instrument which would, if required, make a record of what
was said, so that the exact wording could be studied at
leisure. The German announcer's voice ceased, and the
play began with a crackle of morse.

An expression of speechless amazement crossed Emsworth's face, he shot out one hand automatically to switch
on the recorder and then took his headphones off, looked
at them and put them on again, an idiotic gesture sometimes seen when a man cannot believe his ears.

"To-night," said the guttural German voice, "I sit for
the last time in the little cabin they call the wireless room,
surrounded——"

Emsworth pressed a bell-switch and after a short pause
a messenger came in, but Emsworth held up his hand for
silence because the morse had come on for the second
time. When it ended, he said, "Is Mr. Wilcox still here?
Go and see, if he is ask him to be good enough to come to
me here."

Wilcox came in, an elderly man, heavy and pallid with
years of sedentary employment.

"What's the excitement, Emsworth? You only just
caught me, I was putting my coat on."

Emsworth slipped one headphone forward in order to

hear what Wilcox said with one ear and the German broadcast with the other. "D'you remember telling me the other evening about people transmitting messages from Germany during the war? You quoted three or four call-signs, wasn't T-L-T one of them? Yes—well, here it is again in a morse background to a German radio play about a wireless operator."

"Got the recorder going? Good," said Wilcox, snatching up another pair of headphones and plugging them in. "Oh, he's still talking, I dare say we'll get some more in a minute. Yes, I had your job in those days, but it was a bit more interest——"

He broke off and listened intently, jotting letters down on a slip of paper. "T-L-T. RKEHOSWR39X—" When the morse had ended again, he said, "How many times has that come in?"

"That's the third. Once at the beginning, quite short and nothing but the call-sign repeated, and once since, before this."

Wilcox nodded and went on listening. "More talky-talky, lots of, my hat, how these propagandists do gas," he said. "No, I can't remember exactly which this fellow was after all this lapse of time. After all, it's sixteen years, but I can tell you right away it's not the same fellow transmitting. I remember he had a distinctive, rather pedantic, style. I always put him down as a rather elderly self-taught amateur. You know, of course, that men in the habit of listening to morse come to recognize the touch of other operators they are in the habit of hearing, much as you recognize a man's voice or his handwriting."

"B—but," spluttered young Emsworth, who found Wilcox's calmness positively inhuman, "do you really think it's the same man? After all these years? Do you think it's real?"

"Yes, I think it may be real, but we can tell better when

it's decoded. No, I don't think it's the same man, I've said so already. As for 'after all these years', stranger things have happened and will again. When it's all over I'll have those old codes turned up an—— Sh!"

The morse came in for the last time and was finally drowned by the Horst Wessel Song. The two men waited till it was clear that the play was over, and Wilcox took his headphones off and got up.

"Now I'll leave you in peace to listen to the news," he said, taking the thin steel strip out of the recording machine, "while I go and see if I can worry this out."

The next morning there was a conference on the subject attended by Wilcox and his immediate superior, also an elderly Colonel called up by telephone from the Sussex cottage to which he had retired when he left the War Office years before.

"The code in which these messages were sent," said Wilcox, rustling papers, "was used during the late war by an agent of ours named Reck, who was science master of a school at Mülheim, near Cologne."

"I remember," said the Colonel. "A queer dry old stick. I only saw him once or twice. He never came to England unless it was really urgent, he had become so German that he could hardly speak English at all—he had forgotten it. Very useful man on his job."

"Where is Reck now?"

"Dead. He took to drink, was removed to an asylum at Mainz, and died there," answered Wilcox.

"Either Reck is not dead," said Authority, "or he was careless enough to leave his code behind him and somebody has found it."

"He went out of his mind," said the Colonel. "I am sure of that, for I kept an eye on him. Denton went to see him once and said the poor old fellow complained of bright seraphim crawling up the walls."

"Dear me," said the senior officer present, "how very superior. I thought it was usually snakes in bathing costumes wearing straw hats and playing banjoes."

"He may well have mislaid his code," said Wilcox. "I am sure it was not he who was transmitting. In any case, the question remains, who sent the message? Because at the best of times he only coded and sent messages, he did not originate them."

"If it is genuine," said the Foreign Office man, "it is probably somebody who was in touch with Reck in the old days. Is there anyone who went missing without trace and may have turned up again?"

"Plenty," said the Colonel sadly, "but not, as it happens, connected with Reck. Let me see. Hall died in England after the war. Inglis is in an asylum in the Midlands, poor devil. Saunders was shot in Hampshire. Beckett runs a chicken farm in Dorset. Denton is in the Balkans, and has been for the last couple of years. Hambledon was drowned. MacVicar is in an engineering works on Tyneside. Thorpe is married and living quietly in Salisbury. No, none of Reck's contacts are what you'd call missing. May I hear the messages again?"

"The message was in four parts, in intervals in the play, you understand," said Wilcox. "The first was merely the call-sign repeated. Next came, 'T-L-T. British agent in Germany begs to report thinks he may be of assistance.' Then, 'Your agent Arnold Heckstall will be delivered at Belgian frontier April 5th.' Finally, 'Information in diplomatic bag reaching London April 6th.' That's all."

"April 5th," said Wilcox's superior, "is Wednesday next; to-day's Saturday. I have instructed the British Embassy in Berlin to watch their diplomatic bag like a mother brooding over her sick child. They may find somebody trying to do something to it."

"Otherwise," said the Colonel, "there's nothing for it

but to wait and see what what's-his-name—Hinkson?—has to say, that is, if he turns up."

"Heckstall," said the Foreign Office man. "We knew, of course, that they had gathered him in. We did not expect—er—a happy issue out of his afflictions."

"I'll believe it when I see it," said Wilcox.

．　　．　　．　　．　　．　　．　　．　　．

In Berlin there had been another conference between the heads of the police. "This fellow Heckstall," said the Chief, "is a nuisance. I am perfectly certain he is an English agent."

"Shoot him, then," said the Deputy Chief cheerfully.

"I would with pleasure, but there have been too many Englishmen dying of heart-failure in Germany lately. They will not always believe it, and our Leader does not wish for trouble over it. There was that curate, who would have believed he really was?"

"The curate rankles with you, my dear Niehl."

"I do not like to be misinformed," said Niehl stiffly.

"Had I been in office at that time it would not have occurred," said his subordinate soothingly. "In future we will be more careful with curates. Returning to Heckstall, leave him to me, I will manage him."

"I should be very glad, my dear Lehmann. What plan had you in your mind?"

"If a man is put over the frontier at a quiet spot and found shot on Belgian territory in the morning, what business is it of ours?"

．　　．　　．　　．　　．　　．　　．　　．

The third footman at the British Embassy brought a scuttle of coal into the Ambassador's room, and made up the fire during his Excellency's temporary absence. There were a number of papers on the table, some already tied into bundles for the diplomatic bag for London. The footman glanced hastily at the door, drew a long envelope from inside his coat, pushed it into the middle of one of these bundles, and immediately left the room as the Ambassador returned to it.

.   .   .   .

The conference at the Foreign Office was resumed in the evening of April 6th with one addition to the previous company, the British agent, Arnold Heckstall, who had flown from Brussels that afternoon.

"I was picked up in Berlin on the evening of the day I got there," he said, "and consigned to gaol. That was on Wednesday, March the 22nd. They came and hauled me out for questioning occasionally, but it was not too drastic. Then yesterday evening some S.S. men came in, an officer and three others, and removed me. I thought I was going to be bumped off, of course, but they pushed me into a car and we drove to the Tempelhof Aerodrome. A plane was all ready, so we took off and flew for about two hours and came down near Aachen. There were some more S.S. men there, and we all got into Mercédès cars, four of them, with the officer, two others and myself in the second, and started off again. It was then something after midnight and perfectly dark, but we went through Aachen, which I recognized, that was how I knew where we were. They had refused to answer my questions, or, indeed, to speak to me at all except to give me orders. Some time later the cars all came to a standstill, and in the headlights of the first I saw a frontier marking post at the side of the road just ahead. The officer got out and ordered the cars to be turned round to face the way we had come, which was done."

Heckstall paused for a moment with an odd little smile and then continued.

"They came and told me to get out of the car, which I did. As there were about six of them pointing automatics at me, there did not seem to be much I could do about it. Two of them took me by the arms and marched me along the road towards the frontier, with the officer following behind. At the mark post he sent these two men back and told me to walk on, with him just behind prodding me with his automatic.

"When we were out of earshot of the rest of the party —we must have been out of sight too, in the darkness— he said, 'Keep on moving ahead of me, don't look round. When you hear two shots behind you, run like blazes. Remember what I'm saying, it's important. *Don't come back.* Officially you're dead, so don't let anyone at home see you, either. Go somewhere quiet and keep silkworms, and give my love to the Only Girl in the World!' He spoke the last five words in English with a strong German accent."

"Silkworms," said the retired Colonel thoughtfully.

"He said silkworms, sir."

"Go on, please."

"Then he fired two shots and I ran like blazes, as he said. I glanced back once or twice and could see him walking back to the cars, he was silhouetted against the lighted road. I did not know where I was except that it must be Belgium, but after wandering about for miles in the dark I reached Limburg at about 4 a.m., got an early train for Brussels and flew back by the first available plane."

"Yes," said his Foreign Office chief slowly, "we were hoping you would."

"B-but——"

"We were told you would be released on the sixth."

Heckstall merely stared at him.

"Tell me, did you see this officer plainly? What was he like?"

"Oh, quite plainly. Rather a nondescript little man, grey eyes, rather ginger hair going grey, short but not fat, thin face with duelling scars across his right cheek, quick, energetic walk, rather a pleasant voice, cheerful looking fellow, looked as though he could see a joke. Short nose, wide mouth rather thin-lipped, square jaw. He was evidently someone very important, his men fairly jumped to it when he spoke."

"Duelling scars," said Wilcox. "Evidently a pukka German."

"Which year," asked the Colonel, "was that song about the Only Girl in the World popular?"

" 'The Bing Boys'? Oh, about '16," said Wilcox.

"I am sorry to have come back without the information, sir," said Heckstall.

"We got that to-day," said his chief unexpectedly.

The startled Heckstall stared at him for the second time and slowly coloured to his eyes. "It came in the diplomatic bag from the British Embassy in Berlin to-day," the Foreign Office man went on. "It was written—or rather, typed—on British Embassy notepaper, enclosed in an official envelope, and tied up with a number of confidential documents about another rather important matter which we'd rather they hadn't read. And all this in spite of the fact that not only was the bag not tampered with—and it was not left unwatched for a single instant—but no attempt was made at any time to approach it. The King's Messenger assures me of that."

"Reminds me of Maskelyne and Devant," said the Colonel.

"I suppose," said Wilcox, who had been rubbing his hand over his head till his hair stood straight on end like a scrubbing-brush, "the Messenger is all right?"

"I'll have him watched, shall I?" said his harassed superior. "And the Ambassador too, while I'm about it? Wilcox, I haven't seen you do that since '17."

"I've had no occasion," said Wilcox. "Any suggestions, Colonel?"

"No," said the War Office man slowly. "Only—Reck used to keep silkworms."

CHAPTER II KLAUS LEHMANN

THERE was a German Naval Hospital at the top of the Avenue de la Reine in Ostende in the latter part of the Great War, and in January 1918 a man was brought in, completely unconscious, and clad only in his underwear. He had been picked up on the beach, having evidently swum or floated ashore, and in addition to suffering from exhaustion and exposure, he was wounded in the head. When they had cleaned, dried and patched him up they stood round his bed and looked at him.

"The injury at the back of the skull," said the senior house-surgeon, "may give us trouble, it is impossible to say how much damage has been done to the brain. The facial injuries are trivial."

"He'll have a couple of lovely duelling scars when they heal up," said the medical student. "Simply too Heidelberg for words."

"One is prompted to wonder how he received them," said the ward sister in her prim voice. "The contused wound in the occipital region is more easily explicable."

"He can hardly have been fighting a duel in the sea," said the surgeon, who had a literal mind.

"Oh, I don't know," said the student. "Two fellows desiring to shun publicity while they settle their differences, what could be better? Hop on a raft and shove off, loser's body is automatically and hygienically disposed of

17

by the conger of the deep, winner paddles happily ashore, what?"

"He would appear to have thrown both the seconds to the conger-eels too, my good Muller," said the surgeon.

"Of course, and while he was dealing with one of them, the other clouted him with the paddle, hence the contused wound in the occipital region."

"One is perhaps permitted to doubt whether the explanation is meant to be taken seriously," said the ward sister.

"No doubt at all, it isn't," said Muller, "but it's a dashed good one."

Their patient stirred suddenly, mumbled something, and then said in a clear, commanding voice, "Look at that, you insubordinate hound!" He shifted uneasily, and the sister slipped her arm behind his shoulder lest he should slide down and disarrange the dressings on his head.

"If he is going to be restless," said the surgeon, "he will have to be watched. He may have a morphia injection."

"Yes, sir," said the ward sister.

"He is certainly an officer," said Muller. "All that insubordinate hound business is quite definitely Potsdam."

"I think he may have received his injuries from a bursting shell," said the surgeon, "when there was all that firing from the coastal batteries early this morning—a mysterious light offshore, I understand. As to how he came to be swimming about out there, I have no conjecture to offer, unless he was washed off a submarine."

"Or escaped from Donington Hall and just swam across," suggested Muller.

"I think your remarks are regrettably frivolous," said the house-surgeon, who always disciplined with difficulty. "No doubt he will tell us all about himself in the morning."

But the surgeon was wrong, for his patient was quite

unable to give any account of himself in the morning. While he was being dragged unwillingly back from the fringes of pneumonia, he talked incessantly in the German of the educated classes, but there was never enough continuity in his remarks to give them any clue as to what or who he was. In fact, apart from telling them in a wonderful variety of well-chosen phrases what he thought of some gunners and their shooting, he did not refer to his past at all. So things went on until the day came when the stranger opened his eyes and looked about him intelligently.

The ward sister was informed of it and came to bend over him and give him the usual encouragement. "There now," she said cheerfully, "you are a lot better this morning, aren't you?"

Her patient made an effort to speak, and she expected the usual "Where am I?" but to her surprise he said, "Who am I?" instead. She thought she must have misunderstood him, and answered, "You are in the Ostende Naval Hospital. You'll have some nice soup now and go to sleep again, you'll be——"

"I see it's a hospital," he whispered feebly. "What I said was, 'Who am I?'"

"Never mind that now," she said, "you'll remember presently when you are stronger."

The nurse who brought his soup smiled at him and said, "I'll help you to drink it, shall I?" but instead of thanking her he stared at her and asked, "Who am I?"

"You poor dear," she said. "Don't worry about it now. Drink this and go to sleep. I expect you'll remember when you wake up again."

He obeyed her and dropped at once into the sudden easy sleep of weakness, but neither when he awoke again, nor the next day, nor for very many days to come did he remember who he was. He soon left off asking his pathetic question, but there remained in his eyes the puzzled, hurt expression of a child to whom some inexplicable unkindness has been done, though he was plainly a man in the late twenties. Once the senior house-surgeon, Lehmann, passing through the ward very late at night, heard small uneasy sounds from the direction of the stranger's bed, and discovered him awake and struggling with a frightful attack of panic.

"My dear fellow," said Lehmann kindly, "what is the matter?"

"I don't know—I'm frightened. I don't know who I am. Oh, God! tell me who I am!"

"Hush, gently," said the surgeon, taking a firm hold of the hot hands which clung to him for comfort. "Don't wake the others. Try to calm yourself; you will make yourself ill again. There is nothing to be afraid of."

"But there is! You see, I don't know what I've done, do I? I may be some criminal—and some day somebody may walk up to me and say, 'Ha! Got you at last!' and they'll put me in prison for years and perhaps hang me, and I'll never know what it's all about. Oh, God——"

"Listen to me," said Lehmann in a tone of authority. "You are frightening yourself with shadows. Do you think that we, whose lives are spent in seeing mankind in its worst moments, do not know good from bad? I don't know who you are, but I will stake every penny I have that you are perfectly all right. Even when you were most delirious you never said anything brutal or base, and in your utmost weakness you were courteous and unwilling to give trouble. You a criminal? Nonsense! Turn over and go to sleep again, you are torturing yourself for nothing, believe me."

"But," objected his patient, still only half-convinced, "some criminals are delightful people, I believe. Even a murderer might be. It doesn't mean you're all evil if you

have killed somebody—if you have killed somebody you
—I can't remember——"

"Stop that at once," said Lehmann. "As for killing
somebody, since there is a war on and you are of military
age, I should think it's quite probable you have. You must
pull yourself together. I am going to get you something to
drink, and then you will lie down and go to sleep again,
and we will have no more of this. In the meantime, think
this over. You may or may not have killed somebody, has
it occurred to you that it's more likely that you have
married somebody?"

In the abysmal silence which followed this appalling
suggestion, Lehmann disengaged himself and went away.
When he returned with a glass in his hand he found his
patient lying quietly back on his pillows murmuring to
himself.

"Margareta. Marie. Julie. Helene. Susanne. Elsa—Elsa.
No, I don't think so. Klara. Anna." He looked up with a
sparkle of fun in his eyes. "Do I look married?"

"Not particularly," said Lehmann, "and you don't wear
a wedding-ring. But men don't always wear one, and
besides you might have lost it. Drink this."

"Fancy me with a wife," said the stranger, between sips.
"This stuff is rather nice. I wonder what she's like."

"I should think you'd be a good picker," said the surgeon judicially, "I have noticed you betraying a certain
discrimination in the matter of nurses."

"You are extraordinarily good to me. I wish I had a
name, though."

"You can have mine if you like," said Lehmann diffi-
dently, "till you find your own. I am quite sure it will be
safe with you."

"If you're so damned decent to me," said his patient
chokily, "I shall blub on your shoulder in a minute. I say,
d-do you think I've got a family?"

"I should say at least eight," said the surgeon, patting his shoulder.

"All with noses that want blowing?"

"Oh, go to sleep—Lehmann," said Lehmann senior, and went away laughing to himself.

The next day a committee of nurses round the stranger's bed christened him, after discussion, Klaus, because he came from the sea and Nikolaus is the patron saint of sailors, and Klaus Lehmann, feeling already that he had the beginning of an identity again, started life afresh.

When he was well enough to be discharged from hospital they sent him to Hamburg on the assumption that if, as seemed likely, he had been in the Imperial Navy, he was more likely to come across someone who knew him in a Naval base than anywhere else in Germany. He said good-bye to the only people whom he knew in all the world, and set out for Hamburg in a state of trepidation which he knew he had felt before somewhere, and when he was thinking of something else the memory returned to him. He had felt like that when he was a small boy and was sent, all by himself, to the dentist.

This was so wonderful that his spirits rose with a leap. Then his memory was not destroyed, only stunned, and one day some door would reopen in his brain and he would be a person again, with a home and friends and relations of his own. He still shied at the thought of a wife, probably because he was still too weak to bear the thought of responsibility. He tried to remember more about the dentist, but that was a failure. Never mind, it was a beginning. "When I was a little boy," he said to an imaginary hearer—the carriage being empty—"I used to be sent to the dentist all by myself. Spartan training, what?" Splendid.

He was so uplifted that he stepped out of the train at

Hamburg with his chin well up and his chest thrown out, and began to run up the steps which lead to the road level, when suddenly to his rage and disgust his knees bent beneath him and he found himself sitting abruptly and watching his little suit-case bumping away down the stairs again, right to the bottom, miles away. . . . He closed his eyes and clutched the banisters. Six people rushed instantly to his assistance, three of them tried to pick him up while the other three patted him and told him to sit still and take it easy. Four more people brought him his suit-case, and a porter came with a glass of water.

"Thank you a thousand times," said poor Klaus, feeling horribly conspicuous. "I am so sorry—so stupid of me, my legs gave way."

"It is no wonder, my poor man. You have been wounded."

"But only in the head, gracious lady."

"The head controls the legs, or should do so. Lean on my arm."

"Let me help you on this other side."

"Take it easy, these stairs are steep."

"I have your suit-case, it is safe with me."

"My brother has attacks, just like this."

"My sister's husband also, but he turns quite blue."

"There we are at the top. Would you like to rest a moment?"

"Where do you wish to go?"

"I think you should have some coffee. It is a stimulant."

"I think he should go and lie down quite flat. My brother always does."

"My sister's husband, on the other hand——"

"I think I will take a cab," said Klaus, who felt he would really like to be alone, "the air will restore me."

"You may be right, if the movement does not upset you."

"Have you far to go?"

"Are you going to friends?"

"It is plain to me, gracious lady," said Klaus, "that in the city of Hamburg everyone is a friend."

They chose him the cab with the steadiest-looking horse on the rank, commended him to the personal surveillance of the driver, and Klaus at last drove away.

He was given employment in the Naval depot and spent wearisome days filling up forms indenting for vests, singlets, jumpers, trousers and socks, Naval ratings, for the use of, in the intervals between devastating headaches, but he never met anyone who had known him. He lived in the Naval barracks at Hamburg where men came and went continually, but still no one said, "I remember that fellow. He was with me in the so-and-so."

As the summer of 1918 drew to its close and the news from the Western Front grew steadily worse, the morale of the Navy deteriorated. Discipline became slack and finally bad, little groups of idle men stood about and were harangued by Communist agitators, and ratings were covertly or openly insolent to their officers. Unpleasant scenes were continually occurring, where frayed tempers, undernourishment and despair combined to make men lose control of themselves; on one of these occasions Klaus heard a Naval officer call a seaman "you insubordinate dog." At that the little door in his mind opened for an instant, and he heard himself saying, "Look at that, you insubordinate hound," something to do with petrol, a dump somewhere, and men in field grey. The door closed again at once and he could remember no more, but that must have been in the Army, not the Navy. No wonder the life here seemed unfamiliar and no one ever knew him, he must have been a soldier, not a sailor.

Work in the depot petered out, and in October he was discharged. In pursuance of a plan he had formed in his mind, he left Hamburg just before the rioting broke out and drifted down towards the Western Front to look for his lost identity somewhere in the German Army. He wandered through Hanover, Dortmund, Elberfeld, and Dusseldorf towards Aachen, sometimes stopping several days in one place if he liked the look of it, and sometimes going on again next morning. He stayed for nearly a fortnight at a tiny place called Haspe among the forests northeast of Elberfeld, because there was an old lady there who said that Klaus Lehmann strongly reminded her of her brother at about that age, and he had left a son who had been reported missing. She did not know the son, and Klaus might, conceivably, be he. She produced a photograph of the late Herr Rademeyer to prove her point.

"There you are," she said. "You can see it for yourself, a child could see it. The same forehead, the same nose, one ear sticking out more than the other, the likeness is ludicrous. You are thinner, of course, my brother was well covered."

Klaus looked with awe at the presentment of a portly gentleman with a stuffed expression, and suppressed an impulse to describe him mentally as a pie-faced old sausage-maker—after all, this might be his father—and said, "He has a kind face, kind but firm."

"You might have known him, to say that. Of course, since he was your father you probably did. I mean, since he was probably your father, you did. Georg was a great character, quiet but unyielding. You will stay with me till Thursday week when his widow, your mother, comes to visit me. She ought to know."

So Klaus Lehmann stayed on at the white house among the trees in Haspe, and was introduced to the local worthies, among them the old doctor who had known Herr Rademeyer well.

"Quiet but unyielding," he said, when Klaus quoted this. "Obstinate, she means. Dumb and stubborn as an army mule was Georg Rademeyer, and the more he dug his toes in, the dumber he became. Heaven forgive me, he is now dead."

"You do not seem to have been one of his admirers," said Klaus, much amused.

"There was this to be said for him, he was no chatter-box. He had nothing to say and he didn't say it, heaven rest his soul."

Klaus waited in Haspe for a possible parent, and was fussed over and made much of by a possible aunt. He was well fed for the first time for years, or so it seemed, since, though beef and mutton were almost unobtainable, there were still chickens scratching in the weedy stable-yard and wild-looking pigs ran about in the woods. The store-room shelves of the white house were still full of jams, pickles and preserves, and there was wine in the cellars. Klaus would come out on the verandah after lunch, with a pleasantly replete feeling, and sit in a warm corner in the late sunshine with an overcoat and a book, listening to Hanna singing in the kitchen and the dry beech leaves whispering in the hedges till he fell asleep and dreamed of things he could not recall when he awoke. An idyllic ex-istence, and he grew stronger and better every day, but still he could not remember who he was.

At the time appointed Frau Rademeyer came and dis-pelled the illusion of peace.

"Nonsense, Ludmilla! The young man is no more like Georg than he's like the Shah of Persia, and he's even less like my Moritz. You must be in your dotage, Ludmilla."

"Nonsense yourself," said the old lady stoutly. "There is a strong resemblance."

"Besides, Moritz had scars on his left knee ever since he

fell against the staircase window. Young man, show me your left knee."

"I fear I am not the Herr Moritz Rademeyer," said Klaus, pulling up his trouser-leg. "Quite unblemished, as you see. Well, I must go on looking, that's all—— For pity's sake, Fräulein Rademeyer!"

For the gallant old woman had crumbled into a heap in her chair and burst into tears.

"I wanted him for my nephew," she wailed. "I am so much alone."

"Let's pretend I am," suggested Klaus, and kissed her hand. "It will be just as nice."

"You are a fool, Ludmilla, to let yourself be imposed upon by some good-for-nothing from no one knows where, but what can one expect from an old maid but folly?"

"Leave my house, Mathilde! I will not be insulted!"

"I shall be only too pleased——" began Frau Rademeyer, rising from her chair, but at that moment the servant Hanna burst into the room.

"Oh, Fräulein! Oh, Herr Lehmann! The postman has been and he says the war is over!"

"Control yourself, Hanna," said her mistress. "Go and fetch old Theodor with his truck for the luggage, the Frau Rademeyer is leaving us."

"But, *gnädige Fräulein*, the war——"

"Hanna!"

Hanna went, and so did Frau Rademeyer.

Klaus stayed on for a few days, but the news had made him fidgety. Somewhere out there, beyond these prison-walls of pines, great events were stirring, and he in this backwater——

"I must go," he said. "I will come back, but I must go and see what is happening. Perhaps I shall find myself, and I'll come back to tell you I'm no longer a good-for-nothing from nobody knows where."

"If you quote that vixen to me," said Fräulein Rademeyer, "I will throw the inkpot at you. Yes, go, my dear boy, but do not be away too long."

Klaus Lehmann reached Aachen in time to see the German Army coming home. There were triumphal arches across the streets and the people tried to cheer, but the soldiers dragged their feet and walked dispiritedly along, sometimes not even in step, tired, shabby, defeated. They fell out as the evening came on, and people took them into their houses to sleep, the inns also were full of them, and Klaus went about trying to make them talk. They talked willingly enough, but not about the war, that was too recent and too hopeless, they spoke only of their homes and the quickest way to get there, and grumbled about their bad boots and the food, the weather and the mud. Still no one recognized Klaus out of all those thousands, nor did the Army customs and the Army slang awaken any response in his mind, he felt no more at home there than he did in the Navy. "I must have belonged to one or the other, surely," he said to himself, "unless I was in the Air Force. Perhaps that was it, and I made a forced landing in the sea, and that's how I came to swim ashore. It's a reasonable solution. I will go and look for the Air Force —what's left of it."

CHAPTER III   SOUP-KITCHEN

KLAUS LEHMANN went by stages from Aachen to Darmstadt. He passed through Cologne on the 13th of December, 1918, that was the day the British troops marched in. No German would care to see the Army of Occupation come in, and Lehmann's heart was as heavy as any other man's as the Leinsters' pipes sounded in the Cathedral Square.

At Darmstadt aerodrome he found a number of German war planes waiting to be surrendered for demolition, but very few men about, only just enough for a maintenance party, and to hand over to the British with sufficient ceremony. Klaus drifted on to the aerodrome and leaned against the corner of one of the sheds, looking gloomily at nothing in particular, since that seemed to be the only occupation of such men as were to be seen. Presently he was observed—one of a group of mechanics, after obvious discussion about him, went into a building which looked like an officers' mess, presumably to report. In due course a long, thin officer emerged, and walked towards him.

"What are you doing here?" he asked.

"Nothing," said Klaus with perfect truth.

"What is your name?"

"Lehmann."

"Rank?"

"I have no rank now," said Klaus with mournful resignation.

Several regiments of the German Army had mutinied and torn the badges of rank from their officers' uniforms. The flying man jumped to the conclusion that Klaus' case was one of those which called for tact, so he introduced himself in the correct manner. "Flug-Leutnant Becker, sir," he said, saluting.

Klaus returned the salute casually. "Anything happening here?"

"No, sir, nothing. What should happen? We are waiting for the Allied Commission to come and burn the planes."

"Of course, of course. I cannot think why they do not take them over instead of destroying such valuable machines."

"They have so many already that they don't know what to do with them," said Becker bitterly. "Why should they bother with ours? Will you not come along to the mess, sir?"

"Thank you. Any news?"

"No, none. Only Goering's escapade. Of course, you have heard about that, sir."

"Richthoven's successor. No, what's he doing?"

"Refuses to be demobilized or to surrender his machines in spite of orders from High Command. I don't know where they are now."

"Good," said Klaus judicially. "A little more of that spirit and we should not have lost the war."

"There was plenty of that sort of spirit," said the flying man reproachfully. "It was motor spirit we were short of. Many machines were grounded because there was nothing to put in their tanks."

"I know, I know. Your morale was excellent," said

Lehmann hastily. "When I said that I was thinking of other branches."

The Flight-Lieutenant thought it advisable to preserve a sympathetic silence. The two men had just reached the doorway of the mess when they heard the distant roar of aeroplanes approaching, and turned to look in the direction from which it came.

"The victorious Allies, I presume."

"No, sir, ours! They must be Goering's lot," said Becker excitedly.

Five planes drew nearer as they spoke, circled the aerodrome, touched down and taxied up to the sheds. "Excuse me, sir," said the Flight-Lieutenant, and sprinted towards them while Lehmann followed more slowly in time to hear a man in the leading machine shouting, "Got any petrol?"

"No, sir, none," yelled Becker in reply, at which the new-comer signalled with his arms to the other four pilots, they all switched off their engines and quiet descended again on the aerodrome. The men climbed out of their machines and their leader strolled with Becker across the grass towards Lehmann. He was a big man with a booming voice, and Klaus distinctly heard him say, "Who the devil's that? One of the demolition squad?"

Becker apparently gave some satisfactory explanation, for when they met the stranger was cordial. Becker introduced them.

"How d'you do?" said Goering, shaking hands. "Met you before somewhere, haven't I?"

Klaus' heart leaped up, but all he said was, "It is possible," in guarded tones. He was not, of course, prepared to tell complete strangers about his troubles, but Goering disregarded the reserve which Becker had respected.

"What were you in?"

Lehmann felt a little annoyed. The question was natural

enough, but it was a sore point with him. "Oh, I just made myself useful here and there," he said.

Goering stared, then an idea struck him. "Oh, I see! Intelligence, eh? Do you still have to be so hush-hush about it now it's all done with?"

"Is it?" said Klaus, and left it at that.

Goering looked at him with something approaching respect; as for Becker, his round eyes and awestruck expression were almost comic. "Well, well," said the Flight-Commander, "I know you fellows did awfully good work. I couldn't do it. Give me action." He glanced over his shoulder at the motionless aeroplanes, his face darkened and he relapsed into silence. As for Klaus Lehmann, his brain was busy. It seemed there was no need to tell people things about one's self, if one just preserved an enigmatic silence, people would always find an explanation for themselves, believing it all the more firmly because the idea was their own.

While they were still thirty yards from the mess, a figure appeared in the doorway, a square solid figure which Goering appeared to recognize, for he paused in his stride and said to Becker, "That fellow there! Is that Lazarus?"

"That is Squadron-Leader Lazarus, sir. He has been in command here since Squadron-Leader Fienburg left last week."

Goering muttered something which the tactful Becker thought it wiser not to hear, and walked on again. Becker dropped back a little and Lehmann joined him.

"Look out for squalls," muttered Becker.

"Why?"

"Can't stand each other. Always squalls."

"Good evening, Goering," said Lazarus from the doorstep.

"Evening, Lazarus," said Goering, without attempting to salute. "Got any petrol in this dump of yours?"

"You will address me as 'sir,' " said Lazarus, his long nose reddening.

"Oh, suffering cats, they've started already," said Becker under his breath.

"I asked, sir, whether, sir, you had any petrol, sir," said Goering impertinently.

"What for?"

"To put into the tanks of my machines. Not to wash in, though to be sure it gets the grease off," said the Flight-Commander, staring at his superior's rather oily complexion.

"A painful scene," murmured Klaus sympathetically, to which Becker only replied, "You wait."

"I have no petrol," said Lazarus, "and if I had you would not get it. Your machines are grounded by order of the High Command."

Goering stated what he considered to be the appropriate ultimate destination of the High Command.

"I cannot hear this," said Lazarus, who had the infuriating quality of becoming cooler as the other became more heated. "Your agitation is understandable, Flight-Commander, though your expression of it is unfortunate in the extreme. The Allied Commission is expected to arrive here this afternoon—at any time now," he added, glancing at his watch. "You will be good enough to control yourself and not give the enemy an opportunity of saying that a German officer does not know how to behave in defeat."

"You lousy pig-faced Jew," began Goering, but the doorway was empty. "Some day," promised Goering, "you shall pay for that." He stalked in at the door, disregarding entirely his enthralled audience behind.

"Will they meet again inside?" asked Klaus.

"No. The skipper will go to his room, to await, with dignity, the Allied Commission. Goering will go to the bar, to drown his sorrows. I suppose we ought to do what

we can for these other fellows," said Becker, referring to
Goering's fellow pilots, who were coming up. "It is a bad
day for them, you know."

"Can't we get them away before the—the bonfire
starts?" suggested Klaus, who was beginning to feel that
he had known Becker for years.

"Doubt if they'd go. Like all great performers, a trifle
temperamental—all bar one, that is."

"Who's that?"

"Udet. Sh, here they come."

About an hour later the Commission arrived, to be
received with the utmost formality by Lazarus, while
Goering and his men simmered in silence. The machines
were taken over, receipted, entered up in triplicate, and
destroyed by fire, after which the Commission went its
way again in two staff cars and an Army lorry. Becker and
Lehmann, united by the comradeship which arises between strangers sheltering in the same doorway from the
same storm, looked at each other.

"What happens now?"

"Heaven knows. I can't stand a lot more," said Becker,
who looked white and shaken. "Those machines——"

"I know," said Klaus, and took him by the elbow. "A
foul sight. Come and have a drink."

They found the rest of the party in the bar, talking in
quiet tones and covertly watching Goering, who was sitting by himself on a high stool with his elbows on his
knees, glowering at everyone and drinking heavily.

"What are you going to do now, Kaspar?" one pilot
asked another.

"Oh, go back to my bank, I suppose, that is if there's
any money left in it to count. Funny, being a bank clerk
again after all this. What about you?"

"Back to school, I expect, I was a schoolmaster in Berlin. I shall probably get a job somewhere, money or no money there will always be small boys. What does it matter?"

One of them was evidently a good deal older than the others, a quiet man with resolution in his manner. "Some-one," he said in low tones, "ought to speak to Goering. There will be a frightful scene if he goes on drinking and brooding like that."

"You do it, then," said Kaspar. "Life isn't particularly sweet just now, but I don't want to end it by being brained with a bottle by my Flight-Commander."

The quiet man nodded, picked up his glass, strolled across to Hermann Goering, sitting alone, and asked him if he had any orders for them.

"None," said Goering sullenly. "You can go and take orders from the French now. They might find you a job burning aircraft elsewhere, there are still a few left to destroy."

His senior pilot continued to look at him calmly, with-out speaking, till Goering lifted his head and his almost insane expression softened.

"I beg your pardon, Erich, I am beside myself to-night. No, I have no orders to give you any more—at least, not yet." He paused, and drew a long breath. "There will come a day when we shall meet again, and there will be orders to give and men to carry them out and machines to —to carry them out in." He slipped from his stool and stood erect against the bar, a magnificent figure of a man in those days, with his head thrown back, defiance replac-ing despair. "They think they've got us down, but we shan't stay down," he cried. "Germany shall rise again and we with her, we'll have the greatest Air Force in the world. Then let them look out, these beastly little people who burn aircraft they are unfit to fly!" He turned to find his glass and staggered. "Drink to the new German Air Arm, invincible, innum—" he stumbled over the word—"innumerable, unbeatable. Hoch!"

His men cheered him and Goering smiled once more. "We'll have no Jews in it next time, boys. No oily Hebrews for us. I'll see to that, because I shall lead it myself. Then it'll all be all right. You'll see."

"Rather distressing, what?" said Becker to Lehmann while Goering was being helped to bed. "I think he'll probably pull it off, too, one of these days. I shall be too old to serve then, I expect. I do dislike that braggart manner, though, don't you?"

"A trifle hysterical, perhaps," said Klaus. "One could not wonder if that were so."

"No worse for him than for the rest of us, but Goering was always like that. One of those get-out-of-my-way-blast-you fellows. Now, Udet is different. Udet——"

It was made plain to Klaus that Udet was something quite exceptional, but not all Becker's enthusiasm and friendliness could make Lehmann feel that the Air Force was where he belonged. Perhaps Goering's wild guess was correct, and he had belonged to German Intelligence. If so, he had no idea what steps he could take to establish contact, it would be necessary to wait until somebody recognized him and fell on his neck with ecstatic cries of "Ah! The famous X37! We thought you were lost to us." A pretty picture, if a trifle improbable. None the less, he went to Berlin to look for his lost background.

Here he found for the first time people looking to the future instead of the past, which is a pleasant way of saying that everyone was furiously talking politics. This bored him unendurably because he never got a clear idea of who was who and what they wanted, nor why they had split into such violently opposing parties since they were all Socialists. He gathered by degrees that one party was led by Ebert, the saddle-maker from Heidelberg, and they were moderate in tone, not so much red as a hopeful shade of pink. Then there was Karl Liebknecht who called himself Spartacus, whose party was as red as raw beef and demanded a soviet republic immediately, a working-class dictatorship with all necessary violence. Between these two came a rather nebulous minority party who also wanted a soviet republic, but were prepared to be a little more genial in their methods. Klaus' private opinion was that they all made his head ache, but that Ebert's Social Democrats were faintly less offensive than the others. Klaus was addressed on the subject one day early in January, by the elderly scarecrow from whom he bought his daily paper.

"That there Spartacus," said the old man, "regular upsetting firebrand. Wants to turn everything upside down as though they wasn't bad enough already."

"Just so," said Klaus.

"Him and his Rosa Luxembourg! Huh!"

"Oh, quite."

"And them left-wing minority lot, neither soap nor cheese as they say. Minority's all they'll ever be, in my opinion."

"It sounds probable," said Klaus, only deterred from walking away by the fact that he had nowhere particular to walk to.

"Ebert's the man for me," said the paper-seller. "Parliamentary democracy on the votes of the whole community. What could be fairer?"

"What indeed?"

"I only hope that when we has the elections at the end of the month they gets in with a thumping majority. Show them rowdy Communists where they gets off, that will."

"Yes, won't it?"

"Something we've never had before, that is, parliamen-

tary democracy on the votes of the whole community. I
says to my old woman——"

Klaus drifted off, for something had just occurred to
him as strange. A democracy based on universal suffrage
was something Germany had never had before, yet to him
it had seemed so natural as to go without saying. Where,
then, had he been brought up? Was it possible that he was
not a German after all? No, that was an absurd idea.

The next man he talked to, or rather, who talked to
him, was a young workman waiting for a tram, to whom
Liebknecht was the builder of the New Jerusalem and
Rosa Luxembourg a greater Joan of Arc.

"I think I will go back to Aunt Ludmilla in Haspe for
a little while," thought Lehmann. "I will if I don't get
that post office job," for his money was running short and
he was looking for work.

Two days later the Spartacists revolted and there was
savage fighting in the streets, flaring up and passing, leaving crumpled bundles, which till that moment had been
men and women, lying in the road or crawling painfully
to shelter. Ebert's Government called up the remnants of
the old Imperial Army, and a fortnight of hideous terror
followed in Berlin till the revolt was put down with the
strong hand. Karl Liebknecht and Rosa Luxembourg died
at the hands of the police on their way to prison. Klaus
Lehmann's headaches became so insupportable that he
could not have taken the post office appointment even if
it had been offered to him, so he went to Haspe again.
Here the great news was that Hanna had become engaged
to the postman, and under the fallen leaves in the garden
were snowdrops showing white. Here it was only as a
rumour of half-real happenings that Ebert won his elections and there was established the well-intentioned Con-
stitution of Weimar.

Eventually Klaus obtained a post teaching mathematics

in a school at Dusseldorf, where for a couple of years he was not unhappy. He was earning enough to keep himself and to take the old lady presents when he went home— he had learned to call it home—to Haspe at week-ends and in the holidays. Hanna married the postman, fat smiling Emilie took her place, and the world was not too bad till the mark began to fall in value.

"I cannot understand it," said Fräulein Rademeyer. "The price of everything is rising so rapidly that one's income cannot keep pace with it. I think it is very wicked of people to be so greedy and charge so much."

Klaus tried to explain that the currency was being inflated so that German goods might sell more easily abroad, but the old lady would not have it.

"Nonsense. All I know is that once I was comfortably off on the money my dear father left me, and now I am growing poorer every day. Now you tell me they are doing this so that the foreigner may buy more cheaply. Why does the Government wish to benefit the foreigner at the expense of its own people? Nonsense. They ought to be turned out of office."

"Perhaps there will soon come a turn for the better," said Klaus hopefully, but he was wrong, for things went from bad to worse. Early in 1922 Fräulein Rademeyer's income dwindled to vanishing point, and she sold the white house in Haspe with most of its contents and moved into Dusseldorf to share Klaus' lodgings. The sale took place during the holidays, so Klaus was at Haspe to see it through and to stand by Ludmilla Rademeyer as the auctioneer's men carried the old-fashioned furniture out on the lawn in the cruelly bright sunshine. The old lady sat very upright in a chair under the verandah and watched proceedings, although Klaus begged her to come away.

"I wish you wouldn't stay here," he said. "Come to

the doctor's house and rest there till it is over, it will be too much for you."

"I would rather stay, or these people will think I am a coward. Besides, what does it matter? It is only old furniture, and the people who loved it are all dead except me."

"Who cares what people think?"

"I do, my dear, one must set a good example."

Klaus bit his lip.

"How curiously shabby the things look, my dear, I had no idea that tapestry was so faded. It is time they were turned out."

Her voice was perfectly steady and her face calm, but the thin hands in her lap were twitching, and Klaus turned away his head so as to avoid seeing them. He caught sight of the old doctor making his way round the crowd, excused himself, and went to meet him.

"How's she taking it?"

"Very well. Too well. I've been trying to persuade her to come away to your house, but she won't, she only sits there and gets older every moment."

"I'd like to put her under chloroform," grunted the doctor.

They were fairly comfortable at first in Dusseldorf, though every day saw prices higher and food and clothing scarcer, but the real blow fell when Lehmann's school closed because the parents could no longer pay the fees, and Klaus found himself unemployed. This was the time when the mark soared to an astronomical figure, and people took attaché cases to collect the bulky bundles of worthless notes which constituted their wages. Klaus tramped the streets looking for work, occasionally getting a week's employment sawing timber or loading bricks, while Ludmilla, when his back was turned, trotted out and sold her mother's watch or the gold cross and chain she had worn for her first communion. They moved into cheaper rooms, and then into cheaper ones again, and Klaus almost reached breaking-point the day he went to look for her and found her patiently scrubbing his shirt in the communal wash-house.

"But, my dear boy, it's the only place where there is any hot water. One must be clean."

"I will not have you there," he stormed, "among all those rough women. I can wash my shirt myself."

He said "my shirt", you notice, not "my shirts". As for the rough women, he need not have worried. Apart from a tendency to call a spade a spade not one of them would ever have use a word deliberately to distress or embarrass Ludmilla. Still matters grew worse. There followed the communal kitchen, the soup-kitchen, and the bread queues, the gnawing hunger and, as the winter came on, the cold, and even Ludmilla's courage sank.

"I think I have lived rather too long," she said.

CHAPTER IV
AMONG THOSE PRESENT

FRÄULEIN RADEMEYER came back one day to the two bleak rooms they tried to call home, and Klaus lifted his head in surprise at her air of unmistakable triumph. She shut the door carefully behind her, put her bag down and took out of it half a cabbage, perfectly fresh, a wedge of cheese, a small piece of steak, a loaf, a twist of paper containing alleged coffee, and another containing several spoonfuls of brown sugar.

"Wait," she said. "That is not all."

She brought out of the pocket of her cloak a small parcel wrapped in greaseproof paper.

"Butter," she said in awed tones, "real butter."

"Have you been going in for highway robbery," said Klaus, "or merely petty larceny? Not that the result is petty——"

"There is a man outside the door," she interrupted, "with a bundle. Would you bring it in, my dear?"

Klaus returned with a small sack containing firewood on the top and coal underneath—not much, but some.

"For heaven's sake, explain," said Klaus. "Have you met Santa Claus, or what is it?"

"I met a schoolfriend of mine, that is all, though it is true her name is Christine. Let me come to the fire, dear, I want to make it up. She and her husband have just come to live here. Give me three sticks—no, four. He was one of the architects or master contractors or something who have just built the new Deutches Museum at Munich. Now the coal. They came to live here because her mother's house—would you like to come and blow this while I prepare the stew?—because her mother's house was empty and her husband has retired, and they thought they might as well live here as anywhere else. Oh, dear, how I do run on, I haven't been so excited since—I think I will sit down a moment, I don't feel well."

Klaus abandoned the crackling fire and sprang to help her to the battered old sofa on which he slept at night.

"For pity's sake lie down and keep quite a minute," he said. "I'll put the kettle on, we'll have coffee and bread-and-butter while the stew cooks. I shall buy a collar and chain for you, you run about too much."

"No. The coffee is for later on. We shall overeat ourselves if we are not careful. I will lie still while you peel the potatoes. Peel four."

They feasted at last and were warm at the same time, an almost forgotten luxury, since as a rule one could either buy food or fuel, but not both. Ludmilla went on with her story.

"I told Christine all about you and what a burden I am to you——"

"Then you told her a pack of lies, and the wolf will get you."

"No, for if it were not for me you could go wandering off and find work somewhere."

This was perfectly true, but Klaus had hoped it had not occurred to her.

"Rubbish," he said stoutly. "If it were not for you I should have turned into a filthy tramp, all holes, whiskers and spots."

"Spots?"

"Where I had entertained visitors," he explained kindly. "Go on about Christine."

"She has a son-in-law. Do you know anything about" —she pulled a leaflet from another of her numerous pockets and read from it—"Transport by land, road and railway, construction of tunnels and bridges, ships, aeronautics, or meteorology?"

"No, but I jolly soon will if it means work. Why?"

"Because her son-in-law is in charge of the section of the Deutches Museum which deals with all those things, and he wants steady, reliable men to look after them."

"I think I could manage that. You only have to walk about and tell people not to touch."

"You have to explain things to children when they ask you questions."

"Oh, that's easy," said Klaus happily. "You just tell 'em they'll understand all these things better when they are a little older."

"That wouldn't have satisfied me when I was young," said Ludmilla. "Perhaps the young folk of the present day are less tiresome than I was."

"Even now you haven't told me where all the food came from."

"Out of her larder. We went into her house to talk, and then we went into her larder while she put all these things in my bag. Then I said I must go, so she sent their servant to carry it, and the coal. Also, we are going to dinner there to-morrow."

"Can you cut hair," asked Klaus anxiously, "if I sharpen our nail-scissors?"

They went to Munich in the spring of 1923, a year almost to the day since the auction at Haspe, and found two tiny bedrooms and a sitting-room in the upper half of a workman's house in Quellen Strasse, close to the Mariahilfe Church in the old part of the city. From here

it was only a short walk for Klaus through the Kegelhof
and by Schwartz Strasse and the outer Erhardt Bridge,
to the Isar island which is nearly covered by the immense
buildings of the Deutches Museum. The pay was desperately little in those days, but permanent, and as Lehmann
came to know the Museum personnel, some of the un-
married members of the staff were glad to have Ludmilla
to darn socks and vests for them. Gradually they got a
home together, with chairs replacing packing-cases, and
blankets on the beds instead of coats and sacks and strips
of carpet. They were always hungry and usually cold,
but they had occupation.

Klaus was fortunate in the man who worked in the
same part of a section as he did. Herr Kurt Stiebel was an
elderly man who had been a partner in a firm of solicitors
of some repute in Munich; in common with the rest of
the professional classes in Germany he had been brought
to absolute penury in the slump, and thought himself
fortunate to have obtained a post which would provide
him with a fireless attic in a narrow turning off the Höhe
Strasse, and almost enough food to keep him from starving. Klaus brought him home to Quellen Strasse one evening after the Museum closed, to drink watery but hot
cups of "Blumen" coffee and eat a few leathery little
cakes Ludmilla had saved up to buy for the party.

"You are our first guest, Herr Stiebel," said Fräulein
Rademeyer, "you are very welcome indeed."

"I am honoured," said the old gentleman, and kissed
her hand. "It is long since I had the pleasure of being
entertained."

"Take this chair," said Klaus. "That one has a loose
leg, I have learned the art of sitting on it."

"It is as well," said Ludmilla. "It will cure you of your
regrettable tendency to lounging. Have you had a good
day, Herr Stiebel?"

"I was not asked more than twenty questions of which I did not know the answers. There was a small boy who asked who invented the arch, and when I said the Romans did—I believe that is right—he asked who the Romans were. I directed him to the Ethnological Section."

"He didn't go," said Klaus. "He came and asked me why bricks are usually red and what makes the veins in marble. Even that wasn't so bad as the young man who asked me to explain in simple language the Precession of the Equinoxes. I swivelled him off to what's-his-name in Astronomy."

"We are learning," said Stiebel dryly, "to cope with these emergencies. When I was a solicitor and found myself confronted with a poser I used to say I would consult the authorities. Now my clients do it instead."

"My father used to say," said Ludmilla, "that you can't teach an old hand new tricks, but I have learned many things this last year or so."

"We all have, my dear lady, even to seeing a saddler of Heidelberg Chancellor of a German Republic, and a house-painter from Vienna leading a march on Berlin."

"Where is he now, what is his name—the house-painter?"

"Hitler. Serving a sentence of five years' detention in a fortress."

"Did you ever see him?" asked Klaus. "I have heard much about him. General Ludendorff was behind that, I understand."

"Certainly he was, there is no secret about that; Ludendorff, in my opinion, wanted to turn out Ebert and did not care what tools he used for the work, but as you know, the scheme failed ignominiously. Yes, I have seen Hitler several times and have been to one or two of his meetings. You know," said Stiebel, as one apologizing for a lapse, "one goes anywhere when one has no occupation, it serves to pass the time. To my mind, he is just a stump-orator, I doubt if we hear any more of him."

"He obtained a considerable following, did he not?"

"Among the more excitable and despairing elements, undoubtedly, Fräulein. Unhappy young men, seeing no future, neurasthenic ex-servicemen, Army officers with no pay and no prospects, older men with their life's work ruined, such as these are tinder to his spark. But when prosperity returns to our Germany, as return it must, there will be no place for such firebrands as Hitler."

"Apart from Ludendorff," said Klaus, "did any of the more conspicuous war figures support him?"

"Only Goering, so far as I can remember. He was very severely wounded in the shooting, and smuggled out of the country, I hear. He may have died, I do not know."

"Goering? The air ace? I met him at Darmstadt," said Klaus.

All through the year 1923 the mark, already so low in value that fifty would not buy a box of matches, dropped and dropped until ordinary figures lost their meaning, and English soldiers in the Occupied Area bought good cars for the equivalent of a few shillings, and a factory in full production for a few pounds. Men and women, and especially young people, sold all they had or could give for the price of a meal or a taste of ordinary civilized comfort, and every street, almost every house, had its tragedy when vice, as always, walked hand in hand with despair, saying, "Let us eat, drink, and be merry—or pretend to be—for to-morrow we die." It was so horrible as to be incredible, had it not been so oppressively real, this condition of a nation where nobody at all had any money which was worth anything at all, it was like the awful catastrophic ravings of some inspired prophet of evil.

"Surely," said Klaus to Stiebel, "things must take a

turn for the better soon, this cannot go on. Something must happen or we shall all die."

"Do you recall," said Stiebel in his precise way, "what someone said during the war about the gold-red-black of our Flag? Gold, they said, for the past; red for the present; and black for the future. Well, this is the future, and I see no end to it."

He put his glasses on his nose and they immediately fell off again, he caught them with a bitter little laugh. "I could wish our agonies were not so frequently absurd also. My nose is so thin my glasses will not stay in place."

"Give them to me," said Klaus, and spent ten minutes cutting thicker cork pads and fitting them in the slides. "Perhaps that will be better."

"It is admirable," said the old gentleman, trying them on.

"I wish I could fill all our voids with a little cork and a sharp knife."

"Then there would be a shortage of cork," said Stiebel acidly. "It is evident to me that Heaven is tired of Germany."

In the early autumn someone asked Klaus whether he was going to hear Hitler speak.

"I thought he was in prison," said Lehmann casually.

"Where can you live not to have heard the news? He has been released and is speaking at a meeting on Saturday."

Klaus went, since the hall would be warmed and the entertainment free, besides, he had by this time heard Hitler described alternatively as a gas-bag, a great leader, a firebrand, a stump-orator, a Messiah, a poisonous little reptile, the Hope of Germany and the Curse of Munich, and Lehmann was mildly curious. He hardly knew what he expected—some loud-voiced professional ranter, full of stock phrases and fly-blown arguments. He saw instead a pale young man with a nervous manner and very little self-control. Hitler spoke of Germany as she was and as she might be. He laid the blame for the present appalling condition of affairs on the Treaty of Versailles, the Weimar Government, the Jews, the profiteers, and the foreigner, and worked himself up into a state of hysterical excitement, screaming and weeping and losing the thread of his arguments in a manner which rather repelled Klaus, though there was no doubt that the man was sincere and he carried the meeting with him. Klaus returned home in a thoughtful mood, and Fräulein Rademeyer asked what he thought of the little Austrian.

"I don't know. I can't admire a man with so little self-control—when he gets excited he yells like a madman. But there is no doubt he can sway the crowd, and it is possible that if he were well advised he might yet do something for Germany."

"My dear, have another potato, you have eaten nothing. He is quite a common little man, is he not?"

"He might be a clerk or a shop-assistant, yes. He is neurotic and unbalanced, yes. He shouts and weeps and contradicts himself, but he can make people listen to him."

"So you said, Klaus, but does he say anything worth listening to? What does he want to do?"

"He wants to turn out all the old men who have brought us into this mess, he says that in future Youth shall lead Germany. He blames the Jews and the profiteers for the fall of the mark."

"Very possibly he is right, but what exactly does he propose doing in the matter? Is he an financier?"

"I don't know," confessed Klaus. "I suppose he will have to have financial advisers. As to what he proposes to do, he wants to run candidates from his party at the Reichstag elections, and when they have a majority they will reform the country."

"Ever since I was old enough to read the papers," said the old lady, "leaders of political parties have been saying that. I expect they said it in Ur of the Chaldees."

"Yes, I know," said Klaus, thumping the table, "but this time somebody has got to do it, or we shall all die. I am not overmuch impressed by this fellow Hitler, but at least he is someone fresh. He has ideas——"

"God forbid that I should throw cold water on the smallest spark of hope, but we have been disappointed so often. Neurotic, unstable, incoherent, it does not sound promising."

"I admit it doesn't, but at least here is someone prepared to try and save us."

"And you think he has a chance?"

"I don't know, but I shall make a point of seeing him again. I have come to that state where I would support a convicted murderer or an illiterate village wench if I thought either could help Germany. Hitler, after all, is more probable than Jeanne d'Arc, and look what she did! She raised France from the gutter——"

"Have another potato, dear," said the sardonic old lady.

A week or two later Klaus strolled into a café one evening to drink a glass of cheap beer and exchange views with his fellows, a mild extravagance he sometimes permitted himself when the monotony of his life became more than he could bear. On this occasion there was a group of men gathered closely about one table listening to two of their number who were arguing hotly.

"But you must base the mark upon some definite asset, and we have no gold. Gold is the basis of all reputable currencies."

"That is the way the capitalists talk, and the Jews, who have ruined our country between them. The real wealth is in the land, in fields and mines and forests, and in the good work of our people in factories, not in the pockets of the rich."

"I have heard that voice before," said Klaus to himself, for he could not see the speaker over the shoulders of the men surrounding him. Klaus said "Gu'n'abend" to one or two who were known to him, and they made room for him in the circle; he was right, the speaker was Hitler.

Lehmann sat sipping his beer and listening to the discussion, which became increasingly one-sided as Hitler worked himself up and harangued his hearers without staying to hear what was said in reply, and it seemed to Klaus that Hitler had all the drive, fire and enthusiasm, and personal magnetism too, while greater intelligence and reasoning power remained with the two or three who opposed him. Why must they be opposed, Klaus wondered, if knowledge and skill could be harnessed to the service of this little human dynamo? Something might yet be done, even now.

He was introduced to Hitler that evening and made a point of seeing a good deal of him in the weeks that followed. He remained unimpressed by the little man's mental capacity, but there was no doubt of his sincerity nor of his uncanny power of gaining adherents, in ever increasing numbers, to his party. Undoubtedly the man could be useful, and Klaus joined the National Socialists to be welcomed for his sturdy common sense and resourcefulness. Their leader came to rely upon him as a man whose advice was worth attention and whose reliability was beyond question.

One night in winter Klaus invited his new leader to coffee at the house in Quellen Strasse, and Hitler came. Fräulein Rademeyer welcomed him with the old-fashioned courtesy natural to her.

"It is my greatest pleasure," she said, "to welcome my

nephew's friends to our house. Will you sit here by the fire, Herr Hitler?"

He made her a stiff bow, but hardly glanced at her, and immediately addressed Klaus. "Are you coming to the meeting to-morrow night, Lehmann? Good. I shall speak on the disarmament clauses of the Treaty of Versailles. These clauses have already been broken by every signatory to the Treaty except, possibly, England, and even that may not be true. I expect they have something up their sleeves."

"Will you take sugar in your coffee, Herr Hitler?"

"Thank you. I shall show that a treaty already broken can no longer be binding upon Germany, and I shall announce that an immediate programme of rearmament will be the first care of the Party when it comes to power. It will solve the unemployment problem——"

"Where is the money to come from for all this?" asked Ludmilla innocently.

"The Party will attend to that, you would not understand if I told you, Fräulein. While we are rearming——"

"The first step of all," said Klaus to Ludmilla, "is to stabilize the currency. Herr Hitler is dealing now with what happens in later stages. You were saying——"

It took some time for Hitler to get into his stride again, but presently, in a pause of his flood of talk, Fräulein Rademeyer asked whether there were any women in his Party and, if so, what they did to help him.

"There is no place for women in the Party, Fräulein, their place is in the home. The three C's," he added in a lighter tone. "Cookery, church and children."

"Usefulness and piety."

"Precisely, Fräulein. Now, with regard to the Ruhr——"

When he had gone, Klaus and Ludmilla looked at each other and burst out laughing.

"I am sorry——" he began.

"Please don't, dear, I haven't been so entertained for a long while. Your saviour of Germany is the funniest little man I have ever met."

"I have never seen him in a lady's company before, though it did not occur to me till now. There are stories going round of his rudeness to women, but——"

"Not so much rudeness as—I don't think there's a word for it. Like the way you treat a tiresome fly, shoo! Be off!"

"I will not bring him here again."

"Probably it is the fault of his upbringing. His mother should have slapped him oftener, and a great deal harder. My dear, what a lot he talks."

"That won't matter if he can induce people to act. But —it is a great pity that it's bad manners to slap one's guest. There is a lot to be said for one's nursery days when one would have simply hit him on the head with a tin engine!"

CHAPTER V   AFTER TEN YEARS

DURING THE NEXT TEN YEARS Klaus Lehmann worked for the National Socialists and was rewarded by seeing Germany rise from the dust and stand again among nations as an equal among equals. Prosperity returned, though slowly, step by step, wages meant something again, food was a thing one had every day, and once more the children laughed in the streets. Lehmann was not altogether happy, he disliked heartily many of his colleagues and distrusted their methods and their motives. Hitler he regarded not so much as a leader but as a useful tool for the regeneration of the country; it did not matter who led so long as the right road was taken and the people followed. Lehmann was trusted and relied upon, but not always confided in, not when the action proposed was morally dubious, for there was a sturdy uprightness in him which abashed villainy. He looked with cold distaste upon Goebbels' poisonous invective, Goering's unscrupulous violence and Rosenberg's sham mythology; at present these men served their turn, if they became too much of a good thing steps would have to be taken in the matter and he, Klaus Lehmann, would attend to it in person. He was still a sufferer from headaches and still could not remember who he had been, but he had acquired another personality long ago, and was much too busy to bother.

By 1933 he was a deputy of the Reichstag, high in the more reputable councils of the Party, and living in a flat in Berlin with Fräulein Rademeyer to look after him. She had been greatly aged by the hard years, but was now comfortably stout, increasingly forgetful, and completely wrapped up in Klaus. They sat over the fire one night in late February, and Ludmilla told him the news of the day.

"I saw Christine this morning," she said. "She has been staying with her daughter in Mainz, and who do you think she met?"

"Heaven knows," said Klaus sleepily. "Von Hindenburg?"

"Mathilde. My excellent sister-in-law."

"What, the lady who examined me for birth-marks or something at Haspe? Still as incisive as ever?"

"More so. Christine says she is more like a weasel than ever. She asked after me, it appears."

"Nice of her. I hope Frau Christine told her you are getting younger every day and dance at the Adlon every night?"

"She told her I was living with you in Berlin, and Mathilde was most indignant."

"Why?"

"She said it wasn't respectable."

"The foul-minded old harridan!" exploded Klaus. "How dare she?"

"My dear, if you lose your temper like that you will make your head ache."

"I won't have you insulted," stormed Klaus. "Why—what are you laughing at?"

"It is very depraved of me, Klaus, but—oh, dear—it is such a long time since I was considered a danger to morality!"

"You awful woman," began the horrified Klaus, but at

that moment the door opened and the servant Franz came hurriedly in.

"Fräulein—mein Herr—the Reichstag——"

"What about it?"

"It is all in flames. They say the Communists have fired it."

"Great heavens, I must go. My coat, Franz. Don't worry, Aunt Ludmilla, there is no danger. Go to bed, I shall not be out long. Yes, I will come and speak to you when I come in. Yes, Franz, you may go out provided Agathe does not, I will not have the Fräulein left alone."

He found the trams were not working, so he ran through the streets till he was stopped by the police cordon in Behren Strasse, and had to show his card. Even from there the glare of the burning building lit up the sky, he ran down the Wilhelmstrasse to avoid the crowds he expected to find in the Konigsgratzer Strasse and turned into the Dorotheen Strasse. Here the press was so great that it was not until he had passed the President's house that he was able to force his way to the front of the excited crowd, and for the first time the great fire became a visible reality. He could feel the heat upon his face. He turned suddenly faint, staggered, and clutched at the arm of the man standing next to him.

"Lean on me," said the man, who recognized him. "You have hurried too much, Herr Deputy Lehmann."

"I—this is a frightful sight," gasped Klaus, but in his mind he was seeing another fearful blaze, a country house burning among trees, and a dead man on the floor of a laboratory reeking with paraffin.

"Then I am a murderer," he thought, but had enough self-control even in that moment not to say it aloud. "I have killed somebody, who was it?"

He closed his eyes and did not hear the man suggesting

that if His Excellency would but sit down on the pavement a moment——

"Hendrik Brandt," thought Lehmann. "I remember now, I am Hendrik Brandt from Utrecht, with an office in the Höhe Strasse in Köln."

His knees trembled so much that he sat down upon the ground regardless of kind people, glad to be doing something, who passed the word back for a glass of water, a deputy was taken ill—a judge of the Supreme Court had fainted—the President of the Reichstag was dying. His mind raced on.

"I am not really Hendrik Brandt either, I am Hambledon, an agent of British Intelligence. Bill, where is Bill?"

There was a crash and a roar of flame as one of the floors fell in, and Hambledon looked up. That was the Reichstag burning. "Good God," he thought, "and now I am a member of the Reichstag. It's enough to make anybody feel faint, it is indeed."

Somebody handed him a glass of water, he sipped it and began to feel better, which was as well since in a few moments he was pulled to his feet and dragged back with the recoiling crowds as more fire-engines came rocketing down the Dorotheen Strasse and swung into the Reichstag entrance.

"If the Herr Deputy is feeling better," suggested his anonymous friend, "perhaps Your Excellency could manage to pass back through the crowd and a cab could be summoned——"

"You are too kind," said Hambledon, pulling himself together, "but there is no need. It was a momentary weakness—I ran all the way here. I will rest a few minutes longer and then I must go in and see the President."

"I wonder who could possibly have done such a wicked thing," said the man.

"They say it was the Communists," said another voice.

"They will be found out and punished whoever they are," said Hambledon authoritatively, wondering as he spoke, whether perhaps Bill had done it himself, Bill Saunders, who fired the Zeppelin sheds at Ahlhorn. He thrust the idea from him, mustn't think of things like that just now, he was Klaus Lehmann, a member of the Reichstag, and he had to go and see Goering, the President.

Brown-shirt guards at the gate directed him to a spot near the President's house, where stood a group of men which included Franz von Papen, Hermann Goering, President of the Reichstag, and the new Chancellor of the Reich, Adolf Hitler, talking earnestly together; they looked round as Lehmann came up and greeted them.

"This is a frightful thing," he said.

"It is indeed a monstrous crime," said the leader solemnly.

"Yes, isn't it?" said von Papen cheerfully. "The same thought occurred to me as soon as I saw it," and Goering burst out laughing.

"Is it known who did it?"

"The Communists did it, of course," said Goering. "One of them has been caught—a Dutchman, I believe."

Lehmann's heart almost stopped. A Dutchman—Bill Saunders had passed for a Dutchman when they were working together for British Intelligence in Cologne during the war. Klaus had been Hendrik Brandt, the Dutch importer, and Bill his young nephew Dirk Brandt from South Africa.

"Who is he—is anything known about him?"

"His name is Van der Lubbe, I understand," said Goering, indifferently. "A member of some Communist gang in Holland, according to his papers. I don't know any more about him."

"Lubbe," said von Papen in his light way. "A stupid name, it means 'fat stupid' in English, you know."

"Perhaps the English sent him," suggested the Chancellor.

Hambledon felt that if he had just a little more of this he would be uncontrollably sick, yet he must hear more. "He must have been rather stupid to be caught," he said casually. "What was he doing?"

"Oh, running about with a torch," said Goering. "The police saw him through one of the windows and collared him as he came out."

That didn't sound like Bill, who was never seen if he didn't want to be, and would certainly not walk out straight into the arms of the police, unless he had lost his cunning and taken to drink or something, men did who had lived his life, and he had a slight tendency that way . . .

"Lehmann," said the Chancellor in a tone of authority.

Hambledon looked at him in the light of the fire and noticed as though for the first time his insignificant form, his nervous awkward gestures, and his mean little mouth set with obstinacy. "You moth-eaten little squirt," he thought, but all he said was, "Yes, Herr Reichkanzler?"

"I expect a large majority in the elections at the end of this week, there is no doubt of it whatever, and the natural indignation of the people against the Communists on account of this horrible outrage will only serve to augment it. I am, therefore, making arrangements already to fill the principal posts in my Government. You will, I hope, accept the office of Deputy Chief of Police."

Police—the ideal post. If this fellow Van der Lubbe was Bill——

"I am honoured, Herr Reichkanzler," he said with a bow.

"That is well, you may regard the appointment as settled and you will take office to-morrow. I am anxious to reward my faithful friends as they deserve, and to sur-round myself with men I can trust. I know no one upon whom I place more reliance than I do upon you, my dear Lehmann."

"I shall continue to deserve it," said Lehmann untruthfully, "and I thank you from the bottom of my heart."

"We are all sure you will know how to deal with the Communists," said von Papen. "Rout out the rats' nests, what?"

Goering broke into another of his uproarious peals of laughter, and Klaus Lehmann took his leave.

He walked slowly home, thinking deeply, and indeed he had so much to think about that six minds at once would not have seemed enough to deal with the whole matter. As soon as he started one train of thought, another would present itself and confuse him again. His reawakened memory presented him with innumerable disconnected pictures from his past, von Bodenheim at the Café Palant, the guilty faces of four small boys caught smoking behind the fives court at Chappell's School, Elsa Schwiss saying, "We love each other," Bill in the antique dealer's house in Rotterdam saying, "Must I wear these boots?" and a free fight on the station platform at Mainz between a drunken German private and an official courier. He stood still in the deserted Unter den Linden and said sternly to himself, "Think of the future, you fool, not the past. If Van der Lubbe is Bill——" He shook himself impatiently and remembered that he himself would be dealing with Van der Lubbe in the morning and nothing could be done before then, so there was no object in thinking about it now. Hitler's plans which he had so often heard discussed, the reoccupation of the Rhineland and the Saar, the push to the East, Austria, Czecho-Slovakia, Poland, the Ukraine, the Balkan States, one foot on the Black Sea and the other on the Baltic;

then turning West again, Denmark, Holland, Belgium, the subjugation of France and finally the conquest of the British Empire—Lehmann had often thought the plans too grandiose to be practical, but as a German they had seemed more than admirable. As an Englishman—he walked on again—as an Englishman they were definitely out of the question and must be stopped at the earliest possible moment.

He admitted quite frankly to himself that he had immense sympathy with Germany, he had lived there for years and had shared in the piteous unmerited suffering of millions of quiet, decent people. He had worked for ten years to rehabilitate Germany and had succeeded, and he told himself defiantly that if he had known all the time that he was a British agent, he would have worked to that end just the same. The people were all right, they were fine, it was only their rulers who were so impossible to live with internationally, first the Kaiser and now this fellow Hitler. Someone had said that nations got the governments they deserved, if that were true there was something the matter with a race which could throw up and support a succession of fanatical megalomaniacs.

At this point he stopped again and actually blushed, for he suddenly remembered that few men had had more to do with promoting the rise of this fellow Hitler than he himself.

"The trouble is," he said, "that I'm thinking like an Englishman with half my mind and like a German with the other half."

He regarded this unpleasant predicament for a moment, and came to a decision.

"Since this is largely your fault, you interfering chump, it's up to you to put a spoke in their wheel. And I will."

After which the British agent went home, reassured his adoptive aunt and went to bed. The last thought that occurred to him as his head touched the pillow was a comforting one.

"But oh, what a marvellous, incredibly heaven-sent position I'm in. And to think Hitler's paying me for this! Money for old rope——"

He slept peacefully.

In the morning it was his first care to interview Van der Lubbe at the earliest possible moment, an enthusiastic newly appointed Deputy Chief of Police naturally would, anyway. Van der Lubbe turned out to be about as different from Bill Saunders as was possible within the limits of humanity. The prisoner was a fat, unhealthy, overgrown oaf, practically sub-human in intelligence. Hambledon sighed with relief. On the other hand, it was obvious at sight that this moron could never have thought out a scheme for firing the Reichstag; he did not look capable of lighting a domestic gas-ring without burning his fingers. Then the question arose, if Van der Lubbe wasn't responsible, who was?

At the time of the fire, the police had thrown a cordon round the Reichstag and its environs, and arrested everyone who might conceivably either have had a hand in the crime or have seen something significant which they could be induced to tell. These unlucky ones numbered some hundreds, and Lehmann spent many days in his new office examining suspects. Among their number was a frowsty old man who sold newspapers on the streets; he was well known to the police in that capacity and would not have been the object of the slightest suspicion had it not been for his state of almost uncontrollable nervousness. Why should he be so frightened if he had a perfectly clear conscience?

The old man stood before the desk at which Lehmann

was sitting and replied unwillingly to the questions which were fired at him. An S.S. man in the famous brown uniform, who had brought in the prisoner, now stood by the door, and the news-vendor shot agitated glances over his shoulder at the man from time to time.

"What is your name?" asked Lehmann.

"Johann."

"Surname?"

The man hesitated, and said, "Schaffer."

"Johann Schaffer. Address?"

"Haven't got one."

"Where do you sleep?"

"Anywhere."

"No fixed abode. What were you doing on the night of the Reichstag fire?"

"Nothing. Only walking along selling papers."

"Walking along where?"

"Konigsgratzer Strasse."

"At what time?"

"Just before ten."

"Very late, wasn't it, to be selling papers? Surely the last edition is much earlier than that?"

"I had some left," said Johann Schaffer, and looked for the first time straight at the questioner. What he saw in Lehmann's face did not appear to reassure him. He looked first puzzled, then incredulous, turned even a more unpleasant colour than he had been before, swayed forward against Lehmann's big desk and placed his hands on it for support. He continued to stare and Lehmann, mildly surprised, stared back.

"What's the matter with you?"

"Nothing. Nothing whatever."

Johann began to drum nervously with his first finger on Lehmann's desk.

"What did you see of the fire?"

"Nothing."

"Don't be absurd, man! You were within a few hundred yards of one of the most spectacular fires in history, and you saw nothing of it! Why not?"

"No business of mine. I always mind my own business. Don't like being dragged into things."

The irritating drumming on the desk continued, rhythmic but irregular, dactylic. Lehmann, who had not noticed it at first, suddenly found himself listening to it with interest.

"What was your profession before you sold newspapers?"

"I—have seen better days."

"Heaven help us, I should hope so. I said, what was your profession?"

"I was a schoolmaster," said the old man, slowly and reluctantly.

Lehmann leaned forward across the desk till his face was near the other's, stared into his eyes, and said, in a low tone that could not reach the ears of the S.S. man by the door, "Not a wireless operator?"

Johann Schaffer gasped, closed his eyes and slid to the floor in a dead faint.

"Take him away," said Lehmann as the guard sprang forward. "Tidy him up. Wash him—de-louse him if necessary, and I expect it is—and bring him back here at ten o'clock to-morrow."

At the appointed hour a clean, tidy old man, with his scrubby whiskers shaved off, was brought into Lehmann's room. Klaus looked him up and down, and said to the guard, "Are you sure this is the same man?"

"Quite sure, Excellency," said the man with a grin.

"Merciful heavens, what a little soap and water will do."

"You should have seen what we took off him," began

the man, but Lehmann said with a shudder, "Thank you, I would so very much rather not. You may go, I don't think this prisoner is dangerous."

The man saluted and went. Lehmann beckoned the old man up to his desk, and said, "Next time you are asked for your name, think up a nice one, don't just read one off an advertisement calendar on the wall. It arouses suspicion in the most credulous breast."

"I—my name is Schaffer——"

"It is not. It is Reck. If you are going to wilt like that you had better sit down, there's nothing to be afraid of. You know me, don't you?"

"No, I don't," said Reck, clutching at a chair and dropping into it. "Never seen you before."

"So? Perhaps I can help you to remember. Your name is Reck, before and during the last war you were science master at a school at Mülheim, near Köln. There was a tower to the school buildings with a lightning conductor on it, do you remember now? You were something of an amateur wireless enthusiast in those days, and you had a small wireless transmitter, you used the lightning conductor as an aerial. You knew enough morse to send out messages in code, I will say for you that you were pretty hot stuff at coding messages. Does it begin to come back to you now? No, don't faint again, because if you do I shall empty this jug over you, and it's full of cold water. You remember on whose behalf you sent the messages, don't you? British Intelligence."

Lehmann paused, largely because poor old Reck looked so dreadfully ill that it was doubtful whether he could take in what was said to him without a short respite.

"Well, I think after that a drink would do us both good," said the Deputy Chief, and rang the bell.

"Bring some beer, Hagen, will you, and a bottle of schnapps and glasses."

"Drink this," he said, when his orders had been carried out, "it will do you good. You always liked schnapps, didn't you? I'm sorry I'm not the red-haired waitress from the Germannia in Köln, but I——"

"Stop!" shrieked Reck. "I can't stand it—who the devil are you?"

"I think you know," said Tommy Hambledon. "I think you knew yesterday when you tapped out T-L-T on the table. What sent your mind back to that if you did not recognize me? Incidentally, that's what gave you away, for I certainly didn't recognize you. It's true we have both changed a good deal in fifteen years, but—who am I?"

"I thought you were Tommy Hambledon," said Reck, with the empty glass shaking in his hand, "but you can't be, because he's dead. If you are Hambledon, you're dead and I'm mad again, that's all. I was mad at one time, you know, they shut me up in one of those places where they keep them, at Mainz, that was. Not a bad place, though some of the other people were a little uncomfortable to live with. I was all right, of course," went on Reck, talking faster and faster. "It was only the things one saw at night sometimes, but they weren't so bad, one knew they weren't real, only tiresome, but you look so horribly real and ordinary, and how can you when you've been in the sea for fifteen years? Perhaps you don't really look ordinary at all, it's only my fancy, and if I look again," said Reck, scrabbling round in his chair, "I shall see you as you really are and I can't bear it, I tell you! Go away and get somebody to bury you——"

"Reck, old chap," said Hambledon, seriously distressed, "don't be a fool. I wasn't drowned, of course I wasn't. I got a clout on the head which made me lose my memory, but I got ashore all right. Here, give me your glass and have another drink. I'm sorry I upset you like that, I never meant to, look at me and see, I'm perfectly whole-some. Drink this up, there's a good fellow."

Reck drank and a little colour returned to his ghastly face. After a moment a fresh thought came to alarm him and he struggled to his feet.

"Here, let's go," he said, "before he comes back and finds us in his office. I don't want to face a firing-squad."

"He? Who d'you mean?"

"The Deputy Chief of Police," said Reck. "They told me I was to be taken to him."

"I am the Deputy Chief of the German Police," said the British Intelligence agent.

"Don't be absurd," said Reck testily. "The thing is simply impossible."

"It isn't impossible, because it's happened. Here I am."

"I don't believe it."

"Why not? There was one of our fellows on the German General Staff all through the last war, you know. This is comparatively simple."

"Let me go back to the asylum," pleaded Reck. "Life is simpler in there. More reasonable, if you see what I mean."

CHAPTER VI   THE PLAYWRIGHT

"I'M AFRAID I can't let you go back to the asylum yet," said Tommy Hambledon. "I want you to help me. I don't yet quite know how, but some scheme will doubtless present itself. You see, I have to get in touch with London, and——"

"Not through me," said Reck with unexpected firmness.

"Eh? Oh, you'll be all right, I'll look after you. I think I had better find you a post in my house—can you clean knives and boots? You shall have a bedroom to yourself, and food and wages. Isn't that better than wandering about the streets selling papers and sleeping rough?"

"No. Not if I've got to be mixed up in espionage again at my age."

"Don't be a fool," said Hambledon. "Anyone would think I wanted you to run along and fire the President's palace."

"From what I remember of you," said Reck acidly, "that is precisely the sort of thing you would suggest."

"Listen," said Hambledon patiently. "D'Artagnan is not the character which naturally rises to my mind when I look at you. Definitely no. If I wanted someone to go leaping in and out of first-floor windows with an automatic in one hand and a flaming torch in the other, I shouldn't offer the job to you first, I shouldn't really.

68

What you're going to do is to obtain from various sources the component parts of a spark transmitter——"

"I've forgotten what they are——"

"Assemble it in your lonely bedroom—thank goodness we've got a top flat—and stand by to send out messages to London in the dear old Mülheim code. That's all."

"No," said Reck obstinately.

"You see, normally I could get messages through in various ways, but they might be slow. If I wanted to get a message through quickly, wireless is the obvious method."

"Doubtless. But with some other fool operating it."

"It will also be useful," said Hambledon, disregarding this, "for confirmatory purposes. 'What I tell you three times is true.'"

"I have already told you four times that I won't have anything to do with it, and that's true, too."

"You obstinate old fool," exploded Hambledon, "will you take this in? You—are—going—to—do this, or by Gog and Magog I'll make you sweat for it! Ever heard of a concentration camp?"

Reck winced.

"I am not the Deputy Chief for nothing, you know, and I haven't been in the Nazi Party for ten years without learning how to persuade people, believe me! Now then?"

"Listen," said Reck with unexpected dignity, "I was born in England of English folk, but I have lived in Germany since I was a boy. I worked for England in the last war—yes, I was paid for it, you need not remind me—but Germany is my home, I have almost forgotten how to speak English. Ever since I worked for you I have been afraid, afraid somebody would find out or somebody would talk, afraid of the police, afraid of my old friends, afraid to drink for fear I might talk, afraid to sleep for fear I might dream aloud. Let me alone now, I will not be troubled by you any more. I am tired of being afraid."

The old man sank back in his chair and the animation died in his face and his manner. "Leave me alone," he whimpered. "I do very well, selling papers——"

Hambledon's face softened. "Look here," he said, "where could you be safer than with me? You shall be housed and fed and paid, and who looks twice at my servants? No one would dare suspect you. I am sorry, but it is necessary that you should do this. Necessary, you know what that means? Better men than you or I have died because it was necessary, and I'm only asking you——"

"And I refuse," shrieked Reck, shaking with passion. "I will not, I tell you. I'll tell everyone who you are——"

"And who'll believe you? Don't be a damned old fool! Go to the British Government and tell them Winston Churchill's a Nazi agent, and see what happens. It would be nothing to what will happen if you talk about me here. You must agree, I'm sorry, but I need you and you must. Well?"

"I won't. I don't believe it. Tommy Hambledon's dead and you're just trying to make me incriminate myself. I won't work against the Nazi Government, Herr Deputy Chief, I am a good German, I am really. I talk nonsense sometimes but I can't help it, I was mad once, you know, it doesn't mean anything. I wouldn't do a thing like that——"

"Reck! Stop it at once. You will do as I tell you or take the consequences. Well?"

"I won't."

"Very well." The Deputy Chief rang the bell and the Storm Trooper returned.

"This man's explanations do not satisfy me, but I can't waste any more time over him now. He will go to a concentration camp for ten days, perhaps he will be more willing to talk after that, eh, Hagen? Take him away."

About a week later Gustav Niehl, who was Klaus Lehmann's Chief in the German police, came into his room and said, "There's a man coming to Berlin to-morrow whom I want you to arrest, please. He is an Englishman named Heckstall, and pretends to be an innocent traveller in brewery fittings, but I have reason to believe that he is an English Intelligence agent. He has been over here a good deal in the last year or two without being suspected, but he's done it once too often."

"How very interesting," said Lehmann truthfully. "It enthralls me to have even the smallest contact with enemy espionage, one's boyhood story-books come true! When is he expected and where does he stay in Berlin?"

Niehl gave him particulars, and added, "He is clever. We have always kept an eye on him, of course, but he never gave us the smallest grounds for suspicion and I had no idea there was anything shady about him."

"Then what makes you suspect him now?"

"Our agents in London report that he is in close touch with British Intelligence. Of course, it may be that the Foreign Office and the War Office in London have secret beer engines installed in every cupboard and he merely goes in to see that they are working properly, but somehow I doubt it, Lehmann, I doubt it."

"The idea seems to me so excellent," said Lehmann laughing, "that it might well be adopted in the Wilhelm-strasse."

"You might suggest it to the Führer," said Niehl, "and see what he thinks of the idea."

Instantly Lehmann's laughter vanished. "Our Führer's views on the subject are well known," he said stiffly, "and have my unalterable respect. I spoke in the merest jest."

"I know, my dear Lehmann, I know," said Niehl soothingly, and took his leave.

"Trying to trap me into speaking disrespectfully of the all-highest Adolf," thought Hambledon indignantly, "and then you'd run to him with the whole story embellished with ornate embroidery, you lop-eared lounge lizard, would you?"

Hambledon lit a cigar and sat down to do a little hard thinking. So the German agents in London reported Heckstall to be in touch with M.I., German Intelligence must have some fairly good men. Hambledon's first idea had naturally been to report to London by the earliest possible means, but the more he thought about it the less he liked it. His own position was so desperately danger-ous that one unguarded word, one careless exposure of his name would destroy him at once, apart from these clever agents of whom Niehl spoke, and goodness alone knew who they were. By degrees it became clear to him that he dared not let anyone whatever know his secret, not even the head of his Service in London. "Three may keep a secret," he murmured, "if two of them are dead." Only Reck knew and he was safe, since even if he talked no-body would believe him.

Then the problem arose as to how he was to commu-nicate with London. It would be a sound scheme to give them something dramatic the first time, such as the re-lease of this fellow Heckstall for example, "with brass band *obbligato*," said the unmusical Tommy. Suitably heralded by a fanfare of trumpets, the rescue of Heck-stall should impress even M.I. His return should be an-nounced beforehand, Heckstall himself should have a little story to tell, and there must be a follow-up of some kind just to round it off, to make the third act in the little drama.

Drama. Why not write a play and broadcast it? A play on the Prodigal Son theme. He went into a far-off coun-try among strange people, so did Heckstall, and returned without tangible results, again Heckstall's case.

Too obscure, they'd never understand it in London.

Something definite was wanted. "Heckstall returned to stock undamaged Thursday next," that sort of thing, but one couldn't put that in a play unless it was in code. Code. Reck. A play with morse coming into it. Then the play could be about anything, a wireless operator was the most obvious choice, some of that propaganda stuff, all "O beautiful Hitler, O Adolf my love, what a wonderful Führer you are, you are, you are," besides, that kind of thing would be much more acceptable to the Austrian in Germany than a story about another young man who went into a foreign country and came to horrid grief . . .

Hambledon stretched his arms over his head and yawned. Reck was coming out from his ten days in camp on Friday, three days hence, probably in a more malleable mood, it should at least be possible to persuade him to code the messages as soon as one knew exactly what one had to say. Arrangements must be made about Heckstall, first for his arrest, which was easy, and later on for his release. This last could be announced in the morse accompaniment to the broadcast play. For the finishing touch, there could be nothing better than to supply whatever information Heckstall was sent to obtain, if one could discover what it was.

On Friday afternoon Reck was ushered into the office of the Deputy Chief of Police, and Hambledon greeted him cheerfully.

"Welcome, little stranger," he said genially. "Sit down and have a cigar. Or a bag of nuts. Forgive the implications of the alternative, but you really do look remarkably agile."

"Agile," said Reck scornfully, but he accepted the cigar.

"No, really, you look years younger—you may go, Hagen—what have you been doing?"

"Working. Shoveling concrete, look at my hands. Physical drill, insufficient food and no schnapps."

"Insufficient food," repeated Hambledon. "Then I take it you collected an appetite?"

"I wish to complain of the soap. Bright yellow, smelt disgusting, and stung, too."

"I dare say, but that wouldn't kill you," said Hambledon, with a slight stress on the pronoun. "Anything else?"

"There was an inaccurate notice to the effect that purity of the soul is won through labour. It was displayed where we could see it while shovelling. I find I am not, by nature, a shoveller, and the notice is a lie."

"I take it you don't want to go back?"

"Am I a fool? Besides, it is unjust, I haven't done anything to deserve punishment, it is not a crime to sell newspapers."

"No," said Hambledon coldly, "but it is a crime to refuse to serve your country when it is in your power to do so. Your next visit may not be quite so pleasant."

"Pleasant!"

"Comparatively pleasant. Will you code three or four simple sentences for me?"

"If that is all," said Reck unwillingly, "I will agree this once."

"It is all at present," said Hambledon significantly, and went on in a lighter tone. "So that's settled, good. Will you dine with me to-night and we'll try to remove that hollow feeling?"

Early in the following week Niehl sent for Hambledon and complained bitterly of the difficulty of getting definite evidence against Heckstall. "I am sure he is an English spy," he repeated more than once, "but there is no evidence to prove it apart from Niessen's statement. But he is a good man."

"Niessen?"

"Carl Niessen, a Danish importer who lives in London and is a friend of Herr Heckstall's. His real name is Schulte, but they do not know that in London. He has lived there many years, he knows a number of people in Government circles and they talk to him, my goodness how these English talk—thank heaven!"

Tommy Hambledon winced inwardly, for he knew this was perfectly true. "But hasn't Heckstall done anything? Not even asked questions about anything?"

"Oh, yes. Pipes—the kind water goes through, or gas. In lengths with screwed connections, you know. There are probably some in your bathroom. They are also used extensively in breweries, so Heckstall may be quite justified in asking about them. Only, he started asking at such an awkward time, you know, just when we were short."

Klaus Lehmann nodded comprehendingly, and said, "It looks fishy, certainly, I should be inclined to assume him guilty. Would you like me to try and make him talk?"

"What's the good? If he's made to talk we shall have to shoot him anyway, or there will be a fuss when he gets home, and we want no more of these fusses."

Eventually Lehmann offered to deal with the matter himself, and Niehl gratefully accepted. "I should like an official order to deport him across the frontier," said Klaus, "just in case our bona fides are ever called in question."

"You are very wise," said Niehl. "You shall have it."

Hambledon took himself off with a feeling of good work well done, for he knew now what the information was for which Heckstall had come. Hambledon returned home with a light heart and drafted three short messages which Reck coded for him as a background to his propaganda play.

The play itself was broadcast on Friday, March 31st, as

in the case of a monologue very little rehearsing is necessary. It is possible that that is why the author wrote a one-
character play in the first place, though to those who
commented upon this he said seriously that he was ex-
perimenting with a new art-form, a reply which can be
relied upon to silence ninety-nine people out of every
hundred, and no wonder.

On Sunday evening he said to Fräulein Rademeyer, "I
am sorry to have to leave you alone for an hour or so to-
night. I have business to do at the office."

"What, on Sunday night?"

"I have some papers to study before to-morrow morning."

"Papers, dear."

"Yes."

"Blonde or brunette, Klaus?"

"Good gracious," said Klaus, horrified, "what an idea!"

"I understand," said the old lady, "that when a man has
business at the office out of hours, it's usually feminine."

"You've been reading the comic papers," said her
adopted nephew accusingly, and left the house.

In his official capacity he had access to certain confidential documents. He took out a folder from the safe
where it was kept, and spent an uninterrupted half-hour
copying a sketch-map and a page of notes. He put his
copies in an envelope the flap of which was embossed,
curiously enough, with the Royal Arms of England, and
added a covering letter thumped out, like the page of
notes, with one unskilled finger on a typewriter. "It will
be time enough," he said to himself, "if I speak to Johann
the footman on Tuesday night." He paused, while a
gentle smile illuminated his scarred face. "And he thinks
he's such a clever Nazi agent, bless his little striped
waistcoat!"

.   .   .   .

There was a meeting in London in the evening of Thursday, April the 6th, when Wilcox of the Foreign Office, his immediate superior, and a retired Colonel from Sussex came together to hear a curious story from the lips of Arnold Heckstall. When the British agent from Germany had told all he knew, he was dismissed with kindly words, and the three men remaining settled down to discuss the further enigma from the British Diplomatic bag.

"This map," said the Foreign Office Head of Department, "shows the frontiers of Germany with France, Luxembourg, Belgium, and Holland in detail, merely indicating the others. Along these frontiers, starting at a point near Karlsruhe where the Rhine ceases to be the boundary between Germany and France, and going westward, there appears a line of red ink in places where the land lies low. Where the land lies low," he repeated, and glanced at his hearers. "The notes make this clear. They refer to numbers marked on the map, and in several instances at points where the red line is gapped, they say, 'Broken for such-and-such a ridge of hills'. In the next valley the line begins again. The notes are headed 'Galvanized iron pipe half-inch, screwed connections'. At the bottom there is 'Laid by draining-plough'."

He paused and addressed the Colonel. "You may not have heard the rumour. It was whispered that Germany was laying a pipe-line along her western frontiers to supply gas. Gas, hissing softly through the soil, to drench the valleys through which an invasion must pass. Those valleys might be death to every living thing for months on end."

"So Heckstall went to find out if this were true," said the Colonel, "and was dropped on."

The Foreign Office man nodded, and Wilcox said, "I am a Londoner. This business of a draining-plough?"

"I am a countryman," said the Colonel modestly. "A

draining-plough carves a deep but narrow slot in the earth in which drainage-pipes may be laid, deep enough to be out of danger from the ordinary plough. A quick and easy method, and on arable land leaves no trace at all."

"The Rhineland and the Saar are, of course, demilitarized zones," said Wilcox.

"Yes, but there's nothing in the Treaty to prevent a simple but industrious peasantry from tillin' the soil," said the Colonel.

"Sowing dragon's teeth," commented Wilcox, "and what will the harvest be?"

"Dead men," said the Colonel grimly, for he was at Ypres in '15.

"So our anonymous correspondent has done us a good turn," said Wilcox, with a slight shiver.

"He has done us another," said the superior, "at least, if what he says is true. There is a covering note, I'll read it to you.

"Information required herewith. Also Niessen, Danish importer, real name Schulte, is agent of Germany. He it is who on Heckstall the gaff stridently has blown. Passed to you for action, please!"

"I am beginning to know," said the Colonel, "what women feel like when they go into hysterics. It can't be true, it's fantastic. I think I'm getting old. In my day we had a cupboard which contained restoratives——"

"I beg your pardon," said his host, rising hastily, "so do we. Soda? Or just straight?"

"After a letter like that," said the Colonel, "I think I won't dilute it, thanks. My soul, I needed that. Who is this fellow who uses a German construction one moment and a Civil Service formula the next?"

"A man might easily do that," said Wilcox, "who had lived in Germany so long that his English was rusty."

"All we can suggest about him," said Authority, "is that he is possibly a friend of Reck's."

"Reck's been dead these twelve years," said Wilcox.

"I don't know what you propose to do," said the Colonel, "but Denton used to know Reck personally."

"Am I to recall Denton from the Balkans to hunt for a dead man?"

The Colonel made a gesture of despair. "There's Niessen too," he said.

.   .   .   .

In Berlin, the Deputy Chief of Police made a report to his superior in the matter of the British agent.

"I regret to inform you, sir, that there was trouble at the frontier. I passed Herr Heckstall through on our side in accordance with your orders, but when the Belgian guard challenged, the prisoner, instead of stopping, ran like a hare. As you know, there has been a lot of trouble thereabouts with smugglers, and the guards have been told to be exceedingly firm. They fired, and the prisoner fell dead—on the Belgian side."

"Most unfortunate," said Niehl smoothly. "Very unfortunate, but no one can say it was our fault. A traveller so experienced as poor Heckstall should have known better than to behave so foolishly. Well, it's no use crying over spilt milk, the incident is closed."

"Yes, I suppose so," said Lehmann hesitantly.

"Why, what is the matter? You have no reason, have you, to expect any—er—repercussions?"

"None in regard to Heckstall. I did have a little talk with him in the course of which he gathered that our decision was final, and though his immediate departure rather depressed him he still seemed to be unpleasantly pleased about something. He rather hinted that two Governments could play at that game."

"Can they possibly have found out about Niessen?"

"I wondered that myself, sir."

"I will recall him at once."

So Herr Niessen packed his suit-cases and left London in haste, but two horribly calm men in plain clothes met him at Dover and took him back again, protesting volubly. It appeared that Niessen had been the leading spirit in an organization which smuggled drugs into England, and though he declared with tears that he did no more than sniff occasionally, he retired from public life for a very long time indeed.

CHAPTER VII   THE PURGE

CHARLES DENTON returned from the Balkans without regret and presented himself at the Foreign Office at the end of a fortnight's leave.

"Glad to see you, Denton. Sorry to come away?"

"Not at all," said the young man in a tired voice. "Those people are too damned energetic by half, fight on the smallest excuse. The Younger Nations, what? Simply too nursery for words."

"Perhaps your next job will be more to your liking. I want you to go to Germany to look for a man who is almost certainly dead."

"Do I have to provide my own spade?"

"Do you remember a man named Reck? He used to code and dispatch messages for our Cologne agents during the war."

Denton nodded. "He went bats and died in the giggle-house in Mainz."

"Are you sure?" The Foreign Office man unfolded his tale, ending with, "This has been going on for more than a year now, sixteen months to be exact. We get reports of German rearmament and aviation developments which, so far as we can check them, are scrupulously correct, our agents are assisted in inconspicuous ways and their agents here are identified. One of his best efforts, conveyed in

the passport of a commercial traveller in artificial silk
stockings, informed us last July that Germany would resign from the League of Nations in October, which, of
course, they did. We know where and when to find messages because we are informed by radio in the code Reck
used. We are inconceivably grateful, but we do feel we
should like to know our benefactor."

"Does he sign his communications? Or just put 'A
Well-Wisher' at the end?"

"Nothing at all."

"Is he English, do you think?"

"The form of his sentences is sometimes rather German,
verbs at the end and capitals to all his nouns and so on.
But once he said, 'If I ask for news, will you put a para-
graph in the papers for me sometimes?' and at the end of
yesterday's was 'How stands the old Lord Warden? Are
Dover's cliffs still white?' "

"You'll answer that in to-morrow's *Continental Daily
Mail*, of course, 'Dear old boy, it depends on the weather!'
Has he asked any others?"

"Not yet."

"I take it you want me to find out who he is. Has it
occurred to you that in some way he must be fairly well
in with the Nazis, and that consequently it would be very
dangerous for him indeed if anyone knew who he was,
even you, sir?"

"Yes. In fact, your errand is not so much to find out
who he is as to put yourself in a position to be useful to
him if he desires help. If you fail, it will be because he
does not desire it, that's all."

"Then you really have not the faintest idea who he
is?"

"Absolutely none. We assume, from his knowledge of
procedure, that he has served at some time in British Intelligence, so we looked up everyone on our lists who is

still alive. It is none of them, so it must be someone who is officially dead. I have here the photographs of every British agent who was missing or killed during and after the war, perhaps you would like to look at them. It is only a guess that he is in touch with Reck because he uses that code, but the code may have been written down and Reck may be dead, as you say. I have no guidance to offer, though you will be put in touch with the usual contacts, I only suggest that he must be in Berlin."

"I see," said Denton, "figuratively speaking. In point of fact I don't see an inch ahead in this affair and I doubt if I ever do. May I brood over those photos for a secluded half-hour or so?"

"You can brood in here," said his Chief. "I am going out for an hour and the whisky is in the cupboard."

Accordingly, Herr Sigmund Dedler of Zurich arrived in Berlin towards the end of June 1934 armed with magnificent photographs of beauty spots in the cantons of Zurich, Luzern, Unterwalden, Schwyz and Zug, in search of printers who would reproduce them as post cards in six colours for sale to tourists. He stayed in an inexpensive hotel of the commercial type and prosecuted his inquiries diligently but without haste, he was difficult to please as regards price and quality, and it looked as though his mission would take him some time. Among the people he interviewed was a very German-looking individual who kept a tobacconist's shop in Spandau Strasse near the Neue Markt. The tobacconist was a friendly soul, and invited Herr Dedler to sit with him sometimes in his stuffy little room behind the shop, a room even more stuffy than it need have been, since they talked with the window and doors shut though the summer days were hot. The tobacconist's daughter, in reply to a thirsty howl from her parent, used to come in with wine, and glasses on a tray, and look at Herr Dedler with frank interest.

Since she was undoubtedly a comely wench, Herr Dedler also displayed appreciation, but as her father invariably turned her out again at once and locked the door after her, the acquaintance did not progress.

"I have no suggestions to offer," said the tobacconist. "The Department asked me more than a year ago to look into this, but I am no further forward than I was then. I know some of the Nazi leaders personally, being a good Nazi myself," he smiled gently, "though my unfortunate health prevents me from taking an active part in their affairs—thank goodness. But several of them are kind to me and buy their tobacco here since I take the trouble to stock the blends they prefer. None of them look to me at all likely to be honorary members of British Intelligence. I hope you will have more luck."

"I don't suppose so for a moment," said Denton gloomily. "I have merely been sent over because I used to know Reck. So I am walking about looking for him regardless of the strong probability that he's been in his humble grave at Mainz these twelve years. Reck. Have you ever heard the name?"

"Never."

"I don't suppose you would. If he's still alive he probably calls himself Eustachius Guggleheimer now. Does anyone in Berlin keep silkworms?"

"Silkworms?" said the startled tobacconist. "Shall I open the window a moment? It is true that the weather is hot, but——"

"No matter. I have walked about this blasted city in this infernal heat till my legs ache in every pore and my feet feel the size of Grock's, and I'm not a bit the wiser, at least, not about that. There's something up though, Keppel, there's an uneasy excitement about which I don't like. Something's going to happen, what is it?"

"You are perfectly right. There is a lot of jealousy between the old Brown Guards and Hitler's new S.S. men, and I wouldn't be surprised if there was trouble."

"So. Well, it's no business of mine, at least I hope not. At the first sound of alarm I shall go to bed and stay there, I shall at least rest my feet. I'll come and see you again shortly. You wouldn't like a nice picture of the Lake of Lucerne in six colours, would you?"

"I'd rather have a water-colour of the Pass of Brander as the sun goes down," said Keppel wistfully.

Denton lit his pipe and strolled towards his inconspicuous hotel as the evening was drawing in, and noticed at once that the streets were curiously empty of people. He displayed no interest at all in what he saw, but merely slouched along with his eyes down and his hands in his pockets as one wrapped deeply in thought. He came at last within sight of the turning to his hotel and saw, with an odd pricking sensation in the tips of his fingers, that there was a line of S.S. men across the end of the street who were stopping cars and pedestrians and asking them questions.

Denton quickened his pace slightly and walked on past the picketed turning only to find another line of guards across the road fifty yards ahead. He glanced over his shoulder and saw that a third detachment had formed up behind him. He was trapped.

He decided that nobody could possibly be expected not to notice all this display of armed force, however tactful they might be, so he abandoned his nonchalant manner and scurried along like all the rest of the scattered handful of people whom ill fortune had sent abroad on the night of the Nazi purge.

He saw that the front door of a house opposite to him was ajar, so he ran across the road, dived in, and shut the door after him. In the passage he encountered a gentleman who was presumably the master of the house, for he blocked the way and said *"Wer da?"* in an authoritative tone.

"Sigmund Dedler from Zurich," answered Denton, introducing himself. "I beg ten thousand pardons for inflicting my uninvited presence upon you in this abrupt and ill-bred manner, but if you would permit me to occupy some inconspicuous corner in your house till the streets are a little less unhealthily exciting, my immeasurable gratitude will outlast several reincarnations. I suggest the cupboard under the stairs."

"Impossible," said his host firmly, "my wife is there already. Nevertheless, no one shall say that Hugo von Einem turned out a stranger into a storm more pitiless than the wrath of God, come in."

"Thank you, I have," said Denton.

"Yes," said von Einem absent-mindedly. "Yes, I suppose you have. Listen!"

Running footsteps appoached the door, but passed by without pausing.

"Did you shut the door?" asked von Einem in a low voice.

"Yes," answered Denton in the same tone. "I thought it made the house seem more home-like, don't you know? Did you want it left open?"

"I left it open for a friend, but I doubt if he will come now. He said he would try and come to me if this happened."

"What, exactly, is happening?"

"There is trouble in Berlin to-night."

"I thought they were playing 'Nuts in May'," said Denton sarcastically. "Perhaps they are, only it's June and the wrong sort of nuts."

Von Einem stared. " 'Nuts in May'? What's that?"

"A childish game little girls play in my native canton of Zug."

There was the sound of rifle fire from farther down the street. "There is nothing childish about this game, Herr Dedler. Where are you staying?"

Denton told him and von Einem said, "But that is quite near."

"It is in theory, but there are two cordons of S.S. guards between, which in practice makes it rather far off."

"How true. You might, however, reach it across the gardens at the back if you would not mind climbing a few walls."

"Not at all, a pleasure, believe me. May I look?"

Denton walked through to a room at the back of the house, threw the window up, and looked out. There was a drop of about five feet to a dull little town garden, bounded by the walls of which von Einem spoke, beyond them were more gardens and more walls; one of that row of houses half-right must be his hotel.

He went back to the hall where von Einem was still listening for a footstep he knew, and said, "I think your idea is excellent—I propose to act on it at once. I am very grateful——"

"Listen," said von Einem. The steps of several men were heard outside in the street, they stopped, and there came a quiet knock at the door.

"At last," said von Einem, and opened it as Denton retired modestly to the back of the hall. Three men with automatics in their hands entered hastily, pushed von Einem back against the wall without saying a word, and one of them shot him dead.

Denton was through the back room and out of the window before his host's body had slumped to the floor. "Just a garden wall or two," he thought, "and I'll be——"

As his feet touched the ground something hit him on

the back of the head and he fell through millions of roaring stars into unconsciousness.

He awoke again with a splitting headache to find himself lying on a mattress on the floor, he felt the rough cement, in some place which was nearly dark except for a faint light which trickled in through a barred horizontal slit high above his head. He puzzled over this for some time before he realized that he was in a cellar and that the light came through a pavement grating, probably from a street lamp. His head cleared gradually and he realized that he was desperately thirsty. He sat up, setting his teeth as the darkness whirled round him.

"In all the best dungeons," he said unsteadily, "the prisoner is provided with a jug of water and a mouldy crust of bread."

He felt cautiously about, found a jug of generous size and took a long pull at the water; he soaked his handkerchief and dabbed his head with it, a refreshing moment, though it revealed that the back of his skull was horribly tender.

"I've been sandbagged," he said, and lay back to think things over as clearly as his aching head would permit.

"I remember," he said at last. "They shot von Einem. Wonder what they're going to do with me?"

He felt in his pockets. His automatic had gone and so had his electric torch, but so far as he could tell everything else was there, even his money and his watch.

"Of course, they can always collect the cash from my unresisting corpse afterwards," he said aloud. "Delicate-minded people, these, evidently."

There came a pleasant voice in the darkness from somewhere high up in the wall opposite his feet. "I do hope you are feeling better," it said, in English.

"Thank you," said Denton with a slight gasp. "I survive—so far."

"I hope you will many years survive—survive many years. You must excuse my awkward English, it is so many years since I spoke it."

"Please don't apologize——"

"I do not want to tease you," said the voice, jerkily and with pauses, as of a man recalling a language long disused. "I hope to get you out of this mess, unless they liquidate me next, which seems quite likely."

"Heaven preserve you," said Denton with feeling.

"*Danke schön.* I am sorry we had to hit you quite so hard, but we should not have got you away had they not you dead—thought you dead. Only dead men pass unquestioned to-night."

"But how did you know I was there?"

"I did not, till you looked out of the window. I came to—to succour von Einem."

"Then you were the friend for whom he was waiting?" asked Denton, unconsciously reverting to German.

"I was, but I was too late. Would you mind speaking in English, it is such a pleasure to me to hear it—especially to-night."

"Of course. May I ask who you are?"

"I cannot answer that. I wish I could, but you understand that it would not be safe for anyone to know."

"You are the man I was sent to find, are you not?"

"Yes. I think that stupid a little, you must all know that it would endanger me, and what is worse, spoil my usefulness."

"My instructions were not to seek you out but to place myself where you could find me if I could be of service. I was to say that the Department is inconceivably grateful——"

"But devoured by curiosity, eh?" said Hambledon with a laugh. "I am afraid they must eat themselves a little longer, but tell them that one of these days I will come back and report, if Goering doesn't scupper me first. My English is reviving. Tell me some news, will you?"

A little whisper of suspicion rose in the back of Denton's mind. Set the victim's mind at rest and then question him.

"Certainly," he said cheerfully. "What sort of news?"

"Is José Collins still alive?"

"She was last week, I saw some mention of her in the *Sphere*: And a photograph."

"I daren't be seen reading the English papers," murmured Hambledon. "Do you know Hampshire?"

"Parts of it."

"Is Weatherley much changed?"

"No. They've turned the Corn Exchange into shops on the corner of the Market Square. There's a certain amount of building in the county, on the slopes of Portsdown Hill for example, and all round Southampton and places like that, but the country is unchanged."

"The country is unchanged," repeated Hambledon dreamily. "You asked just now if you could help me. There's one man I should like to help me if the Department would send him out—Bill Saunders."

Denton bit his lip and said nothing.

"Perhaps you don't know him."

"Yes," said Denton, slowly and distinctly, "I knew him very well indeed."

There was a short pause, and Hambledon said sharply, "What happened and when?"

"He was found shot. That was in—er—in '24. He ran a garage in a Hampshire village after the war, and one morning the woman who looked after him went in and found him dead. It was apparently accidental, he had been cleaning his automatic."

"So you didn't get anybody for it?" said Hambledon in a savage tone.

"No. There was no evidence to show that anyone had done it. Suicide or accident was more probable. He was not a very happy man."

"Not married? You said a woman went in——"

"Yes, a village woman to do the housework. Yes, he was married, but separated from his wife."

"Not Marie Bluehm?"

"Marie Bluehm?" cried Denton, starting up. "Who the devil are you—oh, of course, I know now. You must be Hambledon. Marie Bluehm was killed in the rioting in Köln just before the British marched in, I—I saw it done. I think it broke him. That's why I think it may have been suicide, he just didn't care for anything much any more."

"Suicide six years later? Don't believe it. Who did he marry?"

"Some colonel's daughter, don't know who, never met her. Tiresome wench, I believe."

"Were you with Bill, then, after I disappeared? What's your name?"

"Denton, sir. I was sent on to Köln from Mainz."

"I remember. Bill mentioned that you were there. Well, I think I've heard enough news for to-night. You can tell the Department that Tommy Hambledon is not dead, that is, unless they call on me in the next few days. Goebbels loathes me, but Hitler still thinks I have my uses, so I may survive. I dare not tell you who I am here, don't try to find out."

"Of course not, sir."

"And don't 'sir' me every second word, I am not in my dotage yet. Besides, it reminds me of Bill. Denton, there's something fishy about that business. I'm going to look into it. If it was arranged and I find out who did it, God have mercy on the man, for I won't."

Denton said nothing.

"The most brilliant brain in the Service, shot like a dog. What were you all about to let it happen? Wasn't he guarded?"

"The police, I understand, had the usual——"

"Police!" exploded Hambledon. "The village constable, no doubt, had instructions to keep a look out for suspicious characters, as though such men ever look suspicious! My God, if I'd been there——"

He stopped and sighed deeply. "I suppose you think I'm making a fuss over nothing, because it was an accident. Well, perhaps it was, but somehow I don't believe it."

"Perhaps you will be able to clear it up," said Denton, just biting off the "sir" in time.

"I'll have a damned good try. Now about you. I'm sorry I daren't bring you out of that foul coal-hole to-night or, probably, to-morrow, it's the only place I know of which is even approximately safe at the moment, but I'll bring you some creature comforts and try to make it a little more bearable. To-morrow night I'll try and get you across the frontier. Wait a bit, I'll go and fetch some rugs and something to eat and drink. And you are not going to see my face, either, I have no wish to be recognized as the Lord High Panjandrum of All the German Armies or something equally spectacular. I don't look very like Tommy Hambledon now, you know, so it won't be any use digging any of my late scholastic colleagues out of their retirement at Bath or Bournemouth to come over and give the Nazi Party leaders a look over, because they won't recognize me if they do. I have a false nose grafted on, a thick bushy beard, and plucked eyebrows. How my English inconceivably improved has, even during this short interlocutory or what-have-you, ain't it? Is old Williams still alive, I wonder?"

"Who?"

"Williams. At one time Headmaster of Chappell's."

"I could not possibly say, sir, I was at Winchester myself."

"Never mind, these things can be lived down. I will go and fetch your ameliorations."

There was a faint sound of departure, and silence sank again upon the cellar.

CHAPTER VIII   PRIVAT HOTEL

THE CELLAR was not completely dark even at night when one's eyes became accustomed to it; by day light came in through the pavement grating and even a shaft of sunlight, and at night there was a patch of light upon one wall from a street-lamp near by. Sounds also entered by the grating, traffic noises, and voices talking. It was even possible, if people passed close enough, for Denton to get a worm's-eye view of part of them from the feet up. He noticed how men and women alike made a little detour to avoid his grating, and this rather annoyed him. There was a church clock somewhere in the neighbourhood which struck the hours; when sleep would not come he found it companionable.

He slept, or drifted into unconsciousness, for most of the first night after Hambledon had made him as comfortable as possible. The next day passed easily with the help of a basket of provisions and fruit and a feeling of lassitude so intense that he was glad to be away from everyone somewhere where there was not even need to speak. Towards evening he began to recover a little and to wish for a break in the monotony of his imprisonment. He did not desire the dark, either, there were too many spiders in that cellar, and in his weak state he had a morbid horror of their crawling upon him.

Soon after nine o'clock, when it was still daylight, sud-

denly the traffic ceased and there came a stillness which
reminded him of one Armistice Day when he had been in
London and the Two Minutes' Silence had caught him
unawares. Denton rose on his elbow and listened.

From somewhere farther down the street there came a
hoarse command, another, and then a short crackle of
rifle fire. Immediately, as though a spell had been broken,
followed the sound of running feet, irregularly running
as if those who ran looked over their shoulders as they
fled. Some passed over his grating, several men and a
woman or two, one was leading a child who fell down
wailing, and was snatched up and carried on. One woman
came to a stop just above him and leaned against the wall
gasping for breath and sobbing, "Oh, Jakob, oh, Jakob,
oh, Jakob," over and over again. Denton fumbled for his
automatic, and felt naked to the storm when he remembered it was not there.

Next came the sound of disciplined marching, coming
nearer, and the weeping woman ran away. A voice outside
cried, "Here, you there! Halt!" and a man stopped just
where the woman had been. Charles Denton could see
part of a grey tweed trouser-leg and one brown shoe, a
well-to-do man, evidently. He said, "Do you mean me?"
in a quiet, steady voice.

"That's the man," someone said. There followed another command, again the sound of shots, four in rapid
succession. "Automatic," said Denton to himself. The
man above crumpled, and suddenly the cellar was completely dark, for his body covered the grating.

Denton sat up shaking, and fumbled for the cigarettes
and the matches Hambledon had left him on his promise
not to strike one in Hambledon's presence, and on no
account to allow a light to be seen from outside. There
was no need to worry about the light now, the aperture
was effectively blocked and shut out sounds as well, but

Denton listened intently for a moment before striking the match. All he could hear was a trickling noise like the sudden overflowing of a gutter during a storm. "Rain," he thought, "that'll calm them down." Then he remembered that a moment earlier the sun had been shining . . .

He scrambled back into the corner farthest away from the window regardless of spiders and loose lumps of coal, and with eyes open only the merest slits, enough to see his own fingers and nothing more, lit his cigarette. He had some difficulty in keeping both match and cigarette steadily together long enough to light it.

The trickle slowed after a little and became a steady drip—drip—drip, irritating enough to the nerves even if it had only been water. He desperately wanted a drink, but it took all his courage to go forward in the dark and fetch it for fear there should be pools of wetness on the floor and he should put his hand in one of them. More courage, after that, to subdue attacks of panic prompting him to hammer on the door and yell to someone, anyone, to let him out, let him out, let him out before the tide rose.

When Hambledon came an hour later, an interminable hour which seemed like days, he found his prisoner perched on a box in the corner with his feet up, repeating the *Lays of Ancient Rome* to himself aloud.

" 'The harvests of Arretium, this year old men
        shall reap,
    This year, young boys in Umbro shall plunge the
        struggling sheep,
    And in the vats of Luna, this year the must shall
        foam
    Round the white feet——'

Damn! Can't I think of anything that doesn't suggest blood?"

"My dear fellow," said Hambledon hastily, "I am most frightfully sorry—I had no idea this had happened. Are you all right?"

"Oh, quite, thanks," said Denton in a rather cracked voice. "Quite chirpy, thanks. I can't see to read so I was repeating poetry to myself, that's all. Habit of mine, always done it since a kid, when I couldn't sleep, you know." He laughed, and Hambledon did not like the sound of it. "When's the funeral going to be, d'you know?"

"You are coming out of this, whatever happens. Will you excuse me a moment while I write a note? I will come back again at once."

"Please don't hurry," said Denton airily. "Not that I am not delighted to see you—hear you, I mean—at any time, but don't let me be a nuisance. It's quite all right down here—quite homelike when you're used to it."

"*Du Gott allmächtig,*" said Hambledon, and left.

He came back a little while later and said, "Have you ever eloped with anyone, Denton?"

"Not exactly eloped," said Denton cautiously. "Why?"

"Because in about an hour's time you will be en route for Switzerland with a charming lady whom you have persuaded to—er—fly with you is, I think, the correct phrase. You will travel in haste, her enraged father is upon your trail."

"You do think up some lovely parlour games, don't you?" said Denton admiringly. "First you slog me on the head and lock me in a cellar with a dripping corpse overhead, and then marry me off to one of your girl-friends. Come to Germany and see life. What's she like?"

"Quite a credit to be seen with, believe me. She will travel into Switzerland with you and then she can go to her aunt's for a holiday. She will be no trouble to you. You have seen her, by the way, Fräulein Elisabeth Weber."

"What, the tobacconist's daughter? A sightly wench, I agree with you. More, I commend your taste, sir."

"I told her to come at once—shall we speak English now for a little if my lack of fluency does not worry you? I expect she will an hour require her baggages—to make up her baggages."

"Does the baggage make up?" murmured Denton. "Look a bit undressed, nowadays, if they don't, don't they?"

"I shall be obliged to leave you before she comes. She knows me, I permit myself English cigarettes sometimes which the good Weber stocks for me. Besides, I cannot be absent from home too long to-night, they might think I had hidden myself, and that would not seem well, you understand."

"Oh, quite, quite. Tell me, what is all this uncivil disturbance?"

"The Purge," said Hambledon solemnly. "You will understand that in the body politic, as in the human body, undesirable elements agglomerate—accumulate—of which we wish to rid ourselves. So we take the necessary steps."

"Lead pills, eh? Couldn't you have done anything to prevent it?"

"On the contrary, I architec—engineered it. There are some people the Government would be better without. In fact, most of the Government would be nicer in a state of peace. So I thought."

"D'you mean to say you're responsible for that unpleasantness in the window? Surely not, von Einem——"

"Von Einem was my friend," said Hambledon harshly, "and those who killed him will pay, do not be afraid. This Purge has gone wrong a little. I thought the Brown-shirts would do best, but the Black Guards have done best instead. So many things have happened I did not intend. In fact, every step I hear on the stairs, I stroll out to meet

them with both my hands in my pockets, you understand? If I go I will take an escort with me."

"Splendid," said Denton approvingly. "Two-gun Sid
in the flesh. I beg your pardon, sir!"

"Not at all," said Hambledon, laughing. "If you knew
how nice it is to meet someone who is not afraid of one!
I am so tired of people who either bully or cringe. Look,
I must go or your so charming lady will catch me, and
then the cat would be in the soup, eh? Best of luck, and
tell the Department I will come back and report some
day, please God. Good-bye."

Denton was left alone in the dark again, but when he
had time to notice himself he found that he had entirely
left off shaking, and that the obstruction on the grating
was no longer an obscene horror but just some man he
didn't know. It seemed only a short time before he heard
steps on the stairs and a light appeared in a broken fan-
light over the door. Denton stood up as there came the
rattle of a key in the lock.

"Herr Dedler, are you there?"

"Yes, Fräulein Weber," he answered, and bowed politely, which was a mistake, for he immediately turned
giddy and staggered straight into the girl's arms.

"Oh!" she said, pushing him off, "how could you when
I've only come to help you?"

"I beg your pardon, I do indeed. The action was quite
unintentional, it was really."

She turned her torch on his face, which was quite white
where it was not streaked with coal-dust, and saw that he
was really ill.

"Come out of this horrible place," she said, taking him
by the hand. "Can you walk up the stairs?"

"Yes, rather," he said, "you watch me," but she had to
help him to the limit of her strength before they reached
the top. They emerged in the hall of a small house of the

artisan type, which appeared to be untenanted, although
there was furniture in the rooms.

"Come and sit down a moment."

"No," he said, looking at his filthy hands, "I'd like to
wash first if I may."

"You are in a mess, aren't you? There's water in the
scullery if that will do, and here's your suit-case if you'd
like to change."

"The scullery is luxury, Fräulein Weber, believe me.
Thanks, I can manage quite well. No, I can wash my own
face, I've done it myself for years now. You go and sit
in the front room, I shan't be long."

He emerged twenty minutes later, washed, shaven,
changed, and refreshed, to find her waiting by the luggage in the hall looking at her watch.

"We have just half an hour," she said, "to catch the
train for Basle. Do you think we shall do it? How are
you feeling?"

"Positively dewy. Shall I leap out and catch a taxi?"

"No, I will," she said, and was out of the door before
he reached it and running like a hare down the street.

"How very sudden," he said languidly, and demon-
strated his independence by carrying three suit-cases
across the pavement, after which he was glad to sit on
them. She was back in five minutes with a taxi and they
drove through a frightened, silent town to catch their
train with a few minutes in hand, in spite of having been
stopped three times by S.S. men at cross-roads. Elisabeth
Weber showed these men a card, at sight of which they
saluted and stepped back. Each time she glanced at Denton with an air of pride, and looked disappointed when
he made no comment.

"Don't you wonder how it's done?" she said at last.

"Fräulein, I never cross-question guardian angels," said

Denton blandly, but he was thinking of Hambledon and not the lady as he spoke.

The interminable train journey ended at last with the customs officials at the Swiss frontier. At Basle the travellers got out, Denton swaying slightly with a line of pain between his brows as he stood waiting for a porter.

"You are tired," said Elisabeth Weber.

"I have got the most damnable headache," he said slowly, "and the train is running round and round on my brain. I should like to go to bed for a week and be delicately nurtured by silent-footed houris. Let's go to Albrecht's."

"What's that?"

"Albrecht's Privat Hotel."

"Do they keep houris there?"

"You are the houri in question, Fräulein Liese. You won't desert me just yet, will you?"

"Of course not. My father told me to take care of you. Here's a cab. Albrecht's Privat Hotel, please. I hope they'll have room for us."

"Albrecht will make room. Tell me, Fräulein Liese, how did you hear that I was in that cellar, and who induced you to come?"

"My father told me that Herr Dedler had been accidently hurt and was hiding from the Black Guards, and that I was to go and get you out. He said we were travelling to Switzerland, he had the tickets all ready, and your suit-case too. But I think there was somebody else——"

"Thank heaven here's Albrecht's. How wonderful to be in something that stands still and doesn't make noises. *Guten Tag*, Albrecht. Two single rooms with bath, please, and lead me to it."

Albrecht's was a small hotel as hotels go in Switzer-

land, white, with balconies on every floor and a roof of
thick green glazed tiles which caught the sun and reflected the sky. Albrecht himself was short, diplomatic,
and a born hôtelier. He started his career by inheriting
Albrecht's from his father; now, at the age of fifty-seven,
he owned two other hotels in Basle, large decorative
hotels with large decorative managers to match, out-
wardly omnipotent, but in private clay in the hands of
the inconspicuous little man who came, saw and scolded.
Albrecht himself regarded these ventures as money-mak-
ing concerns only, the real passion of his life was Albrecht's. Rich and sumptuous tourists went naturally to
Albrecht's palaces, the wise and discerning traveller to
Albrecht's itself.

Charles Denton went to bed in a darkened room and
stayed there for a week, suffering from delayed concus-
sion. Elisabeth Weber saw to it that the doctor's orders
were carried out, at least as far as was possible with a
thoroughly cross patient. At the end of two days she had
discovered that the way to make him stay quietly in bed
was to say, "Don't you think it would do you good to go
out for a little while?" and if it was desirable to renew the
cold compresses on his head she had only to forget to do
so. Having discovered this, she smiled when he was not
looking, and proceeded to enjoy herself.

Albrecht's served a five o'clock tea at about six, with
tea slightly unusual to English palates, but marvellous
cakes. At this time, and also after dinner, a small orchestra, embowered in pot palms, played in a corner of the
lounge music of the cheerful type called "light orches-
tral". In case even this should become, in time, monoto-
nous to patrons, Albrecht had engaged a singer also, an
Austrian baritone who sang of love and springtime, of
maidens and of partings. Occasionally, in more robust
mood, he sang of hunting, battle, and honourable but

regrettably premature decease. He was a stout young
man with dark curly hair, he would have been improved
if his mother had added a cubit to his stature, and generally speaking his appearance was gently reminiscent of
a prize short-horn bull. He had creamy manners, a really
fine voice which had been immortalized on a number of
excellent gramophone records, and modesty was not his
most outstanding virtue.

There was a noteworthy shortage of personable young
women among the patrons at the time when Liese Weber
arrived, and Herr Waltheof Leibowitz would have been
blind and dumb if he had not noticed her. He was
neither. Besides, owing to the regrettable illness of her
escort, the poor girl was all alone, and it is a pious duty
to brighten the lives of our fellow-creatures.

His eyes wandered round the room as he sang, and
ceased to wander when they reached Liese. When she
applauded, with the rest, at the end of his songs, he had a
special little bow for her among the gestures with which
he graciously accepted these natural tributes to his ex-
cellence. After the concert was over, as he walked
through the room on his way out, he passed near her table
and made her a little bow in passing, with the early rudi-
ments of a smile. So ended the first day.

On the second day he met her in the passage just before
dinner and said, *"G'n'abend, gnädige Fräulein,"* and
after dinner, when she was on the terrace watching the
setting sun all rosy upon some distant alp, he approached
and asked if this was her first visit to Switzerland, and
she said it was.

On the third day he did not see much of her because
Charles Denton was ill, and restless if she was long out
of his sight.

On the fourth day Liese was again in the lounge, and
Herr Waltheof had somebody to sing to, which is always

such a help to the artistic temperament. "Im Monat Mai," he sang, "In the month of May a maiden passed by, a maiden so unsophisticated that she had never been kissed," or words to that effect.

Liese Weber was fairly unsophisticated and had travelled very little, certainly she had never stayed in a hotel practically by herself before. Nor had she ever been singled out for attention from among a number of people before, and she found it pleasant.

By the end of a week Charles Denton had recovered sufficiently to sit up in a chair on his balcony, look at the view, and enjoy a little cheerful companionship.

"That's a sizable little hump over there, surely," he said, indicating an outstanding peak in the far distance.

"That's Rigi," said Liese. "Waltheof says it's five thousand nine hundred feet high."

"Waltheof?"

"Herr Leibowitz."

"Oh. The song-bird. Your Austrian hedge-warbler."

"He has a beautiful voice."

"And is full of instructive information too, evidently, thus combining beauty and usefulness. Like an anti-macassar. Let's talk about something interesting, shall we?"

"Just as you like, Herr Dedler."

"Do you think you could leave off calling me Herr Dedler? Try saying Charles."

"Car-lus," she said.

"Charles."

"Charlus."

"Much better, Liese. Does Waltheof call you Liese?"

"Have you had your soup? It's past eleven."

"No, thanks, I'm tired of soup. Does what's-his-name call you Liese?"

"You're tired of being up here," she said, "and no wonder. Come down to the lounge for a change."

"Don't know that I want to," he said. "But don't let me keep you. Frightfully boring for you up here."

"Don't you want me to stay?"

"Of course I do. Don't you want to go down?"

"No, I don't."

"You know," he said judicially, "you've been pretty decent to me and I've been rotten to you."

"Father told me to look after you."

"Did you only do it because Father told you to?"

"I'll ring for your soup," she said.

"Damn the soup. Put your hand on my head again as you did when I was ill."

"Does it ache still? There, is that better?"

"Keep it there a little. What nice soft hands you have, Liese. I remember a girl once who had soft hands like yours, her name was Marie."

"Did you have headaches in those days?"

"Don't take your hand away. No, but Marie would have tried to cure it for me—unless Bill's little finger had ached, then she'd have forgotten my existence."

"Who were they, Char-lus?"

"Friends of mine. They were—well—rather fond of each other."

"What happened to them?"

"They died. I'll tell you some other time."

"Did they die together, Char-les?"

"You're getting my name better every time. No, she died in Cologne and he in England, years later."

"Perhaps they're together now, Char-les."

"You're rather a dear. Would you really like me to come down to the lounge with you?"

"Yes, I would, please."

"Why would you?"

"Well, it's a little awkward, sometimes, being the only person here who's all alone."

"Good Lord, why didn't you say so before? I'd have made an effort instead of lounging here. I ought to have thought of it. Not but what making efforts is thoroughly alien to my character——"

They went into the lounge, which was nearly empty at that time in the morning, and presently Herr Leibowitz strolled through, ostensibly to put his songs in order, but actually to look for Liese. He sheered off when he saw the long-legged Denton lounging in the next chair. Liese nodded to him and said, "That's him."

"Who? Your tame linnet?"

The two men looked each other up and down as Waltheof walked out, and Denton said, "Umf. I've seen things like him at agricultural shows. In pens, with a rosette on their curly top-knots. He reminds me of a polled Angus."

"But he sings much better," said Liese.

Next day she brought a pile of magazines into Denton's room to amuse him while she went for a walk, and among them was a photograph, signed "With homage from Waltheof Leibowitz." Denton found it when he was alone, and seethed within.

"The blue-nosed, hairy baboon! Not that I'm jealous, of course, the girl's nothing to me, but she's a nice kid and I won't.see her being made a fool of by a fat Austrian crooner, blast him! He's no good to her, probably regards her as a passing amusement. She'd better go home to her father." However, when Liese came in he did not refer to the photograph, nor suggest her returning to Berlin. Instead, he came down to tea, and Waltheof sang, "Ah, can it ever be, That I must part from thee." In spite of friendly overtures from several kind ladies who thought the tall languid young man such an interesting invalid,

Denton said he was tired and went to bed early. No, he didn't want to be read to, thank you.

On the following afternoon he tapped at Liese's door to borrow their mutual ink, and found her looking through a little pile of gramophone records. "Hullo," he said, "been shopping?"

"No, I had these given to me, they're Waltheof's. Look, here's 'Im Monat Mai'. It's a lovely one."

"Oh. When did you hear it?"

"On his gramophone, last night."

"Did you go to his room to hear it?"

"Why not? I had nobody else to talk to."

"I see."

He fidgeted about the room.

"You didn't stay so late as one might have expected, did you? Thought I heard you come up rather early."

"No, I—I didn't stay long."

"Why not?"

"Well, if you must know, he kissed the nape of my neck and I didn't like it."

"He did, did he? Well, if you will ask for that kind of thing, my girl, you'll probably get it."

Denton stalked into his own room and slammed the door.

It was a peaceful scene in the lounge of Albrecht's Privat Hotel at tea-time. There was a cheerful clink of tea-cups, the orchestra played a selection from "L'Arle-sienne" above a subdued but happy chatter, which was only stilled when Waltheof strolled to the front of the platform. The pianist struck a few preliminary chords, and at the same moment the swing door of the lounge opened, and Denton entered.

Waltheof did not notice this. He clasped his hands lightly in front of him, fixed his eyes soulfully on Liese Weber, and began, "Im Monat Mai."

Denton walked delicately between the tables till he was face to face with the singer, when he stopped, and so did the song.

"I'll teach you to remember the month of May, you pie-faced choir-boy," he drawled, and landed the unhappy Waltheof a jolt to the jaw, sending him flying into the grand piano, which complained with a long singing noise. Denton, completely unhurried in the excitement, wandered across to Liese's table and said, "Come on upstairs, we'd better start packing."

"Packing——"

"Come on," he said, and she got up and followed meekly.

"Did you see that girl's face as she went out?" said one elderly lady to another. "Outrageous little minx! I believe she was laughing."

In the cab on their way to the station, Liese said, "Where are we going?"

"To Paris, of course, Lieschen. Good heavens, I've forgotten something."

"What, d-dear?"

"I meant to send your father a picture-postcard of the hotel—in six colours."

THEY HAD A RUSH to catch the train, and, of course, they had no reservations, so it was necessary to resign themselves to spending the night in an ordinary railway carriage till they arrived in Paris at three in the morning.

"But why are we going to Paris, Char-les?"

"Charles."

"Charles. Why are we going to Paris?"

"Because it's the nearest place I know where I can marry you."

"*Herr Gott!* Suppose I don't want to?"

"If you don't now, you will when you've known me another seven hours."

"Who told you that, lordly one?"

"My unconquerable soul," said Denton magnificently. "Come and—no. We are not married yet, so I'll approach you. I want to sit next you, not opposite."

"Shall I have to come when I'm called if I marry you?"

"Running."

"Oh. Just like living with Father," she said in a flat voice.

"Not in the least like living with Father——"

" 'Liese! Fetch my slippers!' "

"A very good idea, but——"

" 'Liese! Fill my pipe!' "

109

"I wouldn't trust you to. It's a fine art——"

"I have acquired it, sir. 'Liese! Bring the beer!' "

"Better and better. In fact, better and bitter. I always knew I was a good picker, but you exceed expectations."

" 'Liese! Bring me the English *Times!*' "

"Does your father read that?"

"Yes. He says that when he was a schoolboy he learned English, and reading the English *Times* is the best way to keep it up."

"I dare say he's right. Can you speak English, Liese?"

"A little," she said. "I read it quite easily, but to speak it is much more difficult. Father made me learn poetry," said Liese, and quoted:

> " '*To be, or not to be, that is the question:*
> *Whether 'tis nobler in the mind to suffer*
> *The slings and arrows of outrageous fortune——*'

That is by Shakespeare, but it is very hard to say. There were some other things Father taught me that I like better. Do you understand English, Charles? Then listen to this:

> '*So through the strong and salty days,*
> *The tinkling silence thrills*
> *Where little lost Down churches praise*
> *The Lord who made the hills.*'

Father says that there are some hills called Downs in England. Father has been there I am sure, though he never talks about it. Have you ever been in England, Charles?"

"Listen to me, my darling. You're going to marry me to-morrow, God help you, and you don't know the first thing about me. I am English, Lieschen."

She looked at him with round eyes and parted lips.

"My name is not Dedler, it is Denton. Charles Denton. So you will be Mrs. Denton, not Frau Dedler. D'you mind?"

"Charles."

"Yes?"

"Was it very dangerous for you, being in Germany?"

"Not at all," he lied stoutly. "Whatever makes you think that?"

She shook her head in disbelief. "Father had so many queer people come to see him——"

"Including me?"

"Yes, dear. They used to talk in that little room at the back of the shop with the doors and window shut, just as you did. I never did believe they all sold pipes or tobacco. I think there was something funny about Father, too."

" 'All the world is queer, dear,' " quoted Denton in English, " 'excepting thee and me, dear, and even thee's a little queer, dear!' "

"You see," she said, refusing to be put off, "Father's a good Nazi, and goes to meetings and things and pays all his subscriptions, but sometimes they come into the shop and talk about how wonderful they all are, and when they've gone he looks amused. I don't think the Nazis would amuse a real Nazi, would they?"

"You notice too much. Tell me," he went on in a serious tone, "have you ever spoken of this to anyone else?"

"Never. And I wouldn't to you, only you're English."

"That's right. Don't talk about it at all, even to me."

"Why not?"

"Somebody might overhear you. Let's talk about something else now, shall we?"

"Is it as serious as all that?"

"Yes, quite."

She nodded understandingly, and presently her eyebrows went up. "Isn't it funny?"

"What is?"

"To think that this time to-morrow I shall be an Englishwoman."

The corners of Denton's mouth twitched, but all he said was, "An Englishwoman who's never seen England. Well, we'll go straight on there and look at it. Are you—aren't you——"

"What?"

"Aren't you really just the least bit scared?"

"Why?"

"It's a long way from home."

"Home is where you are, *liebchen*," she said. "So long as you're there it will be quite safe. You won't leave me, will you?"

"Not more than I can help, my darling. But even if I do, Liese——"

"Even if you must, Charles, what then?"

"Even then, it will still be quite all right, because my heart stays in your little hands, Lieschen, my wife——"

The train slowed down and stopped at Strasbourg, and Denton promptly got up and spread their luggage all over the unoccupied seats of the compartment.

"What's that for, darling?"

"So that people shall think all the seats are taken and we can keep the place to ourselves," said the true-born Englishman. "Try and look as though the stuff didn't belong to you."

Liese wrinkled up her nose and glanced disdainfully at three suit-cases, a hatbox, and two brown-paper parcels, one of them flat.

"Is that the right expression? Oh, but the gramophone records are mine!"

"Feathers from the pet canary."

"He was really very nice, and it was very wrong of you to hit him so hard."

"But it did me such a lot of good," said Denton plaintively, "my head hasn't ached since."

"I think it was horrid of you, Charles. Are you often violent like that?"

"Whenever the moon is full on a Thursday, I grin like a dog and run through the city banging people over the head with lengths of lead piping. Why?"

"Why, indeed," said Liese.

"Oh, just to release my inhibitions. Cheers, the train is moving off and nobody has got in here. See what a clever husband you're going to have, dozens of people looked in at the window and all went peaceably away again, it always works."

A shadow darkened the door into the corridor, and a tall old man with a thick brush of hair entered apologetically.

"I beg a thousand pardons, but could you tell me if all these seats are taken? The rest of the train is so———"

The carriage lurched violently over the points, the old gentleman staggered, clutched at the rack and missed it, and sat down heavily on the flat parcel. Denton let out a yell of delight.

"God bless my soul," said the agitated stranger in English. "What have I done?"

"A noble deed, believe me," said Denton in the same language, "yet one which I should not, myself, have dared. Waltheof's voice is cracked."

"I beg your pardon?"

"The canary has gone off song."

"Dear me," said the old gentleman, gathering up his umbrella and a music-case he had dropped, and making for the door. "How very distressing. I think I———"

"Please don't go away," said Denton, controlling himself. "I didn't mean to alarm you. I get like that occasionally. They are gramophone records in that parcel."

"Are they, perhaps, your wife's?" asked the stranger, with a bow to Liese. "I could, no doubt, replace them."

"She's not my wife yet, but she will be as soon as we get to Paris."

"God bless my soul. May I wish you many years of happiness?"

"*Danke schön,*" said Liese, her English deserting her. "*Sie sind sehr gütig.*"

"Thanks awfully," drawled Denton, "please inaugurate them by not replacing the records. I shall get the bird for that, I expect, but I prefer it to the other bird."

Liese made a face at him, and the old gentleman said, "Some secret, evidently. May I sit here?"

"I do beg your pardon," said Denton, springing up. "Please. Let me remove our truck." He opened the window, and with a simple gesture hurled the records far into the night.

"I'll go and fetch my violin, if I may," said the stranger. "I cannot allow it to travel in the van." When he returned he introduced himself. "My name is Ogilvie, and I am a third-rate fiddler."

"I doubt the adjective," said Denton, looking at the long sensitive fingers. "This is Fräulein Elisabeth Weber, and I'm Charles Denton."

"Have you come far to-day?"

"Only from Basle."

"I have had two days in Strasbourg," said Ogilvie, "but before that I was in Rome. My nephew gave a recital there on Monday, and another in Strasbourg last night. In fact, we have made quite a tour, but he is staying a few days with friends while tiresome business calls me home."

"I am completely uncultured," said Denton, "but somehow the name of Ogilvie suggests music to me."

"You are thinking of my nephew, Dixon Ogilvie, who is a pianist. He is—well, rather famous."

"Dixon Ogilvie."

"Perhaps you have heard him somewhere. I have here," Ogilvie rummaged in his music-case, "a programme with his photograph upon it, here it is."

"Has he played in Berlin, sir?" asked Liese in her careful English. Miranda calls Prospero "sir", and Shakespeare must know.

"Not yet, but perhaps he will some day. He has a foolish prejudice against going again to Germany, he was a prisoner of war there, my dear young lady."

"But," said Liese, "if he is a great musician, he will be very welcome in Germany. We—they—are very musical."

"He knows that quite well. In fact, he has been invited to go, but he says he is afraid that if he hears German spoken all round him again, he will get that locked-up feeling. It must be terrible, to be in prison. You have heard him play somewhere, possibly," to Denton, who was looking at the photograph.

"No," said Denton, "but I have seen him play."

"Seen, but not heard—like a good child?" But Denton did not smile.

"He was playing five-finger exercises on a packing-case when I saw him. Someone who was with me said that was Dixon Ogilvie, a musician."

"And this was——"

"A very long time ago," said Denton, looking away out of the window into the dark, and Ogilvie was too tactful to pursue the subject.

"Are you going to stay in Paris, sir?" asked Denton, returning to the present day.

"I fear not, this time. I am going straight through."

"Couldn't you stay for one afternoon to perform another good deed? If it is a good deed to abet us in a rash one? Will you be a witness at our marriage?"

"My dear fellow," said Ogilvie, "for a thing like that I would postpone any business. I am really honoured that you should ask me—I cannot think why."

"It's a stupid reason," said Denton, leaning back, "but there was a man who would have been at my wedding, and you are connected with a friend of his, if you would stand proxy, I should be most frightfully obliged—sentimental of me, isn't it, but these are sentimental occasions——"

"Tell me the time and place," said Ogilvie.

"Dear Charles, does your head ache again? You look as though it did."

"A little, *liebchen*. I don't know yet, sir, but I'm going to the British Embassy in the morning to see about it——"

"And you will both lunch with me at Maxim's at one, eh? Splendid, and now I think we should all try to sleep a little, it is getting late and those must be the lights of Nancy."

.   .   .   .

Hambledon went to Weber's, the tobacconist's, to buy cigarettes and found him in a state of mental disturbance. He knocked things over, produced the wrong brand, muttered to himself, and forgot the price.

"I'm afraid something is worrying you to-day," said the Deputy Chief of Police sympathetically.

"It is kind of you to notice it," said Weber. "I have had distressing news, Herr Lehmann, that is all."

"I'm sorry to hear that. Can I do anything?"

"No one can do anything. I have lost my daughter."

"Great heavens!" said the startled Hambledon. "That charming child dead! What can have happened?"

"She was to go and spend a little while with an aunt in Switzerland, and in the disturbed state of affairs at the moment I thought it better she should travel with an escort rather than alone. She went, therefore, with a Swiss friend of mine, Herr Dedler, whom I could have sworn to be a man completely trustworthy. But what happened?"

"For pity's sake tell me," said Hambledon earnestly. (What the devil had that fool Denton been up to?)

"See this telegram, gracious sir. I received it an hour ago."

It ran:

Paris, 15.45 16.7.34. Married to-day entreat paternal blessing letter follows.   Charles and Liese.

"Cheer up," said the relieved Hambledon. "They're only married."

"She is lost to me, Herr Lehmann," said Weber mournfully. "I want my little daughter."

"Nonsense, my good Weber. She will return bringing her sheaves with her—probably."

"Sheaves?"

"A poetic touch. Grandchildren, Herr Weber."

"Grandchildren," said Weber, "are all very well in their place, but will they order the dinner? No. Engage and dismiss servants? No. Fetch my pipe and slippers, perhaps, in about six years' time but not before, and in the meantime I shall have to pay a housekeeper who will order me about and probably rob me. Grandchildren, no. I want my daughter. I want Liese."

"There is another disadvantage attached to these particular grandchildren," said Hambledon, with his eyes on the other's face.

"What is that, Herr Lehmann?"

"Herr Dedler is, I think you said, a Swiss? They will not be Germans."

The tobacconist dropped his eyes instantly, but Hambledon had seen in them the gleam which he expected, also the slow colour rose to Weber's temples.

"I—had not thought of that," he muttered.

"They will come here to see you, of course. But they will be brought up in another land, go to distant schools, and play in fields that are very far away."

Weber bit his lip and did not answer.

"I did not mean to distress you, Herr Weber. I will come again some day soon," said Hambledon, and walked out of the shop.

"Distress me!" said Weber to himself. "That German said the one thing that would really comfort me, if he only knew it. I have a good excuse, now, in going to see my married daughter, and who cares if an obscure tobacconist stays in Switzerland or goes on to England? Then I myself will walk again in those fields which are very far away."

"Poor old buffer," said Hambledon to himself. "I bet he bolts off to England via Switzerland before many moons have waned. Why am I so poetic? Oh, yes, honeymoon of course; who'd have thought it of Denton? That thump on the head must have been much too hard, it's softened his brain. He's a lucky man, though, she's a nice little thing—that is, if you like nice domestic little things—— Fancy my telling him to go and elope, and he actually did it, what a frightful responsibility."

He reached home without incident, since the Purge had ceased its more active manifestations some days earlier, and went in search of Reck with a bottle of sparkling Moselle in his hand. He found the old man in his bedroom, sitting slumped in an armchair staring at nothing.

"Cheer up, old thing," said Hambledon breezily, "and have a drink. I've got a toast for you to honour."

"Eh? What? I'll have a drink, certainly, though I don't like that gassy stuff. What is there to drink to; has the shooting stopped?"

"Days ago, you old dormouse," said Hambledon, extracting the cork. "Why don't you go out and see for yourself instead of frowsting in here this lovely weather? Do you good."

"No it wouldn't," growled Reck. "I hate these hearty cold-bath ideas of yours about health. The window's open, what more d'you want?"

"Here you are," said Hambledon, handing him a glass. "It should be Veuve Clicquot, of course, but that's unpatriotic so we drink Moselle. The happy pair! *Hoch!*"

"*Hoch.* But we aren't a happy pair, at least I'm not if you are."

"No, I'm still completely single. We are drinking to two people you've never met. Yes, of course you did. Denton, remember Denton? He was in Köln with Bill after I left."

"Was that his name? He called himself Wolff then, I remember, Ludwig Wolff. An impertinent youth in those days. Is he married? Serve him right, I hope she beats him."

"You're a cheerful sort of devil to celebrate with, I must say. Never mind, here's luck to them. Now, here's a message I want coded and sent out to-night . . ."

.   .   .   .

Denton came to the Foreign Office to report to his Chief, and the old Colonel from Sussex, who could not let this riddle alone, was there also.

"I found out who it is," he said. "As you were, that's

wrong. I didn't find him out, he found me. It is Hambledon."

"Hambledon," said the Foreign Office man. "Good Lord, it can't be, he's dead."

"Hambledon," said the Colonel. "Thank God."

Denton told his story in full detail up to the point where Hambledon left him for the last time.

"So we don't know now who he is in Germany," said Denton's Chief, "and instructions will be issued forthwith that no attempt shall be made to find out."

"From what I remember of the man he is probably impersonating Adolf Hitler," said the Colonel, "having thrown the original, wrapped in wire netting with a couple of flagstones as anchor, down the well of somebody he doesn't like."

"He is certainly a star," said Denton. "If I'd organized a man-sized revolution in a foreign capital city and it had 'gone wrong a little' as he put it, I should bolt at once. Not he. He opens the door to callers, with a gun in each of his pockets, and waits till the storm subsides. All the same, I wouldn't like to be the man who shot Bill Saunders, if anyone did."

"Were there many people—er—I think liquidated is the fashionable phrase?" asked the Colonel.

"I don't know, sir. I was too busy skulking in a cellar to inquire."

"By the way, you have not told us how you got out."

"Oh, quite easily. Hambledon provided facilities and I came home via Switzerland. I had a week in bed at Basle as my head came back at me, and then pottered home."

"Facilities," repeated the Colonel, and smiled.

"Anything more to report, Denton?"

"No, sir. Except that I've committed holy matrimony."

If he expected surprise he was mistaken, for the

Colonel merely smiled again and the Foreign Office man uncovered a short memorandum.

"I have here," he said, "congratulations for you, which have been awaiting you here since 4.15 a.m."

Denton took the paper. The message ran: "T-L-T Denton Foreign Office a.a.a. Congratulations fast work a.a.a. told you to elope didn't I a.a.a. present follows a.a.a. sincerest good wishes."

Denton's jaw dropped. "How the devil did he know?" he said slowly.

"Don't ask me," said his Chief. "Congratulations, Denton, wish you every happiness."

"Congratulations, Denton," said the Colonel. "Lucky fellow. And when may I see the lady?"

"Now, sir, if you'd care to? She's waiting outside in a taxi."

"Lead on, my dear fellow. And—er—when you want a christening-mug, let me know."

HENRY WINTER went to Germany to buy fancy leather goods for the large departmental store to which he belonged. He went from place to place unhindered, a short fat man with a bald head, sincerely welcomed by all who had to do business with him and quite unnoticed by anyone else. In late November 1935 the Exchange was no longer so favourable to the foreigner in Germany as it had been, but he was still able to buy advantageously goods which would sell profitably in the English market. He spent a few pounds on the carved wooden and ivory goods of the Black Forest area as an experiment to see if they would go, bought, as he always did, a present for his wife, in Cologne this time, and settled himself with a sigh of relief in the train for the frontier, homeward bound.

"I'm always glad when I've completed a buying tour," he said. He had made acquaintance with a German commercial traveller in the same compartment, he usually found someone to talk to, for he was a sociable man. "It's a great responsibility, and though I have always given the firm satisfaction so far, one always wonders. It isn't as though it were one's own money one is spending."

"It is evident from what the Herr says that he is a conscientious man," said the German politely, "and the efforts of such men always deserve appreciation."

"It isn't enough just to be conscientious. One has to

use imagination, for it is a sheer gamble to try to please the public."

"It is a gift, not a gamble, to be able to please the public. Besides, you speak our language so well."

"I ought to," said Winter with a laugh, "I spent nearly three years learning it. I was a prisoner of war."

"Were you indeed? I myself fought on the Western Front. Where were you captured?"

"Near Souchez in '15. You know, just north of Arras. I was out with a wiring party, when——"

"Souchez in '15? Why, our lot were down there in '15. Let me see, that would be August onwards. August the 22nd if I remember rightly."

"Oh, I was captured before that. May the 12th, not likely to forget that date, eh? You see, I was out with——"

"May the 12th? Why, my brother was near there then. He was killed on the 30th of May. I wonder if his lot gathered you in. What regiment were they, d'you know?"

"Well, it was like this. I was out with a wiring party, when all of a sudden——"

After which the conversation proceeded on the lines customary in all war reminiscences. "Gave us bread and soup——" "My father was a sergeant of Uhlans, terribly proud of it." "Awful boredom, couldn't stick it. So when I was sent on a farm——" "I was wounded in '16——" "Thawing out frozen turnips——" "The British blockade——" "Decent old fellow, used to write to him till——"

When at last the train slowed down for the frontier station at Aachen Winter said, "Never known this trip pass so quickly. See you again after we've passed the customs? Right. Damned nuisance, these customs. There, see how talking over old times brings 'em back, don't believe I've said 'damn' for ten years except when I've hit my thumb with a hammer or some such. Well, see you later."

Winter pushed his suit-case across the counter to be searched for surplus currency with the unconcern of habitual innocence, and waited for it to be passed. He was very much taken aback when the customs officer asked if he would please step into an inner room, there was a little difficulty. They would not detain him a moment. If he would just step inside and sit down, it would only be for a moment . . .

Winter, protesting volubly, was pushed into the inner room. He sat down, fuming, on one of the hard chairs and was preparing a neat speech for the customs official's superior officer, when he heard the key turned in the lock.

.   .   .   .

Hambledon reached home rather late for lunch that day to find Fräulein Rademeyer rather fidgety.

"I'm so sorry," he said, "to have kept you waiting. You should have started without me."

"I would rather wait, I detest eating alone."

"I'm sorry," he repeated. "I was busy, the time passed before I was aware of it."

"You are always so busy these days, even in the evenings. Can't you take a little time off sometimes?"

Hambledon sighed inaudibly. The old lady was very dear to him, but as the years passed she became more feeble in body but not in spirit, and the increasing limitation of activity was most irritating to her. Besides, it was true, he did leave her alone a great deal.

"I'll take a whole day off early next week," he said. "We'll pick a fine day, drive out somewhere and have lunch. You are quite right, it's an age since I had any time to myself."

"That will be very pleasant," said Ludmilla. "I cannot

think it is good for you to work so hard and come so late to your meals. It is nearly two o'clock."

"I'm sorry," said Hambledon again, glancing at the clock. It was later than he had thought, in five minutes' time the Cologne train would stop at Aachen for the usual hunt through travellers' baggage to see if they were taking more money out of Germany than was permitted by the regulations. Suppose that funny little man Winter had changed his mind and broken his journey somewhere. Suppose Ginsberg had had one of his gastric attacks and been unable to do his job. It might sound a simple matter to undo the lining of a suit-case, slip some papers inside, and do it up again so that it did not appear to have been tampered with, but it took an expert to do it properly. Ginsberg had been apprenticed to a firm of luggage makers, what a find! It was only necessary to tell him that he was concealing secret orders for transmission to German agents abroad for him to take an artist's pleasure in the work. Now the ham-handed Schultz——

"Klaus dear, would it be too much trouble to talk to me when you do come in? I have had no one but the servants to speak to all the morning."

"I am a complete pig, Aunt Ludmilla. I am a mannerless baboon. If it wasn't for certain physiological objections, I would say I was a cow, too. I have had a difficult case to deal with this morning with both sides lying themselves purple in the face, and I was still trying to make up my mind which of them was lying the worst. But that's no excuse for being rude to you. Tell me, what are you going to do this afternoon?"

"I am going to a recital of some of Chopin's Nocturnes and Preludes, and two Beethoven sonatas, by a famous foreign pianist who has never been in Berlin before. I wish you could come with me."

"You don't really. You remember too well what happened last time you tried to educate my taste in music. I snored."

"You were overtired, dear. It was unkind of me to insist on your going."

"That's a nice way of putting it, but you know what the Frau Doktor Gericke said."

"The Frau Doktor Gericke is an evil-minded old cat," said Ludmilla energetically. "As though you were ever the worse for drink! I told her that if that sort of thing was customary in her household, it wasn't in mine, and that if she fed her men-folk properly she wouldn't have so much trouble with that wild Leonhard of hers. Of course, I didn't know that their cook had cracked his head with a rolling-pin the evening before or I wouldn't have said it, but——"

Hambledon roared with laughter. "You didn't tell me that! Where did this exchange of courtesies take place?"

"At Christine's flat. I went there to coffee by invitation, but Alexia Gericke simply walked in. Christine didn't like it, but, of course, she couldn't do anything."

"Then what happened?"

"Oh, Christine started talking at the top of her voice about the reclamation of sand-dunes by planting some sort of grass. You know, her father was an expert at that sort of thing and used to lecture about it. He couldn't read his own writing so Christine had to copy out his notes for him when she was a girl, she's never forgotten them. You wouldn't, you know. So whenever conversations take an awkward turn Christine talks about sand-dunes till it's blown over."

"Frau Christine is a dear."

"She always was. Which reminds me of something quite different. Klaus dear, don't be annoyed, will you? But I cannot abide that horrid old man creeping about the house. Must we have him?"

"Reck? I am so sorry. He is a clever man really, you know. He has had a sad history and I'm sorry for him. Besides, he is useful to me."

"If you really need him, Klaus, there's no more to be said. Only he does look so disreputable, and I'm not at all sure that he is always sober."

"I'll see that he gets some new clothes and smartens himself up."

"His hair wants cutting, too."

"It shall be cut. As for not being sober, if he ever shows anything of that in your presence, out he goes. I would, however, rather keep him under my eye if I can. He will go to the dogs if I turn him out and I don't want that on my conscience."

"You are too kind-hearted, Klaus. I will try and be sorry for him too and then I shan't dislike him so much. If I were to knit him some socks, do you think——"

"You darling! He doesn't deserve that. Heavens, look at the time, I must go. Mind you enjoy your highbrow entertainment. Who are you going to hear?"

"I can't pronounce his queer name, but here's a programme. It has his photograph on it, look."

Hambledon took the programme carelessly, glanced at the photograph, and then looked intently. Dixon Ogilvie's name was beneath it, but that was unnecessary for Tommy Hambledon, once Modern Languages master at Chappell's School. The photograph showed a man in the early thirties, but there was little change from the other picture which rose to Hambledon's mind of a tall, skinny, untidy boy to whom music took the place occupied in the hearts of other boys by toffee, food and cricket, a boy who wouldn't learn French and couldn't learn German—perhaps the guards at the prisoners' camp at Thielenbruck had been more successful teachers.

"A nice face, isn't it?" said Fräulein Rademeyer, who

was wandering about the room collecting tickets, gloves, two pairs of spectacles and a purse, and did not notice Hambledon's expression. "I should think he's a nice young man, wouldn't you?"

Still no reply, so she looked at him, crossed the room quickly and laid her hand on his arm.

"What is it, my dear? Do you think you remember that face?"

"Perhaps," said Hambledon, rousing himself. "It's rather unlikely, isn't it? A chance resemblance, probably."

"He might be a friend, or some relation," she said.

"But he's English," said Hambledon, looking at her curiously. "That would mean I was English, too, and that's impossible."

"I suppose it is," she said slowly.

"Would you mind very much, if I turned out to be English after all? You'd hate it, wouldn't you?"

"No, why? The war's over long ago, Klaus dear, and you and I have been happy together for a long time."

"I'm glad you think like that," he said. "I shan't be so afraid now of—of getting my memory back."

She laughed and patted his arm. "You don't know much about women, do you, Klaus? Besides, the English are quite respectable people. Won't you come with me and see him for yourself?"

"No," he said, "no. I do very well as I am, and besides, I have business to attend to this afternoon."

"Very well, dear. And don't worry, your memory will come back some day, I am sure of it. How tiresome it will be, learning to call you by a new name."

"You never shall——"

"Good gracious, look at the time. Tell Franz to call a cab, will you, while I put—I shall be late—they won't let me in till the interval——"

She scurried out of the room while Hambledon shouted

to Franz to call up a taxi, and himself walked back to his office. He pushed the thought of Dixon Ogilvie out of his mind for the present and returned to the subject of Henry Winter. By this time the little man should have been released, have passed the Belgian customs, and should now be sitting in the slow local to Brussels, having lost the boat train. No doubt he was horribly cross, probably he was bouncing gently on the seat and emitting a faint sizzling sound. Never mind, they also serve——

.   .   .   .

"So I lost the boat-train to Ostende," said Winter to his wife, "and had to take a slow local to Brussels. I caught a fast train from there but, of course, the boat had gone, so I had to stay the night. I went to the Excelsior Hotel, too expensive for me normally, but as it's the off-season I knew the charge would be reasonable, and to tell you the truth, my dear, I'd been so worried and upset that I thought I deserved a little extra luxury."

"Did you have an amusing time there, Henry?"

"No, m'dear. Very dull."

Henry Winter had walked into the Excelsior on the previous evening shortly before dinner and asked, in his Britannic French, for a room for one night.

"M'sieu' is alone?" asked the reception clerk.

"Completely alone," said Winter.

He was still seething with a sense of injustice in spite of the floods of apology which had been poured on him at Aachen. His detention was a mistake, the locked door was a mistake, it was to keep people out, not him in, his being shown in there at all was a mistake and the official responsible should be reprimanded—degraded—dismissed the service. But Winter was not appeased. However, the reception which is accorded to hotel visitors in the off-season began to soothe him, and the excellent dinner, with a wine he'd never heard of before but which was recommended personally by the wine waiter, completed the cure. When he had finished the cheese and biscuits—and the half-bottle—he felt at peace with the world. After all, annoying contretemps must sometimes happen to every habitual traveller, the seasoned hands, like himself, look upon such things philosophically as all in a day's work. He was a little ashamed of having been so flustered by it, the traditional British phlegm, he felt, must have unaccountably failed him for some reason. A touch of liver, possibly. He rose from the table, pulled down his waistcoat, and strolled into the lounge.

Since the stock of foreigners of any sort was a trifle low in Winter's estimation at the time, he counted himself lucky to find another Englishman among the few guests present. The two men foregathered to discuss Hitler and play billiards till Henry Winter went up to bed.

The lift was one of those which starts each journey with an aggrieved howl, and Winter guessed rather than heard that the boy asked him which floor. "Third," he answered, winding his watch on the way up to save time because he was sleepy. The lift stopped, Winter got out and walked along to his room.

He opened the door quietly, switched on the light, and noticed at once that his very ordinary brown suit-case on the luggage-stand inside the door had been closed again although he had left it open. He slid the catches and threw back the lid.

There came from the other side of the room an angry wail of feminine outrage and Winter jumped round to see with horror a woman standing beside the bed in the alcove, a woman, moreover, in an advanced stage of disarray. For a second he gaped at her, speechless with astonishment, then, "My good woman!" he gasped, in English, and fled the room, slamming the door behind him.

He hurried back to the lift, rang for it, and demanded to be taken to the manager instantly. *"Instamment, sans delay,"* but the manager was not there and had to be sought. Henry Winter marched angrily about the room trying to summon adequate French to express his sentiments. If only they spoke German he could have been so fluent . . .

The manager arrived. "Monsieur desire?"

"There is," said Winter carefully, "a woman in my room. I do not want her."

"Impossible," said the startled manager.

"I thought," said Winter, after one or two false shots at the past tense of a notoriously irregular verb, "I thought this was a respectable hotel."

The manager said that it was truly an establishment but of the most decorous, but Winter merely snorted, saying that the woman must be taken away at once, *"éprise"* was the word he used, which defeated the manager yet further. *"Je demande qu'elle sera éprise."*

The manager called upon his Maker and added that there must be some mistake, to which Winter tried to reply that there was indeed a very serious mistake, but that anyone who imagined they could get away with that sort of thing with him would find they would—he found himself drowning in a tangle of subjunctives and tore himself free. "I won't have it," he said indignantly. "I don't like that sort of thing. *Je ne l'aime pas.*"

"Is it," said the manager, upon whom a false dawn unkindly broke, "is it that monsieur desires to part with his wife?"

"Heavens above, no!" stormed the baited Winter, in English. "She's a stranger, I tell you. *Elle est étrange, très étrange.*"

The manager, making another desperate attempt to keep abreast of a situation which became momentarily

further beyond him, asked was it that the poor madame
. . . he tapped his forehead and suggested a doctor.

Winter, who was nearly a cot case himself by this time,
shook despairing fists in the air. "Listen," he said. "I
have a perfectly good wife at home, but——"

"*Mais oui, monsieur*," said the manager, sure he had
got it right this time. "That is of the most undoubted.
But monsieur is on holiday, and life is like that, is it not?"

"No, it isn't," howled Winter. "I tell you——"

At that moment the door opened violently, a well-
developed young woman bounced into the room and set
about the unfortunate manager in floods of French so
rapid as to leave Winter gasping. He looked at her
again——

"Here," he said, grabbing the manager by the arm,
"that's the woman."

She flung out her arm with a gesture worthy of Duse.
"That—that is the man!"

"Hussy!"

"*Scélérat!*"

"Minx!"

"*Ravisseur!*"

"Madame," said the manager, pushing his way between,
"Monsieur! All is now clear——"

"He came to rob! He opened my case——"

"You have the wrong room," said the manager firmly
to Winter. "You were on the wrong floor——"

"Gobbless my soul," said the deflated Winter. "I told
the boy the third floor."

"I am second floor," said the lady.

"The little mistake," said the manager airily. "She
comes, does she not? *Deuxième, troisième*, what would
you?"

"Madame," said Winter, horribly abashed, "I am—I
cannot tell you—I beg——"

"I beg monsieur," said she with a dazzling smile, "not to distress himself. One understands, one pardons, is it not?"

.　　.　　.　　.　　.　　.　　.

"Very dull indeed," said Winter to his wife. "Place half shut up, very few people there."

"But quiet and comfortable, I hope. You caught the boat all right next day, though."

"Yes, I got across all right but, believe it or not, I had more trouble over the luggage at Dover. I had some of the firm's stuff to declare, of course, so after the customs people had examined everything I sent the porter along to the train with the boxes and my suit-case whilst I paid the charges. When I went on the platform myself I couldn't find the porter or any of the luggage!"

"My dear, what an extraordinary thing. Didn't you complain?"

"Complain! I'll say I complained. I sent for the station-master, the assistant station-master and the foreman porter; the train was held up while every compartment and van were searched. Not a sign of them. Not any of them. I was ever so angry, Agnes."

"You had every right to be, Henry. What happened then?"

"Well, eventually they had to let the train go when it was obvious the stuff wasn't on board; I walked about at my wits' end what to do, and chanced to go outside. I mean, to the station entrance, where the cars drive up, and there, just outside the door, was all my luggage neatly piled up. All by itself, Agnes, nobody looking after it."

"And the porter?"

"Never saw him again, they couldn't find him or something. Disgraceful! Scandalous! However, all the cases were there, so there wasn't much harm done, I looked inside each one and they hadn't been tampered with so far as I could see. Oh, Agnes, that suit-case of mine is getting shabby, the lining is split."

"Oh, is it? Well, you've had it some time and I dare say we can get it mended. What happened then, did you have to wait for the next train?"

"No, as luck would have it there was a gentleman outside the station with a wonderful car, a sports Bentley he said it was, he'd missed the train himself and was going to drive up to town so he offered me a lift, and I accepted. He was ever so nice, I told him all about what had happened and he was ever so sympathetic. He even went out of his way to drop the firm's boxes at the office."

"How very kind, Henry, how fortunate, too! So much nicer than waiting hours for the next train. What was he like, Henry?"

" 'What was he like'! Oh, you woman! Very tall, with a lazy manner and a tired way of talking as though it was almost too much trouble to speak, don't you know, but a real toff and no mistake. I should think he'd been in the Army, still is, probably. We got on fine," said Henry with a self-conscious laugh. "He simply insisted on my having what he called a spot of dinner with him before I came home. Went to a place called the Auberge de France in Piccadilly, I'd never heard of it before. Not much to look at outside, give me the Strand Corner House for that any day, but my hat, the cooking! And the service! Waiters everywhere."

"What did you have, Henry?"

"Well, we started with . . ." and so on.

Denton took leave of Winter at one of the Piccadilly Tube entrances and himself repaired to the Foreign Office.

"Well, did you pacify him?"

"Oh, Lord, yes, quite easy, no trouble at all. Decent old fruit really. What's in the kitty this time, anything exciting?"

"Don't know yet, it'll be up any minute now. Wonder where they packed it."

"Oh, at Aachen, at the examination for currency. He told me all his troubles. They aren't so subtle as we are, though, they just inveigled him into a back room and locked him up while they got on with it. I imagine he raised—here's your plate of cabbage."

They tore open the envelope which the messenger brought in, the contents informed them that Germany would march into the demilitarized Rhineland in March, in four months' time, and at the same moment denounce the Locarno Treaty.

"Well, I don't blame 'em," said Denton. "How'd we like being forbidden to have a single soldier within thirty miles of the South Coast?"

NIEHL, Chief of Police and Hambledon's immediate superior, had been too close a friend of Roehm to emerge unscathed from the Purge. He was not executed but removed from office, and made a Provincial Governor far enough from Berlin to keep him out of sight as well as out of mind. When Klaus Lehmann congratulated him on his appointment, the new Governor made a wry face, shrugged his shoulders, and remarked that he had long wished to retire from the whirl of city life to grow vines, and now was his chance.

"How happy you must be," said Lehmann enthusiastically.

"If I were an American," said Niehl, who was a film fan, "I should say 'Oh, yeah?' "

"How I envy you your command of English. I wish I had been more attentive at school."

"It is a gift, my dear Lehmann, the power to assimilate foreign languages is a definite gift."

"How very true," said Lehmann without a smile.

So Niehl left, and Klaus Lehmann became Chief of Police in his stead. It was he, therefore, who was sent for to the Wilhelmstrasse when the plans and specification of the magnetic mine disappeared.

"Not only," said the stout figure behind the enormous desk, "have these plans got to be found at once, but the

man who took them and anyone else to whom he may
have talked about it, must be silenced. I suggest a sepul-
chral silence, Lehmann."

"Yes, sir."

"You see, the point is this. Even the plans, important
as they are, are overshadowed by the importance of keeping secret even the idea that such a thing exists. A clever
man could be found in any civilized country, no doubt,
who could design a magnetic mine if it were suggested to
him. Nobody must suggest it, Lehmann."

"I see the point."

"Ninety-nine men out of every hundred, if they learn
something really important, must tell somebody. For
this reason, when you have found him you must also find
his associates and ask yourself to whom a man would
disclose such a secret. To his friends?"

"As he would almost certainly have to admit also that
he was plotting against the Party," said Lehmann, "he
would choose his friends very carefully, I think."

"You are right. His wife, then?"

"I am myself a bachelor, but I thought that men usually discussed with their wives matters concerning house-
keeping, cookery and children."

"Not necessarily in the earlier days of married life.
He talks of such things later on, but perhaps you are right
again. His sweetheart then?"

"As I have said, my experience is limited," said Lehmann modestly, "yet I can imagine an innumerable list
of matters to discuss with a personable young woman before one reached the subject of magnetic mines."

"You are a dry old stick, Lehmann," said the big man
good-naturedly. "I'd love to see you going all romantic
over some expensive blonde."

"I shall never dare to ask for my salary to be increased
after that suggestion."

"For fear I come to see if she's worth it, hey? But we are positively flippant. I leave this matter—this very important matter, Lehmann—in your hands with the utmost confidence. I am sure you will deal with it effectively."

"I endeavour to give satisfaction, sir," said Lehmann, and took his leave, devoutly trusting that his huge companion had never heard of Jeeves.

The field of inquiry was limited. The papers had disappeared between 12 noon on Wednesday, August the 25th, 1937, when they were marked in as having been returned by Goering, and 10.30 a.m. on Friday, August the 27th, when the same clerk who had receipted them two days earlier was told to send them over to the Admiralty. In the meantime they had been deposited in a locked drawer of the writing-table used by the Civil Service Head of the War Office section concerned. Immediately the loss was discovered, a strong breeze blew up through the Department and troubled the waters.

Herr Julius Weissmann, head of the Filing Section, said that if the folder had been returned to files, as was proper in the case of so important a paper, the loss would not have been incurred. Never in all his thirty-one years' experience had he seen such a gross and unpardonable infringement of procedure. Even the most recently joined messenger-boy would know better, but some there were who thought themselves so great as to be above rules.

Herr Marcus Schwegmann, in whose bureau drawer the papers had been left, became completely unstrung under Klaus Lehmann's unpleasantly pointed questions and stated that (a) he had locked the paper up safely; (b) he could not remember ever having seen it; (c) the office charwoman had taken it; (d) Weissmann had taken it, thrown the blame on him, Schwegmann, and sold the papers to the British; (e) Goering had never returned it;

(f) he, Schwegmann, was not at the office that week at all; (g) it was a plot to ruin him, and (h) he wished he were dead. He was at once compulsorily retired.

All six of the clerks in his section denied ever having touched, seen or even heard of the papers, and as they weren't supposed to anyway, this seemed quite likely to be true. After Lehmann had had their homes searched for incriminating evidence and found only proofs of interest in girls in three cases, music in two, and esoteric Buddhism in the last, he crossed them off the list.

The charwoman went for him like a tigress. She said she had six rooms to clean out, dust and rearrange every night and only two hours to do it in; if the police thought a poor hardworking woman had time to do all that and go snooping round into what didn't concern her at the same time, it was a pity they didn't give up accusing persons as innocent as the babe unborn and do an honest day's work occasionally instead, that is, if any of them had ever known what an honest day's work was, which she took leave to doubt judging by their faces, most of them looked as though they had something nasty in their pasts such as she would not demean herself to describe, and had only joined the police to be on the right side and have no questions asked which would be awkward to answer. She paused for breath, and Klaus, finding he had involuntarily bowed his head to the storm, straightened up again to say that there was no question of throwing aspersions upon her moral——

The charwoman said there had better not be, since there was a law to protect poor honest widows from insult, defamation of character and probably assault, and if anyone, even a policeman, laid so much as the tip of one finger——

"Be quiet!" shouted Klaus. "Stop it! Hold your tongue. Nobody wants to assault you. Nobody would want to, anyway, you—you awful woman. Answer my question. Did you, on the evenings of Wednesday the 25th or Thursday the 26th, notice anything or anyone unusual?"

The charwoman shook her head. "Nothin', bar Frau Kronk speaking civil for once, which is a nine days' wonder I'm sure, never having known it happen——"

"Who is Frau Kronk?"

"The woman who does the rooms at the end of this passage."

"Does she come in here?"

"What? Into my rooms? To see if I done 'em properly like? Not—something—likely. Know what I'd do to her if she did?"

Before Klaus could stop her, she told him. He shuddered, mopped his brow, and tried again.

"What I want to know is this. Did you, or did you not, see anything or anyone unusual in this room on the two nights I have mentioned?"

She paused for thought. "No, bar the electricians makin' even more mess than usual."

"Electricians?"

"Putting in wires for a 'lectric fire in 'ere for fear Lord High What's-'is-name gets cold toes, pore dear."

"Speak civilly of your superiors or you will regret it. Anything else?"

"Ho, speak civil——"

"Anything else?"

"No."

"Go. Get out. Hop it. Buzz off, and don't come back. Merciful heavens," said poor Lehmann, wiping his forehead, "I didn't know there were such women. What a—well, never mind. Now, about those electricians."

Upon inquiry it transpired that Herr Schwegmann had successfully applied to have an electric fire installed in his office, and the work was being done by two electricians. One was a permanent employee of the War Office who looked after the lighting and was absolutely above suspicion, the other had been sent by the firm supplying the electric fire in question. It was the duty of the War Office employee not only to assist the other man technically as might be required, but also to keep watch on him to see that he did not do anything irregular or pry into what did not concern him. The stranger was not to be left alone for a moment within the sacred precincts.

"Oh," said Lehmann. "Sounds all right, doesn't it? Can I see these two fellows?"

"Certainly. Heller is on the premises, I'll send him in to you. The other shall be sent for."

"No," said Lehmann thoughtfully, "don't send for him yet, I'd like to talk to Heller first. Does he know there's anything missing?"

"I shouldn't think so, but I should hate to swear to it. The whole affair has been treated as very secret and confidential, but you've no idea how news flies round in a big office like this. No one, of course, ever talks, but you'd think the walls ooze it out. Most extraordinary."

"I expect so. Let me have the other fellow's name and address, will you? Thanks, now if I might see Heller?"

Heller came in, a capable-looking workman with an honest face. "Tell me," said Lehmann, "you were working in Herr Schwegmann's room on the second floor on Wednesday and Thursday nights this week, were you not?"

"Yes, sir. We was puttin' in an electric fire, and as there was no points near the floor we was takin' out the skirtin'-boards and runnin' the wire behind them. We've done now, sir."

"So I see, and a very neat job too. Are there any more jobs like that to be done just now?"

"Yes, sir, Herr Britz, on the floor above, wanted another put in his room, so it seemed best to do both jobs at once while Hauser was still with us. We start up there to-night."

"Who's Hauser?"

"The man the Elektrische Gesellschaft sent with their fittin's. They won't guarantee 'less their own people fit them."

"I see. Now tell me, was there any trouble of any sort on either Wednesday or Thursday night? Anything unusual?"

"No, sir. Excuse me, might I ask if there's anythin' gone wrong?"

"There is a little trouble, but it is in no way connected with you. I have to question everyone who was in these rooms then, but there is nothing for you to fear."

"Thank you, sir. No, nothing went wrong bar the fuse blowing. That's the second time that fuse has gone in three days, there's a short somewheres on this floor. Devil of a job—beg pardon, sir—awkward job to find a short sometimes. Might be anywhere in the circuit."

"What happened then?"

"I reported it, sir, and the firm who did the wirin' must come and look for it. I haven't the instruments; besides, it comes under their guarantee."

"Yes, exactly. What happened on Thursday night—was it Thursday night? The night before, then, when the fuse went?"

"All these lights went out and we was left in the dark. I says—well, I won't tell you what I says, but I told Hauser it was that fuse again and he'd better hang on while I went and replaced it. So he said all right and off I went."

"Leaving him alone in the dark?"

"Yes, sir. I had a torch, he hadn't."

"How long were you away?"

"Quarter of an hour, sir, quite. You see, there was no fuse wire in the box on this floor, I'd used it up when it blew before. So I had to go down to my store in the basement to get it and then fit it in. Took some time, all that."

"Of course. What was Hauser doing when you came back?"

"Nothin'. Just sittin' where I'd left him. Strictly speakin', I shouldn't have left him accordin' to the rules. I ought to have took him all round with me trailin' about after fuse wire, but who would?"

"Exactly, who would? Especially as he was all in the dark. How did you know he hadn't a torch?"

"He said so, sir."

"I see. Thank you, Heller, that'll do."

Otto Hauser, the Elektrische Gesellschaft's fitter, had a room in a small house in the poorer quarter of Berlin, and while he was out that night putting in the second electric fire for the chilly Herr Britz, there came two callers to his lodgings. A woman opened the door, asking who was there, but shrank back into the passage when she got the answer, "Police."

"Which is Hauser's room?" asked Lehmann.

"First back."

"Stay there till I come down again. Come with me, Muller."

They went upstairs and Lehmann turned the doorhandle.

"Locked," he said. "Open this door, Muller."

Muller bent over the keyhole, there came a few clicking sounds, and the door opened. Inside the room the only locked receptacle was a suit-case under the bed. "Muller!" and the suit-case also opened.

"Stand outside the door, will you, to make sure no one comes near," said Lehmann, and started on the suit-case as soon as he was alone. There was a flat parcel at the bottom.

"This is too easy," murmured Lehmann, untying the string. "Either this fellow's a complete novice, or this is only a photo of his best girl, or some poisonous reptile will leap out and bite me and I shall have only time to utter a hoarse, strangled cry before I—ah!"

He drew out a War Office folder containing some correspondence, two or three pages of close typescript and half a dozen engineers' drawings of a globular object. Under these there was a neatly written copy of the typing and four unfinished tracings of the drawings. There was also some spare tracing-paper, enough to finish the job.

"I see," said Lehmann. "We make a copy and then replace the original after having, as I suspect, arranged another short in the War Office electric wiring. Quite good so far, Otto, but you do want some hints about putting your work tidily away. Since there isn't a chimney I should have looked for a loose board under the carpet, Otto, and I think somehow I should have found one. By this means, Otto, my boy, I should continue to live longer than you look like doing."

He replaced the papers precisely as they were in the packet, tied the string with the same knots and repacked the suit-case.

"I hate to interrupt an artist in the middle of a masterpiece, and really, Otto, you do copy quite nicely. So I think you shall be permitted to finish it before I gather you in. I should think you'd do the other drawings to-morrow."

Lehmann opened the door and told Muller to relock the case. "There's nothing here yet," he said, "but I might want to have another look to-morrow. I'm not quite satisfied somehow. Lock the door while I go and speak to the lady of the house."

He went downstairs to find the woman still standing exactly where he had left her.

"What's your name?" and she told him.

"You know who we are, don't you?"

"Police," she whispered.

"That's right. Why are you frightened by the police?"

"I'm not."

"I think you are. Now, listen. No one has been here to-night, not even the police, and no one has been anywhere near your lodger's room. Do you understand?"

"Y—yes."

"If you forget all about the police I will forget about you, but if your lodger hears one word, one hint about this, I shall remember you at once, and come back to see why you are so frightened of the police. Then I shall find that out too, and you wouldn't like that, would you?"

She did not answer, but Lehmann appeared to be satisfied, for he nodded at her and went out with Muller, shutting the door behind them.

On the following night Otto Hauser was arrested as he reached home after finishing the second job at the War Office. The missing papers were found intact in his suitcase, but the Chief of Police made no mention of any copies although he had searched the premises himself. It is hardly necessary to add that Hauser didn't mention them, either.

The Chief of Police went home that night with the uplifted heart which rewards a duty well done; before he went to his office in the morning he wrote out a brief message and took it along to Reck's room.

"Wake up and take notice," he said. "Half-past eight of a lovely summer's morning and you're still snoring? Wake up." He threw the curtains back, pulled up the blinds and flung both windows wide open. "My hat, what a fug. I don't wonder you're always thirsty."

"Oh, go away," said Reck indistinctly, because he was burying his face in the pillow. "Can't a man have a little peace without your bursting in at dawn with your horrible League of Youth ideas about air and sun and all that rot? You'll be expecting me to take cold baths next."

"Couldn't be done," said Hambledon unkindly. "When you hopped in there'd be a loud fizz and the water would boil. Now then, Reck, that's enough joking. I want this message coded and sent off to-night."

"One of these nights," said Reck defiantly, "one of those extra superchromium-plated American cars with a wireless set in them will come cruising down this street at 3 a.m. full of bright young things on their way home from a party, and when they find they're completely deafened by a spark transmitter at close range somebody will tell somebody about it. Then somebody will begin to think, and one day somebody will come——"

" 'My heart is sair,' " hummed Tommy Hambledon, " 'I daurna tell, my heart is sair for somebody.' "

"Yes," said Reck bitterly, "and the last somebody will probably be me. But you'd better be careful of me, you know."

"Why?"

"Because the code isn't written down and I've no intention of writing it. You won't kill the goose that lays the golden——"

"Pips. Cheer up, old goose, I'll look after you."

The message ran: "Agent carrying current number La Vie Parisienne and examining death of Charlemagne Kaisersaal Aachen Town Hall Monday Sept. 1st at 3 p.m. will exchange copy with friendly tourist to advantage."

Ginsberg, ex-trunk-maker's assistant, was justly proud of the fact that he was sometimes selected to do a little job for German Intelligence, though he was only an undistinguished member of the S.A. Usually the work consisted only of secreting papers in travellers' luggage for transmission to our clever agents in foreign countries, but this time it was different and rather more exciting. He was actually to go and meet someone, and give him a copy of a highly coloured French comic paper in exchange for a similar one which the stranger would be carrying. There was something a little unusual about Ginsberg's copy because the pages wouldn't open, but he was told he could read the one he would receive in exchange. Aachen Town Hall; though he lived in Aachen he had never entered that building. A big room called the Kaisersaal with pictures on the walls, one of a king dying.

Ginsberg stared at the frescoes with round eyes, very fine pictures no doubt, but hardly in his line, and a stranger with a colorful periodical under his arm seemed entertained by the German's puzzled stare.

"Wonderful works, aren't they?" said the stranger.

"I suppose so," said Ginsberg. "I was told they was worth seein', so I came."

"Do you like them now you've seen them?"

"Very fine, no doubt, but I must say I like somethin' a bit more lively, myself."

"Something more like this," said the stranger with a laugh, indicating his paper. "I see you've got one too."

"Yes," said Ginsberg, "but mine's an old one, I had it given me. I expect you've seen it."

"Let's look. No, I haven't. I've done with this, would you care to have it?"

"Let's swap, then, if you'd care to?"

So the affair was neatly arranged, and Ginsberg walked out of the Town Hall naturally pleased with himself. He was, therefore, proportionately horrified when on returning to barracks he was pounced on by a couple of Storm Troopers, summarily arrested, and taken to prison.

The Chief of Police received daily a list of Party members arrested for non-Party activities of various kinds, and usually he gave it a purely formal perusal. On this occasion he ran his eyes casually down the list as usual till he was brought up with a jerk by the name Ginsberg, address Aachen, arrested Sept. 1st. Klaus Lehmann leaned back in his chair.

"Now I do wonder," he said to himself, "exactly why he was arrested, and where, and at what time?"

He glanced at the clock for no particular reason except that the beat of the pendulum seemed to be louder than usual, and was horrified to find it was his own heart he could hear thumping.

"Well," he said philosophically, "I've had a damn good run, anyway."

CHAPTER XII
TRAGEDY AT AACHEN

Tommy hambledon considered for a time the advisability of leaving at once without even waiting to pack a toothbrush, for he was very severely frightened. If Ginsberg had been taken with the plans of the magnetic mine on him, the Chief of Police's chance of survival was miscroscopic. Klaus Lehmann had handled the case, Klaus Lehmann was present when Hauser was arrested, Klaus Lehmann himself found the missing file, it could be proved if anyone really tried, that he had been in touch with Ginsberg, and finally Ginsberg, if he were questioned by Party officials, would talk. Naturally, since he had no idea he had done anything but serve his country, probably he was rather proud of it. Then out would come all the pretty details of papers inserted into travellers' luggage, of which the case of Henry Winter was only one example, of memoranda slipped into passports—— Hambledon broke into a gentle perspiration. Probably it was already too late to leave, the next time the door opened there would be a squad of S.A. men no longer regarding him deferentially. He opened a drawer, took out an automatic and slipped it into his pocket. No, it didn't seem much use trying to bolt, better stay and try to face it out. Besides, there was Ludmilla, not that it would do her much good if he faced a firing-squad, but he could hardly depart without a word and leave her to bear the brunt.

However, the next man who came into his office be-
haved quite normally and made no attempt to arrest him,
nor the next, nor the next. Somehow the interminable
day passed slowly by and still men saluted when they met
him and took orders from him, and no one addressed him
as "Hey, you!" adding, "Come along quiet, now." He
went home in safety and to bed in peace, though it cannot be said that he slept particularly well.

The next day he went to his office as usual, not that he
wanted to in the least, but he found it impossible to stay
away. Still nothing happened.

"Too much dentist's waiting-room atmosphere about
life at the moment to please me," said Tommy to himself
on the third day. "I wonder whether nothing's going to
happen or whether they're just waiting to pounce. To
think I might have been in England by now."

Towards the evening reports of Party activities as they
affected the police were brought in, among them was an
item from the S.A. Headquarters at Aachen. "Heinrich
Ginsberg, shot while attempting to escape, Sept. 2nd."

"Dear me," said Hambledon bleakly.

He determined on a bold stroke and sent for the papers
connected with the case. He had a perfect right to send
for any such papers of course, only it was just possible
that the Party leaders were waiting for him to make some
move like that to incriminate himself. He felt as though
he were feeling his way blindfold about a dark room full
of horribly explosive furniture. One touch in the wrong
place and a highly coloured detonation would immediately follow.

However, the papers came without demur and Hambledon learned to his surprise that Ginsberg had been arrested at 8 p.m. on Monday, Sept. 1st, for suspected race-
defilement, to wit, having an affair with the daughter of
a Jewish provision merchant in Aachen. Informant, Georg

Schultz. The prisoner, evidently actuated by a consciousness of guilt, had attempted to escape when he was taken
from prison for interrogation, and was shot in the act.

"If this is true and not a trap," said Hambledon, "he
was shot before interrogation, but after having got rid
of the plans. If this is true and not a trap, a miracle has
occurred and I've got away with it once more. Informant,
Georg Schultz. That's the clumsy oaf who was Ginsberg's
subordinate, very odd. There's something funny going on
here. I wonder if Schultz has stepped into Ginsberg's
shoes. I think I'll look into this further. Poor Ginsberg, a
nice fellow, what a damn shame. I don't believe this tale.
If Schultz has framed him he shall wish he was dead before
I've done with him and then he'll wake up and find he is,
damn him."

At the end of a week in which nothing untoward had
happened, Tommy Hambledon decided to go to Aachen
to try and find out for himself what was behind the murder of Ginsberg. He frankly called it murder in his own
mind because the man had been shot without a trial, and
he did not believe one word of the "attempting-to-
escape" formula. It was usually a lie, and this time he
knew it, for where would a man escape to in the stone
passages and a staircase or so between his cell and the
charge room?

He noted down Ginsberg's home address from the
papers relating to the case, and arrived one evening at a
small house in a row of workmen's dwellings in the out-
skirts of Aachen. He knocked at the door and was kept
waiting while faces peered at him through the lace curtains at the front window. Eventually the door was
opened to him by a thin old man with a frightened brow-
beaten look.

"*Grüss Gott*," said the man. "I beg pardon, I mean
Heil Hitler!" and he gave the Nazi salute.

"*Grüss Gott*," said Hambledon gently. "I am sorry to intrude on your sorrow. I was a friend of your son's. May I come in?"

He was shown into the family living-room which seemed at first glance to be completely filled with large women in black. The old man edged past him as he hesitated on the threshold and said, "Mother, this gentleman says he is a friend of Heinrich's." Heinrich's mother struggled up from an armchair by the fireplace, a short unwieldy woman in which the features seemed half submerged in layers of fat, but the expression of pain in her red-rimmed eyes made Hambledon feel sick, as one feels who looks on torture. She stared at him with plain distrust, and said, "The Herr is very kind, but my son is dead," in a toneless voice which struck Hambledon as more tragic by far than the emotional agonies with which youth confronts bereavement. "My son is dead," she said again, still staring at him. Hambledon felt that unless he took a firm hold of himself he would turn and run.

"I—I have heard," he stammered, "I am desperately sorry."

The old man came to his rescue. "These are Heinrich's sisters," he said, referring to three stout young women standing politely against the wall. "Annchen, Emilie and Lotte."

There was a fourth girl in the room whom no one introduced, a slim, fair girl like one white rose in a garden of peonies, who sat on a stool by Frau Ginsberg's chair and took no notice of anyone, slowly and continually twisting her hands, she did not even look up when Hambledon came in. He wondered who she was, she was so obviously not one of the family.

"There's no need to be so sorry," said the old woman in a harsh voice. "Will not the Herr sit down?"

Hambledon did so, everyone else who was standing did

so too, and all looked at him silently except the girl who took no notice of anyone but went on twisting her hands.

He felt as if he were entangled in some insane charade, a Russian sort of charade like some of those plays Bill Saunders used to go to see in Köln where dreadful families sat in comfortless rooms and discussed suicide. He tried desperately to think of something to say, but found himself wishing so passionately he had never come, that he was afraid to speak lest those words and no others should gush out in spite of himself. "I wish to God I hadn't come. Why did I come? I wish I hadn't come. I was a fool to come——" And still the women stared at him and the girl went on twisting her hands.

"There's no need," said the old woman, still in the same angry voice, "to be sorry. I am told my son broke some of the rules of the Party, that's all."

"I came to—to see if there was anything I could do," said Hambledon desperately. "He—I liked him."

"The Herr is too kind," said Frau Ginsberg, and again silence descended on the room.

"If I had known in time," said Hambledon. "It is useless to say that, I know, but I would have tried to defend him."

"Why do you come and say such things to us? He broke the laws of the Party, I am told, that's enough. Are you trying to make us speak against the Party?"

"Mother, Mother," broke in the old man, "I think the Herr means to be kind."

"Then let him leave us alone. Nobody can do anything. How can we complain of what the Party does? There's no one to complain to, and I don't want any notice taken of us."

"If only he'd stayed with the trunk-maker," said Emilie.

"I should have had a son to-day," said her mother. "I

don't want to lose my husband also, so we won't complain."

"I believe I am a good Party member," said Hambledon, "but that doesn't mean I approve of every single thing that every other member of the Party may do. I hope these walls have no ears. I hoped I should find myself among friends here."

"The Herr can trust us," said the old man.

"I believe you. I tell you quite frankly that I think there's something behind this matter of your son's death and I am going to find it out."

"Leave it alone," said Frau Ginsberg monotonously. "My son is dead, you can't bring him back."

"May we know the Herr's name?" asked Ginsberg.

"Lehmann. Klaus Lehmann."

The old man gasped. "You are—sir, you cannot be the Chief of Police?"

"I am," said Hambledon grimly, "and as such it is my duty to investigate murder."

"Better let it alone," said the mother.

The girl sitting on the stool looked up for the first time, and Ginsberg asked, "What does the gracious Herr wish to know?"

"Anything you can tell me. This girl he was supposed to be running after, had she any real existence?"

"Oh, she's real all right," began the old man, but the girl on the stool broke in with a torrent of words.

"But he wasn't running after her, it's a lie to say he was. He was my love and nobody else's. He'd never have anything to say to that greasy Jewess, he didn't like her. He was my very own, and we were going to be married next month."

"*Gnädiges Fräulein,*" began Hambledon, but she took no notice.

"It's all a lie and that pig Schultz ought to have been

shot for saying it. It wasn't that Heinrich liked the Jews too much, he didn't like them enough, that's what was wrong."

"Leonore," said Frau Ginsberg angrily, "be quiet at once. It's no good, I tell you, hold your tongue."

"I won't be quiet. You all sit here letting everybody say horrible things about Heinrich and you don't say a word. I don't care if they do shoot me, I wish they would. Do you really want to know why they killed Heinrich?"

"Yes please, Fräulein," said Hambledon.

"Be quiet, Leonore, for God's sake, you'll ruin us all," said the old woman.

"Not by speaking to me, Madam," said Hambledon sternly.

"I don't care," said Leonore. "It was this. Schultz used to get money out of the Jews when they went over the frontier, Heinrich told me because he was worried about it and didn't know what to do. Something about they aren't allowed to take money with them, but if they gave Schultz some he used to let them take the rest. He wasn't the only one either, most of the others were in it, but not Heinrich. He made them ashamed, so they killed him."

"He could have laid a complaint before a higher authority," said Hambledon. "There are means provided for such a case."

"Yes, he said so, but the higher authority was in it too, so that was no good."

"I see," said Hambledon grimly, "and I am going to see a whole lot more. After that, a number of people are going to wish they had never been born." He got up and bowed over the girl's hand. "Good-bye, Fräulein Leonore. I wish more people had your courage. Ginsberg, if there is the faintest suspicion of an attempt on the part of anyone whatever to interfere with any of you, come direct to me at once."

"It's no use," said the old woman. "My son is dead."

"If only he'd stayed with the trunk-maker," said Emilie.

Hambledon returned to Berlin and set in train certain inquiries into the Ginsberg affair; while these were proceeding he turned his attention to the matter of Otto Hauser and the designs of the magnetic mine. The police had gathered in a dozen or so assorted people of both sexes who were associates of Hauser's in Mainz, where he lived except when the Elektrische Gesellschaft sent him away on errands such as this. Most of them were obviously innocent and could be returned at once to their presumably loving families with a warning to be more careful with whom they associated in the future. Two were plainly guilty and were permitted no futures in which to be careful, and three were doubtful, these were put back for further investigation. One of them was an ex-Army officer named Kaspar Bluehm.

This name sent Hambledon's mind back to Köln and Bill Saunders; there was a girl in Köln called Marie Bluehm who had a brother named Kaspar if he remembered aright, though they had never met. It would be an odd coincidence if this were the same man. If this were the same man it would be pleasant to get him in and make him talk of Köln and the good days when a man had a friend at his back and was not always alone, when there was someone to talk to frankly, someone with whom it was not necessary to act a part, someone with whom one could relax and be puzzled or anxious or afraid, someone who would relieve the strain of this unending tension. "God! How I miss Bill," said Tommy Hambledon. Perhaps this fellow Bluehm would talk about him, that would be something, if, of course, it were the same man.

Hambledon shook himself impatiently, touched the

bell on his desk and told the trooper who answered it to bring in Kaspar Bluehm. While he was waiting he thought that if it were possible he would get the poor chap out of this mess, merely because once he had a sister for whom Bill had cared greatly. "Getting sentimental in my old age," said Hambledon, but he looked up eagerly when the door opened. "You may go," he said to the trooper, Bluehm came up to his table and saluted.

Hambledon looked at him attentively and was reminded of Marie at once, though the blue eyes which in her case had been so clear and true were blurred and faded here, Marie's mouth had shown sweetness and strength while Kaspar's displayed weakness and obstinacy, but the likeness was unmistakable and Hambledon's face softened.

"Sit down," he said kindly. "You are Oberleutnant Kaspar Bluehm?"

"Obersatz Bluehm when the war was over," said the man, and sat down.

"I beg your pardon. I find it difficult to believe that a man with your war record could be guilty of espionage against Germany. I want you to talk to me frankly and we will clear this matter up."

"I am certainly not guilty," said Bluehm, but he did not respond to Hambledon's kindness. "Trying to entrap me into making admissions," he thought, "suspected traitors are not handled so gently as all that, does he take me for a fool?"

Hambledon saw growing suspicion in Bluehm's face and felt like shaking him. "Tell me," he said, "you knew this Otto Hauser, didn't you? Where did you meet him?"

"In Buenos Ayres originally. I was there for a time after the war, working as an engineer, he was in the same works. We were both Germans, he came from Mainz and I knew the place well, my mother lived there. We used to talk about Mainz and—and things like that. That's all."

"Very natural. What happened then?"

"He went home, oh, about four years ago. I came home last year."

Bluehm was fidgeting all the time with the hat he held on his knee, pulling out the lining and pushing it back with nervous fingers, never looking steadily at Hambledon but only glancing at him from time to time. "You may not be guilty of espionage, my lad, but you've something on your mind or I'm the Queen of Sheba," he said to himself. "Please go on," he added aloud. "When you came home you met him again, did you?"

"I found my mother and my aunt desperately poor, I had to get something to do. I remembered Hauser, found out where he lived, and went to see him, he got me a job in the Elektrische Gesellschaft. I was grateful, I used to see something of him sometimes, not much, a man like that—but he had helped me."

"What do you mean, a man like that? Did you know that he was——"

"*Gott im Himmel,* no! I only meant he was merely a workman——"

"Not your social equal, of course not. Did you ever meet people at his house?"

"I never went to his house. We used to go to a café, sometimes to a theatre or the cinema."

"I quite understand," said Hambledon, leaning back in his chair. "Apart from having met him abroad and from his having been of use to you, you were the merest acquaintances?"

Bluehm also relaxed, feeling that Hambledon was convinced and that the worst of the interview was over. "Exactly that. Besides, he was an intelligent fellow, I learned a lot from him about the work."

"On your honour as an officer," said Hambledon formally, you had no suspicion whatever that he was engaged in espionage?"

"On my honour, none. He would not have been likely to tell me if he were."

"No," said Hambledon, noticing the indecisive mouth and unintelligent eyes, "no, I don't think. he would. I believe you. Unless anything else crops up to incriminate you, you are cleared."

"Then I may go?" said Bluehm, springing to his feet.

"Sit down again and talk to me a little longer. Tell me, you lived in Köln at one time, didn't. you?"

Bluehm collapsed into the chair rather than sat in it. "I—my family did," he said. "I was in the Army."

"Yes, of course. But you spent your leaves there, didn't you? You knew many people there?"

"I knew a good many, naturally. Why?"

"I knew some Köln people at one time, we might have some mutual acquaintances, that's all. My dear Bluehm, you'll destroy that perfectly good hat if you tear at the lining like that, what is the matter with you?"

"Nothing, nothing. My nerves are not what they were, that's all."

"Am I so very terrifying? I only thought it would be pleasant to talk over old times."

"What did you want to know?"

"Oh, nothing of any importance," said Hambledon, who was getting tired of all this beating about the bush. "Did you know a man I used to meet occasionally, a Dutch importer, Dirk Brandt?"

Bluehm sprang to his feet, his face working. "You're playing with me," he cried, "I knew you were. You think I was in touch with British Intelligence then——"

"Great heavens," said the startled Hambledon, who had no idea anyone knew about Brandt, but Bluehm swept on.

"I didn't know he was a spy, I thought he was a friend of mine and asked him to look after my sister Marie. But he killed von Bodenheim and Elsa shot herself so Hedwige went to the dogs, and he took Marie and disgraced her, she died too, so when I found out who and what he was———"

He stopped and stared at Hambledon, whose face had grown terrible.

"Yes," said Hambledon in a cold voice. "When you found out what he was, what did you do?"

"I traced him to England and shot him," said Bluehm defiantly. "He deserved it anyway for the harm he did, and there was my sister———"

"Damn your sister. Who told you about Brandt?"

"What is the matter?" asked the puzzled Bluehm. "I deserve well of Germany, I destroyed one of her most dangerous enemies———"

"Don't bleat. Who told you about Brandt?"

"I can't understand you. I tell you, I had nothing to do with British Intelligence; when I found out that that was what Brandt had been doing I hunted him down and killed him. It took me nearly a year———"

"Damn your autobiography. Answer me at once. Who told you about Brandt?"

"Reck," said Bluehm, startled into a direct answer. "You wouldn't know him, a person of no importance, a teacher in some school or other. He went mad, he drank, I believe———"

"Reck," said Hambledon quietly, "a person of no importance," and stared straight in front of him, unheeding Bluehm who went on talking of how he had forced the secret out of Reck in the mad-house, tracked down Brandt in spite of his having changed his name twice and moved from place to place.

Hambledon returned from his abstraction to hear

Bluehm saying, "So you see, I have deserved well of the Reich. What is more, I have further information to give. There is no doubt that the other partner, Wolff, was a British spy too, the older man certainly was, Brandt admitted it. He was drowned years ago, though, so we can't catch him now, I mean the one who passed as Brandt's uncle, I never met him as it happened. His real name was Hambledon——"

Hambledon broke in with a laugh so bitter that Bluehm stopped talking and stared at him again.

"You fool," said Hambledon, "you fool. You boast of having shot him and come to me for reward—to me, of all people. Why, I've been looking for you for years. Oh, I'll reward you all right, if I were you I'd say my prayers, fool."

"What d'you mean?" stammered Bluehm, but Hambledon touched his bell twice and two guards came in.

"Take him away," said Hambledon harshly, "and send Hagen to me." He did not look up as Bluehm was led out of the room.

"I told Denton I'd clear this up and I have," he muttered. "Bill, what were you doing to let that stupid lump get the better of you?"

Hagen entered. "The prisoner who has just left me," said Hambledon, "Kaspar Bluehm, is a danger to the Reich. He must not be allowed to speak to anyone. You know what to do."

Hagen saluted and went out. Hambledon spent ten minutes or so carefully tidying his desk, lit a cigar and walked up and down the room till Hagen returned.

"I have to report, sir, that the prisoner eluded his guards and had to be shot to prevent his escape."

"Do not let it grieve you, Hagen," said the Chief of Police blandly. "He would have been shot anyway."

CHAPTER XIII
MUSIC AFTER DINNER

HAMBLEDON walked slowly home thinking over Bluehm's
disclosures. So Reck had done it, Reck the wireless operator of Mülheim, the transmitter of other men's words,
the person of no importance, the drunken little beast, he
had babbled and Bill Saunders had died. Men who knew
the Chief of Police met him in the street that night, took
one look at that grim face and abstracted gaze and did
not venture to greet him. "Did you see his face?" they
said. "Someone is going to catch it for something, heaven
forbid he should ever look like that at me."

He went up the stairs to his flat, entered his study and
wrote a few lines on a sheet of paper, after which he
walked heavily down the passage to Reck's room and
handed the paper to him.

"What's the matter?" asked Reck, staring.

"Code and transmit that message to-night."

"Has anything happened? What's the matter with
you?"

"Read the message, damn you."

Reck dropped his eyes to the paper and read aloud:
"T-L-T. Hambledon to F.O. London. Murderers of Saun-
ders discovered and dealt with stop Kaspar Bluehm of
Köln and Reck of Mülheim."

"My God," said Reck, dropping the paper, "you must
be mad. I never even knew that he was dead."

"Nevertheless, you helped to kill him. So you will code and transmit that message and then you will die."

"I swear to you I am completely innocent. I'm a drunken old waster, but I'd shoot myself before I'd—why he was one of our men. I don't know anything—when did he die?"

"About thirteen years ago," said Hambledon. "He was shot by that fool Kaspar Bluehm—remember him?"

"Yes—no, I don't think I ever met him. Wasn't he Marie Bluehm's brother?"

"Yes. You met him once anyway, he came to see you in your retreat at Mainz you're always wanting to go back to, the mad-house, you know."

"Did he?" said Reck, rubbing his head. "I don't know —I can't remember. Why did he come?"

"He came," said Hambledon very deliberately, "to ask you for information about Bill Saunders because he had a private grudge against him. He asked for Dirk Brandt, of course, you told him he was Bill Saunders, a British agent——"

"No!" shrieked Reck. "I didn't do that, don't say it, I——"

"You told him Saunders had gone back to England——"

"Stop, for God's sake, you're torturing me. On my honour——"

"Your honour!" said Hambledon unpleasantly. "I expect you told him he was Michael Kingston of the Hampshires, too. Anyway, you told him enough to enable him to walk in on Bill one quiet night and shoot him. So Bluehm died an hour ago, and I don't think you're fit to live, do you?"

"No," said Reck with dignity. "If this thing is true, I am not."

"Of course it's true, who else could have told him? He

traced up Bill's contacts till he came to you, quite simple.
He thought he'd been awfully clever. He told me I was
a British spy, too, that's what he called me, apparently
Bill told him that, since I was dead it didn't matter. He
informed me about Denton, too."

"What year was it, d'you know, when he came to see
me?"

"Bill died in '24. '23, I suppose."

"I was very ill then," said Reck. "I nearly died, I wish
I had. They wouldn't give me a drop of real drink of any
kind, you know, you don't know what it's like when your
brain is full of liquid fire and you can smell drink and
taste it, but they won't give you any. But I can't remember anyone coming to see me, why should they? I do remember once dreaming that Marie Bluehm came to see
me to ask about Dirk, I knew she wasn't real because she
was dead, I might have talked to her. She gave me some
schnapps, or I thought she did. It was a nice dream, most
of them——" Reck shuddered.

"Listen," said Hambledon, who had been watching him
closely. "Can you remember how she was dressed?"

"In men's clothes," said Reck without hesitation. "I
told her it wasn't decent."

"Yes," said Hambledon slowly. "Even now the likeness is striking."

"Do you mean to say that it really happened, and I
took this man for Fräulein Marie?"

Hambledon nodded. Reck leaned back in his chair and
there was silence for a space.

"It's getting late," said Reck, glancing at the clock.
"The message will take a little time to code and transmit,
will you leave me alone to do it? I can't work with anyone in the room. When I've finished I'll come and tell
you, unless you like to lend me your gun."

"I don't think so, now," said Hambledon quietly. "I don't think it's necessary."

He picked up the paper from the floor and tore it into small pieces, piled the fragments into an ash-tray and set light to them.

"What do you mean?"

"I mean that I lost my temper and I owe you an apology. Now I know how it happened I don't think you were so much to blame."

"Then I——" said Reck, but suddenly covered his face with his hands and burst into tears. Hambledon amused himself by poking the burning fragments with a matchstick till they were all consumed, and then patted the old man on the shoulder.

"Pull yourself together," he said, "it's all right. I ought to have known you'd never do it deliberately. Come along to my study and we'll drink to Bill Saunders, God rest his soul."

"As you wish," said Reck, struggling up from his chair, "but that's the last drink I'll ever have, I'm going teetotal. If schnapps could turn me into a traitor once it might again."

"Great idea," said Hambledon, opening the door, and if he smiled a trifle incredulously he did not let Reck see it.

In the study Hambledon rang for Franz, and told him to bring whisky and soda-water; when the servant returned he said, "If you please, sir, the Fräulein Rademeyer rang up and told me there would be four to dinner tonight, she had invited two friends for eight o'clock. I was to tell you, sir."

"Eight o'clock and it's seven-thirty now. Who are they, d'you know?"

"The gracious Fräulein did not say, sir."

"Oh, Lord, that means a stiff shirt, Franz. Black tie."

"Very good, sir."

"I've got some new stiff shirts, Franz, one of those. The old ones have got whiskers on the cuffs."

"As you wish, sir. But the gracious Fräulein took the new ones to mark for you, sir."

"Snatch them back then, and don't make difficulties."

"Very good, sir," said Franz, and left the room.

"I shall have to pour this down my throat and rush, here's yours, Reck. Well, Bill Saunders, rest in peace, I have paid one debt to-day."

"Bill Saunders," said Reck solemnly, "and some day I will repay the other, God helping me."

"Upon my soul," said Hambledon, regarding him curiously, "you look as though you would."

"Don't stand there staring at me as though I were a museum specimen in a glass jar," said Reck testily, "you're spoiling my last drink."

"Heaven forbid. Take it slowly, it'll last longer. Would you like a sponge to suck it through?"

"Oh, go and dress up," said Reck.

Hambledon walked into the sitting-room on the stroke of eight to find Ludmilla already there with two tall men whose backs were towards him as he entered. "Klaus, my dear," she said as they turned, "Mr. Alexander Ogilvie, Mr. Dixon Ogilvie."

The room went black for an instant before Hambledon's eyes as he advanced to meet their guests, when the mist cleared he found himself shaking hands with a white-haired man who was courteously taking pleasure in the honour of his acquaintance in careful grammatical German. Hambledon replied suitably and turned to the younger man.

Dixon Ogilvie was not so lanky as of old and his thick

brown hair was tidier, but otherwise his likeness to the schoolboy he had been was so strong that Hambledon expected instant recognition in return, till he reminded himself firmly how much he himself was scarred and changed. Still there was a puzzled look in the young man's eyes as though some bell were ringing in his memory, so Hambledon became instantly and increasingly German. "What a day," he said to himself as they went in to dinner. "First Bill Saunders, and now this."

Fräulein Rademeyer explained that she had met the Ogilvies at a friend's house after that afternoon's recital, and had been so bold as to ask them to dinner as a faint and inadequate return for the immense pleasure their music had given her.

Alexander Ogilvie said that they were more than delighted to accept, not only for the pleasure of making Fräulein Rademeyer's further acquaintance, but for the privilege of meeting one who was regarded in Britain as typifying all that was best in the Nazi Party, a remark which made Hambledon want to giggle. Dixon Ogilvie said nothing but "Sehr treu," at intervals, and looked amiably at everyone, Hambledon gathered that not even a German prisoners-of-war camp had been able to teach him the language. In fact, his uncle said so.

"My nephew," he said, "has not the gift of tongues."

"Sehr treu," said Dixon.

"It is a great pity, because he misses so much of the amusement to be gained by talking to strangers in their own tongue," his uncle went on.

"Any more gifts," said Ludmilla kindly, "showered by Providence upon your nephew would be positively unfair."

Dixon Ogilvie started to say "Sehr treu" again, but grasped the sense of the remark at the last moment and stopped just in time.

"One meets such interesting people when one travels, doesn't one?" said Ogilvie senior to Hambledon.

"It is many years," said Hambledon truthfully, "since I had the means or the time to travel beyond the boundaries of the Reich."

Dixon Ogilvie turned inquiring eyes upon him, and asked with difficulty whether he had ever been in England; Tommy Hambledon looked him straight in the face and said "Never," without a blush.

"You should come," said Alexander Ogilvie, and Ludmilla said, "You hear that, Klaus? I think I should like to go to England some day."

"Some day, perhaps, we'll go," said Hambledon. "I will take a holiday, some day."

"Nearly three years ago," said Alexander Ogilvie, "I travelled from Basle to Paris with a delightful young couple who were married there the following day, they did me the honour to ask me to be one of the witnesses. I gathered that it was something of a romance; they had stayed in the same hotel in Basle for about a fortnight, and I don't think they had met before. Oh, yes, they had travelled from Berlin on the same train. Charming fellow named Denton and a delightful German girl. Apparently a baritone singer with the lovely name of Waltheof Leibowitz in the hotel orchestra had also realized the lady's attractions and used to sing at her, so one day Denton hit him in the eye at one of the afternoon performances. They left for Paris the same night and were married next day."

Hambledon roared with laughter, since the detail about the baritone was news to him, and Dixon said that it was safer to be a pianist.

"Have you ever," said Hambledon, "met the romantic couple since? One wonders how such an impulsive marriage would wear."

"Oh, frequently," said Ogilvie. "I see quite a lot of them when I'm in town, Dixon knows them too. Contrary to what one would expect, they are ideally happy."

"Mrs. Denton is an—is not ordinary," said Dixon.

"How so?"

"She never asks questions."

"She deserves to be happy," said Hambledon enthusiastically.

"I hope they always will be," said Ludmilla, "they sound delightful. Shall we go in the other room? Franz, coffee in the drawing-room, please."

Later on, the talk turned upon music, and Dixon Ogilvie went to the piano to illustrate some point which he had been discussing with Fräulein Rademeyer, with his uncle acting as interpreter whenever the younger man got bogged. Hambledon, who was only musical enough to recognize a tune which he had heard six times before, was not interested and picked up an evening paper. He found something to read in it and sat down with the unscarred side of his face towards the pianist; presently the talk ceased as young Ogilvie played to amuse himself, with his eyes wandering occasionally to the face of his host. He passed from one thing to another, much as a man will look through a pile of photographs in search of one which will tell him what he wants to know. Presently Hambledon laid down the paper and stared idly into the distance, wondering what train of thought had suddenly reawakened a memory of a class of boys with highly variegated voices singing French songs in approximate unison. The idea was to interest them in the language by providing a change from the pen of the gardener's aunt, but he had always been dubious as to how far the idea was successful. The proper way to teach boys languages, of course, was to send them to live with a family abroad for a year at least and let them work, play, eat, drink and sleep in

German or Italian or whatever it was. If they went young enough this method was unfailing, provided a boy had the smallest aptitude——

Hambledon woke from his musings with a start to realize that Dixon Ogilvie had changed from *"Sur le pont d'Avignon"* to

> *" Il était une bergère,*
> *Et ron ron ron, petit patapon,*
> *Il était une bergère*
> *Qui gardait ses moutons, ron ron,*
> *Qui gardait ses moutons."*

He was playing with infinite delicacy, not looking at Hambledon at all, and presently the music changed again to another from the same little red French song-book. *"Au clair de la lune,"* hummed Ogilvie, *"mon ami Pierrot——"*

"He is just doing it to amuse himself," said Hambledon reassuringly to himself, "it has no connection with you at all. One tune suggests another from the same period."

"Yes, it has," himself insisted. "He tried to remember of whom you reminded him, he tried through music and he's got it. You're unmasked, Thomas Elphinstone Hambledon."

"Nonsense," said Hambledon to himself firmly. "You are getting the wind up, your nerve's going. You'd better retire and take up crochet."

Just then a flicker of pure mischief curled the corners of Ogilvie's mouth as with a few inspiring chords he broke into that touching ballad of the English home, "Tommy, make room for your uncle."

"Blasted cheek," said Hambledon almost audibly. "That settles it, he does know."

"School songs," said Dixon Ogilvie in English, "are rather nice to remember sometimes," and looked to his uncle to translate while he played another marching song.

" Forty years on, growing older and older,
Shorter in wind as in memory long, "

and finally wound up the concert with the Hymn for the End of Term.

The player rose from his seat to be delightfully thanked by both his hosts, though there was a gleam in Tommy Hambledon's eye while he murmured *"Reizend! Ergötzlich!"* which ought to have warned his former pupil.

Less than half an hour after the departure of the guests Hambledon's telephone rang: he went to answer it and returned laughing.

"These musicians," he said, "are really not of this world. You would think they might read the simple directions for complying with police regulations, wouldn't you? Not a bit of it. Then they wonder why they're tenderly reprimanded."

"What has happened?" asked Ludmilla.

"Uncle Ogilvie rang up all in a flutter to say that nephew Ogilvie has been arrested, something wrong with his papers, apparently."

"Oh, Klaus! How dreadful for them! Can't you order him to be released?"

"How can I, if he's broken the law? I am paid a substantial sum quarterly to see that people keep it. No, I won't do that, but I have rung up the authorities to ensure that the prisoner is nicely treated, I told old Ogilvie I would. What is more, I'll see the boy myself in the morning and see if I can get him out of this little mess. Probably a small fine will meet the occasion."

"But, dear Klaus, I can't bear to think of that nice young man spending the night in jail."

"Do him good," said dear Klaus unkindly. "Teach him to respect authority. I'll give him Tommy," he added to himself.

The next morning Dixon Ogilvie was brought before the Chief of Police, who sent the escort away, looked sternly at the prisoner and said, "Come here."

Ogilvie advanced to the desk and Hambledon looked him up and down. "You know why you have been brought here, don't you?"

"No, sir," said Ogilvie in English, with exactly the schoolboy's air of pained innocence. Hambledon's sternness wavered, he bit his lip but failed entirely to suppress a grin.

"If you try that on me," he said in the same language, "I'll give you two hundred lines, and they will be legibly written, Ogilvie."

"Oh, but, sir——"

"Come off it. No, listen, Ogilvie. You've stumbled on a secret which is literally a matter of life and death to me. They know at the F.O. in London that Hambledon is still alive and doing a job of work in Germany, but not even they know that I'm the Chief of Police. Only one other man knew that till you spotted me to-night, and I may say that if I'd known you were coming I should have been detained at the office, by heck I should, even if I'd really had to stay there all alone with the charwoman. I didn't even know you'd come back to Berlin."

"They seemed to like me," said Dixon Ogilvie, "when I was here two years ago, and I certainly like them, so when another tour in Germany was suggested I was very pleased to come. Though I certainly never expected to meet an old friend in such an exalted position."

"And now you have," said Hambledon with all the emphasis at his disposal, "you will please forget it completely and utterly. Put it right out of your mind, never allow your memory to dwell upon it for a single instant. Speak of it to no one, not even your uncle—incidentally, that was why you were arrested in such a hurry last night, so that you shouldn't have time to tell him."

"Of course not, sir——"

"You see, it's not only my personal safety that's at stake, though I admit that's a matter in which I take a delicate and restrained interest. The really important thing is that I'm useful to the Department here, so it's desirable I should live as long as possible."

"The Department?"

"Ironmongery, at the Army & Navy stores. Occasionally we transfer to the Chemist's section and sometimes to the Books, Maps, etc. We all deal in Blinds, of course, but never, never—or practically never—in Fancy goods. Sit down, Ogilvie, why are you still standing?"

"You didn't tell me I might sit," said Ogilvie with a laugh.

"Great heavens, does the awe I tried so hard to inspire last so long? And when I'm eighty, if I live so long, which is very dubious, will hale old men of sixty-five spring alertly to attention from their club armchairs as I dodder past, leaning on the delicate arm of my fair-haired granddaughter?"

"Have you got a granddaughter, sir?"

"Heaven forbid!"

"Well, they wouldn't allow her in the club, anyway."

"Then I shan't pay my subscription. You know, Ogilvie, it is a damn long time since I sat like this and said the first thing that came into my head. Not since Bill and I parted off Ostende, you remember him?"

"Bill?"

"Michael Kingston to you. Ever see him after the war?"

"No, but I met his widow once or twice."

"Oh, really? What's she like?"

"Tall willowy woman who looks at you soulfully out of large eyes. They call her Diane the Wise."

"Is she so clever?"

"No. Because she asks such a lot of them."

"Why—oh, I see. Whys. Bill would have loved that, no wonder they parted. Well, look here, I hate to sling you out but I've got some work to do. I shall see you again —how long are you staying?"

"May I stay on, sir?"

"Of course, why not? Lor', I've caught it now. Ogilvie, you will remember what I said about my identity?"

"I will, sir. Uncle Alec and I were hoping you and Fräulein Rademeyer would dine with us one night?"

"Delighted. Ring us up, will you?"

Hambledon stared at the door for some moments after his guest had gone out. Nice fellow, that, very. Got a nice line, too, a musician like that could wander into any country and meet all sorts of people without anyone thinking twice about it, he might be very useful. Hambledon shivered slightly, useful, till he slipped up or somebody let him down, and then a great musician would be destroyed because of The Job, a pity, that, couldn't be done. But he had wonderful opportunities.

"No," said Hambledon firmly, "it wouldn't do anyway, he's far too unpractical. One must be practical. Now, if only Denton could play a concertina——"

HAMBLEDON pursued his investigations into the matter
of Ginsberg, and found that the practice of allowing
Jews to take about twenty per cent of their movable cash
over the frontier in exchange for the other eighty per
cent was not merely a local custom at Aachen, but a full-
sized racket at every exit from Germany. His determina-
tion to break down the practice hardened; though he
had just as much loathing as any German for the foul
type of Jew who had battened on the miseries of Germany in the bad years, his sense of justice revolted at
making helpless and harmless people suffer for the sins
of the rich and powerful. Besides, it was to safeguard
these robbers and racketeers that Ginsberg had died,
and they should pay for it. Besides again, it was against
the law, and it was his business to see the law was obeyed.
Finally, it would annoy the Nazis, and he was coming
increasingly to dislike the Nazis. The exercise of power
is a touch-stone to character, and by that test there was
very little pure gold in the Nazi Party. "A lousy lot,
when you get to know 'em," said Tommy vulgarly to
himself.

"The only thing that puzzles me," he said to one man
he was interrogating, "is why they are allowed to get
away with twenty per cent. It's quite a lot, twenty per
cent. It's one-fifth."

"Quite right, Herr Polizei Oberhaupt, it's too much. But if we charge more they won't give any at all. They just die and the money vanishes."

"So you think half a loaf is better than no bread."

"Four-fifths of the loaf," said the man with a grin.

The further Hambledon traced the threads of this organization the higher in rank were the Nazi officials whom he found to be involved, till he began to wonder who really was at the top or whether he had better cease his inquiries before he found out more than was good for him.

He came home to the flat one evening and was horrified to find Ludmilla Rademeyer in floods of tears, the maid Agathe hovering round with handkerchiefs, smelling-salts and cushions, and Franz walking distractedly about with a glass of brandy in one hand and a hot-water bottle in the other.

"Aunt Ludmilla, for heaven's sake what is it? Have you had an accident? Agathe, out of my way and don't drop things all over the floor. My dear, what is it? Franz, give me that brandy and put the hot-water bottle under the Fräulein's feet. Drink this and for pity's sake don't upset yourself like this, tell me about it."

"Christine," said the old lady, and sobbed afresh.

"Has there been bad news?" asked Hambledon of Franz.

"Evidently, sir, but we have no idea what it is. The gracious Fräulein had a letter brought by hand——"

Ludmilla pulled herself together with an effort and clung to Hambledon's hand. "Send them away," she whispered, and the servants left the room. Ludmilla produced a crumpled letter from one of her numerous pockets and gave it to Hambledon.

"'Ludmilla, my old friend,'" he read, "'my husband was taken away this morning by S.S. men who came to the house and said they were taking him to a concentration camp because he was a Jew.' Is that true?" he asked.

"His mother," said Ludmilla unsteadily, "came of a Jewish family, but nobody thought any the worse of her for that, a nice fat old thing, endlessly kind. She was a Christian, and one can't help how one is born."

Hambledon went on reading. " 'I was made to give up all our papers and all our money except twenty marks. I gave them everything they asked, I thought if I was patient they would let Ludovic go, but they took him away. Then the men who remained said our house was too good for a Jew's wife, and they turned me out in the street and locked the door.' "

Hambledon paused in his reading and stared before him, hammering with one clenched hand upon his knee, while Ludmilla looked in amazement at the beloved face so lit with fury that she could hardly recognize it. He continued after a moment.

" 'I thought I had better go to my son Hugo for advice, so I walked to Albrecht Strasse——' "

"All that way, and she so lame!"

" '—only to find'—I cannot read this, her writing is suddenly so bad—'my daughter-in-law Magda coming to me with the children, because they have taken my son also, they have taken my son also, and the children were crying——' There is a piece here I can't read, something about Gottlieb's horse?"

"Gottlieb is the baby, he had a toy horse on wheels——"

"I see. She goes on, 'They were also turned into the street, and when Magda said she did not know what to do, one of the men made a suggestion I will not repeat'—God blast them!" said Tommy Hambledon, and Ludmilla said "Amen." " 'So we got on a tram and went to old Marthe whom you will remember was my children's nurse when they were little; it is a tiny house, we meant to leave the children there but she would not let us go since they have taken my son also. Magda will find some work to do even if it is only scrubbing, but I am so helpless I can only mind the children and do a little sewing if our friends have any work to give out. Do not come to see me, it might not be safe for you to be seen with us. Marthe's son will take this note, I do not trust post or telephone. I would not mind for myself but Ludovic is in need of care at his age, and there is Hugo and the children. Magda is so brave, but if they had to punish Ludovic and me I do not think they need have taken my son also.' "

Hambledon's voice ceased and there was silence for a space till Ludmilla said, "No doubt I am too old and stupid to understand, and these people are your friends, my dear, but, oh, Klaus, this is wicked! Dear Christine, who never did anything but kindness in all her life! I would not turn out a dog on the streets like that. What will they do? Klaus, this is a vile thing. I can't admire people who are so cruel. I don't like our present leaders, Klaus, I don't like a lot of things that have happened lately. I hate these loud-voiced bullying young men who swagger everywhere and order people about, the old Germany wasn't like this. I don't trust your Nazi Party, Klaus. I've never said so before because they are your friends——"

"No, they are not!" said Hambledon furiously. "I have acted a part to you long enough, but this is the last straw. The Nazis are a set of lying, cheating bullies, out for what they can get for themselves, with neither honesty nor conscience. They did a great work for Germany to start with and I helped them, but now they are a scourge to Europe and a blot on humanity. I was on their side once, but now if I can pull down this foul regime in blood, God helping me, I'll do it!"

"Klaus, I am so glad. It's been such a grief to me to have you hand in glove with those dreadful people——"

"It'll be more of a grief to them before I've finished, don't you worry!"

"Klaus dear, be careful! One hears such dreadful stories, one hopes they are not true, but——"

"I hope that whatever you have heard has been an understatement," said Hambledon grimly.

The old lady sighed. "Yet they are Germans who carry out these dreadful orders, how can they? Why don't they refuse? Germans used to be such nice people before all this happened—except the Prussians, of course, no one ever liked the Prussians—but now they're all Prussianized, I think. I don't like Germany any more, Klaus, I would rather go and live somewhere else. I think I'd like to live in England, Klaus."

"What makes you say that?"

"I knew an Englishman once, when I was very young. He was at Heidelberg University with my brother, who brought him home once or twice—to the white house at Haspe, Klaus, where you came to me. He used to tell me about England, I thought then I would like to go there some day."

"What was he doing over here?"

"Oh, studying things, and learning the language. He was going to be a schoolmaster, my family thought that was funny because people in our class wouldn't be schoolmasters in those days."

"Unless they were in reduced circumstances, like us in Dusseldorf."

"Ah, that was different. My brother used to make great fun of him, saying he would spend the rest of his life teaching little boys their A B C and making them blow their noses properly. But nothing Georg said made any difference to the Englishman, he said that it was a great and noble task to train the minds of future citizens."

"Are you sure he said 'great and noble'?"

"Of course not. He said 'vitally important, really', but that was what he meant. He said that not only would he do that himself, but if he had a son he hoped he'd do the same. It is only my fancy, I know, but you seem to me to have a look of him sometimes, Klaus."

"Oh, oh," said Klaus, "and I thought you loved me for myself alone! Now I realize I'm only a relic——"

"Klaus!"

"Only a faded rose. No, a bit of dried seaweed——"

"Klaus, I shall throw my knitting at you in a minute. Oh, how heartless we are to laugh like this, think of Christine."

"It won't help Frau Christine if you make yourself ill fretting over her. Tell me, what became of this Englishman?"

"He never came back. We heard that he became a schoolmaster and also a minister of the Church, but he wouldn't be both, surely?"

Hambledon's mind went back to the country Rectory where he was born, a white house not unlike that at Haspe, with a garden full of roses, striped carnations, and hollyhocks high in the air above his head. There were bumble bees in the hollyhocks as a rule; he had an idea bumble bees didn't sting till one day he found he was wrong. His father had been a schoolmaster in his younger days and insisted that his son should be one too, rather against Tommy's own wishes, but there was no arguing with the autocratic old man. "It is a great profession, not appreciated as it should be," he said. "Judges defend the law and punish law-breakers, doctors heal the sick and repair the damages of life, but the schoolmaster builds up the body and the character beforehand for the battle, *mens sana in corpore sano,* my boy." Tommy remembered wriggling slightly on this and similar occasions, thinking that sermons should be confined to Sundays and not loosed forth between times, but a schoolmaster he became to start with, though he turned his attention to other things afterwards. "And now I'm a policeman," he thought. "Wonder if the old man approves?" He returned from his reverie to answer Ludmilla.

"Oh, yes, easily, quite a lot of schoolmasters are in Holy Orders, as they call it, in England, sometimes in later life they give up teaching and have a parish instead."

"I see. You do know a good deal about England, don't you, Klaus?"

"Oh, I meet lots of English people,. especially at the British Embassy, they do like talking about themselves, you know."

"I think most people do, except you, Klaus."

"About Frau Christine," said Hambledon, to change the subject, "try not to worry, I will see what can be done about it. Doubtless something will present itself."

Reck had said that he was going teetotal, and to Hambledon's amused surprise he kept his word. For some weeks life was a misery to him and he was a trial to everyone else, but after the transition period was over he discovered, with assumed disgust, that he was clearer in mind and stronger in body than he had been for many years.

"You used to be an Awful Example," said Hambledon. "Stern but loving fathers used to point you out to their sons and say, 'Look! Niersteiner and bock, Moselle and Rhine wines, gin and schnapps——' "

"Shut up," said Reck.

" 'Methylated spirit and eau-de-Cologne——' "

"I never did!"

" '——are milestones on the road leading to old Reck.' But now, what a difference! You are no longer a warning,

you are a Moral Lesson, you are an Uplifting Influence.
In a word, you're a Tract."

"You're a fool," growled Reck.

"Not at all, I am an appreciative audience. You rise
early, you sing in your bath, you do physical jerks—yes
you do, you didn't buy those dumbbells to throw at cats
—you look thirty years younger, and now I learn that
you even go for walks before breakfast."

"Well, why not? I like the streets to myself, not full of
loitering idlers staring in shop-windows."

"No, seriously, Reck, I didn't think you'd do it, and by
heck I admire you. I mean that."

Reck actually coloured with pleasure, but all he said
was, "I said I'd do it and I have. Of course, one does
feel fitter, but all this early waking is a frightful bore."

"Try writing poetry," said Tommy helpfully.

One morning, a few days after Frau Christine's letter
had arrived, Reck returned from his walk shortly before
eight and saw to his surprise that a poster had been attached to the front door with drawing-pins. He read it
with growing astonishment, glanced round him to see if
anyone were watching him, tore it down and ran up the
three flights of stairs to Hambledon's flat, not waiting
for the lift. He burst into Hambledon's room and said,
"What do you say to this?"

"Thank God for safety razors," said Hambledon, who
was shaving. "What is it, free worms for early birds?"

"The German Freedom League," said Reck. "Know
anything about them? It was pinned on your door."

"They can wait while I go round my jaw. Not so
sculptured as it used to be, seems to be more of it, somehow. 'But beauty vanisheth, beauty fadeth, However fair,
fair it be.' Now let's look. My hat, what a nerve.

" 'German Freedom League,' " he read. " 'Germans,
arise!' Ah, that was meant for you, Reck."

"Nonsense," said Reck, "for you. I've been up for hours."

"One to you, but don't rub it in. 'Germans, undeceive yourselves! The Nazi leaders pretend they are making you strong and free, but in truth they are making you into a nation of slaves. Every day you have to work harder for less money, your liberties are curtailed, if any man complains he is thrown into prison without trial, while your leaders live in luxury and amass huge fortunes. Worse than this, they are indulging in wicked and senseless ambitions of conquest which will inevitably lead to war. There are no winners in a modern war, all suffer alike, even if Germany wins in the end it means privation, suffering, wounds and death. Germans, awake!'—Very rousing, this gentleman, ain't he?—'Stand up and proclaim that it is your desire to live in peace with all nations abroad, and at home to practise in happiness and freedom those pursuits of industry, science and culture which alone can make Germany prosperous and respected.

" 'Follow the Freedom League!

" 'Down with the Nazi Party!' "

"Very nicely put," said Reck appreciatively.

"I doubt if our illustrious leaders think so, wonder how many of these appeared in our midst this morning? There'll be a row over this and I've a horrid feeling I shall be in the middle of it."

Hambledon was not in the least surprised, therefore, to find on arriving at his office that a summons awaited him to discuss a matter of importance at eleven-thirty at the Ministry of Propaganda and Public Enlightenment. He was punctually received by the Minister in person.

"These posters," said Goebbels. "We can't have that kind of thing."

"Assuredly not," said the Chief of Police. "Most undesirable."

"This damned Freedom League, who are they?"

"I have had my eye upon it for some time," said Hambledon untruthfully. "It is an organization of discontented and subversive elements, fishing in troubled waters for what they can draw out to their own profit."

"Doubtless, my dear Lehmann, but who are they?"

"That is precisely what it is my duty to discover. They are very well hidden, but if they think they can make a nuisance of themselves with impunity, I will show them that they are wrong."

"You take the words out of my mouth," said the Minister.

"I meant to," said Hambledon to himself.

"I am sure you will deal with the scoundrels effectively and promptly."

"The matter already has my attention."

"Good. Your zeal and industry are examples to us all, I am sure. This brings me, my dear Lehmann, to the other point I wanted to discuss with you."

"Now we come to the real nigger in the woodpile," thought Hambledon, but he merely assumed an attitude of intelligent alacrity and waited in silence.

"I understand," said the Minister, playing with a pen-wiper on his desk, "that you have been inquiring into the details of a certain financial latitude which is sometimes permitted to Jews leaving the country."

"I am concerned," said Hambledon with lofty nobility, "to put a final stop to corruption and law-breaking wherever and whenever I find it."

"Admirable—in principle. But in practice, there is no harm in a special arrangement being made in some cases —in some cases, I repeat."

"Your Excellency will be as horrified as I was," said Hambledon earnestly, "to hear that so far from this practice being an occasional exception, it is in fact the common practice. No one knows better than Your Excellency the disastrous effect of financial corruption from subordinates. It destroys their natural honesty, it depraves their consciences, it ruins their morals and finally it undermines their loyalty. I would not trust a man so far as I could see him, who would take a bribe to break an order I had given him."

"Very true," said the Minister, slightly overcome by this spate of integrity, "but I think you exaggerate——"

"It is my business to be exact," said Hambledon coldly. "I will send a *précis* of the results of my investigations for Your Excellency's perusal, together with a complete list of the names and addresses of every man whom I have proved to be involved in this traffic, and the approximate amounts by which each man has illegally benefited—the last will be underestimated, believe me."

"There is no need," said the Minister hastily. "We have every confidence in your executive ability. There is only one thing, Lehmann, in which you have ever been known to fall short."

"And that is——"

"The ability to take a hint."

"I must beg Your Excellency to be plain with me, I am only a policeman, not a diplomatist, and it would be better to state clearly what you wish me to do."

"Leave the matter alone, then," said Goebbels irritably, "if you must have it in so many words, don't interfere."

"I am to understand that this corruption is to continue unchecked?" said Hambledon frigidly.

"Turn your superb detective abilities to the problem of the German Freedom League, Lehmann, and you will continue to earn the gratitude of the Reich."

"I understand," said Hambledon rising. "I have the honour to wish Your Excellency good morning," and he stalked out.

"Obstinate, pig-headed old die-hard," said the Minister to himself. "Pity, he's a useful man, but it looks as though his usefulness will come to an end soon if he can't be more accommodating."

"Sour-faced, evil-tongued, club-footed scoundrel," said Hambledon to himself as he walked back to his office. "Another moment and I'd have rammed his inkstand down his throat, pens and all. I think my time here is running short, I'm not so patient with these swine as I used to be. They make me sick. I wonder just how much a year he gets out of that racket."

He told himself that it was ridiculous to get so angry over this trivial matter, what did it matter to him if the Nazi Party went on corrupting itself till it was rotten from top to bottom? The sooner the better. It was really only his professional pride that was hurt, fancy being proud of being Chief of Police to this mob of gangsters. "I am a British agent," he said, and straightened his shoulders. "All the same, I have a feeling this game is nearly up. I don't think I can keep it up much longer."

He went home to lunch, turning over in his mind the question of Ludovic and Hugo Beckensburg, Frau Christine's menfolk. He had seen to it that they were as well treated as was possible in a concentration camp, but that wasn't saying much, and the old man was feeling it. It would be as well to get them out of Germany as soon as possible, or perhaps the women had better go first. Frau Christine, anyway, the younger woman could wait. If Frau Christine could be got into Switzerland, the others could join her, that is, if she could travel alone.

"What's the matter with Goebbels," he concluded, "is that he's funny and he doesn't know it."

He went in to lunch whistling.

"I went to see Christine this morning," said Ludmilla.

"I'm glad to hear it, how did you find her?"

"Not very well. I wish we could do something for them."

"I'm going to. They would be better out of Germany altogether, there is no future here for anyone of Jewish descent. If I could get Frau Christine out first, it would be best, I think."

"Dear Klaus, I was sure you would manage it. What will you do, get her a forged passport?"

"You desperate criminal! Where did you get that idea from?"

"I read something about forged passports in the paper, and they wouldn't let her go out with her own, would they? I don't suppose she's even got one, now."

"I'll bear your suggestion in mind," said Klaus gravely. "Tell me, haven't you got anything the matter with you?"

Ludmilla stared. "Matter with me? No. I've always been perfectly healthy, and apart from old age and a touch of rheumatism, I still am. My heart isn't too sound, but that's nothing, and I don't see so well as I did, but you couldn't expect me to. My last doctor said I had a dropsical tendency, but the man was a fool and so I told him. I have a tendency to heartburn but that's my own fault, I will eat fried potatoes. No, I'm perfectly healthy, why do you ask and what are you laughing at?"

"Nothing. I think you're wonderful, only it would be convenient if you could have something for which it's necessary to have treatment in Switzerland."

"Why?"

"You would want a companion, I mean somebody to talk to, you'd have Agathe, of course—I think Frau Christine would do very well. No one would question an old lady travelling with the Chief of Police's aunt."

"Klaus, of course not! How clever you are—but would that mean I should have to leave you?"

"Only for a little while," he said soothingly, "not for long. Then either you could come back or I could come and join you—more likely the latter, I think."

"Do you mean," said Ludmilla, laying down her spoon and fork, "that you are really thinking of leaving Germany?"

"Sh—sh," he said, "don't speak of it. Don't even think about it, but I don't think I can go on with these people much longer. We don't get on as well as we did, somehow," he added grimly.

"Oh, Klaus dear, let's go away! Let's get out of this dreadful land now the Nazis have spoiled it. It won't matter if we are poor again, will it, we'll find a little house somewhere and I can still cook."

"I think even if we do go, we shan't starve. Push all this to the back of your mind for the present, it will need a good deal of arranging, you know. I only told you now so as to give you time to think it over, I didn't want to spring it on you at the last moment."

"If you knew," she said, "how I've been longing for you to say this! Do you think we shall ever have enough money to go to England?"

"You've been very interested in England lately, haven't you? Ever since the Ogilvies were here, why is it?"

"He told me," she said, "that if you're in difficulties in England you go to the police and they help you. Here, if you're in trouble, you avoid them. I'd like to see a policeman who wanted to help you, Klaus, why aren't your men like that?"

"Why, indeed," he said.

CHAPTER XV   LUGGAGE LABEL

Tommy hambledon received a coloured picture post-card of the Kursaal at Wiesbaden, taken across the ornamental water. The message written upon it said, "Playing here to-morrow, Coblentz Saturday, Cologne Monday, going home Tuesday, *auf wiedersehen* some day, greetings, good-bye," it was signed D. Ogilvie. "Lucky devil," said Hambledon, threw the card in a drawer of his writing-table and went to a meeting of the Party Chiefs, summoned by the Leader. Now this was January 1938.

One never knew what to expect from these meetings of the Leader's. Sometimes they were addressed on stirring subjects such as a new badge for machine-gunners, or how to stimulate the birth-rate; sometimes they heard of a new tax to be imposed or new measures against the Jews, sometimes there was an announcement about something really important like the reoccupation of the Rhineland or the building of the Siegfried Line, and sometimes it seemed to Tommy that they just gathered together to blow off hot air and tell each other how wonderful they were, just like the Monkey-People in the Jungle Books, only a lot more dangerous. "You never knew," said Tommy, "whether it's gas or high explosive. Wonder what it is this time."

He soon learned, for they were informed in singularly

few words, considering who was speaking, that Austria
would be incorporated in the Reich in March. There
would be internal troubles in Austria, unrest, rioting,
faction fighting in the streets and so forth. The Austrians, realizing that their paltry Government was too
weak to keep order, would naturally appeal to their
powerful neighbour for help, and union with Germany
would naturally follow. Thus so many millions more
Germans would return to their spiritual home, the Reich,
and Germany would become greater Germany. *Hoch der
Anschluss! Hoch!*

It was perfectly obvious that the inner circle of Party
leaders whom Hambledon rudely called the Big Six had
got this scheme all cut and dried, and the purpose of this
somewhat larger meeting was merely to inform the various heads of departments about a decision already
taken. They were not asked for comment, still less criti-
cism; a few well-chosen words of congratulation, yes,
but no more. One less tactful individual asked what
would happen if any of the Austrians fought.

"Fought! Fought whom?"

"Us," said the Deputy bluntly.

"No worthy Austrians will fight us. There are, as I
have said, subversive elements which require suppression.
They will be suppressed."

"But——"

"There is no room for doubt. There is unrest in Austria, that is why we march in. If there is unrest after we
have marched in, that will only show how right we were
to do so."

The Deputy gave it up.

The meeting ended with the executive officers being
told to prepare plans, each in his separate sphere, for
reorganizing the administration of Austria in line with
that of the Reich; posts, telephones, railways, tax collec-

tions, and so forth. Hambledon received written orders
for the reorganization of the Austrian police, superses-
sion would be a better word. He was to submit detailed
schemes for putting these orders into effect. He clicked
heels, gave the Nazi salute, and marched out.

"There goes a good servant of the Reich," said the
Führer approvingly.

"I had occasion to say a few words to him the other
day about minding his own business," said Goebbels.
"They seem to have done good."

"Indeed! What about?"

"He had some views about the Jewish question which
hardly came within his province, that is all," said Goebbels smoothly. "There was nothing wrong—every man
has the faults of his virtues. He was a little overzealous,
that is all."

"I wish every man I had to deal with had only Lehmann's faults. He has one outstanding merit which I
will ask you to remember and cherish."

"What is that?"

"He is the only man in the Party whom we all of us
trust."

"That is true," said Goering thoughtfully.

"Herr Goebbels will remember in future."

Herr Goebbels would, with displeasure, in fact the
Führer had made a dangerous enemy for his incorruptible
Chief of Police.

Hambledon returned to his office to get some books of
reference, said that he would not be returning that day as
he was going to work at home, and returned to the flat.
In point of fact he often did work at home when he
wanted to be uninterrupted, his study there was not to
be approached once he gave the warning, "I shall be busy,
Franz, this afternoon." The meal-time gong was not
sounded, no wireless played, even footsteps passing the

door were hushed, for Tommy Hambledon, who had never raised his voice or lost his temper in his own house, yet knew how to make himself obeyed.

He settled down with maps and reference books to work out a scheme for the effectual policing of Austria, and it took him several hours. He made copious notes, drew up a draft report, and then corrected, amended and annotated it till it was barely legible. When he was finally satisfied he opened his typewriter, put in a sheet of paper, looked at it for a moment and took it out again, replacing it by two sheets with a carbon paper between. "I'll give 'em something to think about," he said with a grin, and proceeded to make a fair copy of his report. By the time he had finished it was past seven and he was stiff, tired and hungry, but there was a little more to see to yet. He rang the bell and Franz came.

"Is Herr Reck in the house?"

"I believe so, sir."

"Ask him to come to me, will you?"

Reck came, Hambledon gave him a cigar and asked him if he knew anything about photography.

"Did you ever know a science master who didn't? I made a hobby of it at one time."

"Got a camera now?"

"Heavens, no. What for? Want a series of photos of yourself for a magazine article entitled 'Great Men at Home'?"

"Of course," said Hambledon, "how did you guess? One of me at my desk with an expression of grim concentration, one with my feet on the mantelpiece nursing the cat, and one with me in the background and the whole foreground occupied by the glass bottom of a tankard of beer which veils, without entirely obscuring, these classic features which are the admiration of the law-abiding and a terror to evil-doers. Oh, yes, another of me setting out to the office in the morning with my chin up and my chest thrown out, and another of me coming home in the evening, haggard and bent with my day's toil for the Fatherland, but my features irradiated with that pleasing inward glow which comes only from a sense of duty well done——"

"Or from whisky," said Reck. "You're pleased about something, aren't you?"

"Why?"

"You always babble like that when you're pleased."

"Or frightened. Perhaps you're right."

"This photography. What about it?"

"Could you take a photograph of this so that the prints will be competely legible?" asked Hambledon, holding up the two sheets of the orders he had received anent the policing of Austria.

"Nice black typing," said Reck. "Top copy, not too large. Yes, I think so. One of those old-fashioned wooden cameras with bellows extension, half-plate size, wide-angle lens."

"Can you buy such a thing?"

"Second-hand. Oh, yes, I expect so."

"What pretext would you have for wanting a camera like that?"

"They are used mainly for photographing architectural features—ancient Gothic archway, that sort of thing. I take up a new hobby."

"What, publicly?"

"It might be as well," said Reck. "I shall moon about with camera on long tripod legs, prodding people wherever I turn round. Focusing cloth. Pockets bulging with dark slides, and so forth."

"What about developing?"

"I shall process them myself—may I use the bath-room?"

"Except when I want it," said Tommy handsomely. "Ask Fräulein Rademeyer."

Hambledon made a detour on his way to the office in the morning, to pay a visit to a shabby man who lived in a slummy street in the poor quarter of Berlin. The shabby man opened the door himself, and when he recognized the Chief of Police he looked alarmed and indignant.

"Herr Polizei Oberhaupt, I've done nothing, honest I haven't, don't even want to, got a good job now writin' copies for the children's copy-books, straight I have——"

"It's all right," said Hambledon reassuringly. "There's nothing against you—at the moment. I only want you to do a little job for me."

For this man had the gift of being able to write most beautifully in any style he chose; he made a living by practising this gift, only unfortunately he sometimes practised on cheques, and that was how he came to know the Chief of Police.

"Anything I can do for you, sir, of course—please come in."

Hambledon went in, when the door was shut behind them he produced a picture postcard of the Kursaal at Wiesbaden and said, "Can you imitate that writing?"

"Bit funny, isn't it?" said the man, studying Dixon Ogilvie's farewell message. "Foreigner, isn't he?"

"Yes, can you do it?"

"Bless you, sir, yes, have to be a lot funnier than that before it stumps me. What d'you want?"

"Only a luggage label, here are some. Write on it 'Dixon Ogilvie'—here, I'll write it down for you. 'Dixon Ogilvie, à Londres via Bruxelles, Ostende et Douvre.' That's all."

"How many d'you want?"

"Only one. Don't post it to me, bring it to my house at nine to-night."

.   .   .   .

Dixon Ogilvie and his uncle, homeward bound from Cologne, sat in the train at the frontier waiting while customs formalities were being observed by passengers not going beyond Belgium. As the Ogilvie luggage was registered through to London, they did not expect to be disturbed, but a porter came to the door and said, "M'sieu' Deexon Ojeelvie?"

"More or less," said Dixon. "What it?"

"A small matter of m'sieu's baggages, if m'sieu' would come?"

They both went, and were told at the customs office that there was a little difficulty because whereas D. Ogilvie's way-bill declared there were only six packages, there were in fact seven, as m'sieu' would see for himself.

"How many did you have, Dixon?"

"I don't know, six or seven. I suppose the man at Cologne counted wrong."

"I expect so. Perhaps we'd better just look at them."

Dixon pointed at one and said, "That's not mine."

"It's a portable gramophone," said his uncle.

"It is, in effect, a musical instrument," agreed the customs officer.

"You can't call a portable gramophone a musical instrument," objected Dixon, "any more than you'd call a sardine tin the Atlantic Ocean."

The customs official begged pardon, and Alexander Ogilvie said, "Don't be so damned high-brow. It is probably classed as a musical instrument, you know, like 'cats is dogs and rabbits is dogs, but tortoises is hinsects and goes free'."

The customs official understood English, but was not a student of *Punch,* so he found this a trifle baffling. However, he let it go and returned to the main subject.

"Gramophones are musical instruments for the purposes of customs," he began, and Ogilvie senior said, "I told you so."

"I'm not going to pay customs duty on the thing," said Dixon languidly. "I don't want it."

"Nobody desires that m'sieu' should——"

"Then what's all the fuss about?"

"As I have already told m'sieu', there is a package in excess of the number on the way-bill——"

"Present it to the local Female Orphanage, they'll probably love it."

"I say, Dixon——"

"Yes, Uncle Alec?"

"The label is in your handwriting."

"Eh?"

"Exactly like all the others."

Dixon walked over and examined it, and it occurred to him for the first time that there might be more in this affair than met the eye. His uncle snapped open the case, which had compartments in the lid for half a dozen records. He drew out the first, wound up the motor and set it going. The song was a French version of "Oh, Mamma!" and the singer was Waltheof Leibowitz.

"Waltheof Leibowitz," said Alexander Ogilvie thoughtfully. "I've heard that name somewhere."

The introduction ended, the singer started off with notable verve. Dixon Ogilvie clapped his hands to his ears and said, "For heaven's sake!"

"I have it, it was that comic hotel baritone Denton punched on the nose in Switzerland."

"He ought to have killed him," moaned Dixon. "Stop it, stop it. How does one stop these dam' things?"

"One takes the needle off, for a start," said his uncle, doing so, "and then one stops the motor, thus."

"Thank you. I suppose the thing would play a decent record by Moskowski instead, would it?"

"Of course it would."

"Present my excuses to the Female Orphanage," said Dixon Ogilvie to the customs official, "I will take the thing on. What do I have to do about it?"

"It is only necessary for m'sieu' to acknowledge owner-ship. I will make out an additional way-bill."

"Thanks awfully, carry on, will you? I am sorry to have given so much trouble," said Dixon. "Allow me to—er——"

"Thank you, m'sieu'. The affair is now in order."

"That's an odd business," said Alexander Ogilvie, as the train moved off again. "Are you sure you didn't buy it as a present for somebody and forget about it?"

"It's more probable that some luggage labels came loose at Cologne and were later tied on the wrong things," said Dixon.

"In that case, you've lost something. I wonder what it is."

"So do I."

"You don't seem very worried about it. By the way, no, you can't have lost one, the way-bill said six packages, and this one was an extra."

"Oh, the man counted wrong, that's all, but if they insist the thing's mine I'm jolly well going to keep it," said Dixon, but all the time he was wondering whether Hambledon had had anything to do with it, and if so, what and why. There didn't seem much sense in it, but Intelligence agents are always mysterious people, and per-haps it was only a joke—a little return for the concert of school songs. Or possibly Hambledon really thought that this crooner fellow was something wonderful. Ogilvie shuddered faintly, but he knew that some people would agree. In that case, why not send it to him openly, without all this mystery, unless Hambledon had got so in the habit of being mysterious that he just couldn't help it. Ogilvie gave it up and dozed in his corner, anyway the thing would be an interesting memento of an interesting man, he was glad to have it and would value it highly, records and all. After all, one needn't play the beastly things.

At Dover, a porter collected their luggage, including the gramophone, and wheeled them on a barrow into the customs shed, the two Ogilvies following. They saw him slide all the things on to the bench, though they were themselves impeded from reaching it at once by a lady with several daughters who passed before them in single file, adhering to each other. A large trunk shot on the counter and masked the Ogilvie luggage for a moment, but at last they arrived where it was and waited for the customs officer, looking about them, with the ghoulish curiosity we all feel when passing customs, to see if anybody else was going to be bowled out. However, no such entertainment offered itself, and at last the customs man reached them.

"Anything to declare?" he said, and held up before them a card bearing a list of dutiable articles.

"One portable gramophone," said Dixon Ogilvie promptly, and looked among the pile of luggage for it.

"What value, sir?"

"No idea, I had it given to me—I don't see it. It's not here. Where is it?"

"You are sure——" began the man, but Ogilvie cut him short.

"I saw the porter load it on his barrow with the rest, wheel them in here and put them on the bench. I saw him put the gramophone on the bench, I was watching him."

The customs officer consulted the way-bill and counted the luggage. "It says six articles, sir, and there are six."

"I know. There was a mistake at Cologne, and the gramophone had a ticket all to itself."

"I have no other way-bill in your name, sir."

"D'you think I'm lying?" stormed Ogilvie, thoroughly losing his temper. "It was in your charge and it's missing. I will have it, it must be found at once."

"A search shall be made," said the customs man, and consulted a colleague.

"Someone has stolen it," said Dixon furiously. "Blasted inefficiency! Infernal carelessness! If one's goods aren't safe in a customs house in an English port, where are they?"

"My dear boy," said his uncle, "did you really want it as badly as all that? You nearly gave it to the Female Orphans before. No doubt if it can't be found the authorities will replace it."

"I don't want it replaced, I want that one," began Dixon, but suddenly became aware that everyone was staring at him, and relapsed into purple silence.

.   .   .   .

Denton returned to his flat in town and Liese ran out to meet him.

"Charles dear, you are so late, be quick, the dinner is spoiling."

"Yes, angel, just a minute, I must look at this thing."

"It's a gramophone, isn't it?"

"Yes. I want to know why the Department sent me all the way to Dover to collect a wedding present in person."

"Oh, who gave us that, Charles?"

"A friend of your father's, m'dear. Records in the lid —my hat!"

"Oh! they're Waltheof's, how lovely. Is 'Im Monat Mai' there? Yes, here it is, let's have that one, Charles darling."

"If you wish," said Charles, putting it on. "Unhealthy distorted sense of humour I call this," he muttered as Waltheof's voice rang out, "confound Hambledon. Fancy having to listen to this."

But to their intense surprise, a third of the way through the record Waltheof's ringing tones suddenly ran down the scale, and came to an abrupt stop.

"So he never kissed the *kleine Mädchen* after all," said Denton, laughing at his wife, "or did he? Something wrong here, where's a screwdriver?"

"Oh, darling, the dinner!"

"Let me just do this, angel, won't be a minute. No room on this table, I'll do it on the floor. Look, it won't take a minute, just these four screws and the whole thing lifts out——"

"*Not* on the carpet!" shrieked his wife, "oh, you pig, darling, on our lovely cream-coloured carpet, all that black grease——"

But Denton was too busy staring to listen to Liese's wails, for the vacant space round and under the motor was packed with papers. One envelope was addressed to him and he tore it open.

"Dear Denton," ran the note inside. "These few nuts for the Dept., with my salutations. Hope your wife likes the records, she can play them when you're out, can't she? Every good wish. T.H."

Denton drew out one thin packet and two thick ones, and put them in his pocket, his wife watching him in that dutiful silence which Dixon Ogilvie so rightly admired.

"Sorry about the dinner, my sweet, got to go out," he

said, and her face fell. "I am sorry, I won't be a minute longer than I can help, and you are a darling not to argue. I adore you——"

"Dearest," she said, as he was leaving the room with a rush.

"Yes, what? I can't stop just now."

"Not even to wash your hands?"

"No—oh, Lor'! As you were, yes."

Denton took a taxi to the Foreign Office, handed over the papers and explained where he had found them.

"I had an idea that there might be something there," said his chief. "Hambledon would not wireless such detailed instructions for collecting the thing if it were only a wedding present and nothing more—how did Ogilvie take its disappearance?"

"When I left he was jumping up and down and making turkey-cock noises," began Denton, but the other man cut him short.

"My godfathers, look at this. Photographic copies of an Order to the German Chief of Police to get out a scheme for the effective policing of Austria after its union with the Reich in March. In March, good Lord! A carbon copy of the said Chief of Police's scheme, not merely a copy, Denton, but a carbon duplicate. How the devil—what are these?" he went on, opening the two fatter envelopes, full of sheets of flimsy paper. "Dossiers of German agents in this country, dozens of 'em. Dozens of 'em." He put the papers down and filled his pipe. "So Germany marches into Austria in March, does she? Hambledon, you ought to have the K.C.B. No, he ought to have the Garter. Dammit, he's earned a halo, only I hope he doesn't get it just yet."

HAMBLEDON, having some work he wished to finish at home, returned from his office a little earlier than usual one evening and went straight to his study. He was investigating a series of fires in various parts of Germany, in some of which (*a*) arson was suspected but not proved, (*b*) it was certainly arson but no arrest had been made, and (*c*) those cases in which an arrest had been made; but Hambledon was by no means satisfied that it was always the right person who had been arrested. He had left the papers in a tidy pile to the left of his desk, categories (*a*), (*b*) and (*c*) each in alphabetical order and, on top of the whole lot, a separate sheet containing a list of all these cases. He sat down at his desk, drew the pile towards him, and after the first glance examined it with curiosity.

In the first place, the list was not at the top, it was at the bottom, but what really made him gnash his teeth was that the rest of the papers, instead of being carefully and methodically sorted as he had left them, were thoroughly and horribly mixed up.

"Damn it," said Hambledon, looking through them, "someone has shuffled them like a pack of cards."

He looked at the other papers on his desk; though they had not been so carefully arranged as the arson cases he was sure they had been changed about. That demand

from Goebbels for full statistics of the number of women
(*a*) single, (*b*) married, or (*c*) widowed who had been
convicted of shoplifting in the last two years classified
so as to show how many of them were (1) country-
women, i.e., dwellers in places of up to 1,000 inhabitants
and (2) townswomen, dwellers in places of 1,000 inhabitants and over, hadn't been at the top of any pile for at
least five weeks. Confound Goebbels, anyway, this recent
and increasing thirst for statistics was becoming a whole-
time nuisance, and Hambledon had a shrewd idea that
Goebbels meant it to be. "He's getting after me," said
Hambledon to himself, "wonder why?" He made a rude
gesture at Goebbels' query and put it firmly back at the
bottom of the "miscellaneous" tray.

Having thus restored himself to good temper, he rose
from his chair and went in search of Fräulein Rademeyer.

"I say, dear, have you by any chance been dusting my
desk lately?"

"No, Klaus, why? Is it badly done?"

"No, that is, it's perfectly clean, but my papers are all
muddled up and it's rather tiresome. Who does it,
Agathe?"

"No, it's Franz' business to wait on you. I am sorry,
dear, if he is getting careless, would you like me to speak
to him about it?"

"Don't bother, I will," said Hambledon, and returned
to his study and rang for Franz.

"Did you dust my desk to-day, Franz?"

"Yes, sir."

"This pile of papers which were carefully sorted are
all in confusion. Do you think you could——"

"I beg your pardon, sir. I had an accident with that
pile of papers, I picked them up and held them in one
hand, sir, thus, while I dusted underneath them with the
other, and they slipped out of my hand and skated all

over the floor, if I may put it like that, sir. I picked them all up, I was not aware they were in any particular order. I am very sorry, sir, I will see it does not occur again."

"That's all right, Franz, only you understand that sort of thing is tiresome when one is busy."

"Certainly, sir. Thank you," said Franz, and left the room.

"Quite a good explanation," thought Hambledon, looking after the man. "It may be quite true, it's a way papers have, but—— Oh, well, I suppose I'm naturally suspicious."

Nevertheless, when he left the study that evening he put most of the papers away in the drawers of his desk and locked them up. Among them was an order to raid the headquarters of the German Freedom League, it was complete except for his signature, but he was not quite satisfied with the bona fides of all the information received. He thought it over, decided to make a few more inquiries, and put it away in its envelope unsigned.

Two days later he opened the envelope again, but instead of the order there was a neatly-written note saying simply, "No good. They have escaped to Switzerland."

"This is too much," said Hambledon, justly indignant. "A joke's a joke, but taking papers out of my desk and replacing them with little notes telling me where I get off is just plain damned impertinence. Who does the feller think I am? Von Papen?"

He considered the matter carefully and came to the conclusion that the culprit must be either Franz, Reck, or somebody from outside. It was almost too much to hope that whoever it was would have left useful fingerprints on the note, but it was worth trying, so he picked it up carefully by its edges and slid it into an envelope which he sealed down, marked A, and put it in his pocket.

"We'll start at the easiest end first," he said. "Franz."

There was a cupboard in a corner of the room where glasses were kept in case Hambledon wished to entertain visitors in the privacy of his study, or even occasionally to entertain himself: he walked across and opened it. It was small and overfull, tumblers on one side, wineglasses on the other, in ranks of three abreast. Hambledon put on his gloves, took a clean linen handkerchief from his pocket, and very carefully polished each of the three wineglasses in the front row.

"There," he said, replacing them, "now it won't matter which one he takes." He rang the bell for Franz and sat at his desk again.

"You rang, sir?"

"Oh, yes. Bring me a half-bottle of Graves, will you? I'm thirsty."

Franz brought it in on a tray and got out a wineglass from the cupboard. He drew the cork from the bottle and picked up the glass to fill it; just at that moment Hambledon glanced up from his work.

"Don't pour it out yet, Franz. I'll do it—I'll just finish this first."

"Very good, sir," said Franz, and departed.

Hambledon put his gloves on again and, holding the glass carefully by the base, swathed it in tissue paper. He then rolled it up in a sheet of newspaper and tied a label on it inscribed B. After which he extracted a wineglass from the very back of the cupboard where Franz would not notice a gap in the ranks, poured out his Graves and thought about Reck. It was a little unlikely that Reck should be of the inner ring of the Freedom League, but not impossible: it was a lot more likely than, for example, that the Chief of the German Police should be a British agent. He would have Reck's fingerprints too, just in case.

He resumed his gloves, took a half-sheet of notepaper and wrote on it in blue pencil, in a hand as unlike his own as possible, the cryptic sentence, "The bee has crawled into the tulip in search of honey." He folded and creased it as though it had been in an envelope, took his gloves off again, drank another glass of Graves, and strolled off to Reck's room. Reck was mixing chemicals.

"Hullo," said Hambledon, "how's the photography going?"

"All right," said Reck. "Expensive hobby, rather."

"Don't let that worry you. Harmless amusements are always included in the expense account."

"Yes, I know," said Reck cynically. "The operative word is 'harmless'."

"Quite. Got any good ones to-day?"

"How can I tell till they're developed? I exposed plates at the principal entrance to the Zeughaus, a collision between two cars and a tram, and a small boy being rude to a policeman."

"On the whole," said Hambledon, sinking into an armchair, "I have had an uneventful day. The only interesting thing that happened was that I found a note when I got home this evening."

Reck was pouring something out of a bottle into a graduated measure-glass; his hand did not shake nor did the flow of liquid vary. "Either he knows nothing about it," thought Hambledon, "or teetotalism is all it's cracked up to be and more."

"Assignation or libel?" asked Reck, when the measure had been filled exactly to the desired line and no more.

"Neither. Here it is," said Hambledon, offering him the folded sheet which he held lightly between his fingers like a cigarette. "What d'you make of it?"

Reck took it without hesitation, unfolded it and read it aloud. "What does it mean?"

"I haven't the faintest idea," said Hambledon with complete truth.

"How did it come?"

"By post. Posted in Berlin last night."

"Evidently someone is flattering you," said Reck acidly.

"Why? Am I the industrious bee or the colourful tulip?"

"Neither. They thought you'd understand."

"You are neither kind nor helpful," said Hambledon in a pained voice. "I thought you might be able to suggest something."

"Oh, I can suggest plenty of things, but I doubt if they'll be helpful. It's a warning of intended burglary, do you know a burglar whose name begins with B?"

"No."

"It has a political significance. Our heaven-sent Leader is going to march into Rumania after the oil-fields."

"What am I supposed to do about it? Arrest him?"

"Goering's going to invade Russia in search of caviar."

"You are incurably flippant," said Hambledon, getting up and taking his paper from Reck. "I shall go and brood over it alone."

He put the half-sheet into an envelope, labelled it C, and took all three exhibits to the fingerprint experts in the morning, asking whether, if there were any prints on A, they coincided with those on either B or C, and if not, were they among the Department's records. He received the report the same afternoon. There were two sets of fingerprints on exhibit A, one being the same as on exhibit B, i.e., the glass, and the other coincided with a set acquired by the Intelligence section during the Great War 1914-18; they were those of a Dutch importer at Cologne named Hendrik Brandt.

Hambledon really felt for a moment as though he were going to faint. A man can plan so carefully: with a little luck he works himself into an unassailable position, he has a flawless identity and a better background than the Leader himself, and all of a sudden Fate rises to her full height and socks him on the jaw. It only remained for Goebbels to obtain one of his fingerprints and make a similar inquiry, and the balloon would go up in a shower of sparks and a strong bad smell. "Oh, dear, oh, dear," said Tommy Hambledon, "I wonder who did that? Von Bodenheim, I'll bet, just taking precautions in the usual routine manner. Fancy a man you'd shot down twenty years earlier rising from the dead to get his own back like this—after twenty years." He clutched his head in both hands. "Goebbels must have hundreds of my fingerprints; he may send them in to-morrow—he may have already done it—I'd better not think about it or he might get the idea and act on it. I must get Ludmilla out at once, and Frau Christine—and her family. Oh, dear, I wish Bill was here, he'd suggest something. Franz—then it was Franz who put the note in my desk. Franz belongs to the Freedom League. He must have duplicate keys to all my drawers and probably the safe as well, heaven knows how much he's read. Oh, dear, I wish things didn't all happen at once——"

He got up and walked distractedly about the room trying to think calmly, but it was very difficult. He felt acutely the need of someone to whom he could talk. The only available person was Reck, so Hambledon picked up his hat and went home. Reck raised his eyebrows as Hambledon walked into his room, and said, "Hallo! Come to arrest me?"

"Don't make these ill-timed jokes," snapped Hambledon. "Come along to the study, will you, I want to talk to you. Franz! Franz, bring whisky and soda into the study, will you? What'll you have, Reck?"

"Grenadine, please."

"Grenadine, please, Franz. Grena—oh, my hat. Wait till Franz has been in and gone again, I could a tale unfold, etc. Lovely weather we're having for the time of year, aren't we? I always think it's so much warmer when the sun shines, don't you?"

"For pity's sake," said Reck earnestly, "pull yourself together. Franz will notice something."

"I will when he comes, besides, Franz knowing a spot more or less hardly matters now, he knows too much already. At the moment I'd like to run round in small circles putting straw in my hair."

"There isn't any straw."

"Franz will obtain some. What have you been doing to-day?"

"Oh, nothing in particular," said Reck, as Franz came into the room. "Walking about looking at things. I'd like to take some night photographs of Berlin, it's only a question of giving a long enough exposure. The only trouble is lighted vehicles passing, they leave a sort of fiery trail which is tiresome."

"I know, I've seen it in photos," said Hambledon. "Scarcely life-like, is it? Thank you, Franz, that will be all. I shall have to have the traffic stopped for you, that's all. How long would it—— Thank goodness he's gone. Listen," and Hambledon told Reck everything, admitting also that he had suspected him.

"Naturally," said Reck. "It would have been absurd not to."

"Yes, but evidently your fingerprints are not recorded, whereas mine are duly docketed as Brandt, Hendrik, importer, Dutch, Höhe Strasse, Cologne. You see

the beauty of it, don't you? Goebbels has got a down on
me already, don't know why; if he starts looking round
for evidence against me——"

Reck whistled dolefully, and the two men looked at
each other in a painful silence.

"You are in the soup, aren't you?" said Reck.

"Not yet, but I'm teetering on the edge of the tureen.
I don't see what I can do. I can't very well have the record expunged."

"Burn down the Record House or whatever they call
it."

"You drastic old man. But something like that will
have to be done. I can't go on living over a volcano like
this day after day. It might be simpler to shoot
Goebbels."

"Frame him," said Reck.

"I'll bear that suggestion in mind, too. Now there's
Franz to deal with, I think I'll have him in and talk
seriously to him. I should think he could be managed; he
knows his life is in my hands, even if Goebbels' isn't, and,
of course, I don't really mind if Germany is riddled with
Freedom Leaguers, Moonlighters, Ku-Klux-Klansmen,
Fenians, Sons of Suction, Ancient Buffaloes, Old Uncle
Tom Cobley and all. Besides, I don't want to lose a good
servant. In my official capacity I have to discourage these
activities, that's all."

Reck merely grunted, and absent-mindedly helped
himself to one of Tommy Hambledon's best cigars.

"I must get Aunt Ludmilla out at the earliest possible
moment, and Frau Christine Beckensburg and her clan
too. As for you, Reck, I think you'd better slide out unostentatiously, too. Can't you attend a photographic
conference in Paris or somewhere?"

"No," said Reck. "I think I'd better stay here."

"Why?"

"Well, judging by the mess you're getting yourself into, somebody ought to look after you."

"Good Lord! Look after me!"

"Yes, why not?"

"B—but——"

"Besides, you keep rather good cigars, and I'd hate the source to dry up."

Reck finished his Grenadine, nodded to the Chief of Police and strolled nonchalantly out of the room, leaving Hambledon gaping.

"The idea of that moss-grown old buffer thinking he ought to look after me. I must be getting old. Oh, well, I suppose I must deal with Franz now." He rang the bell, and Franz appeared.

"Oh, Franz——"

"Sir?"

"Franz, I have got to talk to you very seriously. Don't stand over there by the door all ready to bolt at any moment, come over here."

Franz walked up to the desk with his usual perfect composure, and with no expression on his ugly lined face beyond courteous inquiry.

"I hope, sir, that I have not in any way failed to give satisfaction."

"You are a damned good servant and I'd hate to lose you, why did you go and get yourself mixed up with those poisonous Freedom Leaguers?"

"Sir?"

"Don't stand there saying 'sir' at intervals like a talking parrot, you heard what I said. You took out of a locked drawer—a locked drawer, Franz—an order to raid the League's offices, and left this note in its place." Hambledon slammed down the note in question on the table. "It is of no use to deny it, your fingerprints are on it."

"I was not aware that I had attempted to deny it, sir."

"Look here, Franz. You and I have been together now for a number of years. It is acutely painful to me to find that you are working against me in my own household."

"Oh, no, sir. Believe me, I have never worked against you and I never would. What you were good enough to say just now about——"

"Franz. You belong to the German Freedom League, therefore you are working against the Government."

"Certainly, sir," said Franz calmly, "but so, I think, are you."

Hambledon leaned back in his chair and looked at the man with so savage an expression that most men would have turned and fled. Franz merely shifted his weight from the right foot to the left, and continued:

"For instance, sir, it is known that the man Otto Hauser, who stole the specification of the magnetic mine, made a copy of it which was never found; he told a friend of mine about it. I think you searched for it yourself, did you not, sir?"

"Go on," said Hambledon quietly.

"Coming nearer home, there is Herr Reck and his transmitting set, which he keeps in the roof-space above his bedroom. It was purely by accident, sir, that I discovered that the plug in the wall above his chest of drawers, to which he connects his tapping key, was not the ordinary power-plug it resembles. I endeavoured to work the vacuum-cleaner from it, sir."

Hambledon's grim face relaxed a little, but he merely said "Go on" again.

"Though I must admit, sir, that all our efforts to decipher the code he uses have so far failed completely."

"I am glad I still retain a few secrets from my domestic staff," said Hambledon.

"Yes, sir, certainly. On the other hand, there are a few things I could perhaps tell you, if you would permit me. For example, is Your Excellency aware that you are followed wherever you go by the orders of Herr Goebbels?"

"I am not altogether surprised."

"There are two men outside the house now, sir, waiting in case you should go out again this evening."

"Do you know how long this has been going on?"

"I could not say precisely, sir, but it was shortly before you went to see that forger to get the label for Herr Ogilvie's portable gramophone."

"So you know that too," said Hambledon.

"Yes, sir. The man is one of our most useful, if not one of our most respected members. Yes," said Franz thoughtfully, "it was just before that, about the time when Herr Reck took up photography."

"You know, Franz, I'm awfully sorry, but I'm afraid I shall have to have you painlessly destroyed—as painlessly as possible. You know too much, you must see that."

"On the contrary, sir, it is precisely because I know so much—not only about you—that I could be of use to you."

"What do you mean by 'not only about me'?"

"To answer that, sir, I must tell you something about the Freedom League. When the Nazi Party first received any notable measure of public support, some of us who remembered an earlier Germany were not favourably impressed, and a careful study of *Mein Kampf* confirmed us in our opinions. For after all, sir, it is all set down there, what he meant to do and how he meant to do it, the only mystery is why so many people are surprised at what he does. Why did they not simply believe him? Well, we did, and we regarded the future with such forebodings that we formed a League to protect what we foresaw

would be most endangered, our personal freedom. That
was in 1924, and since then, with the growth of the Nazi
Party, the Freedom League has also grown till now there
are thousands upon thousands of us. It is a lowly and inconspicuous organization, sir, we have no mass meetings
and we carry no banners, but we do a lot of good work—
literally," added Franz with a smile. "The ivy is an inconspicuous plant, sir, but it has been known to pull down
the forest oak."

"Please go on," said Hambledon, "I am most interested."

"We thought you would be, sir. I may say that if you
had not brought about this *éclaircissement*, I should
shortly have initiated it myself. To return to the Freedom
League. We decided that it was necessary to install ourselves into positions of confidence in the Party without
having to take any share in its iniquities, so as most of us
had fairly good manners and knew how things ought to
be done—I was a Captain of Uhlans myself—we readily
became butlers, valets and so forth. We were fortunate
in obtaining situations with most of the Party leaders, I
came to you because from the earliest days it was evident
that your outstanding capabilities and integrity of character would carry you far——"

"Stop a minute," said Hambledon, "you're making my
head ache. Do you mean to say you have a whole network
of—of supervision running through the Nazi Party?"

"Among all the more important members, sir."

"And that you planted yourself on me on purpose to
—er—supervise me?"

"Yes, sir. Of course, until recent years I thought you
were as convinced a Nazi as any of them, but when I
discovered you were not, I was only all the more interested."

"Naturally. Er—sit down, Captain——"

"Thank you," said Franz, but not supplying his name. "I think perhaps I'd better not, someone might come in. Thanks all the same, I appreciate that."

"Tell me, who do you think I am?"

"To tell you the truth, I haven't the faintest idea and I've never been able to find out. It annoys me—it is a failure on my part," said the man with a frank smile. "I think, however, that you love Germany as we do, and loathe the Nazis as we do. We have seen you defending the cause of simple, honest people against tyranny in power, that is our aim also. We mean to pull down this foul regime which is making the name of Germany a stench in the nostrils of decent men of all nations, and we will set up in its place a Government founded on justice, humanity and peace."

"If you succeed," said Hambledon carefully, "you will no doubt receive a large measure of support from, as you say, decent men everywhere."

"We shall want a new President," said Franz, his eyes kindling with the visions his mind beheld, "a man who can be trusted, whose instincts are sound, whose heart is upright, whose word is his bond."

"Such men are scarce, Franz."

"I think I know of one, sir. I have served him for some time and I should be glad, if he would rescue Germany, to serve him till I died."

Franz clicked his heels, bowed to Hambledon, and marched out of the room before his master could find words to reply.

"Good Lord," said the horrified Hambledon when he was alone, "that settles it. I must get out, I couldn't stand that. President—what a frightful thought. Franz looks quite capable of it—oh, gosh! No more beautiful blondes, and I should have to live on cabbage. This is where I go home."

THOUGH THE DAYS PASSED by without any overt attack upon Hambledon, he was always aware of being watched and followed, and the thought of his fingerprints, neatly docketed and filed, waiting in their proper place for Goebbels to ask for them, made him feel sick. The neatest way to solve the problem would be simply to substitute somebody else's fingerprints for his own, but he had not the technical ability to do this, as he told Reck. "I don't even know how they photograph the dam' things," he said irritably. "They powder them, don't they? What with? Besides, how do they file them? Alphabetically, between Brain and Brawn?"

"No," said Reck, "I don't think so. I think they're classified according to pattern, as it were."

"That's what I'm afraid of. If I got the wrong sort of loops into that place, the experts would spot it at once. That is, supposing I could get hold of it, or having got it could fake an imitation. Besides, there may be two copies under a sort of cross-reference system. I wish I'd taken an intelligent interest in the business earlier, I daren't now. I only used them when necessary and asked not how nor why. I'd like to plant a bomb in the place, but there are technical difficulties even in such a simple scheme as that. Now Bill would have persuaded Goebbels that it

was in the Nazi interest to have the records destroyed,
and Goebbels would have beamed on him and asked him
to attend to it himself."

"Ask Franz to attend to it," suggested Reck lazily.

Tommy Hambledon looked at him much as Balaam
must have looked at his ass, and walked thoughtfully
away.

The next evening, when Franz came into the study as
usual to switch on lights and draw curtains, Hambledon
said: "By the way, I have no desire to meddle in any way
with that organization of yours, but I did hear a piece of
news to-day which might interest you."

"Indeed, sir?"

"Your emissaries scattered quite a large number of
leaflets about in most of the larger towns of Germany
some time recently."

"That is so, sir, and not one of the distributors was
caught in the act."

"No, Franz, but most of 'em left their fingerprints
behind."

"I warned them," said Franz anxiously, "to be careful
about that—having been careless myself."

"Yes, but you can't separate papers in the dark with
gloves on. The fingerprints have been collected and filed,
Franz, and if any one of them can be identified he will
either be dropped on and persuaded to talk, or watched
to see who his contacts are." This happened to be true,
which, as Hambledon remarked to Reck, was convenient,
because he'd probably have said it anyway. "I can't do
anything, this is the Gestapo's work."

"It looks as though some steps should be taken in the
matter, sir."

"I leave it to you, Franz, with the utmost confidence,"
said Tommy blandly.

Franz fidgeted about the room for some moments. "It

would be very wrong, sir, of me even to wonder what advice you would give."

"It would be positively immoral of me to offer any," said his master.

"Yes, sir. Would it be inconvenient to you, sir, if I were to go out for an hour to-morrow afternoon? It is not my usual day."

"Not at all, Franz, by all means go. There is a very exciting film being shown at some of the cinemas, it is called, I think, 'Flames of Desire', or some such title."

"Sir?" said the surprised servant.

"It is, of course, well known to everyone that photographic records are inflammable," said Tommy patiently.

A slow smile spread across Franz's face, and he left the room without replying.

A few days later Franz came to Hambledon and said without preamble, "There are certain men, sir, who are prepared to burn the fingerprint records in possession of the Government, if they could obtain access to the building."

"It so happens," said Hambledon, "that I know the place fairly well. At night it is, of course, always locked up and the night caretaker will not open to anyone. If any person in authority should want to turn up a record after the office shuts for the night, he would have to go with one of the three principal heads of Departments, who would take him there, let him in with his own key, stand over him while he transacted his business, and convey him out again. The outer doors have an ordinary lock which opens by turning a handle like any sitting-room door, and in addition, a Yale lock or something very like it. You know, it locks itself automatically when you pull the door shut after you and you can't open it again unless you have a key."

"Are the doors locked all day, sir?"

"No, the catch of the spring lock is held back by a snib, which you slide up to put the lock out of action and pull down again to release the catch. By day, the lock is not working, it's only after office hours that it is used."

"If one could get——" began Franz, but Hambledon interrupted him.

"So you see, if one night someone were to come out of the door and absent-mindedly slip up the snib as he went, any man who happened to be outside at the time could merely turn the handle and walk in."

Franz nodded eagerly. "And the night caretaker?"

"He's a very decent old fellow named Reinhardt, a veteran of the war, a Saxon; he fought at Ypres in '16, he tells me. Reinhardt must be got out of the way somehow."

"If the gentleman who was going home would send him for a taxi," suggested Franz.

"Gentlemen," corrected Hambledon. "There will be two of them, because one will be an official with a key."

"Of course, you said so just now. If Reinhardt were sent for a taxi, the taxi would come."

Hambledon nodded. "To-day is Tuesday. Friday night about 10 p.m.? The side door, not the main entrance."

"Yes, sir," said Franz, suddenly becoming the servant again. "Certainly, sir. Very good, sir."

. . . .

"I must really apologize," said Hambledon to the Records official, "for dragging you away from your family like this. A man should have his evenings undisturbed."

"Not at all, Herr Polizei Oberhaupt. Besides being my duty, it is a pleasure to serve the Herr."

"You are too kind," said Hambledon, as the other man

put his key in the lock. "I only heard to-night that this man had been traced, and to-morrow—to-morrow is Saturday, is it not?—he is going to Holland and it will be too late. Good evening, Reinhardt."

"Why do you not arrest him at once just in case?"

"It is not a political offence," explained Hambledon, "it is a case of private blackmail, a crime which I hold in such abhorrence, Herr Gerhardt, that I would not even accuse a man of it unless I were morally sure of his guilt."

"It is evident that the Herr has the scales of justice implanted in his soul," said Gerhardt with poetic, but confused metaphor. "The dossier you require should be in this folder—here it is."

Hambledon spent some time making notes from the dossier of a gentleman who had indeed been convicted of blackmail in the past, and then glanced at his watch to discover to his horror that it was five minutes past ten.

"I have completely ruined your evening," he said. "What will Frau Gerhardt say to me? On such a night, too, there is rain beating the windows again. I'll send Reinhardt for a taxi and drop you at your house on my way home. Reinhardt! Are you there? Oh, get me a taxi, would you?"

"I beg the Herr Polizei Oberhaupt not to inconvenience himself——"

"It is no inconvenience, it is a pleasure——"

"The Herr is too polite——"

"Besides, I owe you a little return——"

"On one condition, then, that the Herr will deign to come in and take a little something. Frau Gerhardt will remember the honour all her life."

"I shall be glad to make my peace with the gracious Frau," said Hambledon, who had the best of reasons for wanting an impeccable alibi for the next hour or so. "I shall be delighted. What a wonderful filing system you

must have here," he went on. "Do you keep the fingerprints here too?"

"The fingerprint section is on the floor above this,
directly over our heads," said Gerhardt, and went on telling Hambledon about it regardless of the sound of a taxi
drawing up outside till the Chief of Police permitted
himself another glance at his watch, Gerhardt took the
hint, and they walked towards the outer door.

"Where is Reinhardt?" asked the Records official. "He
should be here to open the door for us."

"We can easily open it for ourselves," suggested Hambledon, but his host continued to fuss.

"Reinhardt!" he called, turning back from the door.
"Where are you? This is positively discourteous."

But Hambledon had already opened the door and was
standing holding the handle. "Please don't trouble, Herr
Gerhardt; no doubt he has a perfectly good explanation,
perhaps it is time for one of his rounds. Come on," he
added, taking the man by the arm in friendly fashion,
"let's go; you have been on business long enough to-night
already." He slammed the door behind them and the two
men got into the waiting taxi and drove away.

When Reinhardt had been sent for the taxi ten minutes
earlier, he had walked briskly down the street whistling
under his breath in spite of the rain. There was a taxi-
rank at the end of the road, he was thinking, as he walked
towards it, how lucky it was that this had happened to-
night, for Herr Lehmann always tipped well, and now
they would be able to have a goose for dinner on Sunday
instead of just ordinary veal; it would make a real feast
for the boy's birthday, twenty-two on Sunday, a good
lad. Reinhardt's mind went back to the day when first
he knew he had a son, when the letter came to the sodden
trenches before Ypres in '16. He had been lucky that
night, too, because his crowd were unexpectedly with-

drawn and replaced by the Prussian Guards, tall arrogant men whom nobody liked, but there was no doubt they were grand fighters. It was just as well they were, too, for in the dawn of the next day the English attacked, and the fighting was savage since they were no ordinary English, though these were bad enough, but the awful 29th Division who were reported to eat rusty nails and broken glass for breakfast. Reinhardt in his walk came to the entry of a short cul-de-sac, leading only to the door of a church, silent, dark and deserted at that hour of the night. He started to cross it, thinking of the ear-splitting roar and the blinding flashes of the artillery barrages which preceded an attack—there were those flashes now before his eyes, searing bursts of flame, and in his ears the unbearable shock of explosion. He staggered, tried to run and could not, his feet would not move—the mud, of course. He threw out his arms feebly and crashed to the ground.

So it was all a dream that he had ever come home from the war and seen his son grow up; probably he had fallen asleep on his feet as men did when they were so very tired, and had a sudden vivid dream. If he opened his eyes now he would see again the seas of foul mud, the wet trench in which he stood, that hanging rag of slimy sacking at the corner of the next traverse which was only sacking by day but at night turned into something stealthy and menacing which always stopped moving when you looked at it. After a while it occurred to him that the place where he lay was curiously quiet for a battlefield and smelt cleaner too; curiosity opened his eyes, and he saw a doctor leaning over him and a man in uniform at the foot of his bed.

"Congratulations, Reinhardt," said the doctor, pleased at the return to consciousness.

"Thank you," said Reinhardt feebly, "but I don't think it's a very nice time for babies to be born, just now."

"My dear soul," said the doctor, laughing quietly, "you don't imagine you've had a baby, do you?"

"Of course not," said Reinhardt. "My wife has, though. I've been hit, I suppose."

"With a sandbag," said the doctor. "Thank the good God who gave you such a lovely thick skull."

"Sandbag? Off the parapet?"

"He thinks he's back in the trenches again," said the policeman at the foot of the bed. "Hope he hasn't lost his memory."

"No, no," said the doctor. "A little confused for the moment, that's all. The war has been over these twenty years, Reinhardt, you are night caretaker at the Record House, and last night somebody slogged you with a sandbag."

"I remember now. I went to get a taxi——"

Directly after the taxi had driven off with Hambledon and Gerhardt inside, a car drew up at the same door and two men with suit-cases got out. The car moved off to a point fifty yards down the road and stopped again with its engine running quietly; the driver lit a cigarette and waited, his eyes on the driving mirror reflecting the street behind him. The two men carried their suit-cases across the pavement, opened the door by simply turning the handle, and went in, locking the door carefully behind them.

"Have a good look at how this catch works, Erich," said one. "If this stuff flares up properly we may have to make a dash for it. Hans has pinched Eigenmann's car for an hour or two because the police will always pass it through; you know, Goebbels' secretary."

"Good idea. I know all about those locks; we've got one like that on the front door at home. Where'd we better start it? Anywhere in this long passage? I've never been inside this place before."

"This leads to the central hall where the stairs go up, there at the end, you can see them. If we start in a room near the stairs and open the window first, there'll be a good draught. Come on."

They entered the last room, next to the hall, and one pushed up the windows while the other opened the suit-cases. The walls of the room were lined with wooden pigeon-holes, full of papers, and there were besides screens six feet high across the room at intervals of a yard apart, screens themselves all pigeon-holes of papers, neatly filed.

"What a wonderful spot for the job," murmured Erich. "Why, you'd think one match would be enough without what we've brought."

"Yes. I don't think we need use it all in here," said his friend. "We'll start one here, and if we're quick, another one farther down the passage as well before we go."

He took handfuls of cinematograph film, cut into short lengths, from one suit-case and strewed it on the floor along the walls while Erich threw coils of film over the screens in all directions.

"I should think that would be enough, then," said Erich. "Going to light it now?"

"Of course."

"But won't they see the flames from outside?"

"No, this window looks on an inner court. Stand back —no, get right out in the passage. Take the suit-cases, I shall have to jump for it."

"All right, I've got them," said Erich. "All clear."

The other man struck a match and applied it to one of the coils; immediately there was a spluttering crackle and the flare of burning celluloid. He lit another and another, tossed the match onto a heap on the floor, and sprang into the passage.

"That'll do for that," he said, "let's find another. What's in here? Books—not too good. This one—tin boxes, no. This'll do, it's very like the first."

"My hat," said Erich, glancing back, "that's taken hold. Looks like the doorway of hell already."

"Come on, don't waste time."

"This room looks out on the street," said Erich, as they tossed the stuff about and pulled papers down to make them burn more readily.

"No matter, we shall be out before the flames show. Pull the blinds down. That's right, now get out while I finish off."

Erich heard the crackle of the lighted film as he turned away and the second man joined him in the passage. "Better than the other, I think," he said. "Now—— Good God, what's that?"

It was a rattle as someone tried the handle of the outer door, followed by hammering on the panels and the shout, "Open, in the name of the Reich!"

"It's the police," said the older man calmly. "They must have found the caretaker."

Erich turned to run back along the passage but checked at once. "We can't get through now," he said. "Look at it." The flames had barricaded the passage and even the floor was flaring.

"Dangerous stuff, linoleum," said his friend. "No, we can't go that way."

"The windows, then?"

"They're all barred. No. I'm sorry, Erich, I brought you into this."

"Can't we—— What's that?"

"They're trying to shoot the lock off, they'll probably succeed."

"Can't we do anything?"

"There is just a rather feeble chance that there may

not be many of them, and if they're silly enough to come in we might shoot them down and get clear away before reinforcements arrive. I've a good mind to go and open the door for them, you know, they've no need to come in, they've only to wait till the fire forces us out. I think I'll do that. Listen! There's the car moving off, if we do get out we shall have to run for it."

"Has Hans gone off and left us, then?"

"Of course, he had orders to do that. What could he do if he stayed? Nothing. Erich, look at that door! It's opening! Into that doorway!"

The two men dodged into doorways as the outer door burst open and the police charged in. There was the repeated crack of automatics, and the sergeant who was leading doubled up, stumbled, came running up the passage under his own momentum, and collapsed like a sack at Erich's feet. A constable by the door uttered a yelp, clasped his arm, and jumped back, the others threw the door wide open and withdrew hastily into the street outside, from whence they could see down the passage with its creeping inferno of fire behind the two desperate men in the doorways.

"They've done us now," shouted the older man. "They can see us and we can't see them. Better get shot, it's pleasanter than burning. Let 'em have it!"

The exchange of shots went on, lessening suddenly from within and finally ceasing altogether. The fire engines came, and the fire brigade leader asked if it was safe for his men to start.

"The fire don't look too safe to me," said the surviving sergeant of police. "I reckon the men are harmless enough by now."

By this time the fire had taken secure hold of the building and was spreading from room to room and bursting through ceilings to the floors above; windows shattered with the heat and flames gushed out, lighting up the decorous streets and squares of the Government quarter with an incongruous dancing bonfire light. Crowds gathered and were shooed back by the police, telephone wires buzzed and celebrities arrived, among them Goebbels in person, to whom the Superintendent of Police reported.

"Arson, sir, there's no doubt," and he told the story of the two men. "Reinhardt—that's the caretaker, sir—was decoyed out somehow and sandbagged. He's now in hospital."

"Did anyone visit the place to-night after closing hours?"

"Yes, sir, Herr Gerhardt came with Herr Lehmann, the constable on duty saw them go in."

"Herr Lehmann, eh? Did they come out again?"

"I couldn't say, sir. The constable's beat takes him right round the square, and they might well have gone while he was out of sight."

"Lehmann," said Goebbels thoughtfully to himself. "Lehmann. Then the two men——" But the idea of the respectable Gerhardt loosing off an automatic at the police was quite beyond credit, if one of the men was Lehmann the other certainly wasn't Gerhardt. After all, it was equally ridiculous to suspect the correct Lehmann of such behaviour, only Goebbels was getting into the habit of suspecting him of having a finger in any unpleasantness which might crop up—not even quite a suspicion, more a hope that the incorruptible Chief of Police would slip up. "Has Herr Gerhardt been informed?"

"Apparently his telephone is out of order, sir, we can't get an answer. I have sent a constable to his house to inform him."

Goebbels grunted.

The firemen confined their efforts to saving the farther

wing since this one was clearly past praying for, the flames leaped higher into the thick rolls of smoke, and the crowd said "A-aah" as the roof fell in with a crash and a shower of sparks. Very reminiscent of the Reichstag fire this, with the important difference that this one was inconvenient, damned inconvenient. All those irreplaceable records——

He started violently as a quiet voice behind his elbow said, "An appalling sight, Herr Goebbels, yet impressive in its grandeur and disregard of human endeavour."

"Lehmann! When did you leave here—where have you been?"

"At my house, Herr Minister, at my house," said Gerhardt's agitated voice. "For the past hour we have been taking a little refreshment in the Herr Polizei Oberhaupt's esteemed company. We went home together from here, soon after ten. All was well then."

"The devil you did," said Goebbels to himself. "A little job for you, Lehmann. Find the miscreants," he added aloud.

"The search will be the subject of my unremitting care," said the Chief of Police earnestly.

JAKOB ALTMANN was a railway porter, not in one of the passenger stations of Berlin where there was nice clean luggage to be carried and tips to collect from grateful passengers, but in the goods yard, where he spent laborious days dragging heavy boxes about and staggering under the weight of awkward parcels. His wife Gertrud said repeatedly, and usually in the same words, that it was entirely Jakob's own fault that he was never raised to the passenger grade; no one could expect gentlefolk to have any dealings with such a rough, clumsy, loutish, mannerless, loud-voiced, ham-handed bullock of a man. She knew what was what, having been with the same family of gracious ladies till she was insane enough to throw up her good place to marry such a lout, a lump, a baboon——

"I wish you were with them still," growled Jakob.

"But they're all dead."

"That's what I mean," he said, and swaggered out laughing.

He drew his wages one Friday evening as usual and returned to the porter's room to get his lunch-bag before he went home. Most of the men had lunch-bags alike, the black American-cloth shopping bag familiar to the poor in most countries; some were shabbier than others but there was otherwise little difference unless one wrote one's name on the lining, but why bother? If they did get mixed up it did not matter much as they never had anything in them at the end of the day. On this occasion there was something in Jakob's; for some reason he had not been hungry at dinner-time and had only eaten half his sausage, so he was naturally taking the rest of it home again. One does not waste good food. Since his name began with A he was paid among the first; when he reached the smoke-blackened brick hutch called the porter's room the space under the bench was full of black bags, with a basket or two for variety, one tin box and several cardboard ones. Jakob picked up his own bag, felt the lump inside to make sure it was the right one, and walked home as usual with his friend Buergers who lived two doors down the street.

They went into a place of refreshment on the way home and had one or two, since it was pay-day, and then ambled off to their respective wives.

"Late again," said Gertrud, "as usual. Been gossiping with that mutton-head Buergers, I suppose. Been fined this week?"

"No," said Jakob good-naturedly. "Been lucky this week, didn't bust anything. Here's the money."

"This isn't all," said Gertrud, counting it.

"Had a drink on the way home," explained Jakob. He explained this every Friday, and every Friday Gertrud received it as though it were a fresh enormity. "Buergers stood me one so I 'ad to return the compliment as they say in 'igh social circles, among the toffs you're so fond of."

"Taking to drink, now. If Buergers' wife is such a soft fool she'll put up with only getting 'alf the money as is her lawful due, I'm not, Jakob Altmann."

"Buergers' wife is one as 'as too much sense to nag at a man the minute he comes in," said Jakob enviously.

"Happy, they are, if she isn't everlastingly buying things for the 'ouse as is no use when they're got. Antimacassars, bah!"

"If Buergers' wife is such a slut as to be content with an 'ome looking as if the brokers 'ad been in——"

"An' if you call two glasses of beer at the end of a day's work 'taking to drink' you're the biggest fool in the street."

"That's right!" screamed Gertrud. "Call me names!"

"And Buergers' wife isn't a slut, she's a decent, quiet, clean woman——"

"That's right! Taking up with another woman! I suppose Buergers——"

"Will you stop!" roared Jakob in a voice which shook the windows. "*Herrgott*, I can't stand this, I'm goin' out. I shall kill you one of these days, then you'll be sorry."

"What's that in the bag?" asked Gertrud, noticing an unaccustomed bulge in it. "Brought somethink 'ome?"

"Only some of the sausage," answered Jakob, diving into the bag for the parcel. "Didn't eat it all."

"Wasn't good enough for Your Lordship, I suppose?"

"Oh, just the same as usual. Only when I was eatin' it I 'appened to think of you, my love, as the song says, an' it put me right off." He pulled the packet out.

"That's right! Be rude! There's the fire goin' out now," said Gertrud, diving at the stove and producing a frightful clatter with the poker. "Go out to the shed an' bring me another bucket of briquettes, quick."

But Jakob neither moved nor spoke.

"Did you 'ear me?" said Gertrud, pushing a few tired-looking twigs into the stove. "Suppose I'm goin' to slave for you all day long when you're out an' then carry 'eavy buckets in while you sit in an armchair an' twiddle your thumbs? This wood won't catch, now."

Still no answer, and Gertrud lost her temper completely. "*Will* you do as I say?" she screamed, and hit the top of the iron stove a terrific welt with the poker, which bent. "Now that's gone, I wish it had been your head, you——" she said, turning round, and suddenly her voice changed. "What's that you've got there?"

"Money," said Jakob in a shaking voice, "lots of money."

"Give it to me," said Gertrud, diving at the table, but he caught her by the wrists and whirled her across the room, casually, without looking what he was doing, with an easy strength.

"I must have picked up the wrong bag," said Jakob in a puzzled voice.

"How much is there there?"

"Shan't tell you. Here's some for you," said Jakob, counting out ten-mark notes. "Go an' buy some more antimacassars if they make you 'appy, and for 'eaven's sake get drunk on the rest, maybe you'd be pleasanter company than you are sober."

Gertrud watched him as he shuffled up the other notes, a fat wad of them, and replaced them between the cardboard covers he found them in, squares of cardboard with elastic bands round them.

"Where are you going?"

"Out. I told you that before."

"Not with all that money," said Gertrud, and made a lightning snatch at the packet. Jakob did not attempt to evade her, he held firmly to the money with one hand and with the other dealt her a stinging slap on the side of her head which sent her spinning to the floor, almost too astonished to cry, because in spite of incessant provocation he had never hit her before. Jakob did not even look to see if she were hurt, he put the money carefully in an inner pocket and walked out of the house.

He started the evening by taking Buergers and his wife

to a restaurant where they got good food, appetizingly
cooked and cleanly served, after which Frau Buergers,
who was an understanding woman, went home and left
the men to enjoy themselves after their own fashion.
Unfortunately, their tastes in pleasure were limited and
unrefined, and by ten o'clock they were hopelessly drunk.
They staggered, arm in arm, along a dignified street which
was new to them, since they had lost their way, singing
the German equivalent of "Dear old pals—jolly old
pals——" in anything but harmony. They came to the
entrance of a short cul-de-sac leading only to the door of
a church, dark, silent and deserted at that hour of the
night, and turned into it, not intentionally but because
their feet happened to go that way. Half-way along it
they tripped over something and fell down.

"What's that?" asked Jakob. "You fall over something,
too?"

Buergers felt about in the obscurity. "Not something,"
he announced. "Somebody."

Jakob also investigated. "Qui' right. Somebody. I say,
he's had some, had lots. Lots more than us. We're bit
tiddley, he's blind. Corpsed."

"Poor ole corpse," said Buergers affably. "Wake up,
catch cold."

"Qui' right. Wake up, corpse."

They shook him, but Reinhardt took no notice.

"Can't leave 'm here, die of cold," said Jakob. "Not
Clish—Christian."

"Pick up," suggested Buergers. "Take 'm home."

"Not my home," said Jakob firmly. "Gertrud—
wouldn't like 'm. Very respectable woman, Gertrud. Too
'spectable. Don't like her."

"Well, take 'm somewhere," urged Buergers, and they
hoisted him up, holding him under each arm, and carried

him along without effort though his feet were trailing, for the two porters even when drunk were stronger than most men when they are sober.

" 'Minds me," said Jakob, "carrying ole Hoffenberg."

"Yes," agreed Buergers. "Jus' like funeral. Sing!"

So they emerged into the very dignified street again, proceeding in zigzags and dismally chanting that dirge of German funerals, "I had a comrade, A better none could be," and met the constable completing the circuit of his beat.

" 'Ere!" he said sharply. "What's all this? Stop that noise."

"This feller's corpsed," explained Jakob. "Take 'm away. I'll give 'm to you."

They let go of Reinhardt, who immediately collapsed like a sack in the road, face downwards, and the constable, seeing that this was more than a one-man job, blew his whistle for reinforcements, and waited. Jakob and Buergers sat down on each side of Reinhardt and went on singing till the constable hushed them again, whereupon Buergers said he was unkind and burst into tears, while Jakob went to sleep.

Another constable and a sergeant arrived and the first policeman explained the circumstances.

"Know who they are?" asked the sergeant.

"No, sir. Don't belong round here, that is, I haven't seen the middle man's face, but they were all together."

"Let's look," said the sergeant, so they turned Reinhardt over and shone a torch on his face. In spite of the mud smears on it the constables recognized him at once.

"*Herrgott!* It's Reinhardt, night caretaker at the Record House."

"He'll lose his job for this," said the sergeant ominously.

"He can't be drunk, sir, I saw him an hour ago stone sober, and just after that Herr Lehmann and Herr Gerhardt went in; he wouldn't get drunk with them there."

"Besides," said the other constable, "he never does."

"There's something very odd here," said the sergeant. "Get an ambulance, Georg, and have him taken to hospital. Handcuff these two to the railings, can't bother with them now. Johan, come to the Record House with me."

When they looked through the letter-box of the Record House they saw the end of the passage a mass of flames, and two men walking towards them.

After the shooting had ceased, the fire-brigade arrived and took control of proceedings at the Record House, and the constables remembered their charges which they had left handcuffed to the railings. They were still there, with the crowd surging round and tripping over their legs, but nothing troubled them nor made them afraid, for they were sound asleep. Efforts to awaken them having failed completely, they were lifted on to wheeled stretchers and taken to the police station.

Here in the morning came the Chief of Police in person, pursuant upon his promise to Goebbels that he would look into the affair himself. Here were two men who had been in company with the damaged Reinhardt; very well, he would start with them.

It was quite easy to start, but quite impossible to go on. The police stated that they had found a large number of ten-mark notes, eleven hundred and eighty-two to be exact, upon the person of the prisoner Altmann, who could give no satisfactory explanation as to how he came by them. There were also two squares of cardboard which, with two rubber bands, had held the money together; one of the pieces of card had notes scribbled on it in pencil. The cards and the money were handed over to the Chief of Police.

Interrogated, Jakob Altmann deposed that he found

the money in his bag when he got home. That he had no idea whose it was or how it got there, and suggested, in a flight of fancy for which the police rebuked him, Santa Claus. That he had noticed a lump in the bag but thought it was sausage. That he had gone home, had a row with his wife, given her some of the money to keep her quiet, and then gone out with the rest of it and taken his friends the Buergers out to supper. That after supper Frau Buergers had gone home to mind the kids while Buergers and he went on the binge. No, he could not recall where they went, just to one place and another. No, he didn't know how they came to fetch up in that quarter of Berlin, supposed they must have lost their way. No, he didn't remember meeting Reinhardt, didn't know anybody of that name, though, of course, they'd met and talked to a lot of people they didn't know in the course of the evening, and who was this Reinhardt, anyway?

Buergers, a gentler and less truculent man than Altmann, but also of a lower mental grade, remembered even less of the evening than his friend, but what he did remember corroborated Altmann's statements. No, he didn't know where the money came from. Old Jakob said he'd found it in his bag and Buergers had simply believed him. Why not? It was no business of his, it wasn't his money.

Recalled, Altmann said that the only explanation he could suggest was that he had inadvertently exchanged bags with someone who had got his sausage in exchange for the notes, he explained how much alike most of the bags were.

"That I can understand," said the Chief of Police, "but what I don't believe for an instant is that a man in your position would lose a sum like that without making an uproar about it. Would you?"

"No, sir," said the prisoner promptly.

"That is, if he ever had such a sum. Has there been any complaint about a serious loss of money among the goods yard porters?"

"No, sir," said the Superintendent present. "Inquiries have been made."

"So you see," said Lehmann, addressing the prisoner again, "it doesn't seem as though your story could be true, does it?"

"But it is, sir," insisted Jakob.

"Would you believe it yourself, if you were in my place?"

Jakob hesitated.

"No, sir," he said, facing Lehmann squarely. "I don't believe I would. But it is true, sir."

"Dammit, I believe the fellow's telling the truth," muttered Lehmann to the Superintendent. "Remanded in custody for a week, both of them. Have that car looked up, you've got its number."

"The Herr Oberhaupt has a funny way of examining prisoners," said one Inspector quietly to another.

"What odds so long as he gets at the facts?" said the other.

"Supposing this man to be speaking the truth," said Lehmann, talking to the Superintendent in private, "it is perfectly obvious that the man who lost the money had no right to it. Nobody swaps eleven thousand marks for a couple of ounces of sausage without howling about it, not in these days, thank God."

"No, sir. Looks like proceeds of a robbery, sir."

"So I think. Either that, or they're forged. I will take them away and have them investigated. I'll sign a receipt for them if you'll make it out."

It was soon established that the notes were not forgeries, so Hambledon sent a list of their numbers to the various banks, with a request to know when they had last been passed out and to whom, and sat down to consider the pencilled entries on the cardboard cover. They ran:

> "April 7th
>
> | Gagel | 600 |
> | Dettmer | 1,200 |
> | Kitzinger | 800 |
> | Tietz | 500 |
> | Rautenbach | 2,000 |
> | Militz | 2,200 |
> | Eigenmann | 1,500 |
> | Baumgartner | 3,200 |
>
> May 4th"

"Message ends," said Tommy to himself. "Since the faculty of reasoning is what mainly distinguishes us from the brute creation, what do we deduce from this? How much did Altmann have on him after his night out?" He turned up a note on the amount. "11,820. And to think of him lying asleep on the pavement with all that mob surging round him and nobody picked his pocket! However, I think that Herr Altmann spent one hundred and eighty marks on his evening beer. What a jag! I wonder how much of that he gave his wife."

He looked at the two dates and the list of names. "April 7th, that was the night of the fire. I think there was going to be a share-out that night among the Herren Gagel, Dettmer and Co., but when they got there the cupboard was bare and so the poor dogs got none. I wonder what they said to the treasurer when he offered them two and a half ounces of sausage instead." He looked again at the list of names, some of them were familiar. "Rautenbach, Militz, Eigenmann and Baumgartner are creatures of Goebbels," he said thoughtfully, unlocked his safe and took a book out of it. "Let's see if we have any notes

about them. Yes, I thought so. Eigenmann is up to the
neck in this Jewish racket, Militz, s.n.p.—suspected, not
proved. Nothing against the other two. Kitzinger, I think
I've heard of him before. Yes, Jewish racket again, and so
is Dettmer if I don't mistake—I don't. He is. Tietz, s.n.p.
again. Gagel, no mention." He locked up the book again
and lit a cigar. "The bag turns up on the railway, and the
railway people are deep in this Jew swindle. We are getting on, we really are. I don't think this is quite an ordinary robbery, somehow, I think it's a share-out of some of
the cash extracted from our Jewish emigrants, poor shorn
lambs, and if Herr Goebbels takes any interest in the case,
I shall know I'm right. It will be interesting to see what
the banks report and in the meantime I think I'll copy out
this little list."

He made a copy, locked it up in his safe, and spent ten
minutes in going through a police report which came in.
He smiled secretly to himself when an S.S. trooper tapped
on the door and announced, "The Herr Minister-of-
Propaganda Goebbels."

"I beg your forgiveness, my dear Lehmann, for breaking in upon your labours like this. I am anxious to know
whether you have been able to get any light upon the
abominable fire at the Record House."

"Please sit down," said Hambledon, setting a chair for
his visitor, "I trust that you will never think it necessary
to apologize for coming to see me. I am firmly of the
opinion that the effective functioning of a Government
is only possible when the heads of Departments are upon
terms, not merely of formal interrelation, but of genuine
collaboration."

"How true," said Goebbels, "but——"

"But you did not favour me with minutes of your valuable time to hear my platitudinous remarks upon Govern-
mental efficiency. Exactly. With regard to the fire at the

Record House, I think there can be no doubt but that it was a case of deliberate arson."

Goebbels gulped slightly. "I had no idea that anybody doubted that for a moment," he said acidly. "The facts speak for themselves." The old fool Lehmann must be entering his dotage; it was inconceivable that he was daring to pull Goebbels' leg.

"Not necessarily," said the Chief of Police. "I have known facts which lied like—like Ananias, till one found out some more. However, I think we may safely assume this to have been arson. The two men who, presumably, caused it were so completely destroyed by fire as to be quite unrecognizable when found. Unfortunately, the sergeant who saw them through the letter-box slit also perished, so we shall never know whether he recognized them or not."

"So you've got no further in the matter?"

"On the contrary," said Hambledon, leaning back in his chair and putting the tips of his fingers together, "several interesting points have emerged. There have been, as no doubt Your Excellency knows, a number of cases of arson in various parts of Germany during the past twelve or fifteen months. I now know them to be the work of criminals already known to the authorities, since they were so anxious for the destruction of all records of such criminals as to be willing to take the risk involved in destroying by fire a large and important building in the——"

"Yes, yes, my dear Lehmann, but that is all rather vague, is it not? It would have been encouraging to hear that you had found out something a little more definite."

"Your Excellency brings me to a point which, if you had not done me the honour to visit me, I should have called upon you to discuss. A constable who was passing the Record House shortly before the alarm was given—

the same who found Reinhardt—noticed a car standing
by the roadside about fifty yards from the door, with
its engine running. He took its number."

"Well?"

"The moment the alarm was given the driver threw
in his clutch and drove off at a furious rate. My men regarded the incident as suspicious."

"Quite right."

"They could not chase him because they had no means
at their disposal, but they subsequently looked up the
number. It was that of a car belonging to one Eigenmann who is, I understand, one of Your Excellency's
private secretaries."

"The car must have been stolen," said Goebbels instantly.

"Inquiries were made," said Hambledon, fitting his
fingers together in a different order, "of Herr Eigenmann
personally as to his movements that evening, with a view
to elucidating that point. He told my representative that
he had spent that evening driving the car in question
to a house near Lindow where some of his cousins live."

"That is true——"

"That he arrived there soon after seven and did not
leave again for Berlin till after eleven. As Lindow is fully
sixty miles from Berlin——"

"It is plain," said Goebbels, "the car by the Record
House had false number-plates."

"That may be," said Hambledon. "I—forgive my careless inattention! Let me offer you a cigar. You may possibly prefer these, let me give you a light. I was about
to tell Your Excellency that a robbery took place near
Gransee that evening, and as the thieves had escaped in a
car all the roads were picketed and every car stopped.
Herr Eigenmann's car was not in that neighbourhood
that night."

"He exchanged cars for some reason," said Goebbels hastily. "Possibly he had a breakdown."

"He particularly assured my man that he had driven his own car all the way," said Tommy blandly. "We thought of that."

"This is ridiculous," said Goebbels angrily. "This is a mare's nest you have found, Herr Lehmann. I will ask Eigenmann to tell me clearly what happened, and inform you in due course."

"That is precisely what I was going to ask Your Excellency to do. If Herr Eigenmann was involved that night in some little indiscretion, it is natural he should not wish to tell the police about it, though, of course, it would be no concern of ours—probably. At the same time, I should be glad to have the fullest possible details of the movements of that car that night."

"Yes, yes, of course. Another point, what about that money?"

"We think it must have been the proceeds of a robbery. I am having inquiries made."

"If you find out nothing?"

"It reverts to the Treasury, of course, who will give me a receipt for it."

Goebbels looked as if he could have killed the Chief of Police, but merely said, "An odd complication. How much was there?"

"Eleven thousand eight hundred and twenty marks by the time it came into our hands, though apparently it was twelve thousand marks originally."

"How do you know?"

"I assume it by the notes on this card," said Hambledon, handing it to him. "The notes were held together— I fear you are not well, Herr Goebbels. You are quite pale. The cigar, perhaps——"

"I have a slight chill, it is nothing," said Goebbels carelessly. "Common names, all of these."

"It would have been better if we had had their initials also," agreed Hambledon.

"I will not take up more of your valuable time," said Goebbels, and took his leave.

"Considering," said Tommy after he had gone, "that you knew perfectly well Eigenmann was waiting with the rest of the hungry crew somewhere in Berlin for the cash to arrive, that's a pretty stout effort."

"Damn the fellow," thought Goebbels. "I'll get rid of him somehow, only he's so infernally incorruptible. Wonder if there's anything in his past; I'll have him looked up. Heidelberg man, by his scars. Before my time, of course. Wonder which Student Corps he was in?"

CHAPTER XIX
LAND AND FIELD CLUB

A WEEK LATER Jakob Altmann and Gregor Buergers came up again at the police-court to answer for their doings on the night of the fire. As it was perfectly obvious that they could not have had anything to do with the fire, not even with the sandbagging of Reinhardt, since they were far too inebriated at the time, they were merely charged with stealing by finding the sum of twelve thousand marks, the property of some person or persons unknown, Altmann as principal and Buergers as accessory. They were sentenced to periods of two years and nine months respectively of forced labour on the roads of Westphalia.

"Nice long way off," said Jakob, with a glance at Gertrud who was sitting in court weeping ostentatiously. "Thank you, gentlemen." Buergers said nothing.

It was another ten days before Hambledon received a reply from any of the various German banks to his question about the mark notes. Eventually, one of them reported that the notes in question, together with others of considerably larger denomination making a total of eighteen thousand five hundred marks altogether had been paid out on March the 25th to Herr Rolf Weinecke of Aachen. Since they knew that the inquiry came from the Chief of Police they added all the information they could give, particularly the numbers and denominations of the larger notes. They added that some of the notes

were again in circulation in Aachen, and that the whole
sum was produced by the sale of bearer bonds deposited
with them ten months earlier by the said Herr Weinecke.

"So," said Tommy to himself. "What proportion do
they allow these wretched Jews to get away with? Twenty
per cent, I believe. Now twenty per cent of eighteen thousand five hundred is—er—three thousand seven hundred." He wrote the figure down and looked at it.
"Strange. That's just the total of the few notes of really
large denomination. Now, if a Jew were bolting out of
Germany with the paltry marks allowed him by the Government, he would change one of his big notes as soon as
possible, I think. Going from Aachen, that would be
Brussels, or possibly Ostende if he were going to England. I'll try both. Twelve thousand plus three thousand
seven hundred is fifteen thousand and seven hundred.
Subtracted from eighteen thousand five hundred, it leaves
—er—two thousand eight hundred. I think Herr
Weinecke pocketed two thousand eight hundred marks
for his trouble—and the risk, of course. Dealing with a
Jew, naughty. Helping a Jew to evade the law, very
naughty."

Four days later he learned from his agents in Brussels
that an hundred-mark note, bearing one of the numbers
quoted, had been changed into Belgian money on March
29th last by a Jew named Reuben Schwartz, who was now
living in rooms in the Street of the Candle at Brussels,
having apparently settled there.

"Splendid," said Tommy Hambledon, and sent two of
his police to bring him the person of Rolf Weinecke from
Aachen, instantly, in haste. Next morning Rolf Weinecke,
ruffled and uneasy, was shown into Hambledon's office.
Hambledon did not ask him to sit down, but sent the
troopers away and came straight to the point in a voice
as hard and cold as stone.

"You are Rolf Weinecke from Aachen?"

"Yes, sir. May I ask——"

"No. I will do all the asking that may be needed. On Friday, March the 25th last, you went to your bank in Aachen and drew out the sum of eighteen thousand five hundred marks."

"I believe I did, but——"

"I know you did. This sum was made up of thirty-seven hundred-mark notes, fifty-six fifty-mark notes, and the rest in tens to the value of twelve thousand marks."

The man merely looked at him.

"This money was the proceeds of the sale of bearer bonds which you deposited with the bank about ten months ago."

"That is so," said Weinecke. "The bonds were——"

"You transferred the thirty-seven hundred-mark notes to a Jew named Reuben Schwartz, at present living in the Rue de la Bougie, Brussels."

"But, sir, that is——"

"You were about to admit that that is a crime against the State. Are you aware of the penalties attaching to it?"

"Yes, sir, but——"

"But what?"

"But there are so many people—it is so often done," stammered the man.

"It will be done a lot less in future, believe me. While I am Chief of Police I will not tolerate such irregularities, perhaps if an example is made in a few flagrant cases such as yours, it will be realized that I mean what I say. This practice will stop," said Hambledon incisively, and banged the table.

Weinecke looked as though if he had much more of this his knees would give way.

"But, sir, I am a good German and a good Nazi. I pay

all the taxes without grumbling, I subscribe to Party funds, I give generously to the Winter Help——"

"You cannot buy the right to sin," said Hambledon magnificently, "with these subscriptions. No man is a good German who gives help to the enemies of his country as you have done. The Jew, the Jew, always the Jew behind these abuses." ("Streicher ought to hear me now," he thought.) "What is there about these Jews that you must defile yourself by serving them? One would think you were a Jew yourself."

Weinecke's face turned green with terror. He had never liked his Jewish grandmother; when he was a little boy that heavy white face, the dark smouldering eyes, the hooked nose approaching the jutting chin, had seemed to him to embody all he had heard of witches; and the strange unknown rites from which he was rigidly excluded, but of which he heard garbled accounts from his Lutheran nurse, were doubtless witchcraft. The fact was that his mother hated her husband's Jewish connection and imbued the boy with her prejudices. Later in his life Weinecke realized that most of his ideas about the Jews were childish nonsense and his hysterical dislike reacted into a sort of inquisitive sympathy, but by that time his parents and the old grandmother were dead, and as he had never had any intercourse with his Jewish cousins the connection had dropped. It was, he believed, entirely unknown by the time the anti-Jewish agitation began in Germany. He would help a Jew if he could, just as he would a non-Jew, that is to say, if there were any money to be made out of it, but admit a Jewish connection, never, never. And now here was this terrible and powerful man, who knew everything, dragging out this ghastly secret also and shaking it in his face. His knees bent inwards, his back curved, his shoulders went up in spite of all efforts to straighten himself, and his eyes showed a line of white all along below the iris.

Tommy Hambledon watched this in amazement, for he had no idea that there was any truth in a suggestion he had merely thrown out to frighten the man. "I must be getting Jews on the brain," he thought. "The creature's turning into one before my eyes."

"Oh, I am not, gracious sir," protested Weinecke, "I am Aryan all through."

"Protest that to the court when you are brought before it. You must know that it will be quite easy to prove you are a Jew," said Hambledon, meaning merely that the evidence could be fabricated if necessary, but Weinecke took the words as proof that his ancestry was known. He still denied it, however, hysterically.

"I am not," he shrieked, instinctively turning up his palms in the age-old gesture of protest. "Revered sir, I am not, on the head of my father I swear——"

He stopped abruptly. On the head of my father, what evil demon had put the betraying phrase into his mouth? Tommy Hambledon leaned back in his chair. Evidently his chance arrow had sunk to the feather and he had got this man where he wanted him.

"You see," said the Chief of Police loftily, "it is useless to try to deceive the Reich. I think you are in rather bad case, Herr Rolf Weinecke."

The man actually fell on his knees. "I am a good Nazi, all the same," he wailed. "I never liked them—the Jews, I mean. It was only my grandmother, I couldn't help my grandfather marrying her, could I? Kind, gracious sir, you are too just to punish a poor man for what isn't his fault!" Tommy was, but he had no intention of showing it at the moment. "Let me off, don't tell anybody. I will do anything you wish, anything——"

"You are a disgusting and repulsive sight," said

Hambledon from the bottom of his heart. "However, I will give you one chance to serve the Reich, just one. If you satisfy me fully in that, it may incline me to mercy."

"Tell me what you want," said Weinecke instantly, rising to his feet and clasping his hands in a gesture of submission.

"Put your hands down by your sides for a start," snapped Hambledon, who found the man more intolerable every moment. "Stand up straight and answer my questions. You will not, I think, lie to me. Now, about the twelve thousand marks you sent to Berlin——"

Weinecke supplied a great deal of very useful information. He was the head of the Aachen branch of the organization which fleeced the Jews at the expense of the Government, for that was what it amounted to. The Jews declared to the Government for forfeit, a mere fraction of their actual possessions. Weinecke, and others in similar positions on every German frontier, not only connived at this but actively assisted the Jews by banking the rest of the money as their own. When the moment came for the Jew to leave Germany, he was given one-fifth of his property to take with him and the organization applied the rest to its own uses. Weinecke explained that they always—or nearly always—kept faith with the Jews, and gave them so high a proportion as twenty per cent, to induce other Jews to deal with them in the same way. It paid the Jew and it paid them.

"Yes," thundered Hambledon, "and the only one that suffers is the Government of the Reich, and what do you care for that? Go on. These people in Berlin."

Weinecke said plainly that Herr Goebbels was the brain behind the affair, but never appeared openly. The Berlin Committee, so to express it, were the eight gentlemen whose names the gracious Herr had deigned to read to him—Gagel, Dettmer, Kitzinger, Tietz, Rautenbach,

Militz, Baumgartner and Eigenmann. They received, of course, subscriptions from all parts of Germany, not only from Aachen, at their monthly meetings. This twelve thousand marks in which the Herr was interested was not, naturally, the whole of the month's supply from Aachen, as amounts were transmitted weekly. It so happened that in that week there was only one windfall, but a large one.

"So when they got there the cupboard wasn't really bare," said Tommy to himself. "Only one plum missing. When's the next meeting?" he added aloud. Weinecke said, as Hambledon expected, May the 4th. It was the second date on the card found with the money.

"Where do they meet?"

"I don't know, honoured sir, I've never heard. On my honour I've no idea."

"Your honour! You mean, on the head of your father."

Weinecke, to whom speech had given a certain amount of confidence, shrivelled up again, and Hambledon improved the moment by extracting full details of the Aachen end of the business, names, addresses and all, with a view to effective action. "Now," he said, "what about Ginsberg?"

"Ginsberg?"

"Ginsberg was a member of the Frontier Guard at Aachen. He was shot at Aachen in August last year—nine months ago."

"Oh, I remember now. Ginsberg, yes. He took it upon himself to disapprove of this business. He made trouble. He was one of those would-be superior people——"

"Silence!" roared Hambledon, really angry this time. "He was my servant, and you dared——"

"Oh, my God, what have I done? I did not know, noble sir, I didn't know—I didn't do it, I didn't even complain of him, Schultz did that, I had nothing to do with it, Schultz complained to the local court and they shot him, I didn't, I——"

Hambledon touched the bell-push on his desk; two troopers came in promptly. Hambledon pointed one finger at Weinecke and said, "Take him away, he annoys me. Return for orders."

Weinecke collapsed on the carpet and was dragged, howling and struggling, from the room. Hambledon poured himself out a drink and swallowed it, lit a cigar and took a turn or two up and down the room till the trooper returned and saluted.

"The man is guilty of murder," said the Chief of Police. "He will be shot at eight to-morrow morning."

The trooper saluted again and went back to his mate in the ante-room outside.

"Speakin' generally," he said, "the Chief is easy though stric', an' not given to tempers, not like some I could mention. But when he gets going proper, *Herrgott,* give me Goering!"

Hambledon took another turn across the room.

"There is also Schultz," he said to himself. "One of these days, Ginsberg my servant, I will deal with Schultz."

A day or two later he spoke to Franz. "I think you once told me that you and your friends between you served most of the Nazi leaders in private service."

"That is so, sir."

"If it so happened that among your patrons were any of these men, it would be interesting to know where and when they are going to meet on May the 4th. Their names are Gagel, Dettmer, Kitzinger, Tietz, Rautenbach, Militz, Baumgartner and Eigenmann."

"On May the 4th," said Franz.

"On May the 4th—that's next Thursday. To-day's Saturday. Not too much time."

"I will do my best to ascertain, sir."

"Thank you. It will, I fear, be my painful duty to arrest eight members of your German Freedom League at that meeting."

"Sir?" said the startled Franz.

"Yes. Their names are Gagel, Dettmer—and so on. I repeated them to you just now."

"I should be very surprised, sir, to learn that any of these gentlemen are Freedom League members."

"Not half so surprised as they will be, Franz, if all goes well."

Franz stared at his master for a moment, and then broke into a low but distinct chuckle. "To serve you, sir, if I may take the liberty of saying so, is not merely a duty, but a pleasure."

"I reciprocate your sentiments," said Tommy solemnly. " 'You're exceedingly polite,' " he hummed, as the man left the room, " 'and I think it only right to return the compliment.' Some day, please God, I'll sit in the stalls at the Savoy again and see a Gilbert and Sullivan opera right through from the overture to 'God Save the King.' "

There was a small lecture-hall attached to the Rektor Art School in Berlin, a room about thirty feet by twenty, with a stage at one end adorned by a backcloth representing the Rhine at Ehrenbreitstein, and double entrance doors at the other. There was also, of course, a door at each side of the stage giving on to dressing-rooms behind, two bare rooms with looking-glasses on the walls and pegs for hats and coats. One of these rooms communicated with the Art School, the other had a door which opened into a side street. This door was kept locked, but Tommy Hambledon had seen to it that the lock was well oiled, and what is more, he had a key to it, for it was in this hall that the Land and Field Club held their monthly meetings.

"Land and Field Club," said Tommy, when this was reported to him. "Lynx and Fox Club. Association of Stoats and Weasels. Thank you, Franz."

There was a full meeting on the night of May the 4th. Eigenmann as chairman and Rautenbach as treasurer sat at a table in front of the stage to conduct proceedings, while the other six grouped themselves in gracefully negligent attitudes on the chairs facing them. The entrance doors at the end of the hall were guarded outside, but not the side door giving to the dressing-room, since that, of course, was locked. Eigenmann had tried it himself. The table was covered with papers, interesting and informative in themselves, and there were also eight fat little packets of notes which the company found even more interesting than the papers. Business was proceeding in an atmosphere of peace, comfort and security. "A good month, on the whole," said Rautenbach, settling his eyeglass more securely in his right eye. "I will begin as usual with the ports. Stettin, seventeen thousand five hundred marks. Lübeck, two thousand six-fifty. Kiel, seven thousand two-seventy-five. Hamburg, twenty-four thousand three hundred. Bremen, only seven——"

Rautenbach saw Dettmer, facing him, suddenly sit up and stare past him towards the stage with a look of horror.

"——hundred and twenty," finished Rautenbach, turning his head to see what the other was looking at. Dettmer had seen the left-hand door open quietly, Rautenbach saw a file of police come rapidly through it, jump off the stage, and hurl themselves on the assembled company, including himself. Eigenmann, having his back to the stage, was taken completely by surprise and promptly handcuffed, but the others put up a good fight and there ensued a very notable uproar. In the struggle the table was upset and papers and money slid to the floor in a heap; the gigantic Tietz, flinging from him the two policemen who had attached themselves to his arms, made a dive

at this and started tearing up papers with the muddle-
headed idea of destroying evidence. One of the police immediately hit him on the head with the leg of a chair,
and Tietz passed into unconsciousness still clasping a
double handful of lists and memoranda, snatched up
haphazard from the ground.

When the fracas died down and the prisoners had been
quelled and handcuffed, victors and victims, alike panting, saw the Chief of Police return to the stage. His
dignity was a little marred by his collar, which stuck out
at right-angles behind his left ear, but he surveyed the
scene with a benignity which the Land and Field Club
disliked intensely.

"Well, well," he said. "Dear me, you have done it
now, haven't you? Sergeant, have those papers on the floor
carefully collected and taken to the police station; they
are important evidence. Let a bucket of water be poured
over the large gentleman, it may revive him. I think
the gentlemen's coats are in the cloakroom we came
through; they may resume them and then be handcuffed
again. The gentlemen will be searched at the station,
locked up for the night and charged to-morrow afternoon, I will go through the evidence in the morning. I
suppose the smaller fry outside the door have also been
netted? Good. I commend the police for their efficiency.
I am now going home. Good night, gentlemen."

Herr Goebbels was not himself present at the police-
court proceedings the following afternoon, but he went
nearly insane with anger when his representative gave an
account of what had taken place.

"The Herr Polizei Oberhaupt himself gave evidence.
He gave a detailed account of the way the Jewish money
business is worked, and it appears he pounced at Aachen
last night too. Every member of the organization there
was hauled out of bed and arrested. Schultz evaded the

police and came up here on a motor-cycle, riding all night, to report it. But that is not the worst."

"What——"

"All the papers at the Rektor Art School Hall were of course impounded, and the eight men are charged, not with defrauding the State of the Jews' money as you'd expect, but with being members of the German Freedom League."

"*What?*"

"The German Freedom League. Not ordinary members, either, but a sort of local executive committee. Important documentary evidence was found, not only on the table but also in the gentlemen's pockets, and worse still, in the houses of some of them when they were searched. Eigenmann's, Rautenbach's and Baumgartner's, to be exact."

"What happened?"

"The magistrate sentenced them to ten years in a concentration camp, each. I don't know what's happened to our people at Aachen."

"Damn the people at Aachen," said Goebbels hoarsely. "Go away and let me think this out—if I can," he added, as the man went. "Freedom League! That devil Lehmann has worked this somehow. It can't be true. It's impossible. No, it's not impossible, but I don't believe it. Eigenmann would never—but he's easily led. Rautenbach is capable of it, but he wouldn't dare. On the other hand, where do the Freedom League get their funds from? Must be from something like this and somebody runs it, why not Rautenbach? No, it's ridiculous. Lehmann has done this somehow, and the Leader will be so pleased. Who are those two men——" He rang the bell and his informant returned.

"Who were those two men we put into Lehmann's police? Send for them at once, I want to speak to them."

"They may be on duty——"

"I said, send for them!"

They came, and found Goebbels white and shaking with fury.

"What do you know about these arrests last night?"

"We were there, sir. We were among the police selected for the duty."

"Oh, were you? Good. Now, those Freedom League papers were planted. Tell me how it was done."

"They couldn't have been, sir. There was some among the papers on the table and some in the gentlemen's pockets."

"They were put there beforehand."

"If you say so, sir. But why didn't the gentlemen see them on the table?"

"They were brought in afterwards."

"Impossible, sir. I found some of them myself, almost before the fight was over."

"They were——" Goebbels fought for self-control and stopped. "You may go," he said, and the men were glad to do so.

"It seems true," he said. "But I don't believe it. This is Lehmann's work; pompous, sententious devil, always talking about virtue and morality, blast him. Rautenbach could do it—— If it's the last thing I do in this life I'll get Lehmann——"

"Quite easy," said Tommy to Reck. "I distributed papers in their coats while my gallant police charged in, then I followed them into the fray, fell over the table, which upset, papers cascaded from under my overcoat and the helpful Tietz clasped them to his bosom. Always remember this, Reck, my pippin. When men are fighting, they aren't *looking*."

CHAPTER XX   THE SCAVENGER

GOEBBELS' EIGHT FRIENDS arrived at the concentration camp; a group of pampered, arrogant men who hid their uneasiness behind a screen of defiance. The Camp Commandant looked them over and decided he did not like them, after which they ceased at once to be pampered, their arrogance vanished, and even their defiance wore thin.

In one part of the camp there was a row of cells with a warders' room at the end which was sometimes used for interviewing prisoners. It was a bare, ugly room with a wide window in front looking on to the parade ground; at the back of the room was a row of horizontal ventilating windows well above eye-level, set wide open on this sunny May morning. Outside the back wall of this room, below the ventilators, a wide garden bed ran the whole length of the row of cells, and here one of the prisoners, with a line, a dibber, and a can of water, was setting out young cabbages.

He heard talking inside the room but took no interest at first in what was said. Nothing that anybody said could ever make him less of a Jew, and as that was the only offence he had committed there was no atonement possible. He had a large share of the fatalism of his race; he knew perfectly well that compared with most of his fellows he was extremely lucky so long as the same Camp

Commandant remained, and he had sunk into an uneasy apathy with his lot, broken only by occasional frenzied attacks of craving for freedom, freedom, and the air again. So he worked on placidly, sometimes murmuring to the cabbages about their roots, till his attention was attracted by a voice raised higher than before.

"Of course they were planted, Herr Goebbels! The police brought them in."

Goebbels. Talking to his prisoner friends, no doubt. The gardener moved even more quietly than before and listened.

"Not the police," said Goebbels' incisive voice. "That swine Lehmann."

There followed a confused murmur, presumably of assent, and presently Goebbels went on:

"I have been looking up his past. He joined the Party at Munich in the early days, he was a curator in the Deutches Museum then. Before that again, in '18, he worked in the Naval Establishment at Hamburg. It is known that he came there from a hospital at Ostende, so presumably he had been wounded, but what branch he served in or where he came from, I can't find out. The hospital staff scattered and the books were lost or destroyed when we retreated at the end of the war, and he never talks about himself."

"Sounds like a thoroughly worthy citizen," said somebody, with a sneer.

"It does seem as though there's nothing in his past to bring up against him—unlike most of us," said Goebbels, with a sardonic laugh. "Besides, if there were it wouldn't do any good, the Leader trusts him."

"So you've just got to sit down under it," said a deep voice, "while we rot in here."

"I can't attempt to get you out while he's in office," said Goebbels, "but I'm certainly not going to sit down

under it, Tietz. I'm going to do something very definite
quite soon; in July, to be exact. If I don't, he'll frame me
next, and then where will you be?"

"Showing you round the camp, I expect," someone said,
and laughed.

"There is a very important commission going to Danzig
in July," said the voice of Goebbels, "they are going to—
er—arrange and expedite future events. They are arriving
unostentatiously, so they can't have the usual conspicuous
guards, but as they are very important I think I can persuade the Führer to send the Chief of Police with them in
person. While he is there he will be assassinated by the
ill-mannered Danzigers."

"How will you persuade them that he's the right man
to assassinate?"

"I shan't attempt it, of course, I shall send two men to
do it, and the Danzigers can take the blame. The anti-
Nazi Danzigers, that is. I'll send Schultz for one, he's done
one or two little jobs for me before, and I'll find someone
to go with him."

"Thought Schultz was at Aachen," said another voice.
"Wasn't he roped in with the rest?"

"No, he wasn't at home that night when they called for
him and the rumour got round. He hopped on a motor-
cycle and left for Berlin, he's there now."

"Why wait till Lehmann goes to Danzig?" asked the
deep voice. "Why not do it now and let us get out of
this filthy hole?"

"Do you want a heresy-hunt started in Berlin, with
everyone looking round to see whom Lehmann has annoyed recently? Don't be a fool——"

Two guards turned the corner and came strolling down
the path towards the cabbage-planter, who suddenly
awoke to the fact that he had not done a stroke of work
for ten minutes, so he hastily went on planting. The

guards passed him without comment, but stopped a little farther on to discuss some matter of dog-breeding, he had to appear industrious in their presence. In a few minutes the voices in the room ceased and he heard a car drive off, the interview was over. He ought to have been grateful to Goebbels, who had given him that priceless boon in a prisoner's life, something fresh to think about, instead of which he spent many hopeful hours invoking new and ingenious curses on the sleek black head of the Minister of Propaganda.

It was nearly a week later that the camp had another distinguished visitor, the Herr Polizei Oberhaupt. He drove his own car, an Opel saloon, and went a little out of his way to drop the Fräulein Ludmilla Rademeyer at the small house where her friend, the Frau Beckensburg, was living in terrified obscurity.

"I am very unhappy about Christine, dear. She has aged so you would hardly know her, in fact she seems to be breaking up. I am really afraid if you can't do something soon she won't live much longer."

"Tell her to be brave and hold on," said Tommy. "I hope it won't be much longer now. I am going to the camp this afternoon mainly to see the Beckensburgs and have a look round the place, I hope that may give me an idea. It's not easy, even for the Chief of Police, to get two Jews out of a concentration camp."

"I know, dear, I know. I feel a tiresome old woman to keep on worrying you about her, but we have been friends for nearly sixty years. After all, you must have much more important things to deal with——"

"Don't talk like that," said Hambledon almost roughly. "I haven't forgotten a winter's day at Dusseldorf when we were cold and starving. Someone gave us firing and food—do you remember the real butter? When I forget that——"

"Klaus dear," said the old lady, "I wish it wasn't so public, I should like to kiss you."

"Better not, I should probably run us into a lamp-post. Here you are, give her my love and tell her to hold on a little longer. Shall I call for you on my way back?"

"No, don't bother, I'll take a taxi. Had I better take the rug with me?"

"No, why? It'll be all right in the car—I'll throw it in the back."

"Well, don't lose it, Klaus. I shall see you this evening, then."

The guard at the gate of the camp stood to attention as the Chief of Police drove his car past them and up the drive. He pulled up outside the Commandant's office and went in without delay; he had various matters to attend to besides the welfare of the Beckensburgs, with whom he wanted a short interview. He also wanted a much clearer idea than he had previously had about the way the camp was run, it would be quite impossible to make even the simplest plan for getting the Beckensburgs out until he knew exactly what he had to cope with. Induce the Commandant to talk, that's the idea. Quite a decent fellow, by all accounts, considering his job . . .

Hambledon was so deep in thought that he saw without noticing a prisoner who was wandering about the drive with a sack over his shoulder, armed with a stick which had a long steel spike at the end, his job was to collect any stray bits of paper which might be blowing about. The prisoner recognized the Chief of Police, and his face lit up, but he made no move to attract Hambledon's attention and merely went on with his work while the Chief of Police disappeared within doors.

The sun shone and the wind blew. Two warders came up with two prisoners, father and son, the Beckensburgs, summoned to an interview with the Herr Polizei Oberhaupt. The guards at the gate left off looking up the drive and turned their attention elsewhere, in the distance a line of men were digging, watched by armed warders. Their bodies moved rhythmically, their spades flashed in the sun; a peaceful scene if one did not know what was hidden behind it. The man with the spike worked gradually nearer to the car.

Presently a raucous bell clanged from a turret on the top of the office; the diggers straightened their backs, shouldered their spades, and marched off out of sight. All over the camp unhappy men ceased work and gathered in long sheds with trestle tables down the middle, for it was the hour of what passes for supper in a concentration camp.

The scavenger ceased work with the rest, cleared a few fragments of paper from his steel spike into the sack, and walked towards the car, he had to go that way, there was nothing suspicious about that. When he was close to the Opel he cast an anxious glance at the guards by the gate, but Providence prompted an enthusiastic young Air Force officer, passing overhead, to loop the loop at that moment, and the men were watching him. The prisoner dodged round the car, opened one of the rear doors, and shot in, taking his sack and his unpleasant-looking weapon with him. He threw himself on the floor, and by putting one foot against the door-post, managed to shut the door properly without slamming it. After that, he covered himself, the sack and his tool completely with Frau Rademeyer's rug, made himself as small and flat as possible, and waited with a beating heart, for the car's owner to return.

Unendurable ages dragged past before he heard footsteps and voices, the Chief of Police being seen off by the Camp Commandant in person. They stood on the doorstep while the Commandant talked about his pet system of checking prisoners several times a day. "There is one call-over almost due now," he said, "at the end of supper; would it amuse you to see it? It is rather——"

"If he does," thought the prisoner, "if he does I shall be missed, they will hunt, I shall be found here, God of mercy, make him say no. Make him say no——"

"——staggered times for guard-changing," continued the Commandant, "so that there is no moment of the day or night when all the guards at once are distracted from their duty."

"Admirable," said the Chief of Police, "quite admirable. The organization and management of this camp should be a model for every such camp in Germany. But no, my dear fellow, I mustn't stay any longer, taking up more of your valuable time. Besides, I also have one or two unimportant matters to see to this evening——"

"I have detained you too long——"

"On the contrary——"

"I bore everybody with my systems——"

"Everything I have seen has been of absorbing interest."

"But where is your driver?" asked the Commandant, laying his hand on the handle of the rear door.

"I drive myself," said the Chief of Police, "whenever possible. It fidgets me to sit in state in the back of a car with someone else driving."

"All really good drivers feel that. Will you not have the rug over your knees? These May evenings turn chilly."

"No, thank you, your excellent Niersteiner—besides, it would be in the way." Hambledon started the engine. *"Auf wiedersehen*, Herr Commandant, and thank you." He moved the gear lever.

"A pleasure," said the Commandant, standing at the salute, and at that moment the bell rang again. "That is for the call-over, will you not—no. *Auf wiedersehen*, Herr Polizei Oberhaupt."

"Oh, God," whispered the prisoner under the rug. "Oh, God, all this politeness; oh, God——"

Hambledon let in the clutch, turned the car and went slowly down the drive. He had to stop at the gate to let some traffic go by, and one of the guards came up to the car to say something civil to the distinguished visitor. The prisoner broke into a perspiration so violent that he could feel it running off his face, till at last the car moved off, turned into the road, changed into second—third—top. Hambledon leaned back in his seat and said, "Thank God that's over. Foul place," aloud, but the prisoner did not hear him, for he had fainted.

He came back to consciousness with a violent start from a dreadful dream that he had been buried alive in a coffin too short for him, flung back the rug and sat up. The next instant he remembered where he was and sank back again at once. There was, however, no need now to stifle under the rug, at least not for the present, and he drew long breaths of the cool night air. Street lights appeared and the traffic increased, they were approaching Berlin. "I ought to have stopped him in the country," thought the prisoner, "where we'd have been alone, it's too late now, too many people about. If he opens the door himself it'll be all right, but if a servant opens it——"

They passed swiftly through the streets, for the car of the Chief of Police was given precedence, occasionally the prisoner risked a glance out of the window and recognized buildings he knew. They went through the Government quarter without stopping. "Good," said the prisoner, "he's going straight home." He lay down again on the floor and arranged the rug carefully over himself.

At last the car slowed down in a quiet street and came to a stop before the entrance to a block of flats. The driver switched off the engine, opened the door, kneeled upon the seat where he had been sitting, and snatched the rug off the prisoner with the words: "Hands up! I've got you covered!"

The prisoner obeyed at once, for he could see an ugly but familiar object in Hambledon's hand.

"Now! Who are you, and what the devil are you doing in my car?"

"Squadron-Leader Lazarus, sir, and I've escaped from the camp."

"Lazarus," said Hambledon thoughtfully. "Lazarus. I've heard——"

"Sir, I must speak to you privately, I've something desperately important to tell you. Do let me speak to you and then let me go, I'll take my chance, I don't want to be a bother to you."

"Squadron-Leader Lazarus," repeated Hambledon, in the voice of a man trying to remember something. "Yes, better come up to my flat." He opened the rear door of the car for the man to get out and walked up the stairs a little behind him, still unostentatiously keeping him covered with the automatic. "Ring the bell, will you?" said Hambledon, because it is not easy to hold a latch-key and a pistol in the same hand at once, or to watch a prisoner and look at what you're doing at the same time. When Franz came to the door, however, Hambledon slipped the automatic in his pocket, though he still kept his hand upon it.

"Franz, show this gentleman into the study, and bring in some—what'll you drink? Whisky and soda?"

"Don't believe I've tasted it since '18, I'd love some," said Lazarus with a smile.

Hambledon's face cleared, the reference to '18 supplied the clue for which he had been searching. "Of course," he said, "of course, I remember now. You were at Darmstadt the day the Allied Commission came to destroy your machines, Goering was there, you had a little trouble with him if I remember correctly."

"Were you also a pilot?" said Lazarus, staring at him. "I am so sorry—I ought to remember you, no doubt——"

"No, no, I was—I merely happened to be there. I was not in the Air Force and had not the honour of being presented to you."

The Squadron-Leader smiled bitterly. "I think that was the last day upon which it was an honour to be presented to me," he said. "Now I am only a Jew, and who says Jew says muck."

"Is that the only reason why you were sent to that camp? Have a drink."

The man nodded. "You can see it in the records. Not too much, please, I'm not used to it now, and I have something to tell you."

"Sit down and drink that first," said Hambledon. "You look all in. Had a rotten time, of course."

"Not too bad," said Lazarus. "I was lucky. The Commandant was one of my Flight-Lieutenants, and he did make things as easy for me as he could. Never got anything really foul to do, gardening most of the time, gave me cigarettes sometimes, and the guards looked the other way if they caught me smoking behind the tool-shed— talk about catching me, how did you know I was in the car?"

"Saw you reflected in the driving-mirror when you sat up," explained Tommy. "Knew you must have stowed away at the camp. Quite safe, nobody slays the driver of a fast car when it's moving. That's why I drove so fast," he added with a disarming smile. "I was wondering whether you'd brought your spike with you, you were the man in the drive, weren't you?"

Lazarus nodded. "It's in the car, I had to bring it. And

the sack, of course. Now, what I had to tell you was this. You know, of course, that eight of Goebbels' men are in the camp?"

Tommy smiled. "I should know, I sent them there."

"Yes? Well, Goebbels came down to see them the other day, he talked to them in a warders' room there for privacy, but I was planting cabbages at the back and I heard a good deal of what was said." He repeated the conversation as accurately as he could, and Hambledon listened intently.

"Schultz," he said, when Lazarus had finished. "Schultz. It's rather a coincidence that he should be looking for me, because I am looking for him. I have a little bill to pay Herr Schultz. It is also borne in upon me, Squadron-Leader Lazarus, that I am also deeply indebted to you. Even if I'd seen Schultz, it might not have occurred to me that he was after my blood. Wonder how he'll set about it? Apparently I'm safe till we all arrive in Danzig—first I've heard of that, too. Thank you. I must do something about you first."

"If I could get out of the country," said Lazarus eagerly, "into Switzerland, say, but it doesn't matter where, I'd be all right. I think I'd go to America and get a pilot's job, fancy flying again——"

"Of course," said Hambledon slowly. "You can still fly, can't you? One doesn't get hopelessly out of practice, does one? I know nothing about it."

"No, at least, not for a long time, especially if you've done a lot, and I was a regular commercial pilot till they pounced on me two years ago. I've kept fit, too, I told you I was lucky, they never knocked me about, in the camp I mean."

"Do you think you could fly a plane to Switzerland?"

"Yes, sir," said Lazarus promptly. "I was on the Swiss route the last nine months I was flying."

"Good. You'll have to hide up while I make arrangements, you may have to fly two old ladies across the frontier—this way up, handle gently, fragile, do not bump, eggs with care, you understand?"

"They shall not know they've touched the ground," said Lazarus with shining eyes, "till the bus stops."

"In the meantime," said Hambledon, "it's the loft under the roof for you, I'm afraid, but we'll make you as comfortable as we can. There's a wireless set up there already, but we'll add a few more amenities. Come along and meet a friend of mine who'll look after you; his name is Reck."

"So Goebbels is looking into my past and finding it inconveniently blameless," said Hambledon to Reck, when Lazarus had been fed, stowed away, and provided with a few comforts. "I wonder how long it will be before it occurs to him to look up my fingerprints?"

CHAPTER XXI   FINGERPRINTS

THE BEDSIDE TELEPHONE RANG furiously. Tommy
Hambledon awakened with a start and reached out
for the receiver, throwing at the same moment a re-
proachful glance at the clock which said, with an air of
apology, that the time was 5.45 a.m. "Chief of Police,"
grunted Hambledon into the telephone, and sank back on
his pillow. "Did I what? Collect four prisoners yesterday
from the concentration camp. No, why? I don't collect
prisoners, I prefer postage-stamps, and at the moment I
am trying to collect a little sleep. Why, have you lost
some? Well, inform the Commandant. Oh, you are the
Commandant. Good morning. It is always a pleasure to
me, Herr Commandant, to have any dealings with you,
but my office opens for official business at nine every
morning, and in the meantime surely the local police
station—— Oh, you have. Well, you could hardly expect
them to find the men in five minutes. No, I am not in
the least annoyed, but I do try to keep regular hours,
and 5.45 a.m. is—— Yes, but why ring me up? I can only
tell the police to look for them, and I assume they are
doing that already, you surely don't expect me to leap
out of bed and chase the men myself in my pyjamas.
Sign the order? It is not necessary for me to sign any
order for the pursuit of escaped prisoners; upon receipt
of news that prisoners have escaped, the necessary action

is taken at once. Did I sign an order yesterday? Yes, dozens. To remove four men from your camp? Certainly not."

There came a bubbling noise from the ear-piece of the instrument, and Hambledon rolled over on his pillow and sighed patiently in a manner which he hoped would be audible at the other end.

"Let me see if I have got this clear," said Hambledon eventually. "A sergeant and six men in the uniform of my police came to the camp yesterday morning—at 10.30 a.m. precisely. Well, that's in the morning, isn't it? They produced an order, purporting to be signed by me and bearing my seal, for the removal of four prisoners, whom you duly handed over. The sergeant signed a receipt and marched off with the prisoners, and you haven't seen them since. Well, I'm afraid you've been had, and I will certainly look into the matter with my accustomed energy when I arrive at the office, but I cannot believe that the Reich will totter on its foundations if I get another two hours' sleep first, what's all the hurry about? Herr Goebbels? What the devil's he got to do with it?"

The crackles at the other end explained that Herr Goebbels had happened to be on the premises when the prisoners had been taken away, and had appeared interested. That the sergeant in charge had explained that the prisoners were only required for interrogation and would be returned that evening if possible. That when they were not so returned, the Commandant had examined the order and thought there was something a little unusual about the Herr Polizei Oberhaupt's signature, and finally, that Herr Goebbels had rung up in the small hours to ask if the prisoners——

"Will you please understand this," said Hambledon in a tone of voice which silenced the other as by violence, "unworthy as I am, I hold my office direct from our

Leader, and am not subjected to question, command, or comment from the Ministry of Propaganda or any other Ministry whatever within the Reich or outside it!"

He paused, but as the other end of the wire maintained a tactful silence, he slammed down the receiver and lay back on his pillows sizzling with anger. It was perfectly plain that what had happened was that Goebbels had faked the order and the sergeant's guard of police; they had taken away four prisoners who would never, of course, be seen again, and Hambledon would be accused of having connived at their escape. Quite good, with only two mistakes. One, being so eager to see that everything went well that he had to be there in person at 10.30 a.m., and the other, forging the Chief of Police's signature so clumsily that even the Commandant noticed it. No, that might not be a mistake. If Klaus Lehmann denied the signature, saying that anyone could see it wasn't his, Goebbels would say that, of course, he wrote it like that on purpose, in order to be able to deny it. A typical Goebbels touch.

There remained the seal of his office, and there were two facsimiles of this. One was kept securely in safe-deposit by the Government in case Lehmann's should be destroyed or irretrievably lost, the other was held by the Führer, who had duplicates of all seals of office. There was, however, one minor difference between them, and it was just possible, though unlikely, that Goebbels did not know this. The seal actually in use by each Government office was quite perfect; the copies held by the Führer had each one tiny dot in the angle of the left-hand arm of the swastika, and the copies in safe-deposit had two dots in the same place. One glance at the wax impression on the order would tell him which one Goebbels had used, probably the Führer's, borrowed without permission. If so, the engineer would be hoist with his own petard indeed.

Hambledon's own seal never left him; even at night it was in his bedroom, so Goebbels could not possibly have got at that, and the one in official keeping was quite out of the question.

Hambledon, with a seraphic smile on his lips, fell peacefully asleep and did not wake till Franz called him at seven-thirty.

Hambledon breakfasted in haste, telephoned the office to say he would be there later, and drove himself to the concentration camp. To his annoyance, his car was stopped at the gates instead of being passed through at sight.

"What is all this?"

"New regulations, sir. Too many escapes lately; all cars to be searched."

"Excellent. Though I never heard of anyone trying to smuggle himself into a concentration camp."

"No, sir," said the corporal stolidly. "But we was told to look for tools and such-like."

Hambledon said no more, but sat fuming while the men looked under cushions and carpets. When he was allowed to proceed to the Commandant's door, he found another man on duty there who quite openly took charge of his car till he should need it again. Hambledon remembered the escape of Lazarus three weeks earlier, surely no rumour of that had got back. Lazarus, with the two old ladies, Ludmilla and Christine, had been safe in Switzerland these ten days, but he would not have talked. No, this was just another of the Commandant's systems.

The Chief of Police was shown into the office, where a wild-eyed Commandant greeted him in very much the manner of a dog who has torn up a sofa-cushion while master was out.

"I cannot describe to you," babbled the Commandant,

"how distressed I was to have had to—at such an hour—
I did not know what—those prisoners——"

"My dear fellow," said Hambledon kindly, "please
don't distress yourself. It is I who ought to apologize, I
am always like a bear with a sore head before breakfast."

"Your Excellency is too kind——"

"You were, of course, perfectly right——"

"Only the most imperative commands of duty
would——"

"I know, I know. It was the doubt about my signature
which rightly impelled you to communicate with me at
once."

"And the prisoners, Herr Polizei Oberhaupt."

"And the prisoners, of course. Yours is a great responsibility, Herr Commandant. Now, if I might see this
forged order, some idea might——"

"Certainly, certainly," said the Commandant, snatching up a bunch of keys and attacking a safe with them,
"but those two prisoners——"

"Two? I thought you said four."

"There were four. I was thinking of the two whom
you interviewed three weeks ago, I understood you to say
you might wish to see them again."

Hambledon turned perfectly cold. The Commandant,
getting no answer to his remark, explained more fully.

"The Beckensburgs, you remember. Ludovic Beckensburg, the father, retired architect, and his son, Hugo
Beckensburg——"

His voice continued for some time, but Hambledon did
not heed it. Goebbels must have found out that the
Beckensburgs had been friends of his, so he had taken
them, partly, no doubt, to make the accusation seem more
credible, but mainly to annoy; the rat-faced, crafty,
sneering devil. Well, this time he'd overstepped the mark;
Germany was no longer big enough to hold Goebbels and

himself. Goebbels—— Hambledon awoke to the fact that he was being offered a paper, he shook himself together and took it.

"This is an unmistakable forgery," he said mechanically, and went on staring at the paper while his mind was screaming questions. Where were they now? Alive or dead, or being tortured to make them talk about Klaus Lehmann?

"I fear Your Excellency is really not well," said the Commandant, who was watching his face. "A little cognac, perhaps——"

"Thank you, no," said Hambledon hastily. "A touch of indigestion; it will pass." He thrust the Beckensburgs to the back of his mind. The seal, there was something to notice about the seal. Oh, yes, of course, a dot in the corner.

"This wax impression is very rough," he said, and carried the paper to the window. It was rough, but there was definitely no dot where one should be, so it was not stamped with the Führer's seal, but with his own, or with an exact copy.

"The seal is a forgery, too," said Hambledon, and took his own from his pocket. "Look, Herr Commandant, it does not fit."

He laid the seal gently upon the wax impression, but it did not bed down as it should have done. "You see? Another forgery."

"But how could such a thing——"

"Quite simple, provided you have a good wax impression. You take a mould from the impression, warm modeller's wax, or a softened candle will do. You take a cast from that in plaster of Paris, and cast it again in lead. Quite simple, but it won't, of course, be so smooth and full of detail as the original."

"The criminal was too clever," said the Commandant happily. "His misguided ingenuity has resulted in entirely clearing Your Excellency of any complicity in the matter."

"Who suggested I was an accomplice?" asked Hambledon coldly, and took his leave without waiting for an answer from the abashed Commandant.

"This is the same idea as the clumsily forged signature," he thought, as he waited for the car to be searched again at the gate. "Goebbels will say I forged it myself in order to be able to disavow it."

He passed a gloomy day at the office wondering how he was to tell poor old Frau Christine of the disaster; the only satisfaction he obtained was in arranging for Frau Magda Beckensburg and the children to be sent out of the country at once. "They shall have something saved out of the wreck," he said, and sent two men he could trust to arrest the little party and put them over the Swiss frontier as quickly as possible. He was pleasantly surprised when this went off without a hitch, and still more astonished when several days passed without any accusation being brought against him. No police investigation into the matter produced any result at all, he did not suppose it would, nor were any of the prisoners recaptured.

Hambledon remained depressed by the whole affair, even when it began to seem possible that it held no evil consequences for him. He felt he had failed in his promise to look after the two men, and the idea that Goebbels had outwitted him was intensely irritating. The flat, too, was a dull place without Ludmilla there, and a letter from her including the phrase, "Dear Klaus, how kind and resourceful you are," doubtless referred to the safe arrival of Magda, complete with babies. No doubt Franz noticed his master's low spirits, and one night, when the servant brought in the evening whisky and soda, he hung about the room and coughed as he did when there was something he wanted to say.

"What is it, Franz?"

"I beg your pardon, sir. I thought you might be interested to hear that the four prisoners who escaped from the concentration camp are safe with their friends in Switzerland."

"*What?*"

"Arrangements had been made, sir, to get the Herren von Maeder and Behrmann out, and it was as simple to get four out as two. The gracious Fräulein, sir, was grieving over the Herren Beckensburg. I could not bear, if I may say so, sir, to see so kind a lady unhappy."

Hambledon's glass slipped from his hand and rolled unheeded on the carpet.

"I seem to have surprised you, sir," said Franz, picking it up and wiping it carefully.

"Surp—— Do you mean to tell me that you forged that order and faked up that sergeant's guard?"

"My organization, sir."

"Do you realize that I thought Herr Goebbels had done it to incriminate me, and that I've been expecting arrest any moment for the past fortnight?"

"I am extremely sorry, sir. Such an idea never occurred to me. I thought that since your seal was used you would conclude I had done it, but you would not, of course, inquire."

"Well, I'm damned!"

"I trust not, sir."

"How did you get hold of my seal?"

"Your Excellency," said Franz with a faint smile, "has the inestimable blessing of being able to sleep soundly."

"I'll sleep with it round my neck in future. But, look here, it didn't fit."

"I soaped it, sir, to prevent its sticking, but the soap

made the wax bubble in a most unexpected manner. Very disconcerting, sir. But when I realized how like a forgery it looked, I left it, thinking it would be easier for you to disown it if occasion should arise."

Hambledon sat still in a reverie so profound that the servant prepared to leave the room, but at the sound of the door his master aroused himself.

"One moment, Franz."

"Sir?"

"Get another glass out of the cupboard, will you? I should like you to drink with me."

"It will be an honour, sir."

"It will—but I am not sure to which of us," said Tommy Hambledon.

. . . .

Goebbels had been perfectly right when he told his friends of a Commission which was going to Danzig. Ostensibly they were to discuss conditions of trade with leading Germans in the Free City, actually they went to arrange with the Herren Foerster and Greiser for the complete Germanizing of Danzig, and the stamping out, by fair means or foul, of any opposition to the Nazi regime either from Polish sympathizers or from those who wished to see the once Free City remain free. It would be necessary for a *coup d'état* to have a large number of German troops in the City, yet it would be unwise merely to march them in. Danzig, and especially its seaside resort, Zoppot, cater for tourists. Very well, let there be tourists, thousands of them, some in uniform and some not, but all S.S. men ready for action, for who holds the gate against the carefree tourist? Very clever, and it worked admirably.

This, however, is anticipation, for when Klaus Lehmann was told to protect the Commission against the enemies of the Reich, Danzig had not yet capitulated and there was sometimes trouble in the narrow, ancient streets, for this was only July 1938.

The day before the Commission started for Danzig, Tommy Hambledon went to the Record House to obtain, if possible, photographs and an official description of the man Schultz for the information of his guards. Hambledon's personal party consisted of Reck, acting secretary, and two reliable men selected by himself from the police under his command, besides a number of plain-clothes detectives whose business it was to look after the Commission. Schultz seemed to have gone to ground since he came to Berlin from Aachen, but information had trickled through to the police that he was going to Danzig at the same time as the Commission, together with one Petzer.

Hambledon was lucky; there were official records of both men. Petzer did not seem a particularly interesting person apart from his tendency to fight with a hock bottle—preferably full—as a weapon, but it was noted that he was a native of Danzig. Evidently he had been selected for his local knowledge, probably Schultz had never been there before. Hambledon took down particulars of the appearance and habits of the two men and waited, chatting with Herr Gerhardt, while copies of their photographs were found for him.

"You must have had a terrible task," said the Chief of Police sympathetically, "reducing chaos to order after the disastrous fire four months ago."

"I cannot describe to you how dreadful it was. It may sound a curious thing to say, but the task would have been easier if the destruction had been more complete. No one who watched that awful blaze would have thought that anything in the building would survive, and yet, strange to relate, there was really a vast mass of material comparatively undamaged."

"That is odd," agreed Hambledon, "yet we must all have discovered at some time how difficult it is to burn a book."

"Exactly, exactly. When the floors gave way they seem to have crushed out the fire beneath them, and the immense number of valuable records were only charred at the edges, and, of course, sodden with water. The dirt, the mess, my dear Herr Lehmann, if I may call you so, words fail me to describe it. Believe it or not, I bought myself a set of workmen's overalls—several sets—and wore them for weeks and weeks. My good wife looked in horror at my black face and hands, and said she never meant to marry a chimney sweep."

"Please convey my homage," said Hambledon, wishing they would hurry up with those photographs, "to the charming Frau Gerhardt and your delightful family. I shall hope to renew my acquaintance when I return from Danzig."

"When I tell her what you have said," answered Gerhardt, beaming all over his round face, "her gratification will be beyond measure. How kind you are, Herr Lehmann, how condescending. But to return to the records, the labour was worth it. Only yesterday Herr Goebbels was good enough to congratulate me upon the amount we have saved." He spoke rather acidly, and Hambledon gathered correctly that Herr Gerhardt did not like the sharp-tongued Minister of Propaganda, probably he had been snubbed.

"So Goebbels was here yesterday, was he?" said Hambledon in a careless tone. "I imagine there can be hardly one of the Government Departments which does not have to apply to you for help at some time or another."

"That is so, and it is our pride as well as our duty to produce whatever information may be required accurately, fully, and instantly. There was an odd coincidence about Herr Goebbels' inquiries which might interest you."

"Indeed! What was that?"

"Your Excellency will remember that a short time before our fire you yourself sent us some fingerprints for identification if possible. One set were on a glass, I think. We identified one set as those of a certain Hendrik Brandt, a Dutchman, who during the last war had an importer's business in Cologne. Herr Goebbels came yesterday with a set of prints which also proved to be those of Hendrik Brandt."

Hambledon had naturally seen the course which Gerhardt's story was taking, and was not even mildly surprised. "The coincidence is probably more apparent than real," he said. "It is quite possible for the same man to attract the attention of several Departments at once—it all depends what he's been up to," he added lightly.

"Of course, of course. We had to have—it was very insubordinate of us, of course, but we experts must have our private jokes—we had to have a little laugh at Herr Goebbels. When he was told to whom his prints belonged, he stared and said he didn't believe it; and when further we assured him that there was no possible doubt about it, he actually queried the reliability of the whole fingerprint system. He seemed to think we were making a fool of him, he was quite angry, we really had to have a quiet laugh about it—after he had gone, of course."

"I think it was extremely funny and I don't wonder you laughed," said Hambledon truthfully, for indeed the idea of Goebbels getting hold of that damning piece of evidence and refusing to believe it was almost farcical. "Ah, here are my photographs, I think."

He exchanged with Gerhardt the stately courtesies in which the German's soul delighted, walked thoughtfully home and went along the passage to Reck's room.

"When we leave to-morrow, old horse," said Hambledon, "we'll kiss Berlin a final good-bye. Goebbels has had my fingerprints identified."

"The devil he has!"

"Yes, and the funny thing about it is that he didn't believe it. Me, the Chief of Police, a suspected agent of a foreign power! Why, he's known me for years. It does sound a bit tall, doesn't it?"

"He'll believe it when he comes to think it over," said Reck with conviction.

"Doesn't matter much now, he's made arrangements with Schultz," said Hambledon, "and an automatic in the hand is worth a dozen fingerprints in the Record House any day."

CHAPTER XXII
A MURDER HAS BEEN ARRANGED

THE COMMISSION travelled to Danzig by the ordinary train, not a special, and merely had compartments reserved for them since they did not wish to be more conspicuous than was unavoidable. Hambledon and Reck had one compartment to themselves, as soon as the train had settled into its swing the Chief of Police sent for his two plain-clothes men and addressed them in private.

"There are two men somewhere on this train among the ordinary passengers, their names are Schultz and Petzer. Here are their official descriptions and photographs, you had better, perhaps, study them here and now." He lit a cigar and sat in silence, looking out of the window, till the men handed him back the papers. "Schultz and Petzer are going to Danzig. On arrival at the station, you will follow these men and see everything they do. When they have found quarters for the night, one of you will come back to me and report but the other will remain on the watch. They are not to be lost sight of, night or day, or the consequences may be very serious."

"If they should part company while only one of us is on duty, which are we to follow?"

"Schultz. Now go and identify them, but don't come back here, it would be disastrous if they saw you with me. You know where I shall be staying in Danzig."

When the men had gone, Hambledon turned to Reck and said, "You're very quiet, what's the matter?"

"I have lived in Germany," said Reck, without looking at him, "since 1901, that's thirty-seven years. What shall I do in England?"

"It's odd you should say that, I was thinking much the same myself. I've been here almost continually since '14, and for fifteen years I believed I was a German."

"I am one," said Reck, "in everything but birth."

"Yes. Latterly, you know, when things have been getting a little too exciting for comfort, I've thought how wonderful it will be to live in England again and sleep in peace with no fatal secret—that sounds well—in the background waiting to blow me sky-high."

"No Gestapo," said Reck, in a tone of forced cheerfulness.

"No concentration camps."

"No S.S. troopers swaggering about, no bumptious Hitler youths."

"No Goebbels. Sounds like heaven, doesn't it?"

"Yes. But d'you realize I've almost forgotten the language?" said Reck.

"Oh, it'll soon come back, I've got a strong German accent myself, but it'll wear off. You know, if you don't like the Government in England, you can stand up on a soap-box in Hyde Park and say so——"

"In a strong German accent?"

"And if anybody tries to knock you off it the police will arrest him."

"Sounds just too marvellous," said Reck sardonically, "that is, for anybody who wants to stand on a soap-box and abuse Chamberlain. But what else is there to do?"

"I tell you one thing there'll be to do," said Hambledon cheering up. "Go to the Foreign Office and collect twenty years' arrears of pay."

Reck brightened up a little. "Do you think they will pay it? We didn't do much for them for fifteen years, you know."

"We'll tell them we spent the time making useful contacts," said Hambledon, "and heaven knows we succeeded. It'll be fun trying to make 'em pay up, anyway. By the way, following the example of most of my revered colleagues, I put away a tidy sum of my savings where I can get at it presently."

"You won't starve, anyway," said Reck. "But what I still want to know is, what shall we do all day?"

"Oh, we shall find some trouble to get into, I expect. Moreover, if German Intelligence spots us, we shan't have to find trouble, it'll find us. I think I'll live quietly in the country and grow pigs."

They arrived in Danzig towards evening, and Hambledon was busy arranging for the protection of his Trade Commission from battle, murder, and sudden death. There were sundry conferences arranged, some in Danzig itself and one out at Zoppot, where Hambledon passed the time wandering about the Casino. The baccarat room fascinated him, with its Moorish arches outlined with electric lights, the unreal landscapes painted on the walls and the vast open fire-place. He learned with awe that baccarat was only played from 5 p.m. till 8 a.m., whereas roulette could be played all day long, why, he never discovered.

The police reported that Schultz and Petzer had taken rooms in a not too reputable apartment house behind the Heilige-Geist Kirche, near the Fischmarkt, and one morning when the Commission was escorted round the sights of Danzig, he was led away from the party at the Butter Tor and had the house pointed out to him.

The Commission was to stay in Danzig for a week, and Hambledon's idea was to take rooms for himself and Reck in some sailors' boarding-house down by the docks and slip away when the rest of the party went back to Berlin. He was never a believer in having plans very cut and dried beforehand, because too much prearrangement only gave scope for things to go wrong. "Some scheme," he would say, "will doubtless present itself," and it usually did. "When I have seen all my little lambs safely into their fold, I shall have time to deal with Schultz. Till then, my police can keep these two in order."

"Little lambs," grunted Reck, who was not impressed by the Trade Commission. "Old goats, most of 'em. What do you propose to do with Schultz?"

"He is guilty of murder," said Hambledon quietly. "He killed a man named Ginsberg who worked for me and trusted me, so Schultz is going to die. I think I'll ask him to go for a little drive with me in my fine car"—the Danzig Nazis had provided cars for the Trade Commission and Hambledon had one for his own use—"take him out somewhere in the forests round here and shoot him. I shall tell him why first, so it will be quite fair."

Reck was on the point of saying, "Suppose he refuses to go?" when he glanced at Hambledon's face and somehow the question seemed foolish, so he omitted it and substituted another. "What happens after that?"

"After that we leave, as inconspicuously as possible, in a ship bound for England if we can find one, if not, in a ship bound for anywhere except Germany. Have you ever been a stowaway, my wandering boy?"

"Never," said Reck, "and I——"

"Never mind," said Tommy cheerfully. "You will. We had better go and buy ourselves some clothes, any slop shop will do, and a couple of cheap suit-cases. We can then walk out of this hotel in these suits, change in any secluded spot which seems convenient, and proceed on our way to the docks."

"It might not be a bad plan," suggested Reck, "if we

went to the docks beforehand and had a look round. We might be in a hurry when we do leave."

"Sound idea," said Hambledon. "We might go this afternoon, I shouldn't think my flock would get into serious trouble between 2 and 4 p.m."

They found the sort of shop they were looking for, and bought clothes of the sort that seafaring men wear when they spruce up to come ashore. They changed into their new suits in a place where a desire for privacy is respected, packed their other garments in the suit-cases, and emerged into the hot sunshine of a Baltic summer's day. Hambledon, strange to relate, had his head bandaged, the Chief of the German Police had become fairly well known by sight in Danzig.

"I can't imagine," said Reck, turning his wrists uneasily in his coat sleeves, "why we think of the poor as thinly clad. These are the thickest garments I ever wore."

"I know what is meant," said Tommy, easing his coat collar where it chafed his neck, "by hard-wearing cloth. It means hard on the wearer. How do I look?"

"Too clean and tidy. How do I look?"

"Too respectable. Couldn't you look a bit more—I think 'raffish' is the word I want? Leer at the girls."

"Leer yourself," said the horrified Reck. "At my age—— I tell you what. These clothes want sleeping in, I remember now. When I was selling papers, a woman gave me quite a decent suit once, at least, it had been cleaned and pressed, I think it had been fumigated too, but never mind. I felt quite smart for a day, but I had to sleep in the things that night—it was cold—and next morning— well, I was myself again, that's all."

"I'll treat these to-night. Do you think it would do as well if I crumpled them up and slept on them?"

"No," said Reck unkindly. "Where are we going?"

"To take a room in some dockside tavern. We don't

want to have to wander about seeking accommodation if we ourselves are being urgently sought, we want to be able to dive in and stay there. We will make sure the proprietor knows us again, too."

"I think this'll do," said Tommy, a litle later. "It looks to be more or less what we want, and I don't think I wish to walk any farther this afternoon, anyway. I have exercised the pores of my skin quite enough, and as for this bandage, phew! The Seven Stars, even if someone crowns us with a bottle we ought to be able to remember that. Come in."

"I am still a teetotaller," said Reck firmly.

"Not here, my lad; at least, not so as anyone would notice it. Perhaps there's an aspidistra you can make friends with. Here goes."

There was no aspidistra, but there were some ferns in pots along the bar in places where they would not inconvenience customers. Reck took his stand by one of them, and it is to be hoped that *Pteris cretica* likes schnapps.

After that, they inspected a room which was vacant, approved it, and paid a deposit. More schnapps and a little light converse with the innkeeper completed their business, and they left the place, changed back into their ordinary clothes on the way home and returned to Hambledon's hotel. One of the police whom he had detailed to follow Schultz and Petzer came in to report.

"The suspects spent the morning quietly in the vicinity of their lodgings," he said, referring to a note-book. "They visited various taverns, I have a list of them here."

"Omit the list," said Hambledon.

"Very good, sir. At one-fifteen they came to the neighbourhood of this hotel and hung about, one in front and the other, Petzer, in view of the side entrance. Pursuant upon your instructions, I concentrated upon Schultz. At two-fifteen precisely, the suspect Petzer came rapidly round the corner from the side entrance, spoke to the suspect Schultz, and both walked away at a good pace."

Hambledon allowed his glance to stray carelessly in the direction of Reck, who gave no sign of having heard anything interesting. Nevertheless, two-fifteen was the hour at which they themselves had left the side entrance to the hotel.

"The suspects walked fast at first and then more slowly through several streets towards the poorer quarter of the town. I have a list of the streets."

"Omit the list."

"Very good, sir. They hung about for some time in a small street off the Johannis Gasse, started again towards the river and again waited just inside the north door of the Johannis Kirche. Here they stayed about twenty minutes. There seemed to be a certain amount of discussion as to what they should do next, they were plainly arguing, and as they passed me I heard Petzer say, 'I don't think it is,' and Schultz answered, 'I do. I'm sure it is.' They then proceeded in the direction of the wharves along the Mottlau and came to another stop in an archway opposite a tavern called the Seven Stars. The time was then three-forty-eight. They waited here until four-thirty-two and then returned to the Johannis Kirche where they stayed for only twelve minutes. They then walked smartly in the direction of this hotel. When it became evident where they were heading, I rang up Bermann as arranged and he took over from me outside here at the moment when the suspects went away. That is all I have to report."

"Very good," said Hambledon, rose to his feet and took a turn across the room and back. "I think it probable," he went on, "that they have now gone home. Find out, and telephone to me."

"Very good, sir," said the man, saluted, and left the room. Hambledon looked at Reck and laughed.

"So much for our beautiful disguises," he said. "Schultz and Petzer have been trailing us all the afternoon."

"Apparently our disguises were good enough for your police," said Reck.

"They weren't looking for us, and anyway, they were busy. Ever tried trailing anybody through crowded streets without getting near enough for him to see you? It's a hell of a job, you don't notice much else. But you see what's happened, don't you? They know where we're going, what we're going to look like, and most serious of all, the fact that we are arranging to get away—they must have guessed that. They know a lot too much."

"What are you going to do about it?"

"Have something to eat, for a start, I can't do anything till that fellow telephones. I hope he'll be quick, because some of the Commission want to go for a stroll round Danzig to-night and I shall be expected to go with them. I should, anyway, because heaven knows what mischief they'd get into if they were out on their own."

"Bear-leading, eh?"

"No. Puppy-walking."

Half an hour later the telephone rang, Hambledon lifted the receiver and said "Yes" at intervals. He ended by saying, "Very good. You and Bermann can both go off duty now. Yes, there is no need to continue the watch to-night. Report here for duty at 10 a.m. to-morrow." He put the receiver down. "They have gone in, the police are going off, and I am going out. See you later."

"Don't you want me?" said Reck.

"No. Yes, you can sit in the car, it may save questions, and you might be useful keeping Schultz in order on the drive. I shall leave the car by the Heilige-Geist Kirche and you will stay with it. Bring your automatic."

Hambledon walked along the street behind the Fischmarkt, turned into the entrance of an apartment house
and walked up the stairs without hesitation. It was a
shabby building with paint peeling off the walls, worn
stone stairs with an iron handrail leading straight up from
the door, and a fine mixed smell of cookery, oilskins and
damp stone floors. There were two doors on each half
landing, Hambledon went up three flights with his right
hand in his coat pocket, opened the first door with his
left hand and went swiftly in. In fact, it might be said
that he burst in except that he did it so quietly, but the
precaution was wasted, for the room was empty.

There were two rooms in the apartment, a sitting-room
first and a bedroom opening out of it, Hambledon listened
intently for any sound in the further room, but there
was none, so he walked through and investigated it. It had
two beds, a dressing-table and a washstand, with signs of
masculine occupation in the way of shaving-tackle, spare
boots and a coat or two. One of the coats, hung from a
nail on the back of the door, had a pocket which looked
heavy. It contained an automatic.

"Careless, careless," said Tommy, and thoughtfully
unloaded it. "Possibly one of our friends is unarmed."

He returned to the sitting-room. There was a table in
the middle, with playing-cards lying in confusion on it, a
pipe, a tin half full of tobacco, a packet of cigarettes and
some matches.

"Good," said Hambledon, surveying this. "They won't
be long, they've only gone to fetch the beer."

The window was wide open to the hot evening, and
directly opposite to him, only about fifteen feet away, was
another window, also open. Tommy glanced down, there
was a well between, probably intended by an optimistic
architect to supply ventilation to the building all round
it, but it was completely airless and smelt of onions. He

drew back again rather too late, for there was a movement in the room opposite, a girl came to the window and leaned out, her elbows on the sill, watching him. He turned away, but she only laughed and shouted a remark across to him. He scowled and withdrew modestly into the bedroom where she could not see him so long as he stayed near the door, though this room was, of course, equally commanded by the window opposite to it.

"Trudi!" called the girl to some unseen friend elsewhere in the block. "Just fancy. A new man opposite, an' he's shy!"

A voice below called up a reply which Tommy felt sure was better inaudible. "Confound the girl," he said irritably, "if all these windows fill with Delilahs I am sunk. As it is, if she sees me with a gun in my hand she'll tell the world."

However, the window opposite the bedroom remained vacant, Hambledon pushed the door almost shut, and waited.

Presently the outer door of the apartment opened and two men entered, talking. Objects were set upon the table with bumps, chairs were drawn up, and there were sounds of settling down.

"Have a drink," said one voice.

"Thanks, I don't care if I do," said the other.

"You look worried," said the first voice, to the accompaniment of pouring noises. "Buck up."

"I shall be glad when it's over; didn't reckon on being mixed up in this sort of game."

"You don't 'ave to do nothin', on'y come with me an' help in the get-away. You'll be good at that."

"Did you say it was to-night?"

"To-night, yes. Listen, it's easy. Some of that high-an'-mighty Commission are goin' out to-night on the binge, an' Lehmann's goin' too to keep 'em in some sort of order.

Well, you know what those sort of toffs are when they're on holiday. 'Show us somethin' tough,' they say, an' off they goes an' all piles into some dockside pub they'd turn their noses up at at home. ' 'Ow quaint,' they say, ''ow interesting.' I've 'eard 'em."

"Well?"

"Well, I'm havin' some of the boys keepin' a look out for 'em. When they goes in somewhere where the likes of us can go, we all piles in and soon somebody starts a bit of bother over somethin'. In the ensooin' uproar, guns are drawn an' the Chief of Police is unfort'nately shot dead. After which we all leaves in 'aste, as is natural, an' you an' me comes back 'ere, picks up our bits and pieces, and takes the first train for Berlin. See? Simple."

"Don't see what you want me around for at all," objected Petzer.

"Gawd knows a strip of dried cod 'ud be more generally useful," said his candid friend, "but you will at least know the way back 'ere from wherever we are——"

The bedroom door opened noiselessly, and Hambledon appeared on the threshold, with his hand in his pocket out of regard for the lady in the room opposite, who was still leaning on the sill. In the same moment he saw Schultz's automatic on the table within reach of his hand, no time for argument here.

"Talking of shooting," said Tommy conversationally, "do you remember Ginsberg? That's for Ginsberg," he said, and shot Schultz through the head. The man slid to the floor, the gun he had snatched up spinning from his hand, and immediately pandemonium broke loose. The girl opposite uttered an ear-splitting shriek and followed it with cries of "Murder! Murder! Help!" Petzer gave a yell of rage, and rushed at Hambledon with his bare fists.

"Here, hold off, you fool," said Hambledon, parrying

the attack, "I don't want to kill *you!* Stop it, you idiot——"

Sounds of shouting filled the house, hurrying feet clattered on the stairs, somebody tried to open the door and failed, because it was bolted inside, so they hammered and kicked it instead. Hambledon was getting an unpleasant surprise from Petzer, whom he had assumed from the previous conversation to be something of a pacifist, but apparently the man only had a conscientious objection to murder, especially when directed against himself. Petzer landed heavily on Hambledon's left ear and made his head sing.

"This practice will now cease," said Tommy, through clenched teeth, hit the man in the wind, which made his head come forward, and then hit him under the jaw. Petzer threw up his arms and dropped to the floor.

"Now," said Tommy, surveying the scene of battle, "what does A do? After all, I am the Chief of Police, but I do hate making a public exhib—— That door'll be down in a minute."

Petzer, who was only half stunned, saw Schultz's automatic on the floor under the table, picked it up and staggered blindly to his feet. While he stood swaying, and shaking his head to clear his brain, Hambledon retired hastily to the bedroom as the outer door fell in and two men with it, backed up by several others who jammed up the doorway and stared. They saw one man dead on the floor, obviously shot through the head, another man standing over him waving an automatic, and drew the obvious conclusion.

"He's shot him!"

"Shot his pal!"

"Murder!"

"Catch him! Tie him up!"

"Police! Murder!"

Petzer finally lost his temper and his head. He didn't know much but he did know he hadn't killed Schultz, and this was too much. He fired a couple of shots at random which happily hit the wall and not his fellow Danzigers, and made a rush for the door. Room was made for him, as it usually is for an angry man with an automatic, and he bolted down the stairs, colliding with people coming up, and finally dropped over the handrail of the last flight into the hall, dodged out into the street, and ran like a hare, with a couple of policemen and half a dozen agile citizens in hot pursuit.

The two men who fell in with the door very wisely stayed down and let the wild ass stamp o'er their heads. When Petzer left the room they picked themselves up, not in the least surprised to find a third man there who seemed to have come from nowhere in particular, and all charged down the stairs in pursuit of Petzer together.

Herr Schumbacher, the cobbler, had just made himself some coffee when the uproar broke out. He lifted the pot off the fire to prevent it from boiling over, and went to the door with it in his hand. Immediately the crowd, in passing, gathered him in as a twig is swept away in a current, and the boiling contents of the pot went over the heads and shoulders of Herr Pfaltz, stevedore, and Frau Braun, wife of Heinrich Braun, scavenger. From spectators in the uproar, they became participants, and matters were not mended thereby.

Nobody had time to notice Hambledon.

Once out in the street, Tommy ran as fast as he could round two corners, dropped into a walk, and rejoined Reck in the car near the Heilige-Geist Kirche, panting slightly.

"Not got your man?" asked Reck.

"Oh, yes, I got him. Ginsberg may sleep in peace," said Hambledon, tenderly caressing his left ear. "It didn't turn out quite as I expected, there was something of a brawl. There was to have been another meeting of the Joy-through-Shooting League to-night, with me for target, but I should think that's off now. Schultz's boy friends were going to pick a quarrel with the Commission——"

As for Petzer, he made his way to the goods yard, having an idea they might be looking for him at the passenger station. He dodged round trucks and stumbled over rails; somebody shouted at him so he dived into a truck of which the doors were open and crouched behind bulky packages. Probably the truck would go to Berlin; he had a muddled idea that most things went to Berlin from Danzig, but it didn't matter. Anywhere out of the place, anywhere——

Five minutes later somebody came along, slammed the truck doors and bolted them, whistles blew, the truck began to move, bumped over points and gathered speed. Petzer was off on the long run to Constantinople.

SOME HALF-DOZEN of the younger members of the Commission set out on a tour of Danzig at about nine that night. They had a Danzig driver for their seven-seater Mercédès, and Hambledon, with Reck beside him, followed in the black saloon which had been lent to him. He thought that they might just as well have gone out in the afternoon and let a fellow get to bed in decent time, since the only difference between 3 p.m. and nine at night was that most of the shops were shut, as it was, of course, broad daylight at that hour in those high northern latitudes.

"What's the programme?" asked Reck, as the cars moved slowly off.

"Broadly speaking, a pub-crawl," said Hambledon. "We visit a few assorted cafés in Danzig itself, some new, with chromium plate; some old, with hereditary smells. After which, we drive along the beautiful tree-lined road to Zoppot, to see the girl dancing in the fountain, play roulette till they chuck us out, and so to bed. My job is to see that the outing proceeds in a stately and preordained manner, and now that Schultz is dead I expect it will. I wish I could leave my left ear at home, tenderly wrapped in cotton-wool in a small box with 'A Present from Danzig' on the lid."

"Girl dancing in the fountain? What's that?"

"At the casino at Zoppot. There is a fountain. There is a girl. They turn on the fountain, also coloured flood-lights beneath it. She gets in and dances under the arches of water in the changing lights, you understand. A pretty sight, I'm told, if a trifle French, the Commission'll love it, bless their little cotton socks. What's this? Oh, stop number one. I suppose I must go in, are you coming?"

"Mine's a Grenadine," said Reck, who privately thought the programme sounded rather amusing. The first café was very modern, of a type to be found in any city from San Francisco right round to San Francisco, and it did not detain the Commission long. There were plenty like that in Berlin, they wanted to see something different.

The next place strongly resembled the under-croft of Rochester Cathedral, and had a damping effect on the spirits of the party which even schnapps failed to counter-act.

"Is this tour all prearranged?" asked Reck.

"Of course it is, what did you expect? Those singularly sober men holding large pots whom you see in all the corners are police."

"Oh. Suppose the Commission wants to go somewhere else?"

"The driver will dissuade them, that's part of his job. Besides," added Hambledon cheerfully, "Schultz is dead, so I don't suppose it would matter."

The third port of call was frankly vulgar without being funny and the Commission became restive.

"Now we go to Zoppot," said the driver persuasively.

"No we don't," said the Commission. "Aren't there any real dockside taverns here with sand on the floors and Norwegian seamen singing choruses?"

"No Norwegian ships in at the moment, gentlemen. It is nearly time to——"

"Swedish seamen, then. Now, in the St. Pauli district of Hamburg I could show you——"

"Harbour's very empty of ships at this season, gentlemen, and most of the taverns close for July and August."

"That be hanged for a tale——"

"Gentlemen," broke in Hambledon, "the time is going on and it is nearly seven miles to Zoppot. It would be a pity, would it not, to miss any of the entertainment there?"

The driver threw him a grateful glance and some of the Commission wavered, but the stalwarts stuck to their point.

"Look here, driver, if you can't find us something more amusing than this we'll find it for ourselves. You hop in and drive where we tell you to drive, and when we say stop, you stop. See?"

The driver looked at Hambledon who merely made a gesture of resignation to the inevitable, so the cars moved off again.

"You can hardly blame them," said Hambledon, "the tour as arranged was not particularly inspired. There's not likely to be any trouble if we keep these fellows in a good temper."

The procession took a devious route in the general direction of the Vistula, since the Commission did not know the way and the driver sulked and refused to tell them. Eventually someone recognized the Kran-tor at the end of a street and remembered that that was on the quayside, but they had passed the turning by the time they got their bearings so they took the next street instead, which was the Heilige-Geist Gasse with another river-gate across the end. At the bottom of this street they saw something which looked a little more hopeful.

"Here, what about this?"

"This looks better."

"Stop here, driver, we'll try this one."

Hambledon slipped out of his car and had a hasty look inside while the Commission was disembarking. The place was certainly old and picturesque, with the requisite sanded floor and polished brass fittings, it really looked the sort of place where tuneful seamen might burst into song at any moment if there happened to be any tuneful seamen there. At the time, however, it was practically empty and seemed harmless enough. Hambledon withdrew again and the Commission entered.

"Shouldn't think they'd get into mischief in there," he said to the driver. "Hardly anybody there."

"Ah," said the driver. "It's quiet enough when it is quiet, if you get me. Aren't you going in, sir?"

"No," said Hambledon, "I'd rather look at the river. Coming, Reck?"

"I'll just turn the car round," said the driver. "Save time afterwards."

"Quite right, I'll do the same." They turned the cars to head up the street and all three strolled through the gate on to the quay. To their left the Kran-tor towered against the sky, wharves and warehouses faced them across the glassy river, upstream tall houses masked the sunset. A motor ferry crossed the river lower down and the ripples broke up the inverted gables in the water, gulls cried, someone laughed in a group of people twenty yards away, and somewhere far out of sight a steamer hooted.

"Do you get much foreign shipping here?" asked Hambledon.

"Not a lot here, mostly barges and that from up the river. The foreign ships mostly put in to the Free Harbour down at Neufahrwasser, that's the real port, like. There's always ships in there, German, Swedish, English, Italian, French—all sorts."

"Is it far down there?"

" 'Bout three and a half to four miles. No, not far. I tell you, there was a row down there last night. Some men off an English ship got into a row in a pub down there— just such a place as this one. Two of 'em was properly laid out. The ship'll have to sail without 'em, for they're in hospital and she's going out in the morning."

"What will happen to them?"

"Oh, nothing. Get another ship when they come out, I expect. British Consul 'ull look after them."

The conversation languished, and Hambledon looked at his watch.

"Do you think if you blew your horn it would hurry them up?"

"I doubt it," said the driver, but he strolled off, climbed into his seat and blew the horn. He was quite right, nothing happened.

"You heard that about the English ship, didn't you, Reck?" said Hambledon. "When I've got this school- treat home again I think we'll slide quietly away and board her. I've paid Schultz, so there's nothing to wait for, if we leave it too long Goebbels might replace him with somebody more efficient."

Reck grunted assent and they leaned against the quay- side rails and waited while the day sank into twilight and the colour faded out of the sky. Two sailors passed talk- ing animatedly in Italian and somewhere among the wharves across the river a dog barked. The street-lamps came to life, and a man in a peaked cap, under one of them, took a long time to say good night to a girl in a gaily smocked white blouse with full sleeves like a bishop's. Hambledon and Reck walked back through the archway and leaned against their car watching the door of the tavern patronized by the Commission, it seemed to have livened up a little, snatches of song floated out, and sounds of merriment. The driver of the big car had apparently fallen asleep. Various people approached the tavern door and entered, others came out, but none of them looked particularly truculent.

"I suppose I ought to go in and rout those people out," yawned Hambledon, "but I'm blowed if I do. I don't care if they never go to Zoppot."

An elderly man in a neat grey suit came down the street, pausing every now and then to glance behind him. He reached the tavern door, decided to go in, looked in, decided not to, and strolled past the cars towards the river. Before he passed under the arch he cocked his eye up at the evening sky.

"Sea Captain," said Hambledon, "looking at the weather."

"Sea Captain or not," said Reck, "he's the living image of you."

"Nonsense. My face has its drawbacks, but not warts on its nose."

"I meant, in build and general appearance."

"I am not unique," admitted Tommy modestly.

A woman came down the street closely followed by a man. Husband or lover, presumably, for when she looked at Hambledon in passing, the man glowered. They went under the archway and disappeared, but the neat grey man returned. He stopped near the cars and brought a cigar out of his pocket, pinched it, smelt it, cut the end off with a knife, stuck the cigar in his mouth and finally lit it. He took one or two puffs at it which appeared to please him, and strolled past.

He was just approaching the tavern door when there came a change in the tone of the sounds which floated from the half-open door, and he stopped to listen. Instead of song there was shouting, instead of merriment, anger. Hambledon straightened up and began to run towards the door, and at that moment two shots rang out.

Instantly the doors burst open and a gush of customers poured into the street. The Mercédès driver awoke, started up his engine, and kept on tapping the accelerator, producing a rhythmic series of roars. Hambledon leapt at the car and threw the doors open just in time for the Commission to fling themselves into it.

"You are a fool, Andreas," said one angrily.

"I thought all Danzigers were good Germans," said Andreas in a pained voice, while another voice from the doorway told them what sort of Germans they were. The adjective used was not "good".

Hambledon slammed the doors and shouted, "Drive on!" The car moved off and was rapidly gathering speed when there came a fresh rush of men from the tavern and one of them fired several parting shots after the car. Several of them hit, for the impact was audible, but one at least missed, for the elderly man in the grey suit, who was hurrying away, suddenly threw up his arms as though he were going to dive, and fell headlong in the road in front of the car. The driver had no chance to avoid him and perhaps did not even see him; the heavy Mercédès ran right over him, shot up the road, round the corner and out of sight.

"Now they have killed somebody," said Hambledon in an exasperated tone. "There'll be trouble over this."

He looked round for Reck and saw him emerging from the doorway in which he had prudently taken cover, for he was not one of Nature's warriors. The other people in the street melted away so quickly that it seemed some of them must just have vanished where they stood; already the tavern lights were out, blinds drawn and doors locked. In an incredibly short time the Heilige-Geist Strasse was deserted except for Hambledon and his car, Reck, and the neat grey man who was a great deal greyer and not nearly so neat.

Hambledon observed with surprise that Reck, instead of hurrying to the car, was bending over the body in the road. Tommy, supposing him to be animated by purely humanitarian motives, did not call to him, but started the car and drove it to the spot where the man lay.

"Come on," said Hambledon, after one glance at the victim of malice and accident, "you can't do anything to help him."

"Quick," said Reck in peremptory tones, "get him in the back of the car. Come on, lend a hand."

"What the devil——" said the surprised Hambledon.

"Don't argue, help me!"

Hambledon slid out of the car, opened the rear door and helped Reck to hoist the body into the back. "Though why on earth you want to saddle us with a corpse just when——"

"Don't argue," repeated Reck, slamming the door. "Get in and drive like blazes!"

Hambledon obeyed, very astonished at himself for doing so, and it was not until they were several streets away that he said, "May I know what all this is about?"

"Certainly. That poor thing in the back is you."

"But he's not in the least like me in the face."

"Face! Did you notice his face?"

"No," said Hambledon. "I thought you'd put something over it—a rag of some kind."

"No. There was nothing over it."

"Oh," said Hambledon, and shivered.

"You see, the Mercédès——"

"That'll do, thank you. What were you thinking of doing with him?"

"Driving the car to some quiet spot and leaving him there to be found. Then we can go away and live happily ever after, because even German Intelligence won't look for you when they've buried you with full honours and an oration by the Führer."

Hambledon slowed the car on purpose to look at Reck. "I hand it to you," he said admiringly, "on a gold plate edged with rosebuds." He thought it over for a moment. "But this means I shall have to change clothes with him."

"It does," said Reck firmly.

"Oh, Lor'. Well, the Department will damn well have to pay me twenty years' arrears after that. I shall have earned 'em."

"Do you know of a good place to go?"

"I only know the Zoppot road. It runs through forests, I should think we could find a track turning off it somewhere."

.   .   .   .

"No marks on his underclothes," said Reck after investigation. "That saves your changing those too."

"No, it doesn't," said Hambledon, "for I shouldn't have put them on in any case. It only saves you picking the marks off. Mind, that's the wrong leg. You'll have his trousers on back before."

"Why the hell do we have so many buttons? Heave him up while I fix his braces."

"Collar and tie. Hang it, Reck, how do you knot a tie on somebody else? It's all wrong way round, besides—— Oh, damn. I shall have to wash again now."

"Hot night, isn't it?" said Reck, who had perspiration running down his face. "Waistcoat. A trifle loose, he didn't live so well as you, evidently. Tighten that strap at the back a little. That's it. Now your watch in his pocket."

"I liked that watch," said Tommy plaintively, but it had to go.

"Now his coat. No, it's not so simple as all that, his

sleeves will ride up if we aren't careful. Here's a bit of string, tie his cuff-links to his thumbs, and don't forget to remove the string afterwards and twist the cuffs round."

"I would give the whole of that twenty years' arrears," said Hambledon violently, "for a tumblerful of John Haig—neat."

.   .   .   .

The ship was ten hours out from Danzig, bound for Cardiff with a cargo of sugar, when one of the firemen thought he heard voices in the coal bunker. He picked up a firebar and went to investigate.

"'Ere, you! Cummon outer that."

They came, slithering down the coal, blinking from the long darkness, cramped for want of movement, and inconceivably grimy.

"'Ere! Look what I've found."

"Stowaways," said the second engineer. "Hoo mony o' ye are there?"

"Two," said Hambledon with dignity. "I want to see the Captain at once."

"Ye'll no need to fret yourselves, ye'll see the Captain quick and lively, but whether ye'll enjoy the interview is another pair o' breeks a'thegither. Come on, now, get a move on. What the deevil ye mean stowin' away aboard this ship——"

"Who the devil are you?" asked the Captain.

"Thomas Hambledon and Alfred Reck. Can I speak to you in private?"

"No, you filthy blasted skulking scarecrows! How dare you stow away aboard my ship?"

"Because we had to. I am sorry, Captain, but there was no alternative. The passage will be paid as soon as we arrive in England. I must speak to you in private."

"You'll do nothing of the sort. Yes, you'll pay for the trip all right—in work. Lucky for you I'm two men short. Take these men for'ard——"

Hambledon took a quick step forward and leaned over the Captain's desk. "Look here," he said, in a tone inaudible to the men clustered round the door, "we are British Intelligence agents on the run, and I must send a wireless message instantly."

"Wireless message my——"

"Don't be a fool, man. You'll soon know when you get the answer. The message is to the Foreign Office."

The tone of habitual authority was unmistakable, and the Captain paused.

"The matter is urgent," added Hambledon coldly.

"Very well," said the Captain. "You shall send your message, but if there's any hanky-panky about it the Lord help you, for you'll need it. Come with me."

In the wireless room Hambledon asked for a sheet of paper and wrote down a message, briefly informing the Department that he and Reck were on board the——

"What ship is this?"

"The *Whistlefield Star.*"

"Bound for?"

"Cardiff."

"Do you put in anywhere between here and Cardiff?"

"No."

On board the *Whistlefield Star* bound for Cardiff, and requested instructions.

"Code that, will you, Reck?"

"Let me see it first," said the Captain, and read aloud, "Hambledon to Foreign Office, London." The rest of the message he kept to himself.

"You may send it."

"Carry on, Reck."

Reck settled down to write a string of letters, with

pauses for thought, occasionally counting upon his fingers. Hambledon found the Danziger's cigars in his pocket, pulled them out, saw they were hopelessly crushed, and threw them in the wastepaper basket. He then walked restlessly up and down the cabin, the Captain sat in a chair and stared at the calendar on the wall, the wireless operator looked from one to the other, and no one spoke out of deference to Reck's mental labours. The wireless operator was a stocky man, with a freckled face and red hair turning grey. He had been aboard the *Whistlefield Star* for a number of years and had served in destroyers during the first Great War.

Presently Hambledon in his prowling came opposite to a small piece of mirror fixed to the bulkhead, glanced at his reflection and said, "Good Lord."

"What's the matter?" asked the Captain.

"I had no idea I looked like that. No wonder you didn't believe me. Dammit, I look like a nigger minstrel on Margate sands."

The Captain unbent enough to smile, and said, "You'll be glad of a wash, no doubt. Won't you sit down?"

"No, thanks," said Hambledon absently, and went on walking up and down, thinking. Dear old Ludmilla in Switzerland, must let her know as soon as he could or she'd grieve horribly. Perhaps they wouldn't find the car for some days; it was well hidden in the woods off the Zoppot road. He must send her a message somehow as soon as possible, better send it to Frau Christine and let her tell Ludmilla. She must come to England; she always wanted to, though how she'd like living there permanently was another matter, with the language difficulty, the foreign cooking and the strange customs. Pity to part from Franz but it could not be helped, Franz would be sorry, probably. He'd have to look elsewhere for the President of his New Germany—thank goodness!

Reck stirred in his chair and began running through what he had written, absent-mindedly tapping out the message with his pencil on the table, whereat the wireless operator spun round, scarlet with excitement, and cried, "Good Lord! Is that who you are?"

"What d'you mean?" asked the Captain.

"Why, British secret agents, of course. T-L-T, that's the call-sign. Used to listen for it when I was on destroyers in the last war. Heard it again soon after I came in this ship, that'ud be six years ago, before you came to us, sir——"

This was enough for the Captain, who rose from his seat, advanced upon Hambledon with his hand held out and said, "I see I owe you an apology, sir. But you must admit appearances were against you!"

The reply to Hambledon's message came a few hours later, instructing the *Whistlefield Star* to rendezvous at a certain time and place in the Channel to tranship passengers to a destroyer, but by that time Hambledon and Reck, washed clean and in borrowed garments, were having dinner with the Captain.

The following evening they were listening to the Berlin radio from the wireless set in the Captain's cabin, for Hambledon showed a certain interest in the German news bulletins.

"It is with heartfelt sorrow and burning anger," said the announcer, "that the German people will learn of the cowardly and brutal murder of our Chief of Police, Herr Klaus Lehmann. His car was discovered this afternoon hidden away in a forest glade near Danzig; inside it was the body of Herr Lehmann, battered almost beyond recognition. It was, actually, only identified by the clothes and general appearance, and by the fact that the honoured and respected Chief had not returned to his hotel two nights earlier. He was not, however, always in the habit of giving previous notice of his movements, so that his absence had not yet caused alarm. He was one of the earliest adherents——"

"Lord love us," said the Captain, who knew enough German to follow a plain statement, "was that why you were on the run?"

"What a question," said Tommy blandly, and the Captain blushed and held his peace.

"—faithful servant and leader of the Reich and a trusted and beloved friend of the Führer himself——"

An inarticulate gurgle came from Reck.

"—who will himself pronounce the oration at the State funeral, which will take place in Berlin on Tuesday in next week. The whole German people will join with their Leader in mourning and resenting this bestial and revolting outrage, perpetrated upon one whose outstanding devotion to duty, meticulous honour and unfailing fidelity made him an example to every——"

"They are doing him proud, aren't they?" said Tommy, fidgeting slightly.

"Wonder if Herr Goebbels wrote this?" said Reck impishly.

"—Immediate steps are being taken to ensure the arrest, conviction, and condign punishment of the bloodstained assassins, who, undoubtedly under Jewish influence, were guilty of this abominable act of treachery. At the end of this announcement, that is, at once, a two minutes' silence will be observed as a tribute to the dead Chief."

Reck lifted his glass. "To the late Chief of Police," he said in German, and drank. Hambledon, with a rather wry smile, followed suit.

"May he rest in peace," said the Captain solemnly, and drained his glass.

"No rest in peace for him, I fear," said Hambledon

cryptically. "There wasn't before," he added, to himself, "and to-morrow is here."

The radio reawoke to life. "We are now giving you a recorded version of the late Herr Lehmann's radio play, *The Wireless Operator,* first broadcast from this station in March 1933. There is only one character, the wireless operator himself——"

THE END